More praise for *Your Oasis on Flame Lake*

"Finely wrought characters populate Landvik's intricately tex-
tured tale. . . . Landvik illuminates what is essential, without
seeming to, and pushes us to break through hard surfaces to a
higher level of understanding. All the while, we are grandly
entertained. . . . She now takes her place next to Maeve Binchy,
Jon Hassler and all the great storytellers who bring you to the
heart of their home places. She carries you with especially delicate detail, amazing resonance, humor and brilliant images."
                                    —*Minneapolis Star-Tribune*

"Quirky characters are a dime a dozen, but truly believable, lov-
able ones are not—a fact that makes Landvik's latest slice of
American life a genuine pleasure."
                                    —*Kirkus Reviews*

"Written with warmth, wit and tart dialogue, the book engages
big themes (love, friendship, loyalty, betrayal and the quest for
meaning). . . . Landvik's quirky and passionate characters, and
her ardent determination to give them dignity, make this a
heartwarming story."
                                    —*Publishers Weekly*

By Lorna Landvik
Published by Fawcett Books

Patty Jane's House of Curl

Your Oasis on Flame Lake

YOUR OASIS
ON FLAME LAKE

LORNA LANDVIK

FAWCETT COLUMBINE
THE BALLANTINE PUBLISHING GROUP
NEW YORK

A Fawcett Columbine Book
Published by The Ballantine Publishing Group

Copyright © 1997 by Lorna Landvik
Reader's Guide copyright © 1998 by The Ballantine Publishing Group, a division of Random House, Inc.

http://www.randomhouse.com

Library of Congress Catalog Card Number: 98-96108

ISBN: 0-449-00298-5

Cover illustration by George Angelini
Text design by Debbie Glasserman

Manufactured in the United States of America

First Hardcover Edition: July 1997
First Trade Paperback Edition: July 1998

10 9

To my daughters, Harleigh and Kinga
I'm glad I'm your mother

and

To my mother, Ollie
I'm glad I'm your daughter

ACKNOWLEDGMENTS

I WOULD LIKE TO THANK Ballantine/Fawcett, particularly my editor, Leona Nevler, for her gentle guidance. Also thanks to Ellen Archer, Helen Dressner, Janice Fryer, Rachel Tarlow Gul, Kim Hovey, Leona Nevler, Jane O'Boyle, and Beverly Robinson for my first New York publisher's lunch; and to my publicists, Rachel Tarlow Gul and Heather Smith, worth their weight in gold Rolodexes.

I am grateful to the McKnight Foundation and The Loft for the generous support they provide writers, including me.

Thanks to my friends in the Minneapolis theater scene (even those deserters who've skipped town) who've given me a lot of laughs, on and off stage: Laura and Lee Adams, Renee Albert, Signe Albertson, Leslie Ball, Kim Bartmann, Bill Bliseth, Peter Breitmayer, John Brady, Andrea Buetner, Michelle Cassioppi, Andy Cerisier, Mo Collins, Mark Copenhaver (thanks also for the computer help), Chris Denton, Melissa Denton, Maille Flanagan, Amy Fisher, Denise Sumpter-Foy, Wendy Freshman, Beth Gilleland, Peter Guertin, Leon Hammer, Robin Hart, Cheryl Hawker, Judy Heneghan, Michelle Hutchison, Drew Jansen, Bridget Jones, Wendy Knox, Rich Kronfeld, Gene Larche, Tony Lee, Kirsten Lind, Mary Lucia, Jimmy Martin, Ann Milligan, Priscilla Nelson, Barb Otis, Mary Jo Pehl, Grant Richey, Joel Sass, Steve Schaubel, Danny Schmitz, Dean Seal, Wendy Smith, Pete Staloch, Dane Stauffer, Sandy Thomas, Jeff Towne, Greg Triggs, Mike

Warren, Wayne Wilderson, Tom Winner, Kevin West, and Phyllis Wright.

Thanks to many others for oodles of things; to my faithful agent, Betsy Nolan; to my cousins, particularly those big book-buyers, Laurie Kleven and Brenda Young; to fellow ECFE mothers for the fun we had at that big round table; to the Minneapolis and St. Paul libraries, particularly the Nokomis and Roosevelt branches; to my friends Bev Baz, Ginny Eckstein, Shelly Haagenson, Betty Lou Henson, Kim and Killian Hoffer, Ann and Mark McDonald, Lori Naslund, Susan Rolandelli, Diane Sasaki, Catherine Schlesinger, Mike Sobota, Katy Krantz-Victor, and Elizabeth and Steven Zaillian, for coffee, conversations, duets sung, laughs laughed, kids watched and kindnesses done; thanks to my brothers, Wendell, Greg, and Lanny, for allowing me to be the youngest and the only girl.

A special thanks to Mr. Spaeth, my sixth-grade teacher at Morris Park Elementary School, who epitomized the best in teaching and whose inscription in my autograph book, "Best of luck for a fine literary career," thrilled an eleven-year-old girl.

Finally, thanks to Chuck, who increases the pleasure factor in just about everything.

DARCY

I ASKED MY dad once if he was sorry he didn't have any sons, and after he made a face he put his hand on my forehead like he was checking for fever.

"Boys?" he said, jerking the brim of my baseball cap down. "Who needs boys?"

I lifted my fishing pole as if I thought there might actually be something on the end of the hook. "Yeah, but wouldn't you like your name passed down and all that stuff?"

"Darce, as long as my superior genes are passed down, who cares about the name? What's so hot about 'Lindstrom' anyway? A rose by any other name would smell as sweet."

"Hey, quoting Shakespeare," said my mom. "Not bad."

We were sitting on the dock, casting for fish that were boycotting worms or something. It didn't matter; catching fish is about one tenth the pleasure of fishing, if you ask me. It was the kind of late-spring evening Minnesota dishes up to make up for winter. The sun was sitting like a big fishing bob on top of the water, staining it all red. The lilac bushes were in bloom by the boat shack, and underneath their perfume was the tangy cologne of pine trees. School was just about to let out and I didn't have a care in the world, except for the small nagging thought that I had been born the wrong sex.

"Well, see, Dad, I was reading this article on all these countries that don't value women—I mean, they throw girls on top of live volcanoes or drown them in raging rivers or give them terrible operations—"

"Darce," said my dad, "I wish you wouldn't read that kind of junk."

"Dick, she's serious," said my mother, digging around in the cooler. She took out a bag of bite-size Snickers.

"So am I," said Dad. "Can't we monitor her reading material, Dev? Make sure it's a little more . . . wholesome? I mean, come on—whatever happened to Nancy Drew?"

"Last I heard she was working homocide in Chicago and going to AA meetings on her nights off."

"That's cute, Dev." He pulled the brim of my cap down again. "They really throw girls into live volcanoes?"

I nodded. "*And* give them clitorectomies."

"Good grief!" said Dad. My mom said something, too, but I couldn't hear what it was.

"Well, all those terrible things aside, Darcy, you don't really think I prefer boys over you and your sister, do you, honey?"

I shrugged. I never thought so before, but that stupid article had got me thinking.

"Well, *don't*," he said, using his you'd-better-listen-to-me voice. "I'm a bigger fan of girls than boys, any day of the week, bar none."

"You're not just saying that?" I believed him, but sometimes he says things to impress my mother and I wanted to make sure this wasn't one of those times.

Mom passed us each a miniature Snickers bar. "I *am* just saying that," said Dad, cramming the whole piece in his mouth. A little square bulged out of his cheek. "And I'm just saying that because it's true. Anytime I see a bunch of boys running around like wild animals, knocking each other down, I think, man, am I glad I don't have any of those."

"Dick," said my mother, "you know if you had a son you'd be crazy about him."

"I'd be crazy about any kid of mine, but I couldn't be more crazy about any boy than I am about my girls."

I flicked a water bug off the dock. "Really, Dad?"

"Sure. Girls are more interesting. I'm a boy and so are most of my closest friends, so I should know. Just look at how much girls have going for them and how much they have against them—"

"Why don't you stop while you're ahead, Dick," advised my mother, unpeeling the wrapper of another Snickers. She's always bugging me and Lin about nutritious snacks, but she's the one whose pockets are full of linty Life Savers and the Hershey's Kisses wrappers she squeezes into little foil pellets.

"What I mean is it's so much harder to be a girl." There were big pauses in between words, like he was translating a language he didn't understand too well. "To me the whole female sex is like an army who's forced into battle with rusty weapons and out-of-date maps and wet matches, and yet as many times as they're beaten, they know they'll ultimately win."

"Aw, Dick," said my mom, "underneath your big chauvinist chest there beats a feminist heart."

Dad burped. "Shut up, woman, and get me a beer." Mom slapped his leg, laughing, and I laughed and Dad laughed and we sat there on that warm spring evening feeling fine and dandy watching the sun sink while our bobbers just sat there.

I PLAN ON being a world traveler someday, mostly for the experience but a little bit for the hats. (I'm what my mom calls a "headware connoisseur"; I'm not that into fashion, but I do love hats, which give you automatic style anyway. I can't wait to get berets and panamas and sombreros in the countries of their origin.) But I think I'd have to cross a bunch of time zones and ten times as many countries to find a place like Flame Lake. We're the only lake in our chain that has an ordinance against powerboats and you can still see your toes when you're standing in three feet of water.

Dad says the lake got its name from a drunk fur trapper who ran a little corn-liquor business on the north shore. His still used to blow up every other month and the fireball would be thrown into the lake. Mom says that's a big lie concocted by the drinkers down at Bardy's Tap—she says all you

have to do is look at a sunset to figure out how the lake got
its name. I vote with Mom on this one; some sunsets really
do look as if they're setting the lake on fire.

I went to this stupid camp one year and all the city girls
went on and on about the smell of the great outdoors, but
believe me, Flame Lake, with its dark green pine and dark
blue water, smells more like the great outdoors than that
dumb old camp whose counselors didn't even let us have a
campfire on the last night because they were too busy talking
babytalk to their boyfriends on the lodge pay phone.

I'd seen enough daytime talk shows and read enough of
my mother's magazines to know that my family situation was
pretty good, too—I mean, we all loved one another (well,
except for my sister Lin, who we *tolerated*). Growing up in
that house on Flame Lake, it was pretty easy thinking that in
the great poker game of life, I was holding a royal flush.

I guess I still think that way, I mean Lin says I've got the
biggest ego in the Western world.

"If you were me, you'd be thrilled, too," I tell her.

The truth is, I don't feel like *me* much anymore. Sometimes it's as if I've aged at warp speed and I'm as old as my
grandma Ardis, who thinks a cup of hot tea and a new
Reader's Digest is a party. Other times I wish I'd never given
up my blankie and my pajamas with feet.

Lin and I don't share a bedroom, so she doesn't know how
many times I've laid in bed, crying myself to sleep, scared
that all the trouble that came to us was just a little preview of
the main attraction.

I try to tell myself that what happened is all over, finis-
simo, water under the bridge; but how can something you're
always reminded of be over? I can't look in a mirror without
seeing how lousy things can be—I've got this row of false
teeth and I haven't even been kissed by a boy yet. I mean one
I'm not related to. Not that I'd want to. Oh well. At least you
can replace teeth, I tell myself. I don't know if you can ever
get back what Franny lost.

Dick

AT OUR TWENTIETH high-school reunion last summer, BiDi
and Devera were both voted "Least Changed." They pranced
around the stage giggling, pumping their cheap little trophies
in the air like they had won the Stanley Cup or something.

BiDi did look good, standing on tiptoe in red high-heeled
shoes with no backs, her tight little body squeezed into this
red leather dress. ("It's leather*like*," she explained later while
we stood eating Triscuits and Colby cheese at the buffet
table, "and I sweat three pounds off every time I wear the
thing.")

Devera looks the same in the face—she should, the jars of
Noxema she pickles herself in—but you can't tell me her
body looks like it did when she was doing back flips on the
Rebelettes squad. When she's got her clothes off, you have to
wonder: How does skin pucker around a butt like that?
When did her breasts take that drop in altitude?

If I asked her, she'd probably say something like, "If you
don't like the view, don't look."

The thing is, I do. I'm just curious about gravity's toll
is all.

Once we were dancing at King Olaf's Hideway and I said
whoa, no more of that shimmying—all that loose flesh is
going to pop me in the face. She just about popped me in the
face after I said that, but instead she grabbed the car keys
right out of my sports-coat pocket and gunned out of the
parking lot, the gravel under the wheels flying like confetti. I

had to hitch a ride home with Glen Pauley, an insurance agent who likes to talk about his work, as if normal people are fascinated by actuarial tables and annuities.

DEVERA MARRIED ME the day after her twenty-first birthday. We both were going to White Falls State, but she had been thinking of transferring her credits to "somewhere exotic"— the Sorbonne or the University of Cairo or UCLA"—but then her dad, Evan "Fair Shake" Bergdahl, was robbed and pistol-whipped (with a toy gun, but Dad Evan said when you're smacked in the face you can't tell the difference between real and fake). After that, Devera put her plans of exotic study on "temporary hold" and decided to stay home.

"Always remember," Devera reminds me, holding up two crossed fingers, "Daddy and I are like this."

I always answer back with my standard joke. "Easy for him, he's not married to you."

They caught the guy who robbed Dad Evan; he was holed up in a shack on Uncle's Lake, ice-fishing and drinking Champale. They arrested him on a bunch of charges, including assault, robbery, and fishing without a license. They must have tagged him for exceeding the limit, too— Sheriff Buck told me there were over two dozen northerns and crappies swimming around in pails in that icehouse. At his trial I wanted to ask the guy what he used for bait but Dad Evan would not understand any mingling with the accused. He takes loyalty very seriously, and I take my new-model Caddies and the future ownership of Viking Automotive pretty seriously myself. I'm in line to run Viking Appliance and Norse Man Liquors, too, but it's the dealership I care most about, being a natural at car sales. So of course, I just sat there quietly in the courtroom, bored, with Devera and her hysterical mother, Helen.

"Just look at that man," she'd say, shredding Kleenex like a hamster. "If he's not put away for life, he'll come after us for the final revenge."

The poor guy was French-Canadian, and his accent, you

can bet, added a couple of years onto his sentence. Around White Falls, people tend to think you *can* judge a book by its cover and foreign accents are most often up to *something*.

AFTER OUR WEDDING reception, Dad Evan and Helen drove us out to a three-bedroom ranch house on Flame Lake. The front door was wrapped in ribbon like a present and Dad Evan tossed me the deed like it was spare change. Dad Evan likes to give big presents away as if he's doing nothing more than picking up a check for pie and coffee. It burns me—his Mr. Casual act—so I go right along with it, like it's no big deal. Of course, as a bridegroom of twenty-two, I hadn't figured this out yet and I jumped right along with Devera, hugging and kissing him like he was Monte Hall.

Last fall we bought a bigger lot and built a new house—five bedrooms and a sauna in the basement—on the east side of the lake, because Devera thought it was time to move up. My wife keeps our upward mobility on a tight schedule.

At thirty-nine, Devvie is going through an early midlife crisis. It's harder on me than our daughter's puberty. The things I'm sure would please her—a "greatest hits" disco CD, a bottle of Jungle Gardenia—now make her cry or get mad. She says things like, "Have I ossified?"

To answer her I sniff the air. "I thought I smelled something."

SHE STARTED TAKING some night courses (she says just because she earned a degree doesn't mean she learned anything) and she takes a book wherever she goes. She tried to read at the dinner table, and even my daughters backed me up in letting her know there is a limit to rudeness.

I'm hoping it's a passing stage. When we moved to the new house, she threw out her little plastic "Least Changed" trophy, saying she now considered that award an insult. I've noticed BiDi still has hers in the glass-and-walnut display case Sergio built for Franny's hockey honors.

Our daughter Lin won't have anything to do with Franny; she calls her a dork with a capital "d" which perturbs Dev and BiDi, who'd like their best friend thing to be passed down to the daughters. I get along okay with Sergio, but I'd known Big Mike, BiDi's first husband, since the second grade, so there was this loyalty thing there. Big Mike and BiDi divorced about four years ago. Big Mike said he needed his freedom. He told me this one late-October day when we were laying on our stomachs in a duck blind. I almost shot my arm off, I was so shocked.

"Freedom from BiDi? What are you—crazy?"

The wad of tobacco Big Mike always had in his mouth traveled the length of his lower lip. "She's a lot different at home, Dick."

"I'll bet," I said, wiggling my eyebrows.

Big Mike laughed and waved his gun at the autumn sky, a big full blue.

"Damn ducks know we're here," he said. "They've changed their flight pattern." His tongue poked the chew into the corner of his mouth. "Believe me," he said, squinting up at the sky, "BiDi puts on a hell of a show, but at home it's like living with a warden. That big cookie jar? The one that's shaped like a caboose that she made in ceramics? Every time I do something that bugs her, I gotta put a quarter in it. A quarter if I chew in the house. A quarter if I don't put the toilet seat down. A quarter if I drink more'n two beers a night. Christ, pretty soon it'll cost a quarter just to put my arms around her."

I wanted to pursue this, but Big Mike just shook his head and spit out a slimy wad of tobacco.

BiDi went through sort of a wild period after the divorce was finalized and Big Mike moved to Wisconsin; she was out dancing at King Olaf's almost every night, getting drunk with strikers from the meatpacking plant and truck drivers who had pulled off the interstate.

Sergio had a booth at a confections and chocolate convention in Fargo and came across King Olaf's on his way down to Minneapolis. He and BiDi were married three weeks later, in our backyard, under a trellis Devera made me rig up. BiDi wore a dress that looked as if it would transfer straight to the honeymoon, no problem. Pastor Egeqvist miffed a line or two; put a cleavage like that in front of any man—of the cloth or not—he's going to get flustered.

Sergio started up a store on Main Street—about five blocks from the car lot—and he's done so well that he's thinking of going national. He'll become a rich man off chocolate cakes, of all things. They are good, though, and I'm not all that big on chocolate in the first place (unlike my wife). Sergio says the original recipe came from his Spanish grandmother who fell in love with a Viennese baker.

Sergio's family has led dramatic lives—his father was an opera singer who lost the use of his voice during his first week in America. He was mugged and punched in the throat by some thug wearing brass knuckles (whenever I think of that story, my hand automatically goes to my Adam's apple). His mother was a psychic, but Sergio says if she had a gift for it, she never unwrapped it. She died last year in a bus crash, an accident, Sergio points out, she obviously failed to predict.

Sergio's an interesting guy, but, man, he's got way too much energy for me. I think the only time he sits down for an extended period is when he's driving his car. Ask him to shoot a game of pool with you and you'll get dizzy watching him run around the table.

Franny's nuts about Sergio, even though she's Big Mike from her shoe size (huge) to her skill on the hockey rink. (Big Mike's hat trick won White Falls its first and only state high-school championship.)

BiDi told us when Sergio met Franny, he actually cried.

"I cannot believe you have the name of my own beloved grandmother," he said, holding her head in his hands. Franny (he never calls her by her nickname, it's always Francesca) had gotten scared and BiDi had to explain that Sergio didn't mean to frighten her, he was just an emotional guy. Now Sergio plays goalie in Franny's pickup games on the lake. He wears boots because he never learned to skate.

Lin won't acknowledge us on Family Skate Nights; she just hangs around in a cluster of teenagers that somehow manage to look surly, even on ice.

Devera just laughs and says, "She's fourteen years old, Dick, what do you expect?" Still, I'm happy that Darcy at eleven lets me hold her hand when the "Blue Danube" or "Tennessee Waltz" is piped through the loudspeakers Alf Johannson rigged up in his icehouse.

Dev is a good skater, better than me and she knows it. She's not fancy—no pirouettes or double axels—but she's fast. She wears black speed skates, and even if I didn't have a mild nicotine habit, I'd never catch her. She skates around the rink that we've cleared off on the lake, bent over and moving only one arm like she's on the Olympic team, and I think how much pleasure it would give me if she wiped out.

She always laughs when I tell her that and then I say, what the hell, show-off, I love a fast woman. Most of the time she unlaces my skates when we're ready to leave and rubs my feet until they're warm. It's one of those married things I never knew I'd be such a sucker for.

BiDi

MY NAME'S PRONOUNCED "B-D"—short for Beverly Diane, which I'm never called except on official forms or by my mother when she phones in from her seniors' condo in Naples, Florida. I wear a size five and brother, do I work at it. After my divorce, I played around with bulimia for a while, but it was never really my thing. I prefer speed. Ted Erck, our family physician, lets me have a prescription whenever I ask; he says I know my body better than anyone else does. I wish all doctors had his sense; of course, Ted's a boozer and still pops the occasional pill plus I've heard he used to have a pretty good ether habit going. So the man understands vices.

I work out on a rowing machine, which Sergio thinks is crazy.

"We got a canoe! Row across the lake!"

He doesn't seem to realize I like my exercise to seem like exercise.

If you asked me what the three most important things in my life were, this is what my list would look like.

1. My body and the maintenance of
2. My husband, Sergio
3. Devera, my best friend
4. My daughter, Franny
5. My house

* * *

I guess I can't narrow it down. The list is pretty much in order of importance, too, although Franny could move up if she started behaving herself.

Honestly, only God or some oddball chromosome could be responsible for a woman like me having a daughter like Franny. I'm as blond as a baby chick (the rinse is only to bring out the highlights) and Franny's hair is flat black. Even Big Mike, her father, is fair, in a redheaded sort of way. Franny's heavy, too. I'd say fat, but she says if she hears that word one more time, she'll run away. As far as the Dairy Maid, I tell her. She's taller than me by three inches and she's only fourteen. It's kind of scary. I'm hoping for a trans-formation—you know, the Ugly Duckling turns into a graceful swan type thing—but I wouldn't bet any cold cash on it. I've found the less attention I give her, the less she seems to want to annoy me. She even said no to seconds on dessert last night—a chocolate mint cake that Sergio's kitchen is testing—and that's news enough to make the front page.

Sergio does all the cooking—you'd think he'd be tired after a day of measuring cocoa powder and flour and butter and sifting and greasing and baking; but no, after his shower he's in the kitchen again, whipping up something like wild-rice soup or steak medallions. It doesn't bother him that I ask for a child's portion night after night; he says my figure is "thee stoff ove laygends." Maybe when the money really starts coming in, I'll go down to the Cities and have my lower ribs removed or whatever surgical procedure gives you back your twenty-two-inch waist. No matter how many hours I spend on that Twist-A-Board, there's no way I can get my waistline below twenty-four inches.

Devera has no shame. When we barbecue on the lake, she'll wear swimsuits or shorts like the rest of us, and that cellulite on the back of her legs shakes like leaves in the breeze. I gave her a book once on how to shape up her thighs, knowing I was hurting her feelings but also knowing hurt feelings ain't nuthin' compared to thighs like that.

See, Devera and I are what you'd call on the same wavelength—always have been—and I feel bad that she's let herself go. It's kind of a reflection on our friendship, what we value, you know? We used to spend hours browsing at cosmetics counters and boutiques, trying on "ocher mist" eye shadows and "ruby fire" lipsticks. Nowadays, of course, you buy your lipstick untested—who wants a fatal disease or, God forbid, a case of herpes?

But anyway, ask her today and Devera acts like an afternoon at the mall is Chinese water torture and our long, two-carafes-of-wine lunches at the Cattle Baron have been cut to forty minutes at the Sub Shoppe.

Devera's changing in other ways, too. We don't bowl anymore on Tuesday nights because she's taking a night class at the college. On Ancient Rome, for crying out loud. Don't get me wrong—I'm all for self-improvement as long as it's applicable to *real* life. Community ed. offers a lot of practical classes like Preserving Your Photographs or Sewing with Your Serger—who in their right mind would want to take a class about a bunch of guys in togas? Devera's got a degree, too (I lasted three semesters at White Falls State before I woke up to the fact that guess what!—this is boring!) so it's not like she *has* to take this class. She says she wants to explore worlds other than her own, to learn for the sake of learning this time, and not just memorize for tests. The "explore worlds" part sounds a little hokey, but I hear what she's saying about memorization. Every single Saturday night I was tortured by my grandma Smoland if I hadn't memorized a Bible verse. If I messed up on one little *ye* or *thee*, I'd get swatted on the hand with a wooden spoon. I swear, to this day I look over my shoulder every time I get near a Bible.

We were sitting in Devera's huge new kitchen, looking out of a window that was big as a wall and facing the lake. She had pulled up the narrow blinds (you'll always find curtains in my kitchen—blinds belong in a dentist's office) so that the sun splashed on the floor like something broken. Devera was telling me about the guy who taught her Ancient Rome class.

"He's been to Europe twice," she said.

"So have you," I reminded her.

She sniffed. "Package tours. Two-week package tours. Once with my parents and once with my parents' money. You know what you see the most on package tours?" Devera pressed some crumbs on her plate with her middle finger. "The back of the head of the person sitting ahead of you."

"Excuse me," I said, like, oh of course, I'm such a stupid idiot to not know such a thing. I dug in my purse for a packet of Sweet'n Low. Devera says the facts aren't in on artificial sweeteners even though they say they are and she drinks her coffee black anyway. I poured in two packets, just to spite her.

"Say," I said, trying to change the subject, "Connie Cole got that Korean baby. She's flying to California on Thursday."

"I know, Dick told me. She was in the store to get a new lint rack for her dryer." She sliced herself another piece of coffee cake and wiped the knife clean with her fingers. "I'd offer you a piece, but what's the point? We both know you wouldn't eat it anyway."

Quick as a light switch being flicked on, tears sprang to my eyes. I cupped my hand by my face and flipped out a contact lens.

"I swear, I'm going to get soft lenses," I said, pretending my eye was irritated. The bright bowl of plastic sat in my palm looking like a hard blue tear.

It's not in my constitution to waste a lot of energy crying; in my view, it just makes you feel worse, besides messing up your makeup. I'm not saying Devera can't hurt my feelings when we fight—boy, we've had some doozies over my divorce, over clothes and children and even bathroom tile—but this time I couldn't quite figure out why in the heck I felt so bad. So instead of laying my head on that ugly faux-whatever countertop and bawling my eyes out, I told Dev that just because I wasn't a fan of lousy store-bought cake didn't mean she couldn't pour me another cup of coffee.

DEVERA

IT IS NOT early menopause, as Dick'll suggest, but some hormones or glands or brain neurons are acting up at my expense. It seems as if my life has tipped—not over, just slightly, like a china cup whose bottom rim doesn't quite fit into the saucer indentation. I sit staring out at the lake after everyone has gone to bed, thinking the strangest thoughts. Last night I almost drove myself crazy thinking about the word *life* as in "she lost her life."

Okay, she lost her physical *life*, her breath forever, the beatings of her heart, the function of her internal organs. She also lost her *life*—the day-to-day routines and relationships that made up her days and her plans; the dreams of something wonderful happening in her future *life*. Maybe she lost a child who was her whole *life*. And where does lost *life* go? I still basically think there's a heaven, but I can look at a night sky and get all panicky thinking this place is far too big for one little *life* like mine, that the universe will swallow me up without so much as a hiccup.

These are very confusing thoughts for a woman whose biggest worry used to be what badge to have the girls work on during a Scout meeting. I've tried to share some of these weird thoughts with Dick, but that's like forcing a man to wear paisley when he prefers checks.

"You're just scaring yourself," he'll say. "Why work yourself up?"

Dick and I knew we were getting married from the

eleventh grade on. I liked his blond straight hair and his turned-up nose (although it's getting sort of piggy looking as he gets older)—he looked like my brother Don would have. When he was twelve years old, Don was killed in a burning paper shack with his best friend, Bruce, Dr. Erck's son. The fire inspector surmised that Don and Bruce had finished their paper routes and went back to the shack for a cigarette. ("Cigarette?" Dad had screamed. "Don was a church acolyte, for Christ's sake!") There was a can of gasoline in the corner, belonging to Dave Caroll, who kept it hidden in the shack so that his mother wouldn't know he was borrowing another boy's motorbike—"a dollar a ride and you supply the gas." Don or Bruce was careless with the matches and the paper shack blew, waking up the whole town of White Falls.

I was eight years old and developed a hero worship for Don I hadn't had in real life. I have only recently allowed memories of brotherly cruelty to sneak in—once he threw my favorite doll, Eva-Marie, into the deep part of the lake and he used to give me snakebites on my forearm until red welts rose—but mostly I remember the times he put up a swing for me and taught me how to dive backward.

I'll state the obvious; Don's death was a great trauma. My mother shut down a big part of herself (in my mind, I see a little "Closed" sign hanging over her heart). It was as if loving, or at least expressing that love, was too risky a proposition. Dad cried and drank his way through his grief, and just when it seemed he'd drown in booze and tears, he emerged on the other side, fairly whole. As their surviving child, I decided I could only be one thing: perfect. I would cause my parents no pain, no worry, no frustration or anger, which was, of course, a goal way too lofty for a kid, but I tried.

I became diligent in my quest for perfection, earning the best marks in school, the most stars in piano class, the blue ribbons in 4-H, all the while biting my nails until blood oozed from their sides; one single habit my mother was repulsed by, a habit that loomed large, casting a shadow over all that bright perfection.

"Honestly, Devera, you've got the hands of a degenerate," she would tell me as I offered her a freshly picked bouquet of daffodils or a cup of coffee (Little Miss Perfect learned how to brew superb coffee in the fourth grade). Dad would intercede, saying in his loud bear voice, "Let me get a whiff of those pretty flowers!" or "I'll take a cup of that joe!"

I could get up early on a Saturday morning and wash and wax the kitchen floor and wipe the windows clean with crumpled newspapers and a vinegar solution and Helen would grab my hands, telling me I should protect them with rubber gloves, but then she'd amend her scolding, asking what was the point of protecting hands with degenerate-person fingernails anyway.

I still give myself manicures by mouth, and although I no longer gnaw them to the quick, it still causes my mother, who believes that you can tell a woman's character by her hands, great suffering. I've told her that's a pretty limited way of judging a person and she always answers, "Limited or not, it's true."

My dad, on the other (nail-bitten) hand, thinks I'm the be-all-end-all of daughters, and in Dick, he found the son he lost. Even though he complains about Dick's lack of ambition ("Why do I need ambition?" Dick asks me, "I'm inheriting everything!") he truly loves him as a son.

Dick's real desire is to be a cabaret singer. He's got a microphone and speakers in the rec room and he sings there every night after the news. He's so conscientious about it that he won't answer any phone calls then; we're supposed to tell whoever's on the line that he's "in rehearsal."

He's built a small stage and now he's thinking about turning the whole rec room into a nightclub with live shows on weekends. He says we'd get especially good trade in the summer when tourists fill every cabin and lodge on our chain of lakes. (Flame Lake is the lake we live on and the one that's within the city limits of White Falls; there's also Uncle's Lake, Spirit Lake, Lake Piper, and Veil Lake, which has the distinction of attracting the rowdiest tourists and killer horseflies.)

Dick accompanies himself on a little Casio keyboard and

sings old standards that have been treated to his lyric changes. "Born Free" turns into a song about old clothes called "Worn Through." "Swing Low" is a song about baseball. Our daughter Darcy cracks up at her father but Lin thinks he's "gross," and me, well, he makes me feel old. I see people on TV who are older than me and they seem years younger. They dress like they're juniors in high school with the kind of hair that looks like it exploded on their heads. On a music awards show, a rapper won what was called a Genius Award. Genius Award? To me, rappers sound like they're yelling at everybody (and in bad rhyme schemes, too) and all their backup dancers look the same—like pistons in a car engine, pumping away. I probably don't understand their whole point, though, which makes me feel, what else: old. But what do you expect from someone who's married to a guy who spins around at the keyboard while singing his version of "Blue Moon," which is, you guessed it, about an Eskimo who likes to expose himself?

My Ancient Rome professor, Gerhart Ludwig, has taught in San Francisco and Syracuse, New York. He speaks three languages and has a beagle named after Isak Dinesen. He got his baby toe cut off by a power mower when he was eleven years old. We had coffee last week after class; I'm nervous as a cat about this week's. Nervous and hopeful. Not that I'm looking for anything to happen, but it sure is nice to have the attention of someone who likes, in his beautiful bass voice, to throw a little Latin into the conversation; who's biggest thrill isn't driving the latest-model Seville before anyone else.

You know how crabby you get when you're driving and even though you thought you understood the directions perfectly, you get lost? That's where I'm at right now; I thought I was headed a straight route and now I'm all tangled up on side streets.

Being a wife and mother, I still believe, is the main entrée on life's plate, but I'm starting to think I missed out on some of the more exotic side dishes. Where's the hot pepper relish? The garlic pilaf? Can I get a helping of that mango aspic, please?

I don't know, sometimes I fantasize about running away to Minneapolis, getting an apartment, having my hair cut in one of those chic places where the windows display neon and not dusty jars of wave set, and going to poetry readings at night. But how do you expect a woman who's afraid of going down to the basement alone at night to do something like that?

SERGIO

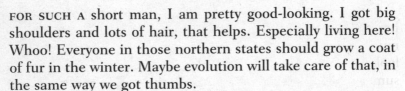

FOR SUCH A short man, I am pretty good-looking. I got big shoulders and lots of hair, that helps. Especially living here! Whoo! Everyone in those northern states should grow a coat of fur in the winter. Maybe evolution will take care of that, in the same way we got thumbs.

I flew to Chicago last week—it is a sure thing, "Cakes by Sergio" will be opening there next winter. I got a nice location by the Lincoln Park Zoo. Minneapolis, too, is a go. Now when the "Fortune 500" list is published, I have dreams.

I say in three years I'll get to New York. It will be nice to go back to New York a businessman, instead of some punk. Do you know the things I miss about New York are the things I used to hate? I miss taking the subway from Brooklyn to the City, the dark tunnels, the scary feeling when the train stops for no good reason and you take a big gulp of air and think: suffocation. I miss building after building hogging up the sky, so when you look up and see a rectangle of blue you think, yeah! This one's mine!

I got a funny life here—I'm doing hockey drills with a fourteen-year-old girl! And keeping track of her game schedules and points per game on a big chart in the kitchen! I love my Francesca, though. I would adopt her in a minute but that Big Mike has his rights, too. Not that he uses them much! Francesca has only been to see him once since BiDi and me got married. I don't know if we could ever be friends; BiDi says our personalities are night and day and besides, he's about two feet bigger than me going both directions.

Francesca calls me Sergie, which is half Sergio/half Daddy. I am trying to talk BiDi into having a brother for her, but she says, "Now let's put a veto on that idea right now."

I think by next year she will be ready, though. BiDi turns thirty-nine soon and I think she will hear the biological clock ticking like Big Ben. I have good instincts about women and I think this is how it will happen.

My wife is really something. She reminds me of the cakes I bake. Like them, she is pretty to look at, sweet, and maybe sinful. I named a Dutch chocolate cake "the BiDi" but my wife said no way, she could just hear all the yokels asking for "a piece of BiDi." I named the cake the Rosina instead.

A funny thing about BiDi, with her fantastic body—really, her skin is smooth as marble—she doesn't like to use it much. I mean with me. She wears these negligee things that look like they might float away like a ghost and in the summer bikinis that are like two ribbons, but when it comes to doing something more than teasing—forget it! I am not all that big a Casanova, but it would be nice to enjoy my wife on a more regular basis.

So I got something going with Noreen Norquist. Noreen's husband was shot up so bad in Vietnam that hardly nothing works, but she's stuck by him and tells me she loves him. She knows I love BiDi, too; there is no misunderstanding there. We just do with each other what we can't do with our spouses.

After Les and Myra Lund punch out at five, that is when we do it. I lock the store and in the back-room kitchen, well, that is where. The air smells of cakes and it is very warm and nice. Noreen is about thirty pounds heavier than me but she makes me feel very much a man. She is kind, too; she volunteers as the activity director at the nursing home and always her own home is open to people in need. Right now Emil Anderson who lost his wife to cancer is staying in her guest room.

BiDi will never find out. We are very careful. Of course, BiDi probably wouldn't care anyway—she knows I am wrapped around her little finger, if not her body, ha-ha, that is a joke.

We are going over to Dick and Devera's house tonight. I am going to help Dick put some track lighting in over a little stage he has built. My friend is thinking of opening a nightclub in his basement! It wouldn't surprise me if he did—not a real one with a liquor license and cash registers and waitresses—just one where people could come and drink and dance (BYOB, he'll make sure everyone understands that). Dick would be able to sing to a crowd and he says anyone could get on stage if they had a song to sing or jokes to tell. He's thinking of calling the place Your Oasis on Flame Lake. All of us like the name, except Devera. She says it's too long.

DICK

WE WERE HAVING what I thought was a nice family dinner; nice if you make allowances for Devera's cooking, which I've had to do lately. Dev's normally a good cook, but for the past couple months I've made regular runs to the stove to turn down the fire under a burning pot, only to find Devera lost in some strange reverie, staring at, but not reading, a book, or looking out at the lake like it's hypnotized her. Meanwhile, we're served dinners which vary in their degree of over-cooking. We're talking charred, singed, or black.

I know I sound like a male chauvinist pig (you'd never know that was an outmoded phrase the way it's bandied about in my house) but she refuses my offers to help. I am allowed to make breakfast, but dinner is still the domain of The Incinerator. Lin's in home ec. now and has these "Cook Night" assignments, so at least when she's in the kitchen there's a lot less carbon on the table.

Anyway, we were sawing through our porterhouses when suddenly Devera announces, "You might have noticed there's not any meat on my plate."

"Going easy on the fillings?" I asked.

Devera smiled at my joke, but there was that little jump in her jaw muscles that told me she really didn't think I was funny.

"No," she said, patting her mouth with these cloth napkins she insists we use, "no, I've decided I can no longer in good conscience eat meat."

"You had bacon this morning," Darcy pointed out.

Devera's jaw muscles jumped higher. "I only decided it this afternoon. After weeks of internal debate." She looked to me to dare doubt her sincerity.

"That's great, Mom," said Lin, shoving her plate aside. "I could skip the meat, too."

"Now wait a minute," I said. "A grown woman can make that kind of decision but not a kid."

"Why not?" said Lin and Devera together. They smiled at one another and Lin said, "Jinx." They hooked their baby fingers together and shut their eyes and, as the dumb ritual has it, made a wish.

"Because you're only fourteen," I said. "And a kid needs her protein."

Darcy swallowed the piece of steak she'd been chomping on. "You can get protein in lots of other food, Dad," she said, and my heart did a little twist because Darcy is always on my side.

"Well, not meat protein," I said, knowing I sounded stupid the minute the words were out. I coughed. "I mean not the complex proteins found in meat."

Devera laughed her pretty tinkling laugh, which I have always loved but not when it was directed at her dim-bulb husband.

"Oh, Dick," she said, "the protein you get in meat isn't any more complex than the protein you get in beans or nuts or tofu."

I scraped up a last forkful of peas and swabbed at my mouth with the napkin. "Darce, you gonna help me and Sergio put those lights up?" I was not going to fly my ignorance at half-mast and ask exactly what the hell tofu was.

My bad mood drifted away when I got into the basement, which makes me feel the same way my tree house did when I was a kid.

"Dad, you think people will really want to come here?" Darcy asked as we were pulling the stepladder out of the Tool Room. (It's kind of embarrassing; there's so much space in this house we've named all the rooms.)

"Sure," I said, "who wouldn't want to come to Your Oasis? You would, wouldn't you?"

"You bet," said Darcy, "I'm here from the git go."

My younger daughter complains she was born too late. She doesn't consider herself dressed unless she is wearing a hat and, while she is "hep to" current slang, usually she talks like a forties radio announcer, using words and phrases like *you bet, nifty, that's swell*, and *ain't life grand?*

Lin teases her about getting her vocabulary from those Valentine candies—those little printed hearts?—but then Lin's at the stage where being cool has its very strict definitions. Right now she doesn't wear any color but black—it's like a pastel would give her a rash or something.

I know that being a teenager is like what it was like being a communist in the former Soviet Union: you'd better follow the party line or risk being sent to Siberia, which I suppose for a teenager is Nerdsville. I'm sure that according to Lin that's where I live. Hell, she probably considers me the mayor of Nerdsville. Lin's defected from me in a big way. Devera says it's just a phase. So was the Civil War, I told her, so was the Spanish Inquisition. Doesn't mean nobody gets hurt.

"So kids'll be able to do stuff here?" Darcy asked me as we positioned the ladder on the stage.

"Well, sure, Darce. We're an equal-opportunity stage. All talent allowed, no matter how small."

"Live, here on our stage," said Darcy, imitating Ed Sullivan. We have a collection of old television shows on tape and my daughter does impressions of everyone from Jackie Gleason to Don Knotts as Deputy Barney Fife. "Those with talent—and those who left it at the hat check."

"Hey," I said, "maybe I'll use you as my emcee."

Darcy hugged my knees as I climbed the ladder and I swayed on the third rung.

"Trying to knock your old man down?" I said, but I couldn't help smiling.

We worked for about an hour—fortified by the late-sixties and early-seventies music that I did everything important to—graduated high school to, got laid in backseats to, got married to—and that I stock our big Wurlitzer jukebox with.

Darcy was boogying around to "Love the One You're With," playing air guitar like the maestro she is, and I was laughing, trying to screw a fixture into its socket, when Sergio blasted through the door like a gas explosion.

"It looks fantastic," he said, twirling around like the little plastic ballerina inside a jewelry box I once bought Lin. Even if I hadn't been high up on the ladder, I wouldn't have been able to watch him—he just made me too damn dizzy.

"Wow," said Franny, who had followed Sergio in. She plopped down on the couch and hugged a pillow to her chest. "It looks just like a nightclub."

Darcy's air guitar vanished and she flung herself on the couch next to Franny.

"I didn't know you were coming."

"I finished my homework," said Franny, "and there was nothing on cable."

"I know what you mean," said Darcy. "It just winds up being more channels showing more shows you don't want to see."

Franny nodded, considering this. Unlike Lin, who automatically thinks anything that comes out of her sister's mouth is less interesting than radio static, Franny listens to Darcy. But I've always noticed that about Franny—she's the type of person who gives everyone their due.

"You want to shoot a game of pool?" she asked. "Unless you want to keep helping your dad?"

Darcy jumped up like she was spring-loaded. "You can get along without me, can't you, Pops?" She slapped the side of the ladder as she passed. I shrugged as if it would be a hardship.

They went off to the far side of the room and the Three Dog Night song Sergio punched in on the jukebox turned their voices into a blur.

Sergio helped himself to a beer from the vintage cooler I had found at a yard sale. He threw me one and I caught it, my chest smacking against a ladder rung.

"Doesn't anyone realize I'm up on a ladder?"

"What, do you think you are going to fall to your death?" said Sergio. "You are up three steps."

I gave my beer a little shake as I opened it and aimed it at his Brylcreemed head. He ducked under the narrow stream of foam and hopped as if we were playing a game of jump rope.

"Take a break?" he asked.

"Aren't we already?" I said, wondering if it's because English is his second language that he has to state the obvious.

We sat down at the bar, turning out on our stools so we could watch the girls play pool. We didn't have the best seats in the house, but we could get a general idea of how the game was going.

"Geez, Franny's getting big," I said. She dwarfed Darcy the way a sequoia dwarfs a scrub pine.

"You're telling me," said Sergio. "And her feet! We are buying new shoes every other weekend." He pulled on his beer and leaned toward me, saying something as his shoulder touched mine. Normally I'm put off by that sort of thing, but Sergio's the type who's got to touch when he talks, no offense intended.

"What's that?" I asked, cocking my head.

Sergio narrowed his eyes and leaned his head closer to mine. "I said, 'She got her period today.' "

"Franny did?" I looked at the big hulk of a girl with the black straight hair that had been pulled into a skimpy little ponytail. "Gee, that's too bad."

"Bad?" said Sergio. "Why bad? You and BiDi—what is the matter with you? She is fourteen after all—it was a high time her womanhood began."

I had to laugh; I mean, who'd suspect two guys sitting around drinking a beer would be talking about menstrual periods? Plus Sergio sounded so proud, as if he was announcing Franny's shots-on-goal record or an A-plus report card.

"She told me first," said Sergio, and his eyebrows tilted

and he looked like he might cry. "Before BiDi, before her own mother, she came to me and said, 'Sergie, guess what happened to me at school today?' "

"Oh, geez, she didn't . . . have an accident or anything, did she?"

I'll never forget Ann Heffelmeyer who started her period in seventh-grade geography and the whole class knew about it when she went to point out the continent of Asia on the map that pulled down from the blackboard like a shade.

Sergio rolled out his lower lip and shook his head. "She discovered the situation in the bathroom. Before any . . . damage was done."

I finished my beer in one big sip and crumpled the can in what Devera claims is my "typical he-man fashion." I think she still thinks they make beer cans out of that heavy aluminum or something.

"Nice shot!" Franny said, loud enough so we could hear her. Darcy wiggled with excitement—she still takes praise like a puppy.

"Dad, watch this," she yelled across the room, knowing with that kid antenna that she was being watched by a grown-up. "Nine ball in the side pocket." She leaned against the table and wiggled her butt in the air and with a nice crack, sank the nine ball, just as she said, in the side pocket. I gave her the thumbs-up.

"She's good," said Sergio. "A regular Milwaukee Fats."

I laughed. "That's *Minnesota* Fats, Sergio."

"I know, I know, of course I know. I only say that because all of a sudden, you look so gloomy."

It's weird, having a conversation with Sergio is like talking to a woman. He'll catch me off guard, he can read me so easily.

I was "gloomy." It bummed me out to think about Franny's period. Well, not hers: Lin's. It seems the day Dev got Lin her own box of teen tampons was the day Lin slammed a door on me. Maybe mothers go through the same thing when their sons start growing their wispy little mustaches and their voices change, but I don't know. I think it's a much more drastic thing with fathers and daughters.

Lin used to sit at my feet and I'd dry her wet hair with a towel and then rub her back a little. She started wearing a bra around the same time her period started and I remember the unspoken self-consciousness that passed between us when I would pat her on the back and feel the outline of her bra through her sweatshirt.

She blow-dries her hair now. I still dry Devera's hair—she says hand drying really brings out the shine—and Darcy's, too. I savor the smell of the baby shampoo Darcy still uses. Call me a sap, but to me it means I'm still her daddy and she's still my little girl who needs me.

DEVERA

THE NIGHT SERGIO came over to help with the lighting, Dick came to bed all weepy.

He's done this a number of times in our marriage—he comes out of the bathroom blowing his nose and then falls into bed as if he's just run a marathon, and I'll feel these little shudders. I used to be so touched, I thought I'd married the World's Most Sensitive Man, but this time I just rolled over and hugged the edge of the bed, hoping he'd think I was asleep.

He sniffled for a while and then he whispered, "Dev? Dev?" and then he leaned over and shook my shoulder. "Devera, are you asleep?"

If I had been, he certainly would have woken me up, but I just mumbled and moaned as if I were in some deep REMs.

"Devvie, I need to talk to you."

I sighed, a big put-upon sigh. "What is it?" I asked, packing aggravation into each word.

Dick snuggled next to me and I thought, big baby. What greeting-card commercial was this six-foot three-inch man crying over now?

He sniffed phlegm into his throat. "Devvie, the Tides of Time are rolling over us."

Where Dick comes up with these gems I never know, but he can say the most ridiculous things with complete seriousness.

"What do you mean, Dick?" I said, looking at the clock and hoping he'd wrap things up by midnight.

Dick slid up on the pillows and rested his cheek against his fist. "Franny started her period today."

I stared at him as if he were the nut he was.

Dick's eyes got all filmy and the corner of his mouth turned down. "Don't you see, Devera? Our little girls aren't little girls anymore."

"Dick," I said. "What do you expect? Kids grow. I'm surprised Franny didn't start a long time ago, but so what? She's not our little girl in the first place."

Dick tucked a pillow against his chest. "You know what I mean. They're slipping away from us. We're getting older."

I reached for the glass of water I always keep on my nightstand (my mother has successfully rammed into my head the necessity of hydrating the skin) and took a big gulp.

"I mean, first it was Lin," said Dick, "and pretty soon Darcy will be curling her eyelashes and chasing after boys and having her period."

"Dick, they're not committing treason. They're just growing up." I drank some more water and some of it sloshed on the front of my nightgown.

"Nice move, Bessie," said Dick, smiling.

I glowered at him. "Bessie" is short for "Messy Bessie," one of Dick's cute nicknames for me. I always seem to wear some remnant of a meal I've eaten, but now didn't seem to be the time to joke about it. I mean, wasn't Dick in the throes of despair over aging, and losing his little girls? All of a sudden he could step out of his misery to make fun of me? I rolled over and switched off the lamp.

"Come on, Devvie, I was just teasing." Dick wrapped his arms around me and pressed up against my back. He kissed my neck. "You're the cutest litle slob I know. Why don't we get down and dirty together?"

"Oh, God," I said, peeling his arms off as if they were leeches. I stood up, untwisting my nightgown which had spiraled around my thighs. "You want to 'get down and dirty'? Gee, Dick, is that invitation supposed to turn me on? *Get down and dirty?*"

A quick blush spotted his cheeks and he shrugged his big shoulders.

"For God's sake, Dick, a minute ago you were blubbering about—what was it—the Tides of Time? And now you want to *get down and dirty*?"

"Geez, Dev, I—"

"Geez, Dev yourself," I said, pulling my pillow off the bed. "Geez, Dev yourself."

I stomped across the room but the thick carpet muffled my sounds of anger.

I tossed and turned in the guest-room bed, pulling the comforter up and then kicking it off. I was disappointed that Dick didn't come in after me; not that I wanted to get down and dirty, but I really do hate sleeping alone.

I woke up mad the next morning—mad because of our argument and madder still because I'd somehow stumbled back into our bed in the middle of the night. I don't remember going back, which makes me think that even while subconscious, I'm still a big chicken. Then at breakfast I accidentally helped myself to the sausage Dick had fried up.

"Suey, Suey," said my dear husband.

"Yeah, well, you're no Redford either."

"He's not insulting you, Mom," said Darcy. "He's reminding you."

I poured syrup all over my French toast, more than I cared for actually, but I wanted to make a point. "Yeah, I know. Reminding me that he thinks I should lose about ten pounds."

Resting his clasped hands high on his chest, Dick sat back in his chair, a smug smile on his face. "Reminding you, Ms. Purity, that you're supposed to be a vegetarian."

I looked away from his smirky little face and to my plate, where a couple links of sausage formed a corral around a pool of syrup. My tongue immediately probed at a piece of gristle between my teeth. I sat down, not knowing what to do.

"It's okay, Mom," said Darcy. "Lin had some, too."

"She said she liked the idea of not eating meat but she liked eating meat more." Dick smiled, and it was a gentle smile, but I wasn't in the mood for his understanding. With my fork I slid the sausage links off my plate and onto the serving platter. I scrubbed the grease off my lips with a napkin.

"A minor relapse," I said, pushing away from the table. "Anyone can have a minor relapse." I grabbed my purse off the rack by the door and told my family not to worry about me, I'd break my fast at the Top Hat, where a person could eat in peace.

I wasn't absolutely sold on fate, but there did seem proof of its existence when I walked into the diner and there was Gerhart Ludwig, pouring ketchup over his Cock A Doodle Special.

"My gauche side," he said, and wrinkled his beautifully shaped nose. "Alas, I can't seem to eat hash browns without ketchup."

I slid into the booth opposite his. "I don't think it's gauche at all," I said. Excitement had raised my voice to a Minnie Mouse register. "Gauche is when you declare you're going to be a vegetarian and then can't stay away from the breakfast sausage."

"Don't ever give up meat," said Gerhart Ludwig. "Your sex life will become as anemic as your soul."

Thankfully, Princess came by to take my order, saving me from any sort of reply.

"Dick get in my zapper yet?" asked the waitress as she poured me a cup of coffee. "My other one's bum—new batteries don't make a difference—I got to get up out of my chair every time I want to change channels."

"How do you manage?" asked Gerhart, but Princess just laughed and wagged her order tablet at him.

"You get a touch of arthritis in both knees and you tell me if you don't miss your zapper."

"My dear," said Gerhart, patting the crumbs off his mustache, "I wouldn't miss it at all. I never watch TV."

"You don't have a television?" I asked.

"Well, of course I have one," he said. "But I can't remember the last time I had it on. Maybe for the last election returns."

"Don't know what I'd do without a TV," said Princess. "It'd get pretty lonely at night without it."

"What on earth is she wearing on her head?" Gerhart asked me after Princess took my order.

I laughed. Princess wore one of those white cloth tiaras that waitresses wear, but she decorated hers with rhinestones so that it looked like a little crown. "Her husband nicknamed her Princess when they were married. Ever since he died, she honors his memory by dressing like . . . well, a princess."

"By God, it's a good thing he didn't call her 'pumpkin.' " I smiled at his joke as he laughed and then we sat in silence for a moment or two.

"So what do you do in the evenings?" I asked finally, forcing myself to stop stirring my coffee and looking him in the eyes.

My professor smiled. The teeth that showed between his beard and mustache were small squares and a little gray. There seemed to be a slight gray cast to everything about him—the pallor of his skin, his shaggy hair, his eye color, and the tweed of his jacket. It sounds unattractive, but actually it was sexy, in an unkempt, artistic black-and-white French-movie sort of way. He looked like what he was, a man steeped in books and ideas, who didn't have time for frivolous cosmetic niceties.

Gerhart tilted his head. "What do I do in the evenings? Have you something in mind?"

I laughed like an idiot because I didn't know what else to do. Gerhart's got a beautiful voice—it's what initially attracted me to him, especially when he used it to praise a particular thing I'd said or written in class—and asking me that question with that voice; well, I was close to hyperventilating.

Gerhart Ludwig picked up the stack of books next to his plate. "I've got a class in seven minutes," he said, "and you know how unruly students get when the professor's late." He reached into his pocket and took out some crumpled-up dollar bills (no wallet, I thought—how free! how bohemian!) and tossed them on the table.

"Think about my question," he said, his voice dripping a dark honey. "An essay one, if you will. We'll discuss your answer after class tomorrow night." He put a quarter next to his coffee saucer and pushed it around with his finger. "We're still on for coffee, yes?"

I nodded dumbly.

Gerhart Ludwig stroked his knit tie. "Good. We have a lot to . . . talk about."

I forced myself not to watch him leave and instead looked around the Top Hat, ready to explain that the chance breakfast I had with my night-school professor was innocent and not a prelude to adultery. But the patrons of the Top Hat needed no explanation. I inspired no curiosity. I was, after all, married to Dick Lindstrom, as if that were some sort of be-all, end-all.

BiDi

I WAS SHAMPOOING my carpet, putting a little dance step in to maximize my aerobic workout, when the doorbell rang. It wasn't a leisurely *ding-dong* either, it was *dingdongdingdong*, so I knew whoever was standing outside pressing the bell had something on his/her mind.

I thought it might be Claire Stenvig from next door. She's always baking up something and running out of ingredients.

I was thinking I'd add a tablespoon of salt to the cup of sugar she'd come mooching off me. She's the type who names all her recipes "Claire's Famous," so there's "Claire's Famous Chili," "Claire's Famous Popovers," etc., etc. It would give me a nice little charge to screw up whatever famous thing she was cooking up now.

"Devera," I said with true excitement when I opened the door. Number one, because it was nice to see her, and number two, because I had been certain it was Mrs. Famous Recipe.

"Hi, BiDi," she said, looking over her shoulder like the FBI was on her tail or something.

"You okay?" I asked as she barged past me, her hair flying frizzy and loose around her face. She was on her way to the couch when she stopped suddenly.

"Oh, you're shampooing your rug again," she said, standing on her heels. "I'm surprised there's any pile left."

"Ha, ha, ha," I said, but I couldn't be miffed, I was so happy Devera had dropped in. She used to always stop by without calling, but lately it seemed we never got together unless we made formal arrangements. "Come on in the kitchen, I'll make us some coffee."

"Coffee's what's getting me in trouble," she said. I didn't ask her to explain, I knew I'd be getting the full story—whatever it was—and a teeny shiver zipped through me.

Of course, Devera made a few snide comments about my housekeeping as I ground up the beans, but I'm used to them by now. She'll ask me if I really believe dust is life threatening or ask what's the difference between BiDi's kitchen and the Superior National Forest? Answer: BiDi's kitchen smells pinier. You get the picture. It used to hurt my feelings until I figured out she's so self-conscious about her own lax housekeeping that she feels a need to cut mine down. Hey, I'm the one with the problem just because I believe in cleanliness?

Anyway, this bantering small talk kept on until I poured the coffee and we sat down, our signal to *really* start talking.

"Beed," said Devera, wasting no time. "I think I'm about to start an affair."

I could feel my eyes bug out and I was surprised my contacts didn't pop right out on the table. Words failed me, but it didn't matter. Devera had a speech to make.

"It's not that I'm unhappy with Dick—well, I am, I guess, some of the time, but it's not really personal. I mean I'm unhappy with myself a lot of the time, too. I mean what else is new in a marriage, right? It's just that I've been feeling something missing lately. I wake up in a panic, thinking, 'Is this all my life is going to be? I'm happy to be a wife and mother, but is that it? That's all?' "

I thought she might want an answer from me here, but she marched on, thank God. What would I have said?

"I mean, remember, I was going to be a foreign correspondent and write about puppet governments in South America?"

Actually, what I remembered was Devera applying to the airlines to become a stewardess but then canceling her interview because she was getting married.

"Doesn't Devera Bergdahl Lindstrom the *person* get a chance?" she was saying. "Don't I get time to figure out how just me, myself, and I fit into the whole picture without the titles of wife and mother? I mean I've been so many things to other people that I don't know what to be for myself."

"Why don't you just be Dev?" I asked.

She took a sip of coffee then, and over the brim of the cup gave me the cold fish eye as if daring me to say one more wrong and/or stupid thing.

I obliged her. "So who's the guy?"

There's something about Devera; sometimes you can say the most innocent thing and she'll act as if you slapped her across the face. Other times you purposely say something to piss her off and it won't bother her in the least.

"Gerhart Ludwig," she said, a little defiantly, too.

"Gerhart Ludwig?" My mind raced, trying to come up with a picture that matched the name.

"My Ancient Rome professor?"

"Oh, yeah," I said, nodding, even as inside I yelled ISH! I never have reason to go onto the college campus, but I remembered a man collecting a tired-looking suit from the dry cleaner's. I had been standing behind him with an armload of fine washables (tip: If the label says *fine washable*, you'd better play it safe and dry-clean it) and I heard Ginger the counter girl call him Professor Ludwig. I remember being surprised, I thought he was some kind of vagrant. Well, maybe not quite a vagrant, but he did look pretty shabby in corduroy pants that had worn off most of their pinwale at the knees and a pathetic beard that could have used some Miracle-Gro. And his eyes—a weak and watery blue gray, the kind that makes me think a person's been inbred or suffers from tapeworm, or both.

"That's why I said coffee was the start of all my problems, because we've had coffee a couple of times and now I really think things are starting to perk!" Devera blushed and a sudden laugh, like car backfire, sputtered out of her.

I got the cookie jar—this cute caboose I made a long time ago in ceramics—off the counter. I had to do something besides sitting there with my mouth open. I held it in front of her.

"No thanks," said Devera, which had to be a first. This was a woman who didn't think coffee could be taken without dessert.

"So what are you going to do?" I asked finally.

Devera shrugged and her mouth puckered as if she were going to cry. I thought good, I'll get to comfort her and how long had it been since I'd done that? But then boom, she was smiling.

"Well, I'm not exactly going to plan anything," she said. "But if it's going to happen, I'll let it." She giggled then, and as much as I disapproved—you would, too, if you ever saw this Ludwig guy—I joined in and we giggled like we used to in the old days, until we were pounding the table with our palms.

"Oh, boy," said Devera finally, wiping her eyes. "I needed that." She got up and refilled our coffee cups. We're the kind of friends who can play hostess in each other's kitchen. "So, Dick tells me Franny finally got her period."

"What is it—out in a newsletter?"

"Sergio told him last night." Devera looked at me in this way she has, like she can figure out exactly what I'm thinking. "It really bothers you, doesn't it?"

Surprise tears came into my eyes and I blinked them back, embarrassed.

"Aw, Beed."

"She didn't even tell me," I said, taking my earring off and looking at it. "Sergio had to tell me."

"Aw, Beed," said Devera again. She rubbed my arm and I thought how ragged her cuticles looked.

"Not that I care a whole lot," I said, and polished my earring on a napkin. "Face it, Franny and I aren't exactly the king and queen of mothers and daughters, but still, when a girl first gets her period—especially when it's taken so long to get here—doesn't she usually tell her mother first?"

Devera smiled. "After they've told all their friends and a couple enemies. In fact, I distinctly remember the pleasure I got in telling my enemies I had gotten my period. Remember how Judy Jenson asked me to prove it?"

"And you called her a pervert?"

"Well, wasn't she? I hear she's serving time at Granite Penitentiary."

"No," I said.

Devera laughed. "No. I'm kidding." She stretched her arms back over her head and then looked at my ceramic caboose as if seeing it for the first time. "Hey, maybe I *will* have a couple of those cookies."

Honest to God, I could have leaned over and given her a big kiss.

To me, Devera saying "maybe I will have a couple of those cookies" was the same thing as reciting lines from a poem; you know, the one where God is in his heavens and everything is all right with the world, or however it goes.

SERGIO

THE PEOPLE AT Johannson's Heating & Air told me to "go crazy"—after all, they said, their company president only retires once—so I frosted the cake with raspberry *and* mocha! A chunk of almond bark in the shape of an air conditioner sat on the top of the cake, and Noreen, who does all the fancy work, painted SO LONG, ALF across it in gold leaf. As usual, she did her beautiful work and I was looking forward to thanking her in a special way (if you know what I mean) but Noreen had to leave work early, to drive her boarder Emil Anderson to the doctor's to have his insides looked at with a probe. He's getting to be a hypochondriac, Noreen says, any little gas and he's sure he's got cancer of the colon, any headache and it is a brain tumor. She says it is common when a spouse goes one way to think you will go that way, too. Although I think BiDi and I will die in completely different ways. Me, probably of the heart from arteries full of sugar and butter and eggs, and BiDi, well, I can't see her body breaking down—she will probably die of old age still a size two. No, probably she would kill herself before letting old age do any bit of harm to her body.

Yes, I am feeling a little bitter. I tell you truthfully, no man loves a woman more than I love BiDi, but still, I am not blind to her meanness. It only sparks up once in a while, but when it does it is no little campfire but one that races across a forest and burns everything in its path.

It is easy to see why she was hurt that Francesca would

come to me with news of her menstruating, but as I told BiDi, it is not as if she has always left the door open for Francesca, with a big sign that says COME ON IN!

"Just what's that supposed to mean?" BiDi said, her voice as cold as January in Flame Lake.

I hated to make an argument, but I had to speak the truth.

"Francesca does not feel she can come to you with her problems. She doesn't feel you listen to her."

"Oh, she doesn't feel I listen, huh? Who's willing to send her to a fat camp for a thousand bucks? Who took her to Mother/Daughter Jazzercize even though it was no picnic having the biggest daughter in the room? Who—"

"BiDi." I had to interrupt her, she was making me so angry. "BiDi, that is just the point. You think all of her problems are because she is a little big for her size—"

"A little big for her size! What exactly is that supposed to mean—a little big for her size!"

I gave her a dirty look. "You know what I mean. There is much more to Francesca than numbers on a scale. Why don't you give yourself the pleasure of seeing that?"

"I guess because she blocks the view!"

We glared at each other for a while, our eyes seeming like weapons.

"And why do you always call her Franny?" I asked, giving the fight more fuel.

"Everyone calls her Franny, for crying out loud!"

"You know that she wants to be called Francesca now."

"Cripes, you spoil her, Sergio. You'd call her Pippi Long-stocking if she asked you to."

"It's an easy thing to call a person by their given name," I said softly. This particularly bothers BiDi when I can remain calm while she is hollering.

"As far as I'm concerned, Franny hasn't earned the right to be called Francesca."

"But that is her name!" I had to yell a little now.

"I'll tell you what," said BiDi with a smile that is so unsmiley you wouldn't believe it, "when she's slimmed down and earned the right to a pretty name, I'll call her Francesca. But not a pound before."

We went to bed with our backs facing each other and enough room for a family of four to sleep between us.

So, my mood was not the most cheerful the next morning even though BiDi's was. (She doesn't seem to hold on to an argument long, and truthfully, I don't know if that is because she is forgiving or forgetful.) She was dancing around the kitchen to the oldies station that is most likely to play Elvis songs and gave me a big kiss, and mad as I was at her, I could not help but kiss her back. I'm gonna turn down something like that when it's offered?

THE BELL ABOVE the door tinkled and I was glad the cake was done, thinking it was Alf's secretary to pick it up, but no, there in the doorway was Francesca.

"Peanut!" I said. It is a pet name she likes, especially, I think, because she is no peanut.

A smile broke through on her face, which looked so sad, and she untangled herself from her heavy backpack. (She carries her schoolbooks home every night and BiDi asks her hasn't she grasped the concept of a locker?) She sat down on the white bench by the window.

"Sergie, can we talk?"

"When can we not talk?" I said, coming out from behind the counter.

"The game is tonight," she said (as if anyone had to be reminded!). "Is it okay for me to play? I mean with my period?"

Francesca never beats around a bush. She always steps right on top of it.

"Sure it is," I said, sitting down. "I have heard that a woman can go about all her daily activities with her period."

This got a little laugh out of Francesca. "Hockey isn't exactly a daily activity."

I shook my head. "There is no problem, I am sure. We'll ask your mother, though, just to make sure."

The look on her face asked me not to.

"Okay, we'll keep it to ourselves. Anyway, I am sure it is fine."

We chatted more about the game. Francesca's team had been knocked out of the finals but had gone further than anyone expected; in fact, White Falls was as excited as if this were the state championship game instead of the regional's consolation one. Francesca was the only freshman—and the only girl!—to play on the varsity squad.

Big Mike was even going to make a rare appearance, but then his appendix burst.

"I had just gotten into my Jeep," he told Francesca from his hospital-room phone, "we were going to do a little off-road driving, when BAM! I thought I had been shot in the stomach!"

Fortunately, his girlfriend Stacy was with him and called the ambulance.

"Thanks for saving my dad's life," Francesca told her politely.

"Thank God," said Stacy. "He did the saving."

"Actually, it was the paramedics," BiDi whispered, her hand cupped over the telephone receiver we were listening in on. BiDi would never admit it, but I knew she didn't like the idea of Big Mike having a girlfriend.

"You never heard of Wayne Gretsky having these problems," said Francesca after I served us some macadamia brownies.

"No," I agreed. "There aren't too many hockey players who sit out because of cramps."

"Or bloating," said Francesca.

"Or general crankiness," I said, which got us to laughing, because when BiDi has her period, she complains of all these things, but most especially, what she calls "general crankiness."

Francesca kissed me on the cheek when she left and told me she would score a goal for me.

"My hero," I said, holding my hands to my heart and fluttering my eyelashes, a regular La Gioconda.

Alf's secretary came in shortly after that and picked up the cake and tipped me even though I refused so heartily. But I have learned as a businessman that there comes a time when it is just bad form to refuse a tip of a similar complimentary gesture, so I pocketed the five, thinking I would give it to Francesca. So the sun was really coming out on my day, especially when Noreen Norquist came rushing in just at closing time. Emil Anderson had come out of his exam just fine. His doctor told him he had the intestines of an eighteen-year-old and Noreen wanted to celebrate.

Les and Myra Lund had already left, so we ran into the back room, each of us trying to win the race to see who could get their clothes off faster.

Afterward, I felt like beating my chest like a big hairy ape, I was so happy and satisfied. So I did, which of course made Noreen laugh and then that got me excited again and I had thoughts of an encore performance, but no, Noreen had to get home to get her husband supper and did I know she was taking him to the game?

Which reminded me of the conversation I had with Francesca and so I asked Noreen if it was all right that a girl played hockey with her period.

"Well, sure," said Noreen. "Olympic athletes compete when they're in their cycle."

I nodded. "That is pretty much what I told her."

Noreen kissed my earlobe and said Francesca was lucky to have me and I said it was me who was lucky and I meant that.

On the way home, I sang a little Rossini, concentrating on *The Barber of Seville*. My father didn't pass down his beautiful voice to me, but still, there weren't any babies in my car who might cry at my high notes, no dogs who could whine, so I let loose, winking at Pastor Egeqvist's wife when her car pulled up to mine at Main Street's only light.

DICK

WHAT A GAME. I decided to tape it for Big Mike (not that he asked, but I thought it would be a nice keepsake) so I watched practically the whole thing through the viewfinder of my camcorder. It's not exactly network quality—every time there was a great play the camera came down, so there are a lot of shots of my feet and the back of the guy sitting ahead of me. But hey, I never said I was Joe Cameraman, and besides, I got the most important thing: Franny's beautiful sudden-death goal.

The Elgin Rogues ("cute name," Devera says whenever we play them, "maybe we should change our name to the White Falls Womanizers") were ahead of the Rebels 5–3 in the third period and we were getting pretty quiet in the stands, thinking oh well, we gave it our best effort, when Corky Johannson intercepted a pass and whisked the puck right between the legs of the surprised goalie.

Ba-ba-bum. Ba-ba-bum. We were all doing our school drumbeat and the bleachers shook underneath our feet.

Corky's grandpa, Alf, stood up and howled like a wolf until he was pulled down by his wife, Violet. We all laughed—it was obvious Alf had dipped heavily into his retirement-party punch bowl and in fact none of the Heating & Air people that came to the game would have passed a Breathalyzer test.

"I'm the designated driver," Violet explained to me and Devera in between periods. "I brought them all here in the company van and each one is more obnoxious than the other. This afternoon, they were valued employees. Now they're all a bunch of drunken idiots and of course Alf's worse than all of them put together."

I guided Devera toward the popcorn stand. Violet Johannson is like a spider who likes nothing better than trapping you into her web of talk. You emerge dazed, hours later, after she's completely recounted her early career as a nurse/anesthesiologist in the Quad Cities or her survival of the Blizzard of '46.

So there we were with only forty seconds left in regulation play when Dave Clovis passes to Alan Bydell, who tips it into the top of the net. Pandemonium. We were like the crowd watching the Americans beat the Czechs in the 1980 Olympics. I hugged Devera hard and lifted her in the air and she laughed and it seemed we were reliving our days as BMOC and Homecoming Queen all over again. Darcy, who was sitting between Dad Evan and me, was hugged by her grandfather and then she jumped on my back, so there I am, holding my two best girls. Lin was sitting in the front with her friends (in their black clothes they looked like they were assembled for a funeral rather than a hockey game) and was bouncing up and down and holding on to that miscreant Kyle Christianson, who doesn't play any sports at all as far as I know.

When the clock ran out and both teams took a five-minute break before sudden death, Dad Evan leaned over and said, "Win or lose, steak dinners for all of us at the Cattle Baron, okay? I'm buying."

Tell me something I don't know, I thought, but instead I said, "Sounds good to me." I suddenly remembered Devera's change of diet, though, and I shrugged my shoulders at her, but she was nodding happily, which is her Pavlovian response to anything her father suggests.

Helen leaned over then and said, "Why don't we ask BiDi and Sergio, too, unless they've got something planned with their little hockey player?"

You couldn't mistake the disapproval in her voice when she said "little hockey player." She thought it was unseemly, unfeminine, and a lot of other "un" words for a fourteen-year-old girl to be playing a rough sport like hockey. "Besides," she said once, "it erodes the sense of sportsmanship among the boys."

I reminded her that Little League had gone coed and it worked out, and in truth, the point of a team is for every member to accept each other, regardless of their differences. She just sniffed as if she was in the presence of some lowlife and said, "If God had meant girls to play boys' sports, he would have given them the same equipment."

"If they had the same equipment, they'd be boys," said Darcy, and I thought, touché for her.

"Precisely my point," said Helen, closing the conversation with one of her tight little smiles.

I looked down the stands at BiDi and Sergio. They always sit by themselves at games because Sergio doesn't want the distraction of socializing.

BiDi, all dolled up as usual, had turned around and was talking to Connie Cole and her husband, offering me and whatever male was lucky enough to be seated above her a pretty good view of her breasts, which were pushed up and peeping out of the plunging neckline of her fuzzy pink sweater. I turned on the video camera and immediately felt an elbow connect with my rib cage.

"Grow up, Dick," said Devera.

"Just filming the local color, dear," I said, putting the camera on my knee.

"I know what you were filming." Craning her neck, she looked down at BiDi. "I didn't know Frederick's of Hollywood sold sweaters."

I aimed the camera at her. "And now let's focus on the real beauty of White Falls."

Devera stuck her tongue out, but I could see she was pleased.

"Yes, and she has inherited the best of her ancestors—classic Nordic features and skin so creamy only the English could claim it as theirs—"

"I don't have a drop of English blood in me," said Devera,

laughing, as she pushed the camera away. Her laugh froze then and a funny look I can't really describe came over her face and she waved.

"Who's that?" I asked, turning off the camera.

"What? Oh, that guy? That's Gerhart Ludwig, my Ancient Rome professor."

"Gerhart Ludwig—sounds like he should be teaching Ancient Frankfurt." I squinted. "He looks like that flasher they caught out at the campgrounds last summer."

Devera gave me one of her rattlesnake looks, but then the players came back on the ice and both school bands tried to drown out each other's fight song, so I was saved from the particularly nasty comment I knew she was ready to strike me with.

Right at the face-off you could tell neither team was going to give the other any slack. They were pumped. Everyone was slapping their sticks on the ice, waiting for the linesman to drop the puck. When he did there was a clash of sticks and the puck went flying. The Rogues' star, Guy Hammond, got to it first and skated away with it, zigzagging and dodging as other players lunged at him in a wild ballet.

"Dad, the camera," said Darcy.

"Whoops," I said, and started taping. And just in time, too. Hammond skated toward the goal like a maniac. No Rebel could catch him, and even if they had, the two Rogues who skated behind him like bodyguards were not about to let anyone get near.

He must have been two feet away from the goal when he blasted in a shot that couldn't help but go in—Hammond had a deadly aim—only it didn't. Ben Opdahl, not the strongest link of the team by any means, leaped and twisted in a miraculous configuration and the puck bounced off his glove. The crowd went wild, especially when Corky Johannson picked up the rebound and sent the puck sailing. A blur of bodies followed it, and within five seconds Alan Bydell had passed it to Pete Arsgaard, who nudged away a Rogue with a nice tap to the hip (okay, it was a check, but the refs let a lot of things go in the play-offs). Arsgaard looked as if he were going to shoot—you knew he was dying to shoot, he hadn't made a goal or an assist in the last couple games, but then he saw someone skate to the side of the net and in a moment that happened so fast you're not quite sure it happened at all, the puck whizzed over to the player by the net, who flipped it in right above the goalie's shoulder.

There was a half second of silence as people absorbed what happened and then the goal light went on and it was bedlam. Absolute bedlam. Kids in the top row of the stands lobbed rolls of toilet paper, which unfurled a little before hitting the ice, or in one case, the back of Helen's head. People screamed and the band played a hundred different notes. Dad Evan was whistling with two of his big fingers jammed in his mouth as the players surrounded the player who'd just won the game.

"It was Franny!" I screamed. "Mike, that was *Franny's* goal!"

"Fran-ny, Fran-ny!" Darcy yelled, and pretty soon the chant got picked up and the ice arena reverberated with the sounds "Fran-ny, Fran-ny." I panned the camera over the rink and down among the stands. Sergio was standing on top of his chair, his arms held straight up toward the ceiling. I couldn't see what BiDi was doing.

"That's for your daughter, Mike," I said softly, feeling both proud and a little weird, as if I was trying to sell Big Mike on his own kid.

Then I focused back on the ice to the Rebels, who were in a blackslapping huddle and I kept the camera going until the award ceremony was over and the crowd began filing out.

BıDı

FOR A SOLID week I couldn't go anywhere without people saying, "Oh, there's the mother of the hockey star." It was a weird kind of déjà vu; I had been through all this hockey-hero stuff with Big Mike in high school. At first it was flattering to be the girlfriend of someone who got so much attention, but then I'd started thinking, "What am I, chopped liver?" So I couldn't shoot a hockey puck—big deal. No matter that I was good-looking and entertaining *all* the time, Big Mike earned glory for that brief moment in time when he was on the ice scoring goals. It didn't matter that he was a big lug during the rest of his waking hours because—applause, applause—he was a sports hero.

And now with Franny in that same limelight, I couldn't go shopping without merchants slipping gifts under my arms. Dale behind the meat counter even wrapped up a rump roast and gave it to me, saying, "Our hockey champion deserves the choicest cut."

Oh pul-leese, I thought, and if you really think that way, why not wrap up some filet mignon?

All the hoopla—Dave Garner of the *White Falls Gazette* interviewed us for the sports page and a TV station from Duluth came down and filmed Franny and her teammates—lasted for a solid week, as I said, but then Maude Milner was found dead in her garden (apparently the mortician had to practically break her fingers trying to pry the spade from her hand) and so the attention sort of shifted over that way.

Maude was sixty and carried mail; she was the big strong
type you thought would last until her nineties, so that's why
everyone was so shook up. Plus then we had the additional
burden of Mac Connors taking over her route; I swear he
didn't get to my house until nearly five o'clock those first
couple days. Still, I'd rather wait until suppertime for my catalogs and decorator magazines than have the whole town act
like I gave birth to a hockey legend. Some legend.

I remember when Franny was still little and still cute. She
had just turned three and her eyes were so big it seemed she
only had an inch of forehead and I dressed her in dresses
with ribbons and flounces and ruffles. (Devera says I deco-
rate my house the way I used to dress Franny—she says I
suffer from "severe cutetitis with a side complication of
rufflese." Remember, jealousy often rears its ugly head in
sarcasm.)

Anyway, she *was* cute and so I entered her in a "Little
Lady" pageant; you know, to build her confidence and meet
new friends and all those other things pageants are supposed
to do for a kid? I had already bought the competition dress—
it had a stiff petticoat so the skirt stuck out to here—and I
had paid the entry fee and set up an appointment at Sheryl's
Style Hut (only a professional could get a curl out of
Franny's poker-straight hair). I had grilled Franny in how to
respond to a judge's questions (believe me, I had thought of
some real cute responses) but none of this mattered, Big
Mike laid down the law: Franny was not about to be
"paraded on a stage and judged like a piece of meat."

I had to laugh. This was coming from Big Mike, a man
who I know for a fact had never missed the Midsummer's
Night Dream wet T-shirt contest at King Olaf's Hideaway?

"That's different," Big Mike said. "Those contests are just
for fun, and besides, nobody's forced to be in them."

"Same here," I said. "This contest is just for fun and I'm
not forcing Franny. She *wants* to be in it."

Big Mike called Franny in from the backyard. "Those contests aren't for kids," he said. "It's their parents who get off
on them."

Franny came in, dirty as a sod farmer.

"Look," I said, triumph in my voice, "just look. If anyone needs a pageant, it's this little mud lover."

"Franny, come here," said Big Mike, and she walked very seriously toward him, holding her small hands in front of her waist.

Big Mike kneeled down and held her by the shoulders. "Franny, tell me something. Are you excited about this pageant thing Mommy's got lined up?"

Franny's big eyes got even bigger and she looked at me so seriously I could not hold her gaze.

"Well," she said finally, "well, I think I would rather play."

Big Mike's smile split his auburn beard open.

"See?" he said, planting a big kiss in Franny's hair. "See? She's got more sense than you give her credit for, BiDi."

"Any kid would rather play than do just about anything." I gave Franny a dirty look that usually went a long way in her seeing things my way, but this time she only stared back at me, unblinking. I changed tack. "Franny, this pageant will be fun. There will be lots of little girls to play with. And I'll tell you what—we'll go out for ice cream afterward." I smiled big and long until my jaw muscles started to ache. "Really Franny," I said, trying one last time. "It'll be fun."

"I'd rather play."

Big Mike laughed and started opening cupboards, rooting around like a big bear until he found a bag of pretzels.

"Then it's settled," he said, sitting down. "No pageant." He smiled at me, victory smeared all over his face like a stinky aftershave. When Franny climbed up on his lap and the two of them started stuffing pretzels in their mouths, I decided the kitchen had grown impossibly small.

"Clean up your mess when you're done," I said, feeling so mad that I knew if I stayed around, someone's big smug face would get bashed in.

I know what it sounds like—Big Mike was the forward-thinking one, protecting his daughter from "objectification," but believe me, his putting the kibosh on the Little Lady Pageant was more about power than it was making a stand to protect and defend Franny's right to be a tomboy. Big Mike just wasn't that interested a father and only paid close attention to Franny when he had a point to make with me. Usually he wasn't so politically correct in his point-making; he must have heard Devera spouting off. We came of age when the feminist movement was in its flower, and for our senior talent show, Devera did a modern dance to the Helen Reddy song "I Am Woman." (Believe me, it was as pathetic as it sounds.) It drove her crazy when I said I was "beyond feminism," and believed in servitude. I meant that, too: I feel everyone should wait on me. Ha-ha. Gotcha.

Anyway, back to Mike. He was never gaga about being a dad the way Dick is, but then again, and I feel funny confessing this, I did not exactly have a natural flair for motherhood either. I hated all my time being taken up and the mess really got to me—the dirty diapers and the spit-up formula (I gag just to think about it); the crayon marks on the walls and the Legos all over the floor. *But*, and here's where I think character comes in, *I tried*. As unnatural as it was for me to get down on the floor and play train or paper dolls, I did it. As boring as it was to push Franny in a swing for three hours or read "The Three Bears" eighty million times, I did it. By sheer force of will I engaged myself in my daughter's life and in motherhood because I knew what it was to have a parent give up on you and I wasn't going to do that with Franny.

Big Mike, on the other hand, retreated like the cavalry. It was his hunting, his stupid car tinkering, his sports (did he ever take his daughter out on the ice?—never), his plumbing business, his poker nights; everything ranked far above his responsibilities as a father and a husband.

So of course I responded in kind—I mean toward him. I wasn't about to take anything out on a defenseless child. And sex, or the lack thereof, became my weapon.

Once I was dumb enough to tell him that and he laughed like he was watching a Three Stooges show. He sobered up pretty quick, though, and his voice had that edge in it that scared me.

"Well, then you must have been mad at me since you've

known me," he said, "because that's how long you've been holding out."

DEVERA ALWAYS GRILLS me about my sex life but I just wink and sigh and roll my eyes around, which makes her think I'm as big a sex maniac as she is. And she always has been, even in high school. She couldn't wait to "say good-bye to my old friend Virginia" and after prom night she spent two hours telling me in loving detail how she and Dick finally did it, how it hurt a little but the hurt was worth the fun and how'd I *make out* with Mike, *pun intended*?

Big Mike had had the same idea as Dick and Devera, but I wasn't allowing anything past second base and I slapped him hard when he tried to hit a home run.

He drove me home in a car full of silence that seemed more poisonous than carbon monoxide; honest, I was in a coughing fit by the time I got out of that Mustang and slammed the door.

Sex. I get depressed when I think that's what makes the world go 'round. Sure, looking at me a person might get the idea that it makes my world go 'round, too, but believe me, that person would be mistaken.

I like formfitting clothes (many of which I sew with my own talented little hands) because I've got a great body, pure and simple. A, if you've got it, why not flaunt it, and B, flaunting isn't an invitation. People can admire a da Vinci without having to possess it, can't they?

It's just like flirting—I consider it a recreational sport, and if there were a Flirt Team USA, I'd be captain.

But I'm in it for the game, pure and simple, and I don't see it as a means to an end. I don't need or want to score a touchdown; the fun for me is the passes, the fakes, the game. Get it, guys? *The game.* But there you go, play the game and not follow *their* rules and you're a tease. Go figure.

I'm not stupid, though; I know when Sergio's resentment level starts to rise, and rather than drown in it, I will put in the old diaphragm (I'd been on the pill for years until Devera finally wore me down with her blood-clot statistics) and roll around with him for a while. I even throw in an orgasm or two (I didn't win the White Falls Drama Desk Award for nothing) and then I reap the rewards of his gratitude and devotion. There's always a present for me after sex; a fair enough trade—especially the Kirby vacuum cleaner. Wow! I almost threw in a bonus round for that.

DEVERA

DICK MADE A big deal out of me ordering a New York strip at the Cattle Baron, but I was not about to throw my father's hospitality up in his face by ordering some puny little dinner salad. Besides, I had been thinking a lot about what Gerhart Ludwig said about my sex life becoming anemic if I gave up meat and it made sense to me. Vegetarianism makes sense to me, too—look what overgrazing has done to this planet—but somehow, big world issues shrink when pitted against those directly affecting me *right at this moment*.

I felt a blush warm my face like a low-grade fever, but I stared at Dick after the waiter took my order, stared at him when he said, "Dad Evan, I was about to tell you the new road your daughter's conscience had taken her on, but I guess she's changed lanes again."

"What?" asked Daddy, but then the waiter asked him what he'd like and Darcy asked BiDi where she got the neato earrings and Mom asked Sergio if he used butter in all his cakes or did he occasionally save money with Crisco, and Dick's comment was deservedly buried. Still, I stared at him until the waiter left; long enough to make him, but not everyone else, uncomfortable. I would have kicked him underneath the table but we were positioned in such a way that my foot couldn't reach his shin. Besides, Dick is just the the type to acknowledge an under-the-table kick by asking, "What did you do that for?"

My stare seemed to work, though. He gave me this funny

little I-surrender smile and didn't mention my spinelessness again.

Just because I was defensive didn't mean I wasn't aware of my weakness. Could there ever be a political or environmental cause big enough for me to change my eating habits? Sad to say, but I doubt it. I could just see myself aligned with a bunch of protestors fasting against U.S. intervention somewhere. While everyone laid around looking wan and idealistic, I know I'd be sneaking out for a Mars bar. It is not a side I am proud of.

I used to ask Dick how he thought he would survive something truly horrible—say imprisonment in a concentration camp. (There was about a year or so when the only books I read were on the Nazis and the Holocaust. Finally Daddy told me to cool it, he had lived through the horror of war once and didn't need to relive Hitler's reign every Sunday at his daughter's dinner table.)

Do you think you'd be part of a resistance, I'd ask him, smuggling information out to the Allies, or maybe the kind who cheered up everyone in the camp, or the type who decided the pain wasn't worth it and gave up any kind of fight?

Dick said, "Gee, Dev, why do you ask me such spooky questions? How do I know?"

I thought he'd be the type to cheer everyone up, joking and singing his hokey little songs, but I didn't want to flatter him, so I didn't tell him that. I was mad that, as usual, he refused to talk seriously with me. Sure, he can expect me to spend two hours discussing the value of a two-door over a four-door, but ask him a thoughtful question and he calls you spooky.

I certainly didn't tell him that I had suspicions I'd be in a category I didn't even mention: the informer, the one who tattles to the Kapo to get an extra crust of bread.

Well, as Dick says, there I go again, plunging into darkness.

THE CATTLE BARON was really humming that night; a lot of players' families were there celebrating.

"That's some daughter you've got there," said Alf Johansson as he stumbled by our table. I knew Violet was pouring coffee down him but he was still on the tipsy side of the scale.

"Great game, wasn't it?" asked Jerry Bydell, Alan's dad, clapping everyone on the shoulder. He's running against Bunny Vold for mayor this year, so he always uses this jovial body language. If there'd been a baby at the table, he would have kissed it. "And that Franny—she's the new Bobby Orr!" He put his hand to his cheek as if he'd made a gaffe. "I mean the new Babette Orr!"

Sergio was constantly nodding his head and smiling, taking in all the compliments like the proud papa (step or no) he was, replaying the game and jokingly signing up people for the "Francesca LaFave Fan Club."

BiDi sat there with a smile plastered on her face, too, but I know BiDi and I know the ratio of showmanship to sincerity was about, oh, ten to one.

BiDi liked attention; you don't dress like the reincarnation of Jayne Mansfield and propose to be demure, but I could see the conflict she was going through in getting secondhand attention through her daughter's victories.

When Dave Clovis's dad was at the table going on and on about taking State next year, BiDi and I happened to catch each other's eye. I threw her a little wink and she shrugged her shoulders ever so slightly, understanding me perfectly. She knew I knew how much Franny's sudden-death goal meant to her and that was not a whole awful lot.

Franny made history; first she fought to be a member of an all-boys' team (girls' hockey is really catching on, but there wasn't a girls' team for Franny to try out for. The bandwagon has to be moving real slow for White Falls to jump on it) and then she turns out to be an important player on it. God, I'd love it if that had been Lin out there on the ice, but I'm afraid Lin's beginning to listen to that old song: Be Cute, Be Popular. She's both, wouldn't you know. Lin has a huge talent in art—when we were putting in our bathroom tile, we let her do this mosaic, and so every time you take a shower you see these incredible jungle flowers growing out of the spigot—but lately it seems the only concession she makes to her talent is dressing like her idea of an artist; i.e., in all black. Of course it doesn't hurt that black seems to be a trendy color in her school this year. Anyway, I try to encourage her gift—I want both my girls to be strong and passionate about something other than their status as girls/women, but for now Lin seems content to follow my wayward path, even as I've tried to show her a different road. BiDi, on the other hand, would love nothing more than Franny to follow in her stiletto-heeled footsteps.

We were on the Rebelettes dance line and both of us were high-school royalty. I presided over homecoming as queen and BiDi was our "Sno Daze" Princess. Nobody came close to "Dev and Beed."

It makes me a little sick to think how smug we were in our rule. We wouldn't have given girls like Franny the time of day—of course, girls like Franny weren't allowed to play hockey with the guys in those days either.

In my senior year I did, to my credit, organize the first "Equality Day" march and I did this feminist dance piece in the talent show, but still, I remember I couldn't go in front of the crowds before my hair and makeup were absolutely perfect.

Fortunately, I have made *some* progress in how I see my worth, but BiDi does not want to relinquish her most important title, "Foxiest Girl," even if it is over twenty years old.

"Franny must be on top of the world right now," I told BiDi as the waiter served our main courses.

BiDi flapped her napkin and wiped the blade of her steak knife with it.

"I asked her to join us but she's gotten too big for us little people."

Sergio leaned over his plate. "Coach Emery took them all out for pizza. It is their victory party."

"Where Lin is, Mom," said Darcy, and then her lower lip swelled out in a pout. "Where I wish *I* was."

"Oh, Darcy," said Dick, putting his arm over her shoulder and drawing her to him. "And deprive us of your company?"

"That's right," said my mother. "We love your company.

Now sit up a little straighter, honey. You're slumped over like a slug."

"Helen," said my dad.

One of my mother's favorite pastimes is to remind people when they're not behaving up to snuff. If you give her a glass of iced tea, she'll tell you that stemware should always be hand-dried. If you get a haircut, she'll tell you how your old hairstyle made you look less jowly.

"I just think good posture's important," said my mother, smiling sweetly. "Who wants to wind up a hunchback?"

Suddenly, in the middle of dinner at the Cattle Baron, just when I was thinking of something snide to say to my mother, I felt the brewings of a panic attack. The general malaise and fearfulness I had been suffering from for a while suddenly, last week, cranked up, manifesting itself into something horrible. I didn't know what it was at first; I just thought I was going crazy. I had been shopping at Rainbow, minding my own business while I tried to remember what peanut butter was supposed to the "peanuttiest," when all of a sudden this huge sense of dread filled me.

I was so surprised—I had never felt such full, sheer terror, but then my mind had no room for surprise, enveloped as it was in total fright.

I heard my heart banging in my chest and I thought I might be having a heart attack. My skin tingled as if the nerve endings were on alert and I stared at the rows and rows of peanut butter—their labels seemed incredibly bright—wondering if I was going to wind up in a morgue or a mental hospital. I wanted to scream, but everything seemed choked and frozen.

I don't know how long I stood there, holding on to the shopping cart so I wouldn't be sucked into this vacuum of black fear, when suddenly Madge Peasley, who's always asking me to join her book club, was standing before me, asking me if I was all right.

Her words were like a slap across the face to someone babbling; immediately I began to feel I might know how to feel normal, which was the greatest relief because I didn't think I'd ever feel normal again.

I was wondering how everyone at the table was going to react as I lost my mind right in front of them, but breaking through the sound of air rushing in my ears was the sound of laughter, and I looked at Darcy, who was sitting up straighter than a four-star general, her chin tucked into her chest, her hands curled into fists on the table.

My brave little girl was making a joke out of her grandma's disapproval, and her bravery kicked aside that percolating panic and I joined everyone else, even Mother, in the blessed laughter. I was so grateful, so grateful to be back in the realm of the normal, that I could have kissed everyone at the table.

We all dug into our dinners then in high spirits and it wasn't until I had a nice piece of strip steak on my fork that I noticed Gerhart Ludwig across the room. He was standing at the hostess's dais, switching on and off the covered-wagon lamp, which seemed to give the hostess a case of the giggles.

All of a sudden, as if radar-led, he looked up, right at me. I slid the piece of meat off my fork with my teeth and he smiled and nodded and then aimed his finger at his heart as if it were a pistol. He pretended to fire and mouthed the word *pow*.

I knew then, without a doubt, that along with my notebook and pencils, I'd be taking my diaphragm to class the next night. Make that my diaphragm *case*, I'd be wearing my diaphragm. Life was too precious, too wonderfully rich, and as long as I was normal, I was going to take full advantage of it.

"What's this?" I asked, coming back down to earth. Dick had dipped his napkin into his water glass and handed it to me. He didn't say anything but looked down at my blouse. I followed his gaze. There was a blob of steak sauce right under my collar and I scrubbed at it until the front of my shirt was watery pink, like blood that had been washed away.

SERGIO

BIDI WAS IN the bathtub, watching one of those horror movies she loves so much. That's right! She has got every Elvis movie available on tape, but even the biggest Coke fan needs a sip of something else now and then. So she watches horror. And not only does she have a TV in her bathroom, but also a VCR! She thinks there is nothing odd about soaking in a tub full of bubbles while watching some monster with steel fingernails slash at human flesh!

I had started a fire in the fireplace. It was the last week of April, but here winter has long arms that stretch into months they have no business bothering. I wanted to create a nice, homey ambience for our hockey star.

Let me tell you, when she came through that door and saw me sitting in the big wing chair, her face lit up. Another photo for my memory album.

"Sergie!" she said, running toward me. I stood up and we met in a big hug.

"Francesca, I am so proud of you!" I said, lifting her a bit in the air, which couldn't have done my back any favors but I figured too bad!

"I just can't believe it, Sergie," she said, and her voice was breathless with happiness. "It was the perfect goal—of course look at how Pete Arsgaard set me up. There's no way I could have missed the net."

"That is nice of you to say, Peanut, but it was your play one hundred percent."

We sat down by the fire and I poured two cups of hot chocolate from the thermos I had prepared.

"You think of everything, Sergie," said Francesca, "except marshmallows."

I held up my pointer finger and than I took a bowl off the table. It was full of, you guessed right, marshmallows.

Francesca laughed, dropping several into her cup. "Where's Mom?"

"She got a tape from her video club today."

"How can she watch that stuff right before she goes to sleep?"

I shrugged my shoulders. "Some people need a lullaby. Your mother needs blood and gore."

We laughed and then sipped our cocoa, listening to the snaps and crackles of the wood burning. Nothing but contentment filled my heart.

"The pizza party was a lot of fun, Sergie," said Francesca.

"I'm glad. We had some fun, too, at the Cattle Baron."

"Pete asked me to sit with him at the hockey banquet." This Francesca said so quietly that I had to ask her to say it again. She did, with a shy little smile pulling at her mouth.

"So, not only is he assisting your goals, but he is interested in you off-ice, too. And you like him, am I right?"

Francesca shrugged but then nodded her head, smiling all the more. "A lot of girls do." She stared at the fire. "Still, it is just a hockey banquet, and not a real date or anything."

"What's not a real date?"

We both looked up, surprised, because we had not heard BiDi coming down the stairs at all. She was tying her bathrobe tie and the little tendrils of hair by her ears were curly from the steam of the bath. All of her makeup had been scrubbed and she looked so lovely, in a new and soft way.

"I'll give that movie a thumbs-down," she said, moving a pile of pillows on the couch so she would have somewhere to sit. (Like rabbits, it seems our pillows are always breeding.) "The fakiest special effects I've ever seen and you practically knew who the killer was two minutes after the opening credits." She crossed her arms and put her slippered feet up on the coffee table. "So what's not a real date?"

By the way Francesca stuck her chin out, I knew she was not going to open her mouth to answer her mother.

"Peter Arsgaard asked her to sit by him at the hockey banquet," I said, hoping that I was not betraying Francesca.

"You know you're too young to date, Franny. We've always said you have to wait until you're fifteen." She patted the back of her hair. "But you're right, sitting next to someone at a hockey banquet isn't really a date. Say, is that hot chocolate?"

I nodded and passed her my cup. She took a little sip and handed it back to me.

"You're using coasters, aren't you?"

I had to give her a dirty look; here she was making sure her furniture was protected and had not said one word about the game of her daughter.

"Good game, Franny," she said, as if reading my mind. "That was really a beautiful goal."

I think that the president makes a promise he intends to keep more often than BiDi gives her daughter a compliment. Okay, maybe I exaggerate, but it is a rare thing.

"Thanks," said Francesca. "Thanks, Mom. 'Course it was all Pete's setup."

I refilled my cup from the thermos and passed it to my wife and the three of us sat there in silence—not an awkward silence at all, but the kind of silence you could find in a full church, when everyone is maybe awed and thankful by what they heard the choir just sing.

A SUDDEN PICTURE of my father jumped into my head, and it hurt, like a pinch. I remembered him all dressed up in his dark blue suit, his shirt collar and cuffs bleached to a whiteness that only my mother seemed able to achieve. She loved getting stains out of clothes, mixing up concoctions like a chemist. If she'd been any good at telling fortunes, she would have seen her true calling was in stain removal.

But now back to my father. He was dressed in the dark blue suit when we went to St. Ignatius Church in Brooklyn, always looking so handsome, his hair black and shiny, matching the shoes he polished every Sunday before Mass. When the hymns were sung, he would open his hymnal and sing along, but because of his encounter with the gangster who beat him up, destroying his vocal box, only a whisper rose out of his throat.

He said he could still hear his voice in his head, so it wasn't so bad, but he died at the age of forty-four of a heart attack. My mother always said his heart was broken when he was robbed of his voice. It was only a matter of time that it gave out on him for good.

I am not saying that BiDi saying something nice to her own daughter was on the same scale of bravery as my father whispering hymns through all those Masses; still, I am not going to shirk any credit. And BiDi deserved some for that. I know how hard it is between mothers and daughters when the daughter goes through adolescence—especially a mother and daughter as different as those in this family.

Bing. Another little jab of pain. Why they bubble up when I am so happy, do not ask me. But in thinking of my family, I was thinking—it is too small.

It is too much for Francesca to bear all our attention, bad and good. She needs an ally. A little brother (we already have a girl, now it is time for a son) would be a gift to us all. I cannot let the Herrera name blow out like a match.

But, I am not the type to be blinded to what I have at the present by what I might have in the future. I was not about to darken this moment with BiDi and Francesca, this moment when we were all together and feeling so good.

How many times I would return to this moment, when the fire was snapping and the room had a dash of the smell of wood smoke and the potpourri BiDi puts around in little jars and we were all drinking hot chocolate, comfortable and cozy, laughing over BiDi's impersonation of the Rogues' cheerleading squad. Francesca's laugh especially—it is high and delicate and unexpected coming out of a big girl like her—and I could tell how BiDi was enjoying it, too, which made her all the more amusing. When she imitated one of the Rogue players—making her face look like a monkey's and dragging her knuckles across the carpet—Francesca nearly choked on a marshmallow because of her laughter and I had to pound her on the back.

BiDi took that good mood into the bedroom—surprise for me!—and what happened there most certainly was to change our lives, but at the time, of course, that was not the night's highlight for me: it was that feeling that we were wrapped up in a happy and safe world, and in that world, my wife desired me.

DARCY

FRANNY AND I were splitting a plate of french fries and guzzling down hot fudge shakes at the Top Hat when Bunny Vold sat down next to me, whacking my thigh with a newspaper so I'd move over.

"Princess and I have a little wager going," she said, nodding to the Top Hat's member of royalty who was busy filling ketchup bottles. "She says it was Ray Milland who starred in *The Lost Weekend*, and I say it was Stewart Granger. Now we've got a big piece of coconut cream pie riding on this, so consider the question carefully."

"I don't have to, Bunny. It's Ray Milland." I raised my voice. "Hey, Princess, she owes you a piece of pie."

Princess adjusted the little tiara she wore and screwed on the cap of a ketchup bottle. "I knew it. See, Bunny, if you'd just get the American Movie Channel, you wouldn't be such an ignoramus."

"Ah," said Bunny, nodding. "So it's the American Movie Channel that would prevent me from being such an ignoramus—I thought it was a love of reading and an insatiable curiosity about the world."

Franny and I laughed. It wasn't exactly *what* Bunny Vold said that was so funny but *how* she said it. She made this moronic face and scratched the top of her head, looking like Stan Laurel's younger, dumber sister.

Franny and I had run into each other after school on Main Street. She'd been at Sergio's bakery and I was over at the car lot showing my dad the Martha Washington monologue I'd written for history class that I got an A-plus on. (Okay, Mrs. Snelling is the easiest grader in the history of history teachers, but I'm sure my speech would have gotten at least an A-minus from any other normal teacher.) My dad was impressed, laughing at the part where Martha says George did in fact lie when he said he chopped down a cherry tree—it was a sycamore. He gave me an extra ten spot along with my usual allowance, so I was feeling pretty flush when I met up with Franny and asked her, "Hey, you wanna get something to eat over at the Top Hat?"

"Well, actually," said Franny, looking at me with this sly look, "I was on my way to Flip's."

"Yeah, you and me both," I said, and we both laughed.

Flip's is *the* cool kid hangout, a soda fountain where a person practically needs a written invitation from a cool kid to go inside and join a bunch of other kids who stand around listening to music they're too cool to dance to. If you ask me, the whole concept of cool has gotten a little twisted. Cool today is way more about image than it is about depth; I mean to me, a nerd who is totally into his nerdiness—into a ham-radio habit, or being a first-chair clarinetist, or a state math finalist—is far cooler than some slacker whose biggest kick is being a human advertisement for brand-name clothes and standing around looking bored, which somehow is supposed to be cool.

I personally think you can't get any cooler than me, and if the rest of the world (or even the rest of my class) hasn't come to that realization yet, well, big hairy deal. There's no accounting for taste these days.

Franny accepted my invitation and we racewalked to the Top Hat, with me winning (okay, so I ran a little at the end).

The Top Hat's one of those restaurants that the fifties did so well—shiny with chrome and Formica and slippery red leather booths. I heard this guy once on public TV say that if restaurant architecture was an indicator of society's mental health, then America started getting psychotic in the late seventies. It sounds true to me—I mean, you don't have to sit on an orange plastic-molded chair in some fast-food restaurant to know, hey, not only is this uncomfortable—it's ugly!

My dad says that's the way they build cars now, too—junky plastic crap—which is why he loves selling Cadillacs.

"People'll pay for style and comfort," he says, "And Cadillac's never forgotten that."

Am I going off on a tangent, or what? But it just makes me mad that I live in the era of McDonald's and Burger Kings when it's obvious I was meant for tearooms and the Brown Derby.

"Are you planning to eat that?" asked Bunny, pointing to the last french fry on the plate, and when we shook our heads, she dragged it through a pool of ketchup until it was three-quarters red and I was thinking anyone who eats french fries like a kid would probably make a pretty good mayor. Bunny sort of read my mind then because she said said, "Hey, you girls want to come down to my campaign office and see my new buttons?"

Franny and I looked at one another, trying to tell from the other's expression if it sounded like a fun thing to do or not—I mean it's not like we hung out all the time and could read each other's mind. But we both must have thought what the hey, because we got up and followed Bunny out the door. Oh, in case you're wondering, we did leave Princess a tip, a big one, too. I mean we're not social retards.

Bunny's campaign office wasn't exactly an office; just the tiny storeroom of Vold's Snack & Gas. There's a big Super-America by the highway, but most of the locals gas up at Vold's and most of the locals' kids buy their candy there. I mean we're talking one delicioso candy counter. You can get your standard Mars bars, Nestlé's Crunch, and Reese's Peanut Butter Cups, but then they've also got imported chocolate like Toblerone and Lindt and Cadbury and then there's this "old-fashioneds" section—candy in jars that old Mr. Vold scoops into a little striped paper sack and weighs on the scale that dangles from the ceiling. They don't sell cigarettes or beer like other gas stations—just car junk, milk, pop, chips and stuff, and of course, candy.

"Hi, Mr. Vold," Franny and I said to the old guy who sat behind the counter, but he didn't look up from the *White Falls Gazette*, only wiggling his knobby fingers at us. I don't remember Mr. Vold ever saying one word to me ever, although Lin said he once told a group of her friends they'd better "fly right" when they came in to buy candy after their middle-school graduation program.

In the storeroom, Bunny was rubbing her hands together like a villain. "You're witnessing history, girls. One day when I'm a senator, these'll be collector's items." She opened up a cardboard box.

It was full of campaign buttons, hundreds of sparkly, glowing campaign buttons.

"Do you like the neon?" asked Bunny. "I thought it might be a little too much with the metallic, but I think it really jumps out, don't you?"

Franny picked up one of the buttons. "Hop to it," she read.

"That's my slogan," explained Bunny.

"I don't get it," I said. "Hop to what?"

"Hop to it and vote for me for mayor."

"Well, maybe you should say that. Otherwise I don't think most people will get it."

"Darcy, everybody knows I'm running for mayor," said Bunny, and I could tell she was getting a little frosted. "When they see 'hop to it,' they're going to associate it with me. Hop. Bunny. Get it?"

"I just think it could be clearer is all," I said, pinning a button to my shirt. "Have your name on it or something."

"It's all implied," said Franny. "We learned all about stuff like this in media arts. These buttons are subtle advertising at its best." She smiled this little nya-nya smile at me and I had to laugh because I knew the know-it-all she was imitating was supposed to be me.

"If people ask me why they should vote for you, what should we tell them?" Franny asked.

"Tell 'em we got city hall in our back pocket," I said in my best Jimmy Cagney voice.

"That's a very thoughtful question, Francesca," she said,

ignoring my little joke. "I'd like people to vote for me because they want change. For a small town, White Falls isn't so bad, but I want it to be better. Bring it into the twenty-first century. Obliterate all isms—sexism, racism, ageism, and every other ism you can think of. I'm for peace and justice and equal rights for all."

"Well, that's a fine kettle of fish."

I looked up to see old Mr. Vold, standing in the storeroom doorway, waving a crooked finger.

"Yuh—just nifty—but what about the pay increase the school board's hollering about? And what'll you do about that minimall proposal? Or those recycling-plant plans? People want to talk real issues, Bunny, not your pie-in-the-sky 'isms.' "

He cleared his throat as if so many words at one time hurt it and walked away, not waiting for an answer. Bunny rolled her eyes but I could tell she was a little embarrassed.

"I was just trying to explain to you girls what I'm about in *general* terms," she said. "I figure if people know where I stand on the big issues, they'll know where I stand on the smaller ones."

She gave us both a handful of campaign buttons to "pass out to the masses" and then out in the store, filled a striped bag with rootbeer barrels as "your payment for button distribution."

Jack Cole came in then to buy a couple quarts of oil and got to yakking with Bunny about their new baby's colic and Franny and I decided it was time to make like a log and split, but before we did I got the bright idea of giving Mr. Cole a campaign button.

"Hop to it," he said, reading it. "Hop to what?"

Franny and I got a big charge out of that and then Bunny yelled at us, saying that was it, she wasn't going to tolerate this kind of insubordination in her troops, and I could have sworn I saw old Mr. Vold crack a smile, but maybe it was just a shadow or something.

* * *

I TURNED TWELVE the next Tuesday and, ladies and gentlemen, it was the worst birthday of my entire life. Twelve's a big deal, too—your last year of being one hundred percent kid. I know you're still officially a kid when you're a teenager, but unofficially, you're crossing a big line.

I'd planned this whole bash—we were going to go roller skating at the rink in Brainerd and then eat at the Leaning Tower of Pizza, where the birthday kid gets a free personal pizza with as many toppings as she wants. So imagine my shock when I woke up that morning with pink spots all over me and itching like I had a major case of fleas.

"Chicken pox!" said my mother, sounding like it was the eighth Wonder of the World or something.

I burst into tears then, which isn't the greatest way to start your first day of a brand-new age, but what was I supposed to do?

The party was canceled, of course—all of my friends are *normal* kids who already had chicken pox when they were little, like kids are supposed to. So I wasn't contagious to them, but I felt so itchy and lousy I didn't want to do anything but lay on the couch smeared with Calomine lotion and watch *The Parent Trap*.

I had just finished the grilled-cheese-and-turkey sandwich my mother had brought me on a tray (one thing about being sick, it does give you good room service) and was laying there feeling pretty sorry for myself when my mom answered the doorbell and there was Franny.

"I'm looking for the coolest twelve-year-old in the world. Do I have the right spot? Oops—no pun intended."

"Franny! What are you doing here?"

She wiggled out of her backpack like it was a tight sweater and dumped it on the floor.

"I'm on independent study in Cragun's civics class. That means I can do anything I want to as long as I have my paper done by Friday.

"It's a drag you're sick on your birthday." She plopped down on the couch. "Oh, *The Parent Trap*. I love that movie, especially when they pour honey all over Vicky."

"It's almost over," I said. "Do you want me to rewind it?"

"Nah. Then I'll want to watch the whole thing and I'll be late getting back to school."

"Did you ride your bike?"

Franny nodded and helped herself to one of the ginger-snap cookies my mother had made that morning when she asked if there was anything special I wanted. (I figure when you're sick on your birthday, you have a right to ask for just about anything.)

We sat and watched the last five minutes of the movie when the parents are reunited and Hayley Mills and her twin live happily ever after.

"So you had to cancel your whole party, huh?" asked Franny when I turned off the remote.

"Well, it wasn't really a big party," I said. "Just Amber and Nichol and some other kids from my class." I felt embarrassed talking about a party Franny hadn't been invited to, even though we never invited each other to our birthdays. She was Lin's age, so we didn't do a lot of formal socializing—but after that day at the Top Hat, I'd been hoping we'd hang out more. Now that she came to see me on my birthday while I was all itchy and oozy, I wanted to be her friend even more. I mean none of my other so-called friends came by, although Amber did call me that night.

We sat around listening to the tape rewind and then Franny said, "Oh—your present!" and got this tissue-paper-wrapped lump out of her backpack and threw it at me.

"What is it?" I said, asking that classic dumb gift receiver's question. I mean the answer everyone thinks but never says is, "Why don't you open it and find out, stupid?"

It was a vintage hat, a maroon felt hat with a little brim, a hat that Ann Sheridan might have worn to an audition.

"Franny, I love it," I said, trying it on. "Where did you get it?"

"The Goodwill."

"It's in great shape." I took it off and sniffed it. "It doesn't stink or anything. Thanks again. It's the best present I've gotten this year."

"Have you opened any others?"

"Well, no. But I can't see how they could be better than this."

By the time Franny left, I was thinking maybe this birthday was going to turn out after all, but no; I was all excited about my 1941 hat and had to run to the kitchen to show my mom. She didn't hear me at first, so I stood there by the refrigerator, staring at her, frozen to the spot even as I wanted to run away.

She was crouched under the kitchen table, saying, "Help me, help me, help me, help me," over and over and over again. Tears were gushing out of her eyes and her hands were held up on the sides of her face like blinders.

"Mom?" I wasn't even sure I said the word out loud, but she jumped like she was the target of a precision peashooter, smacking her head on the bottom of the table.

"Ouch," she said, and we both stared at each other for a minute and I remember thinking that she looked exactly how I felt, which was terrified.

"Oh, Darcy, I was just—" she began, but I didn't wait around to hear whatever lame excuse she came up with. I mean, what could she tell me, that she was feeling a little *down*? I had seen her plain as day, sitting under the kitchen table, cracking up, flipping out, going nuts. I ran to my room, my heart banging away, so scared, but also mad that out of all the days in the year, my mother had to have a nervous breakdown on my twelfth birthday. Oh, the humanity.

DICK

WE WERE HAVING our "Syttende Mai" (May 17) sale down at the appliance store, a big deal to the many White Falls residents of Scandinavian descent—not only because we celebrated Norway's independence but because we offered great bargains.

I had spent the morning glad-handing customers; listening to Alma Soltvedt argue with Violet Johannson over who had contributed most to world culture: Sweden or Norway.

"Strindberg!" shouted the hard-of-hearing Alma.

"Ibsen!" Violet shouted back. I assumed it was the passion of her argument and not deficient hearing on her part that made her match Alma's volume.

"Jenny Lind!"

"Edvard Grieg!"

Get a life, I wanted to tell them. Then Stan Nilsson buttonholed me for one half of a long hour, trying to get me to go ten percent lower on an already discounted iron.

"I've never paid retail in my life!" he reminded me for the third time that day, and my wish for him was the same I had for the dueling Scandinavian patriots: *Get a life*.

I was not in my best selling mode. I was wound up from too many cups of the complimentary coffee Lin was pouring at a table by the front door. Darcy sat with her sister, offering customers krumkakka and other butter-filled cookies and I'd had my share of those, too, so I was running on caffeine and sugar, which is not my most efficient fuel.

Then, thanks to the Viking helmets we of the sales force were wearing (Syttende Mai and the store named Viking Appliance—you don't think we're going to wear yarmulkes, do you?) I had a headache that pulsed through my head like an electric current—*zzzttt, zzzttt, zzzttt.*

There was nothing more I wanted to do than take the stupid helmet off, light up a cigarette, and get the hell out.

"Dick, what do you mean you won't give Jack and Connie a little incentive for buying this humidifier?" Dad Evan held his arms out as if he couldn't believe I'd be so miserly. "Can't have their new baby drying up her nasal passages."

I smiled and Jack and Connie Cole giggled, probably seeing in my smile the message I intended to give them, which was: Aren't you taking this baby thing a little far? Do you expect to get a discount on everything just because you adopted a Korean baby?

"If it were me, I'd *give* it to them," I said, and watched the magnanimous-salesman face of my father-in-law harden just a bit. Dad Evan thinks generosity is his territory and he doesn't like any trespassers.

He laughed then, recovering quickly. "If it were up to Dick, we'd be hanging out in bankruptcy court."

I excused myself, pretending I was needed elsewhere.

"How's it going?" I asked, wandering over to Kyle Christianson, whose job it was to blow up balloons.

"Great," he said, filling a balloon from the helium tank. He tied a string around it and handed it to Stan Nilsson's grandson, who immediately let go of it.

"*Wahhhhhh!*" he screamed, watching it float toward the ceiling, where it bobbed against the tiles along with a dozen other balloons on the lam.

Dumb kid, I thought.

Kyle quickly blew up another balloon. "Here you go," he said, handing it to the boy.

"Me want that one," said the boy, pointing upward.

"I know you can handle this one," I said, clapping Kyle on the back as the little boy's scream got shriller. I must admit it cheered me for a second. I mean, Lin's boyfriend breezes in here for two dollars above minimum wage for just blowing up balloons. Uh-uh. Let him see what true customer service is all about.

Lin was glowering by the time I got to the coffee-and-cookies table.

"Dad, what did you say to Kyle?" Her face was pink with heat. Both she and Darcy were wearing traditional Norwegian costumes. Helen ordered them for the girls every other year, to wear not only for the Syttende Mai sale but other holidays as well. Lin considered it a form of torture, especially since they were full of color, but Darcy liked wearing them, and the hats, even though to me they look like little toaster covers. There were a lot of layers to them and with the heat generated by the crowd—well, it had to be an uncomfortable costume.

"I didn't say anything," I said, helping myself to a couple more cookies.

"He's sure giving you an irty-day ook-lay," said Darcy.

"Everyone else went up to Uncle's Lake for a picnic," said Lin. "We're the only ones in the whole freshman class who have to spend the day in a fucking appliance store."

Darcy actually gasped; me, I guess I must have just stared at Lin pop-eyed. There have been a few *shits* and *dammits* in our house, but for the most part Devera and I try to set a good example with our language.

Lin sat staring at me in all her fourteen-year-old defiance, and I have to admit, a part of me admired her. Yeah! Shock the old man, I thought—go for it! Her face was tilted up and her cheeks were blazing with color, and Darcy was seated inches above the seat of her chair, so tense was her body, silently asking, What're you going to do, Dad? Smack her? Ground her?

I glared back at Lin like I was not only shocked but really pissed and then I threw them a double whammy: I started laughing.

"That's real cute, Lin," I said, my laughter still riding along with the words. "It's always cute when a fourteen-year-old dressed like Inga the Clog Dancer talks with a garbage mouth."

I walked away then, out the front door, and I ducked a little as if I were so tall the horns of my helmet might knock against the top of the door frame.

I would like to have gone over to the car lot and sat in one of my Caddies—we had gotten in a beautiful pearl-gray Fleetwood Brougham just the other day—but Larry O'Herne, the salesman in charge whenever I'm away, is the type who would not enjoy the presence of his boss sitting and reading the paper inside the new merchandise. He was a dullard, destined to let the Blue Book and not his own imagination be his guide, but his father was Dad Evan's golf partner and Larry hadn't made it in St. Paul, where he'd gone to open a fish-and-chips franchise, so what can you do?

I walked around the block instead, holding my helmet under my arm like a football, letting a tender May breeze dry my sweaty, pulsing scalp.

Main Street was fairly empty of commerce—the Syttende Mai sale sucking up all customers—so I didn't have to stop and talk to anyone.

Being a salesman has cranked up my natural propensity toward gregariousness, but like anyone, there are times when the idea of normal discourse with a fellow human being makes me sick.

Sometimes I'd just as soon slug someone as say hi, and on those days I jam my hands in my pocket and steel that old grin.

I stood on the corner next to the hardware store for a while, just inhaling the smells of spring. My big-shot Manhattan-lawyer brother came back here for a visit last summer, laughing at our one-horse downtown. I asked him, "Hey, Bob, do you have lilac bushes on Fifth Avenue? A crab-apple tree in front of the post office?"

I wished Devera was with me; I would have picked a clump of lilacs and given them to her, but she was at home, writing a paper on Carthage and the Pubic Wars.

"Punic Wars, Dick," she had said, not appreciating my joke. "The *Punic* Wars."

She did her homework at the kitchen table and like a kid who wants to ward off cheaters, always curled her arm on top of her paper when anyone came near. When I asked her what she was writing about, she acted as if I were a stranger asking her age and weight. But Devera has always liked keeping a part of herself closed, I think she likes the idea of being thought of as mysterious.

For instance, with both kids, she didn't tell anyone she was pregnant until she started showing. I wanted to take ads out in the *Gazette*, but I had to keep a muzzle on the news until she gave me the go-ahead.

Both times I used the argument, "It's my kid, too, you know," but she said until I carried them, I wouldn't be able to make any announcements without her permission.

She didn't even want to tell Dad Evan or Helen, which really surprised me, considering they're so close.

"I just don't want anyone knowing my business until they have to, Dick."

Well, okay. Geez. She was the pregnant one, though, and I suppose her hormones were playing around with her judgment and reasoning.

I came to enjoy those first secretive months when no one but the two of us knew what was going on in Dev's belly and then I stood by her when her parents and BiDi got all hurt and mad, wondering why she hadn't told them earlier.

"She didn't want to jinx things," I told them privately, believing it, too, even though she had never told me as much.

It seemed to me BiDi and Big Mike conceived the day we told them Dev was four months pregnant because Franny is exactly four months younger than Lin, and back then, Devera and BiDi did sort of copy each other.

This was the first Syttende Mai sale that Devera had missed. She was always there dressed up in her Norske maiden outfit, pouring coffee and chatting with the customers, making it easy for me to pretend that I was a Viking warrior and not some goof in a helmet selling discounted broiler ovens.

Dad Evan had been a little upset—"What do you mean she's writing a paper about Carthage?"—he likes his whole family out in force when he marks down prices for the masses. To him, his Big Sales are political events—no, make that royal events—and he's the king thanking all his subjects for their loyal support.

I had a cigarette and it seemed my exhales were nothing but big long smoky sighs.

I started walking back to the store, feeling lousiness fall on me like a spring drizzle, but then I heard a knock and there was Sergio, standing behind the window of his shop. I had to laugh, the way he was jumping and waving, he looked like a little monkey in a baker's hat.

"My friend, have a piece of cake with me," he said, meeting me at the door.

"Can't. I'm loaded up on coffee and krumkakka."

Sergio looked at the helmet I was carrying under my arm. "So, you are done with your raping and pillaging for the day?"

"Just about," I said, "but first I thought I'd clean out your register."

"Good luck. I've had two customers to your two hundred."

"Feels like two million," I said.

"You'll feel better tonight," said Sergio, taking a chocolate cake out of his display case. "Look what I made for us!" He walked around in a little circle, holding the cake near his shoulder.

"Oh, no," I said. "We're having dinner with you guys, aren't we?"

Sergio put the plate down and looked at me as if I'd smacked him. "That is just the reaction I hope to get from someone who remembers a dinner engagement with me."

I laughed. Sergio could do a wounded number better than a woman. "It's just that I'm so beat. It's draining being a retailing wizard, you know."

"I should know the pain," said Sergio, and he bit his knuckles. I'm used to Sergio's humor—remember, his father was an opera singer—I actually get a charge out of the dramatics.

I looked at my watch. "Well, guess I'd better get back before we run out of stock."

"No, no, stay here and rub it in."

I left his shop, feeling as if my mood had been brightened by a powerful bleach. The idea of a night out with BiDi and Sergio appealed to me in a big way. I could use the laughs as well as the respite from my own dinner table. When Dev's in a bad mood—and it seems she has been in one for a while—she always brings it to the table like a side dish.

Dad Evan acted like I had abandoned ship—what was I gone for? twenty minutes at most?—but I didn't let his Captain Queeg act bother me. Instead, I plastered on the smile, lit up the charm, and *sold, sold, sold* like the heir apparent to Dale Carnegie that I am.

DEVERA

WE GOT OVER to BiDi and Sergio's around seven. I expected Dick to be beat when he came home from the Syttende Mai sale, but he burst through the door like a battering ram. I had just come out of an afternoon wandering through a B.C. time zone, so it was a little hard summoning up enthusiasm over the sales record he had set.

"Not just *three* combination washer/dryers, Dev," he had said, looking fevered, "but two self-defrosting refrigerators, two freezers, four microwaves, a half-dozen irons, *and* that big ugly humidifier!"

Fortunately, he didn't even notice I didn't dig out my old pom-poms and start up a cheer. He was in that ebullient mood that makes him assume everyone else's mood matches his. So all I had to do was sit there and listen to him; in his mind it was as good as applause.

I heard him singing in the shower and as he got dressed. "Mr. Sandman" had been rewritten into "Mr. Salesman."

> *"I'm Mr. Salesman, selling it all—*
> *You buy from me, and I make a haul. . . ."*

Or something like that. I was sitting at the vanity in my slip (I must be the only modern woman who wears a slip—I just like how it feels as a garment) which turned Dick into Brick from *Cat on a Hot Tin Roof* (we'd just seen it on the *Late Show*), except his Brick was a turned-on one.

"Maggie, you shouldn't oughta tempt a man like that," he said in a twangy accent that was more cowboy than southern. "I'm a fixin' to get my pants off right now."

He leaned over and kissed my neck and I was planning to cooperate fully, but then Darcy chose that moment to knock at our bedroom door, and then poke her head in.

"Mom, can I bring your old Monkees sleeping bag to Grandma's?"

Darcy was spending the night at Dick's mother's.

"Sure," I said.

"Why not bring the Rolling Stones one for Grandma?" asked Dick, buttoning (reluctantly) his shirt.

"Dad." Darcy turned the word into two exasperated syllables. "They don't make Rolling Stones sleeping bags. At least I've never seen one. And besides, Grandma wouldn't sleep in one if they did."

Ardis has pretty bad arthritis and slept—in fact, did most everything—in an adjustable hospital bed.

"What's your sister up to?" asked Dick.

"Told you, Dad," said Lin, suddenly appearing at our doorway. Her head was bulbous with steam rollers. "A bunch of us are going to see a movie at the cineplex."

"Does 'a bunch' include Kyle?"

"Well, sure, Dad."

"Who's driving?"

"Carolyn's brother."

"Okay, but be home by eleven."

Lin started to whine about having the earliest curfew of anyone she knew, but Darcy, who knows everybody's business, reminded her that Emily Gustafson and Heather Drust had to be home at eleven, too, and what about Franny? She had to be home at ten-thirty.

"Thanks a lot, dweeb," said Lin. "And besides, Franny never goes out, so her curfew might as well be three o'clock in the morning."

I was so grateful for the normal family scenario, I could have wept.

Since seeing me in the midst of one of my panic attacks,

Darcy had either been ignoring me or treating me like an invalid—asking me if I needed a sweater or could she get me a cup of tea?

Poor kid, I know it's not fun to discover your mother freaking out under the kitchen table.

I called after her as she ran out of the kitchen, my panic completely erased by my need to comfort my daughter. She ignored my knocks on her bedroom door, so, uninvited, I entered. Both Dick and I had agreed when we built this house that bedroom doors didn't need locks on them.

"Darcy, honey," I began, coming toward her.

The fear in her eyes nearly broke my heart—I want to inspire many things in my children; terror is not on the list.

I sat down on the bed, wrapping my arms around my pink-spotted birthday girl. "Oh, Darcy, I'm so sorry you had to see that. You must have thought I was going crazy."

Darcy's head bobbed up and down.

"Well, I think I was for a minute," I said, news which Darcy greeted with a wail. I held her tighter. "But I'm not crazy now, honey. I'm your same old boring mom now."

Darcy loosened her grip and looked at me. "Well, what happened? Why were you saying 'help me'?"

A big sigh inflated my lungs. At age eight, Darcy had handled my "birds and bees" speech with aplomb; was she ready at twelve to handle a discussion of her mother's bruised psyche?

I exhaled. "Darcy, lately I've been getting these panic attacks. I start feeling . . ."

We sat in silence for a moment.

"Like what?" whispered Darcy.

"Well . . . really afraid. Almost claustrophobic in my own skin. I feel that either I'm going to die, or go crazy, or that the world's going to end."

"Oh, Mommy!" said Darcy, her voice years younger, and I wanted to kick myself. Me and my stupid honesty-is-the-best-policy crap—what right did I have telling my daughter something that terrified her?

"What makes you feel like that?" Darcy asked.

I stared across the room at her collection of hats hanging from the rack, wishing desperately I could take my words back. But I couldn't. So misguided or not, I went on.

"I don't know. They just come on. I was in the middle of baking your birthday cake when this one came on and I—"

"Oh, Mommy, will you have to go away? To a mental institution or something?" She barely finished the question before she burst into tears again.

"Oh, Darcy." I breathed in the sweet smell of her hair. "No. No. I'm not going crazy—they're just panic attacks. A lot of people get them—Dad and I have been reading up on them—and oh, honey, I'll be fine. I *am* fine."

"Daddy knows about them?" asked Darcy. "What does he think?"

"Well," I said, petting her hair. "He wants to help me."

When I came home from the grocery store after that first one, Dick knew immediately something was wrong, and when I told him about it, he didn't try to blow me off by telling me I was "overtired" or "it was just in my imagination," but drove me immediately to the library.

"We'll do a little research," he said, holding my hand during the entire drive. "Might as well find out what we're dealing with." (I loved him for saying *we*.)

"Are you taking some medicine for them?" asked Darcy. "Couldn't Dr. Erck write a prescription or something?"

"Oh, sweetheart, there probably is some kind of medicine, but from what I've read, you just have to deal with them. You have to realize that as bad as they seem, you're not going crazy, the world is not ending, and you're not going to die."

"Promise?" Darcy sniffed.

"I promise," I said, praying I wasn't lying.

She helped me frost her cake and that night we presented her with the mountain bike she had wanted, and we made popcorn and watched one of her all-time favorite movies, *All About Eve*.

After Dick tucked her in, I went in for a private audience, and when I hugged her, she held me to her.

"I love you, Mom," she said. "But I love you best *not* crazy. So try real hard to stay that way."

"I will, Darcy."

When I brushed my teeth that evening, I saw the right side of my face was dotted with pink and my first reaction was "How can I have chicken pox?" but then I realized the spots were Calomine lotion, transferred from Darcy's face onto mine in the press of our hug.

AFTER WE DROPPED Darcy off at her grandmother's, we drove to BiDi and Sergio's, giggling like a bunch of teenagers. You know how you can move your pointer and middle fingers so that they look like a pair of legs walking? Well, with one hand on the wheel, Dick kept "walking" over to me with his other hand, hopping and jumping up my thigh and then sliding down it. I kept slapping him away but I was getting slightly turned on. The dichotomy of my feelings is that sometimes when Dick acts like a squirrelly little boy he'll repel me and other times I'll think, I must have him right now. A lot of emotions, especially guilt, made me even more inclined toward the latter because . . . well, because I had started my affair with Professor Gerhart Ludwig.

Coffee at a truck stop off the interstate *had* led to bed, one with bad springs, as a matter of fact, in a motel room outside Fergus Falls. I got there early, and gave the name H. Prynne to the guy at the desk, who surprised me by asking, "Oh, would that be *H* as in Hester?"

I was shivering under the stiff, bleached sheets, wondering what exactly I was doing, when Gerhart came into the room all blustery, almost frantic, telling me next time I decided to register under a code name at least inform him so he'd be spared the song and dance he had to go through with the smart-alecky desk clerk "who probably has a community-college degree and is writing the great American novel in between checking in trysters."

Suffice it to say, it wasn't the best way to greet a housewife who'd just recently begun to suffer from panic attacks and never before slept with anyone but her husband. I was ready to leave then and there, but then Gerhart apologized and said let's start over.

The sex isn't worth writing about (and what if it was—can you imagine Dick reading *that* letter?) but the idea of it is. Its illicitness is as exiting to me as the actual deed itself. I'm sure things could be improved if Gerhart shaved his beard, but maybe I just have to learn to tolerate scratchiness. Anyway, it's not as if I sought out an affair for sex; sex with Dick was and still is fulfilling. What I was looking for was a change—a chance to see how I functioned in a set of completely new circumstances.

So take up scuba diving! part of me yelled, but the other part yelled, *Shut up, I'm not doing anything a billion other people aren't doing.*

And while guilt might be a chain around my leg, it's a weak one, one that I'm sure I'll be able to step out of with the next motel invitation.

SERGIO MADE A fantastic dinner—a chicken polenta dish— and we brought over some good wine Dad and Mom had given us on our anniversary, so everyone was feeling festive in that way you do when you eat and drink something more exotic than burgers and Coke.

Sergio and Dick even did dishes and made coffee, which made BiDi and me feel terribly luxurious. If all men knew to do the unexpected, especially when it comes to the domestic stuff, the war between the sexes would have a cease-fire. At least until they did the next dumb thing.

BiDi and I "retired" to the den.

"Let's smoke cigars and talk politics," I said, putting my feet up on an ottoman.

"No," said BiDi, "let's have fun instead. Tell me all about you and your Professor What's-his-name."

"Ludwig," I said, feeling suddenly shy.

"Look at you—you're all red," said BiDi, pushing my feet off the ottoman and sitting on it. "So what gives?"

Before I could say anything she slapped my knee. "I knew it, I knew it, you slept with him, didn't you?"

"Shhhh," I said, even though the kitchen was on the other side of the house.

"I can't believe it," she said, folding her arms and turning her back on me. "I'm not talking to you."

"Beed, come on, you didn't act like this when I told you it was probably going to happen." I felt like I was explaining why I was out all night to a dorm housemother.

"Well, that's before it did." She turned around, her bright blue eyes glittery with anger. "I can't believe it, Devera, what has gotten into you?"

I bowed my head, chastised.

BiDi shook her head. "You who has the model marriage in White Falls."

"The model marriage?" I said. "You've got to be kidding."

BiDi looked at me as if I had told her she needed a stronger deodorant. "No, Devera, I am not kidding. If they took a poll and asked 'Which couple in White Falls seems the most in love?' I bet you'd win hands down."

"We would?"

"Well, sure you would, and I don't know why you want to spoil it all by having an affair." BiDi held her middle fingers under her eyes; the dam two tears rolled over. I couldn't believe it—BiDi is not a crier.

"BiDi," I said, not knowing what else to say.

"I know, I know, this is stupid, but I've always looked up to your marriage, you know? Especially after Big Mike and I broke up—I mean you two gave me courage to try again with Sergio."

"We did?"

BiDi pinched the bridge of her nose. "Devera, I swear if you say 'we would?' or 'we did?' like that again, I'm going to slug you." She breathed a ragged sigh. "Now I'll have to find another couple to hold up as a model—and who am I supposed to use—Jack and Connie Cole?"

I laughed. "Why do you need a model to hold up?"

"I don't know," she snapped. "I just do."

I should have known BiDi would take this hard—this was a woman who thought perfection was attainable, not impossible; a woman who didn't think you should wear shorts if you had a little cellulite, a woman who not only made her bed every morning but washed her sheets twice a week.

We didn't say anything else until Dick and Sergio came into the room, wheeling in a loaded tea cart.

"Don't tip it over!" said Sergio as Dick came to a rather abrupt stop. He put his hands in the space around a chocolate cake dripping with frosting and walnuts. "This one I slaved over!"

He cut me a huge slab and BiDi a nearly transparent sliver and I ignored the smirk she gave me that asked, "Don't you have any pride?" In fact, I had another piece and made much about the cake's richness, and how exactly did he make such a fudgy frosting?

Afterward, we got out the Scrabble board and BiDi and I played against each other as if we were in the World Finals. Sergio was on my team, so I felt at a disadvantage. He'll lay down these Spanish words and Dick or BiDi'll challenge him before I can tell him to pick up his tiles, doesn't he remember only English words are accepted? Of course, Dick is a poor speller, so we came out about even. BiDi claims she never picks up the Scrabble dictionary, but I know she secretly pores over it, collecting ammunition like *xi* and *em* for her next game. Of course, so do I; why be intentionally handicapped?

They beat us by fourteen points but I had scored a seventy-point word, so I felt somewhat vindicated. We were choosing tiles for the second game when the phone rang.

Sergio's a fairly swarthy guy, but when he came back into the room his face was the color of skim milk.

"BiDi," he whispered, coming to the table, his hands pulling at his shirt collar.

My stomach lurched as if I were on an express elevator to a twenty-story penthouse and I heard BiDi say, "What?", her voice flickering with panic.

For a moment I could hear nothing but the thumping in my chest. I remember looking at my watch; it was ten-thirty, half an hour until Lin's curfew.

Sergio cleared his throat and said as if he were asking a question. "Someone beat up Francesca."

"What?" said BiDi. "What are you saying, she and Kirsten had a fight?"

"No, BiDi, someone—they don't know who—beat Francesca up. She's in the hospital."

BiDi made a sound like a laugh crossed with a moan, and as I got up to go to her, I knocked my chair over and BiDi yelled at me to be careful, what did I want to do, tear the house apart?

BiDi

I REMEMBER DEV'S mom talking to my mom after Devera's brother was killed in that paper-shack fire. They were sitting out on the porch, watching the sunset, shelling peas. My mother loved to denude vegetables out on that porch (she husked corn, peeled potatoes, snapped beans) and she would recruit anyone who came by to help her.

"It's all a blur," Helen was saying about the funeral. "It's as if the past few weeks have been written in pencil and then erased. I can't remember a thing." She kept looking out across the lake and I noticed there were only four peas in her bowl whereas my mother's was nearly full.

Nothing was blurring for me as Dick drove us to the hospital. I can look back and see everything crystal clear.

Sergio held my hand until I told him to cut it out—what did he want to do, break all my fingers? I remember staring at the back of Devera's head and counting her split ends and getting up to eighteen. I remember having to put my hands on my knees to stop myself from kicking the back of the front seat. I wanted to feel my foot make contact through the upholstery leather and into the small of Devera's back. I wanted to pull her split-up hair, I was just so mad at her for having two safe daughters.

When we got to our dinky little hospital, Sergio opened his car door before Dick had completely stopped and he pulled me out with him as if I were no more than a bag of groceries.

The four of us raced into the hospital and I remember the distinct sounds of everyone's footsteps; the *click click* from the Cuban heels of Sergio's boots; a *flumpflump* from Dick's Top-Siders, the *shoosh shoosh* of Devera's thick-soled flats, and my own high heels sounding like someone snapping their fingers to a crazy beat.

Dr. Erck was standing at the nurses' desk, and even an emergency couldn't stop him from giving me the old once-over, which I tried to ignore. While other people might think he looked a little bleary-eyed from a hard day as Healer, I figured he was coming down from one of his private parties.

"BiDi, my dear." His hands shook a little as he took my arm in his, but I figured as long as he wasn't performing surgery, he was probably fine.

"She's resting comfortably," he said in his smooth doctor voice. I think Ted Erck could be completely blotto and still sound like he was in charge.

"Can we see her? Where is she? Where is she?" said Sergio, throwing his arms up.

"She's over here," said Dr. Erck, and we walked down the hall with him, a tight cluster that the nurses tsked sympathetically at.

Sheriff Buck was standing at the door of Franny's room and he started to say something but I pushed right past him, drawn to that hospital bed like a magnet, and then Sergio and I grabbed each other at the shock of what lay in that bed.

It was Franny—I could see that from the flat black hair smooshed against the pillow and I'd recognize her thick eyebrows anywhere, but the rest of her, at least the part showing about the sheet, was a purplish, bluish, swollen mess. Her eyes were squeezed into little black crescents and her lips were plumped up as if she'd had a collagen injection from a quack doctor.

"Francesca?" I whispered, almost afraid that if she answered, then yes, it would really be her.

"She's resting now," said Dr. Erck. "It's what she needs most."

"Can we stay with her until she wakes up?" asked Sergio as he sat down on a chair next to the bed.

"I think Sheriff Buck would like to talk to you," said

Dr. Erck. "Franny should be out for a while. Why don't you speak to the sheriff and come back here as soon as you're done?"

It sounded logical to me but I could tell Sergio was not going to move from that chair.

"I am not leaving," he said, smoothing Franny's hair, "I am not leaving my Francesca."

"I'll go," I said to the doctor. "I'll talk to the sheriff."

We (Dick and Devera insisted on going with me) followed the doctor and the sheriff into the chapel, which I for one thought was a strange place to have a conference. But then everything was strange—I felt like a miner going deep underground for the first time—the air felt kind of skimpy and clammy and there was a very real possibility that I might pass out.

Dick and Devera sat on each side of me, both pressing their bodies next to mine. Sheriff Buck and the good doctor sat down on folding chairs facing us, both men looking so concerned they actually looked a little mean.

"Where did it happen?" I asked, jumping right into it. "How did it happen? She was supposed to be doing her homework, for God's sake." (Who else but my daughter would spend a Friday night doing homework at a friend's house?)

Sheriff Buck rubbed his sideburn with his thumb.

"Apparently, Beverly Diane"—I could tell this was official, he had never called me Beverly Diane in all the years I'd known him—"she left the McAllen home around nine o'clock on her bicycle."

My mind was Spin Art. The McAllens lived a half mile down the road from us—they're the ones that set up that huge water slide in the summer and that huge ice-fishing house in the winter, and Franny spends a lot of time with Kirsten, one of their tall daughters with that ridiculous clown-colored red hair.

"So someone got her between the McAllens and our house?" A cold shiver ran up my back, thinking how close this danger was.

Sheriff Buck rubbed his other sideburn, looking puzzled.

"The ah . . . incident occured on County Road One. By a perpetrator in a silver van, make and license plate unknown."

"Why would Franny be riding on the old County Road at night?"

"My deputy took statements from Kirsten McAllen and her family," said the sheriff, looking at his little notepad. He cleared his throat. " 'All parties claim said victim was on her way home.'" He put his notepad in his back pocket, his Sergeant Joe Friday impersonation over.

"Well, I'm confused," I said. "Why would Franny take the old County Road home? No one takes the old County Road anywhere. And it goes the opposite way. More than the opposite way."

"I guess we'll have to get the answers from Franny when she wakes up," said the sheriff.

"How is she?" Devera asked the doctor, who was sitting there inspecting the hem of his white coat.

"She's got a couple fractured ribs," said Dr. Erck, continuing his tailoring inspection before he looked up straight into my eyes. "I was worried a little about her spleen for a minute, but I think it'll be all right. She's had seven stitches to a cut above her eyebrow . . . and her nose is broken . . . well, you've seen her face." He shook his head. "I haven't seen an assault case like this since those meatpackers beat up that scab a couple years back."

"There was no other type of . . . assault . . . was there?" Dick asked. Silently I was thanking them for asking questions I just couldn't seem to formulate.

"You mean sexual? Was she raped?" Dr. Erck shook his head. "I examined her and found no trace of sperm or torn tissue. As far as her injuries, well, you know kids. They're resilient. She won't win any beauty contests for a while but . . ." He shrugged and I laughed at the idea of Franny being unable to compete in any upcoming beauty contests, but then Devera pressed a tissue into my hand. I gave her a dirty look—what?—didn't she think I could handle this?— but then I tasted salty tears running over my lips and I held the Kleenex over my face, like a veil.

SERGIO

FRANCESCA HAS SURPRISING hands, not ones you would expect on a hockey player; long-fingered and the nail beds are deep. I was almost afraid to touch them, they were so pretty and delicate and still, like two orchid blossoms that had been cut. For the longest time my own hands were lead and I could not lift one up from my own lap to put on top of Francesca's. On the ride to the hospital BiDi had yelled at me for squeezing her hand too tight and I did not want to risk putting Francesca through one more ounce of pain.

I did, though, want to put whoever did this to her through much pain, *huge* pain, pain that would make him first senseless and then dead! I wanted to curl my fists into tight steel balls and then drive them into the barbarian who did this, right into the stomach, and then move upward, smashing his ribs into powder and splintering every bone in his face until one pierced through his brain, killing him slowly and with great torture.

This fantasy kept playing in my head over and over. I slammed my fists into the phantom's face, over and over. I watched blood spurt, heard moans. Over and over.

I felt I might go crazy in the head, might not be able to turn off these pictures, but when a nurse came in the room it was as if a television set had been turned off and the picture went to black.

"The X rays show a couple rib fractures," she said, hugging a clipboard to her chest. For one quick moment I thought she was talking about the victim I had been beating up in my imagination.

"Rib fractures?" I said, coming to, and finally my hand was able to move and I patted Francesca's fingers.

"This is awful," said the nurse. "Who could do such a thing? It makes me wonder how men can be such animals, no offense."

I shook my head, no offense was taken. How could it be when I wondered the same things myself?

"I have an eight-year-old daughter," the nurse said, and she touched Francesca's blanket. "She's quite a fan of your daughter. She wants to play hockey when she's older, too."

I sat forward a little, feeling my heart cave in a bit.

"Yes, we are proud of our Francesca." My words sounded as if they hadn't been used for a while, a little rusty.

"You should be. My gosh, the presence of mind she showed."

I looked at her; what could she mean? Presence of mind where? On the ice rink?

The nurse's thin-penciled eyebrows went up. "Oh, you don't know. Oh my gosh, you don't know!"

"Know what?" My heart was beating as if someone very fast was chasing me.

"She got here by herself. Francesca was beat up and thrown in the ditch and she got up, got her bike, and found her way to the hospital."

I tried to swallow but my throat was blocked.

"There's a bedpan under the bed, if you need it," said the nurse. "Francesca already filled one—my gosh, how she vomited—but we've got plenty." The nurse giggled then, a little uneasily. "Bedpans, that is. I mean we are a hospital and all."

She ducked her head as she left, telling me that she had enjoyed my cakes on several occasions and that if I needed anything to let her and the other nurses know.

I felt that was a strange mix—complimenting me on my business and then offering help, but of course people are not given guidebooks on how to act during emergencies. What a best-seller book that would be! I know I would buy a copy for BiDi—maybe she could read a chapter that said a person shouldn't yell at her husband for hurting their hand when the husband only needed to hold on because he wasn't sure he wouldn't fall off the earth into blackness if he didn't.

You are so dramatic, BiDi always says, but how can a person not be? Life by its nature is one big boiling drama, yes? I am not doing any embellishing, only reporting. I think mostly in English now, but still, there is the Spanish soul that maybe makes my purple darker, my water colder.

Oh, brother! is what BiDi would say to that.

Francesca stirred a little and made a little mouse squeak. I squeezed her hand, but only lightly.

"Francesca, it's Sergie," I said, putting my face near hers. "Francesca, I love you."

"I love you, too," she said, at least I think that's what she said.

"Francesca, I heard you perfectly."

"Good," she said, and maybe it was a little bit of a smile that came over her. At least I saw her teeth, and it was with relief I saw they were all there, white, straight rectangles, unbroken. Thank you, God, for little favors.

"Sergie, I hurt all over."

Right away I wasn't so thankful anymore. "I know you do, Francesca, I know you do." I blinked hard. I knew it would be worse for Francesca if I cried.

"Where's Mom?"

"She's talking with Dr. Erck and the sheriff. She loves you so much."

Francesca squeezed my hand back. "She's not going to like how my face looks, though." She made a huh-huh-huh sound, which was laughing, I guess, so I laughed a little bit, too, to keep her company even though what I wanted to do was jump up on my chair and scream.

"Maybe I won't talk for a while now," she said.

After a little while I could hear her even breaths, so even though I couldn't tell if her eyes were closed or open, I guessed she was sleeping.

I hoped that I had not aided the criminal by not pumping the information from Francesca, but I didn't have the strength and I knew the sheriff knew all there was to know and was telling BiDi at that moment. Still, there was an urge in me that wanted to shake Francesca and wake her up and beg her to tell me everything, to go over everything step-by-step so I could gather all my clues and go out and commit my murder.

But instead, my fingers brushed her hand lightly in a figure eight that went over her knuckles and back down to her wrist.

BiDi came in about fifteen minutes later with Devera and Dick.

"You can go now," she said to them in a snappish voice. "I won't fall apart if you're not here, you know."

Devera and Dick—well, their whole bodies seemed to shrug sadly, as if they had been scolded for doing something they didn't know was wrong. I looked at Dick and apologized with my eyes.

"We'll see you later," he whispered. "If you need anything at all, call."

Devera bent down to hug BiDi, who was pulling a chair up to Francesca's bed, but BiDi did not stop to hug back, she just kept pulling the chair and Devera kept holding on to her, skipping a funny little step. Devera whispered something in my wife's ear but BiDi did not acknowledge it, and then, somehow she and Dick seemed to get out of the room without me seeing them leave.

All I remember is a sudden big quiet, the kind of quiet that fills a place you are lost in.

I looked across the bed to BiDi, and her face, it shocked me. Dick joked to me once, he said that BiDi was a freak of nature; a woman who defied the laws of gravity, and it is true, her face was as young and fresh as a twenty-five-year-old girl's—and her body, well, you have heard my rhapsody on that. I think mostly those Scandinavian genes are responsible; BiDi is all Norwegian. And of course there is that devotion to herself.

Anyway, the change on her face was as sudden as if she had picked up an old woman's mask and put it on. It scared me, that face, and I am not kidding you to say I would not have been surprised if her hair had suddenly turned white either.

But when she moved forward, the shadow fell off her face and I saw it was my same BiDi, looking the worse for wear, of course, but not the old crone she had seemed a moment ago.

"Francesca?" she said, and in her voice I heard a tenderness I had not heard in a long time. "Franny honey, can you hear me?"

Nothing changed; the rise and fall of Francesca's chest was the same, nothing of the face moved.

"She was awake for a little while," I said. "She spoke a little bit."

A sharp look came into her eyes. "Figures. Figures she'd talk to you and not to me."

My head tipped to the side as if she had hit me with a rock or other weapon. How could BiDi say these things?

"I'm sorry," she said, reading my mind as she does sometimes. "I just don't know what's going on." She started to cry and I was glad because it gave me a chance to do something, to comfort her.

I gave Francesca's hand an extra little pat as if to say, It's all right, I will be right back, and then I went to BiDi, gathering her up in my arms, trying in this storm to feel like a big strong tree.

"BiDi, BiDi, BiDi," I said over and over, breathing in the coconutty smell of her hair, and for a moment I forgot my sadness, thinking only how nice it was to hold her so close and have her hold me back. She cried into my shoulder, and the wetter my shirt got, the stronger I felt.

"Oh, Sergio, why would anyone do this?" BiDi wiped her nose like a child, with the fleshy part of her palm.

"I don't know," I answered, and the feelings of powerfulness began to leak away. "What did the sheriff and the doctor say?"

BiDi pressed her head against mine. We were ear to ear,

and even though her earring bit into my earlobe, I did not complain because I felt so close to her, able to communicate without talking. We sat that way for a while, staring at Francesca as she slept, but then BiDi sat up and her whole body seemed to fill up with a sigh and she told me what had happened in what she called "that conference in the chapel."

"She was riding alone on the old County Road," began BiDi, her sweet voice all the way flat in a monotone. "A van pulled up ahead of her, almost knocking her over. She was ready to turn around and some guy jumped out and starting beating on her. She was able to half ride/half walk to the hospital."

BiDi let out a whoop that in one second had turned into a sob, and she sat still for a moment, her hands clamped over her mouth.

"Is that it?" I said finally.

"What do you mean, is that it?"

"That's all there is to the story?"

"Well, that's all Franny could tell before she practically passed out and then they brought her to X-ray."

"That's all she said about it?"

"Sergio!" said BiDi, her voice angry. "That's all she said. It says it all. Some guy got out of a van and beat her up."

"Why?" I asked.

"Well, how should I know!" This she said so loud that a passing nurse backstepped to look into the room and ask if everything was all right.

"No, it's not!" said BiDi. "But you can't do anything about it!" The nurse ran off the way a mouse does when a light's turned on.

"Oh, my God," whispered BiDi, "was that Midge Selitz?"

"Who?"

"That nurse! Midge Selitz! Oh, this is great—we've got the town slut nursing our daughter!"

"BiDi!" I would like to have slapped her, but I never want to get into anything like that, afraid where it would end. She knows I let her get away with a lot of bad behavior, but this was too much.

"Oh, I'm sorry, Sergio. She's not the town slut. She just enjoys a physical relationship with a large body of men."

What could we do? What could we do when our Francesca was laying there blue and purple and swollen, with fractured ribs that gave a little crackle to her breathing? We couldn't break anything or get down on our knees and scream or grab Dr. Erck by his lapels and ask him to make Francesca better *now*, so we did what was left; we just laughed about poor Midge Selitz and her large body of men.

DICK

WE PICKED UP Darcy on the way home from the hospital, which teed off my mother in a big way.

"I thought she was spending the night," she said from her hospital bed, where she and Darcy had been sharing a bowl of popcorn and a game of crazy eights.

"Something's come up," I said.

"What?" asked Darcy.

I took her overnight bag off a chair. "Does anything go in here or didn't you unpack yet?"

"Dad, of course I unpacked—I'm in my pajamas, aren't I? So what came up?"

Devera gave me the eye but we had agreed. Well, we hadn't exactly *agreed*, but I wasn't going to waver on this one—Darcy wouldn't be told about Franny until the next morning. No reason to give her nightmares.

"Don't ask so many questions," I said, playing the hard guy. "Just get your coat and come on."

"Well, I never, of all the . . ." said my mother, gathering up the playing cards with her thick arthritic fingers. "If you don't think I can properly watch my own grandchild—"

"Ma, it's not that." My mother suffers from an inferiority complex. She thinks Dad Evan and Helen with their good health and money have it all over her as far as grand-parenting goes.

"Not at all, Ardis," said Devera. "I'll call you tomorrow." She kissed my mother on the cheek and picked up some pop-corn kernels that were scattered over the afghan.

"I just hope next time she'll be able to spend the whole night," said my mother with a sulk in her voice. "We were going to stay up and watch the Creature Feature."

"Yeah," said Darcy. *"Frankenstein Meets Godzilla."* She stood by the closet, her coat over her pajamas, glaring at me.

I kissed my mother, who smelled like camphor and hand lotion. The smell makes me slightly nauseous. "Ma, I'll explain it all tomorrow."

My mother waved her knobby hand as if she couldn't care less if I ever called again.

Darcy sat in the corner of the backseat, her arms crossed over her chest and I could feel her stare even as I drove. It was like an extra ceiling light or a heat vent aimed at me.

"Geez, Darce," I said, "lighten up."

"You lighten up. You're the one who dragged me out of Grandma's house for no good reason—" She paused for a moment. "Wait a sec, is Lin all right? Did something happen to Lin?" Her voice waggled a little and then she burst into tears.

"Stop the car, Dick," said Devera, and when I did, she got out of the front seat and into the back, carefully buckling her seat belt. No turning around in her seat for her; no, that would mean she'd have to undo her seat belt, an action that goes against the craw of Ms. Car Safety.

"Darcy, Franny's in the hospital."

I slapped the steering wheel with the ball of my hand.

"What did we say, Devera?"

"Dick, I didn't say anything. You did. But Darcy has a right to know what's going on and I have a right to tell her."

"Franny . . . why?" asked Darcy, her voice so high and scared and disbelieving that I wanted to take her in my arms. Instead, I did the only thing I felt I could do well at the moment: I put the car into drive and got back on the road.

"Who would want to beat Franny up?" asked Darcy.

"Someone . . . some . . . guy in a van."

"A guy in a van? Well, who? Did they catch him?"

"No," said Devera, "not yet."

A car behind us honked, and even though I realized I was veering across a lane, I flipped him the bird and honked back. I turned around quickly and gave Devera a dirty look so she'd know I held her responsible for breaking an agreement *and* for my erratic driving.

"Is she all right?" Darcy asked.

Devera sighed. "She has some fractured ribs, a broken nose, a bruised spleen and she needed some stiches, but if anyone is strong, it's Franny. She'll be all right."

Devera said this last part with absolute conviction, but I wasn't fooled. I knew it was more a wish than an assurance.

I swore under my breath, suddenly feeling that I could crush the steering wheel under my fingers.

Devera was very up-front about everything with our daughters—she said she had suffered because of her own mother never telling her anything she *really* needed to know. I think Dev goes too far sometimes—I know she really scared Darce by telling her about these little panicky things she gets, but somehow Dev's like the president and she always gets to veto my vote. Darcy would have been happy with the simple explanation "Franny got beat up," but no, Devera had to give a rundown of the injuries. She had explained sex to the girls when each of them had turned eight. I had been willing to go along with stories of cabbage patches and storks until they reached college age, but Devera always said an informed child was an armed child. They all laughed at my nicknames for body parts—"down there" was "down there" for both sexes; I could no more say *vagina* than I could *penis*.

The only sound as I turned off onto Lake Road was of Darcy crying into Devera's shoulder, and in the big padded interior of the Fleetwood, it sounded like a little bird.

Usually I loved this last part of the drive home from town. Lake Road was curved around the big houses on the east side of the lake and driving it always made me feel a little like James Bond; this successful virile guy negotiating the hairpin curves and turns above the Monaco apartment of his mistress. It's a fantasy, okay? But now it seemed that every slow curve was full of danger; that danger was some dark, hairy thing, ready to jump out of every corner, ready to grab my girls.

Lin was painting her toenails at the kitchen counter, bobbing and weaving her head to music she listened to through electronic earmuffs.

She looked up, startled, when we came into her peripheral vision.

"God, you guys scared me," she said, taking her earphones off. The rest of us all started talking at once.

"Don't say 'God,'" I said, "and get your feet off the counter, we eat off that, you know."

"Did you lock the front door?" asked Devera.

"Lin, Franny was beat up!"

Lin stared at her sister. "What did you say?"

"Franny was beat up!"

"Beat up?"

Darcy nodded her head. "She broke her ribs and her nose and fractured her spleen and there's stitches all over her—"

The counter stool clattered to the floor as Lin hopped off it and rushed to Devera.

Dev opened up her arms and clamped them tight around Lin, and then Darcy, like a puppy, wriggled open a space and the three of them stood swaying gently, all of them crying.

I stood there for a moment feeling like a complete clod, helpless to do anything, help anyone. I noticed the blender, shoved in a corner by the toaster, and felt even worse: I had promised Devera weeks ago that I would fix it, but there it sat, unable to stir, mix, or chop. Another testament to my helplessness.

It didn't take me long to join that bear hug, and as much as I wanted to contribute strength to it, I also needed to draw from it.

I WAS AT the dealership the next day—trying to talk Clayton Hagstrom into buying an Eldorado convertible. It was a futile exercise; Clayton Hagstrom was a Dodge man from his laced-up boots to his bow tie, but he was also a rich man,

owning more farmland than anyone in this or any neigh-
boring county. His sons did most of the hard labor now, so
he had a lot of time on his hands. Time to stop by my lot and
harass me.

"I don't know, Lindstrom," he said, patting the trunk
of the spanking-new red convertible. "How am I 'sposed to
stay warm in the winter with nothing but canvas over my
head?"

"You'll be as warm as toast in this baby," I said. "Cadillac
believes in comfort."

"That's right." The old man sniffed. "Comfort and flash.
Over reliability and road performance, you can bet."

"I don't know where you get your facts, Clayton," I said,
smiling, even though I wanted to knock him over and hit him
with his stupid porkpie hat. We went through this same routine every time he came into town. Couldn't he hang out at
the barbershop or the hardware store like the other old farts?

"You were saying?" Clayton cocked his head, squinting his
cagey blue eyes at me.

I slid my hand along the back end, getting back my concentration. "I was saying, Clayton, that Cadillac matches any
automobile on the road today in reliability and road performance. Simply put, there's no better car on the market."

"Tell that to Mercedes! Tell it to Saab!" The old man was
cackling now, really enjoying this. "Most of all, tell it to
Dodge!"

He spit a slimy gob of old-man spit on the ground and I
was tempted to tell him to get a rag from the office and clean
that vile shit up, but a salesman can't really act on all that
many temptations. At least not if he wants to make a sale,
and I was convinced that somehow, someway, I was going to
sell old Clayton Hagstrom the finest car of his life.

Larry O'Herne was in the office, playing tiddlywinks with
paper clips.

"So, d'you sell him the Allante?"

"Eldorado. I'm trying to get the old man into an Eldorado."

"Fifty says you won't."

"Gee, Larry, what a risky bet."

I poured a cup of coffee in the mug Darcy had given me for Father's Day last year. It said #1 DAD. "You must be hell on wheels in Vegas."

"Touchy, touchy, touchy," he said. He crouched down so that he was eye level with his desk, and pressing a big paper clip against a smaller one, he shot the clip into a paper cup.

"He shoots, he scores!" he said, raising his arms.

I shook my head at the sad case he was.

"So what's eating you?" he said. "Upset because your hand-eye coordination isn't as sharp as Mr. Precision's?"

"Yeah, how did you know?" I said, thinking how slow the day was going to pass if I didn't get off the lot.

"Sure, you're just shook because of what happened to Franny LaFave."

The hair on my arms stood up. "How do you know about that?"

"I'm only boffing Midge Selitz is all." He looked at me and wiggled his eyebrows. "And yes, it is true what they say about nurses."

I sat down, suddenly feeling *really* tired. "Larry, for a change, why don't you shut your big fucking mouth?"

"Well, *excuuuuuse* me." He grabbed his tie knot and twisted his neck and then he swiveled around in his chair so that his back was toward me.

I paged through an owner's manual and folded some of our Viking Automotive stationery into a little paper elephant. Devera says if I wanted to, I could become a master of origami (for a brief moment I thought she was complimenting me on my sexual prowess). She says it's an amazing natural talent— like I'm the idiot savant of paper folding.

It was starting to drizzle out and I knew we were in for a slow day. No sense freezing out the only person I could pass the time with, so I said, "Lare, game of cribbage?"

"Sure," he said, pleased. He got the board out of his middle desk drawer. "I don't blame you for feeling lousy," he said, sorting the pegs. "It's a shame, what happened to Franny."

I nodded, but Larry didn't get that it was the kind of nod that means let's not talk about it anymore.

"Usually there's not much for Midge to report on," he said, fumbling around in his desk drawer until he found the score pad. "Old Lady Dexter's gallbladder, Bart Donner's infected teeth—but this—Jesus—she tells me how the kid rides her bike to the hospital, in the dark and all beat up. Didn't she rupture her spleen or something?"

I was so put off by Larry running off at the mouth that my fists balled reflexively into fists. I looked hard at the cribbage board.

"Yeah," said Larry, who never, as long as I've known him, has been the kind of guy who can pick up signals from people (that gives you an idea of what I have to put up with vis-à-vis his salesmanship). "Yeah, whoever beat her up ought to be shot, but hey, at least she doesn't have to worry about her beauty being destroyed."

Sweeping the cribbage board and pegs off the table with one hand, I stood up, leaning toward him.

"You're fired!"

Larry looked at me as if I were nuts. "You can't fire me, Dick."

I stared at him, knowing what he said was true—only Dad Evan fires and hires at the lot. "You're lucky I didn't punch your stupid face in," I said finally.

Larry pushed back on his chair. "Relax, would you, Dick? I was only joking. Jesus."

He bent to pick up the cribbage pegs and for a minute I thought about stepping on his hand, but instead I grabbed an umbrella hanging from the hat rack and went out in the drizzle.

I had a sandwich at the Top Hat and BS'ed with Bunny Vold, who's running for mayor and wears buttons like GREEN POWER and PRO-CHOICE and W.A.M.M. A lot of people think she's off her rocker, but I like her. I even think she's sexy, for an old broad.

"First thing I'd do is declare war unconstitutional," she was saying to me and Princess, the waitress. "It goes against the basic precepts of life, liberty, and the pursuit of happiness."

"Gee, Bunny," I said, salting my french fries. "I don't think the mayor has the right to change the Constitution."

"Aw, the mayor's office is just a stepping-stone. I'll get to Washington someday."

Princess rolled her eyes at me. "Well, heck, Bunny. Anyone can get to Washington. I mean, Northwest flies there, right?" She winked at me just in case I didn't get her sophisticated joke. I smiled and pointed to my empty coffee cup.

"You'll vote for me, won't you, Dick?"

"Sure I will, Bunny," I said, watching as Princess filled my cup. "You'll make a great homecoming queen."

Bunny's got a wonderful laugh—it's like Santa Claus's—ho-ho-ho—and you've got to laugh with it.

"My constituents," she said, shaking her head. "A smarter bunch could not be found."

When I got back to the lot I sat in the Eldorado I had been showing Clayton Hagstrom. I don't know how long I was in there—maybe an hour, just sitting and listening to a light rain drum the top. I could have stayed there all afternoon—it was so peaceful—but finally Larry O'Herne's nervous looks out the office window got to me and I went inside.

DARCY

WHEN FRANNY ASKED if I could keep a secret, I asked her what did she take me for—a palooka, a squealer, a rat?—thinking she was gonna tell me something like, "Once I laughed so hard I peed in my pants," or "I've got a crush on Mr. Baylor." (He's the band teacher and he *is* a hunk.)

I mean, *come on*, I am the all-time secret keeper, never telling on Lin when I walked into her bedroom and found her and Kyle laying on her bed kissing, with Kyle's hands up inside her shirt. ("Finding anything you like up there, Kyle?" I asked before Lin jumped off the bed to whomp on me.) I didn't tell anyone when I saw Jenni Froholff smoking behind Eaves Dairy even though Jenni's only a year older than me and everyone knows a nicotine habit should be nipped in the bud. So imagine my surprise when Franny decides to unload the secret of the year on me.

We were downstairs sitting at the bar of Your Oasis, drinking Cokes and scarfing Chee•tos.

"Darcy," she said, looking left and right like she was casing the joint, "you're sure what I tell you will never leave this room?"

I nodded and held my lips tight so my teeth wouldn't chatter, I was so excited. Franny looked around the room again and took a deep breath.

"Okay." She cleared her throat. "Okay. It wasn't a stranger in a silver van who beat me up. It was two guys from the Rogues hockey team."

I sat there like a big lug for a minute, like I had taken a bite of something terrible and didn't know if I should swallow it or spit it out.

"What?" was all I could finally say.

Franny brushed at her corduroy pants. "I said I got beat up by two guys from the Rogues hockey team. It wasn't any stranger in a silver van."

I visited Franny the day after she got beat up, and I thought she looked like a sumo wrestler who lost his match; her face was huge and swollen and full of all sorts of colors you don't really want to see on a face. But now, two weeks later, it was pretty much back to normal, except for little smudges of yellow under her eyes and a scar from the stitches that ran through her right eyebrow like a little train track. Her nose had a new bump on it, but I thought it gave her character and I had told her so.

"Darcy," she said, "how does a broken nose give someone character?"

"I don't know. Isn't stuff like broken bones and scars and wrinkles supposed to give you character?"

"I don't see how. I think what happens to you gives you character, not what happens to your face."

I nodded. I had been captain of my sixth-grade debate team, but I was never paired against anyone who made sense the way Franny did.

Now we were sitting on bar stools, both of us sort of swiveling back and forth just a little, the secret Franny had just told me feeling like a real thing, like a stranger sitting with us at the bar.

"So you're telling me there was no silver van and that some Rogue hockey players beat you up?" Maybe it would make sense the more I said it.

Franny nodded. "Don't talk so loud," she said, even though I'd been whispering.

"Well, *why*? Why'd they do it in the first place? *Where'd* they do it?"

Dad and I had just put up a smoked-glass mirror above the bar and Franny was staring into it, and when she spoke, her voice sounded like a stare, too, if you follow me.

"I was riding down the old County Road on my bike, I just like riding there sometimes, you don't have to worry about traffic. I was going fast and pretending I was the leader of the Tour de France or something when a car cruised by. When it stopped and went in reverse to back up to me, I thought it was just someone who wanted to stop and say hi. My biggest worry was that whoever it was was going to squeal to my mom that I was out riding my bike when I was supposed to be at Kirsten's, figuring out what A equals B-squared was. Anyhow, this car is sitting there idling away and like the dork I am I say, 'Hi, nice night, huh?' to whoever it was sitting on the passenger side."

"You couldn't tell who it was?" I whispered.

"'Not until the door opened. And then, like the *real* dork I am, I said, 'Hey, Ricky'—Ricky Walsh, he's a Rogues' defenseman, doesn't get a lot of play—'so, who do you think's gonna win the Stanley Cup next year?'

"'Not you,' he said. He stunk like beer and kinda swayed as he stood there. 'You're never gonna win a Stanley Cup.'

"*Well, duh,* was all I had time to think because the next thing I knew he knocked me off my bike and threw himself on top of me."

I took my beret off, it was too hot on my head. I couldn't think of one single word to say.

"I laid there a little while—I mean, I was like stunned—and then my brain woke up and yelled at me to do some-thing, so I started hitting him. He tried to pin my arms down with his legs, but not before I hit him in the nose.

" 'The bitch hit me!' he yelled, and I felt his blood drip on me like little raindrops.

" 'Well, hit her back, stupid,' said the guy who got out of the driver's side. It was Guy Hammond—the Rogues' *star*—and he stood over us like a wrestling coach or something, saying, 'Hit her harder, harder!' Which Ricky Walsh seemed to have no problem doing. And then Guy Hammond started kicking me. I guess that's how I fractured my ribs."

Franny took a big swig of Coke—really, it was like she swilled down nearly the whole bottle. When she was done she said "ahh" and then sighed.

"You know," she said, "I probably could have taken one of those guys—I mean, Ricky Walsh is pretty scrawny—but there's not much you can do when you're pinned on your back with two of them pummeling you." She finished the last of the Coke. "When it finally seemed like they were done—I mean, they were breathing hard like they were tired out and they weren't kicking me or hitting me so fast. I don't think they had much stamina because they were so loaded. Anyway, I thought maybe the bad part was about over when Guy Hammond said, 'We could always rape her!' "

"Oh, Franny." I felt like the breath had been punched out of me.

" 'Rape her?' said Ricky Walsh. 'Don't fucking gross me out, man.' Then they laughed like that was the funniest thing he ever said and then Guy Hammond kicked me again and pushed me with his foot and I rolled into the ditch just like a beer can they'd thrown out the window."

Suddenly we reached out to each other like Fred and Ginger, like it was planned choreography. We held each other and I felt Franny's tears on my face and she had to feel mine on hers because it was all of a sudden like Niagara Falls, I mean, there was water everywhere. We sat there inhaling each other's tears and snot until it got so gross we had to laugh.

"Oh, Franny," I said when we finally let go of each other and wiped the gunk off our faces. "We'll just have to rub them out."

"Rub them out?"

"Yeah. Exterminate them. Smoke 'em. Make their days on earth short ones. I don't know how but we'll figure it out."

"Oh, Darcy."

" 'Oh, Darcy' what? If we don't kill them at least we've got to turn them in. Send them up the river, to the big house, to the slammer—"

"Darcy, they said if I squealed, they'd kill me."

I laughed and a little Coke burp bubbled up. "Oh, come on, Franny, they couldn't kill you if you squealed. Everyone would know they did it."

She nodded, although she didn't look too convinced. I got up and took the wall phone off the hook.

"I'm gonna call the sheriff right now."

Franny's cheeks had gotten really red while she was telling me the story, like it was making her madder and madder, but when I told her I was going to call the sheriff, it was like she dunked her head in bleach. It was the weirdest thing.

"Don't call the sheriff, Darcy," she said as if she couldn't get a full breath of air. "I can't tell the sheriff."

"Why not?" I said, still holding the phone.

Franny held her face in her hands for a while, and when she finally lifted it, I felt more scared than ever. I hung up the phone.

"Darce, you know how you promised to keep what I told you a secret?"

I nodded.

"Well, this part is even a bigger secret. I mean, you can't tell any of it, but this part especially. Promise?"

"Franny, what—"

"Promise?" she whispered in a yelling way.

I nodded again and crossed my heart.

She took a deep breath and then, her cheeks filled out like Alvin the Chipmunk, blew the air out slow.

"I was with Pete Arsgaard. Or I was supposed to be with him. We had both ridden our bikes to meet each other on the County Road—I mean it's a private place and we could go there and talk and stuff and nobody would know about us. I mean you know how people are always wanting to know stuff that isn't any of their business. . . ."

I just sat there nodding, even though she could have been talking to me in Albanian for all I understood.

"See, a lot of girls like Pete—you know how popular he is—and no guys have ever liked me, at least not like a girl-friend, and when we sat together at the hockey banquet some of the other guys got on his case"—Franny's voice slowed down here—"and so we just decided it would be less of a hassle not having anyone know we liked each other, you know?"

"Seeing each other on the sly, on the q.t., keeping mum—"

"Yeah, I guess," she said, interrupting. "See, we had met out on the old County Road a couple of times—just to talk, although last time we kissed good night. We'd leave our houses at the same time and meet halfway, but when Guy and Ricky's car came, we hadn't met up yet.

"It wasn't dark yet but it was getting there. The sun had just gone behind the lake when I left Kirsten's house. I told her I had forgotten to clean my room and my mom would ground me if she found out I hadn't—Kirsten'll fall for any lame excuse you give her.

"Anyway, our usual halfway point was by that old billboard that advertises that lodge that burned down a couple years ago? Well, I was about a quarter of a mile from it when the Rogues pulled me over, and just when Ricky Walsh had pushed me off my bike and I was flying through the air—it was so weird—at that exact moment, before I hit the ground, I saw Pete pedaling toward me and I had the strangest feeling of like peace, you know? Even though I knew in one second I was going to be diving into that gravel road, I felt calm. Everything made sense—Pete was here and was going to save me. It was like even though I knew I was going to crash, the car had an air bag. Then I hit the road, and boy, it did hurt, but still, knowing Pete was on his way made it hurt not so bad because I knew it would stop soon."

I could barely stand what Franny was telling me—I felt like I had when I saw that movie with Audrey Hepburn playing a blind woman and I just knew that guy was going to jump out at her.

"But then, right before Ricky Walsh flipped me over to start smacking my face, I saw something that at first I couldn't believe. I saw Pete turning around on his bike and pedaling back to White Falls. I wanted to holler out to him, but I also didn't want either of the Rogues to see him. I think now it was a pretty stupid move—or nonmove—but that's what I did. Nothing."

"And he kept riding away?" I asked, and when Franny

nodded, I said, "What a creep. What a cad. What a lily-livered, yellow-bellied coward. You've got to tell on the Rogues first and on that little wimp second."

"No!" said Franny. "I don't want to get him in trouble!"

"Why?" I asked, seriously stupefied. "Why wouldn't you want to get a lowlife like that in trouble?"

"Because I like him," said Franny softly. "And I don't want to . . ."

"To what?"

"To completely blow my chances with him."

Really, you could have knocked me over with a Nerf ball. This was Franny LaFave, the first girl ever to play for the White Falls hockey team, talking like one of those women you see on those battered-women documentaries?

"Franny," I said, "you *want* to blow your chances with a guy like this. A guy who'd—" Suddenly I remembered something. "Hey, my mom told me how you'd ridden your bike to the hospital after you got beat up."

"Yeah . . . so?"

"So couldn't Pete the Wuss have called somebody or told somebody to help you when he got back to town? Like the sheriff or his own parents or somebody? I mean he could have even done it anonymously!"

Franny bowed her head and shrugged. "I haven't talked to him him yet."

"*What?*"

"I called him the second day I was in the hospital . . . but he was on his way out . . . he said."

"That's it," I said, getting up and going to the phone again. "He's almost as bad as those Rogues. *On his way out.* I'll show him out. I'm calling the sheriff now."

"No!" Franny stood up and I froze for a second, her voice was that scary. "No!" she said again, this time in a whisper. "I've already told my story and it was in the paper! People believed it! I just want it to end here."

We stared at each other, and really, to me it felt like we were enemy soldiers, coming across each other in the jungle, not knowing what the other one was going to do.

DEVERA

FOR NEARLY A week after Franny got beat up, I would get up in the middle of the night to go sit in the hallway between the girls' bedrooms. I didn't go in either room because I wanted to protect them equally and the only way I knew how to do that was to stand (or in this case, sit) guard outside their doorways. I'm afraid of too many things and that shames me, but I knew that if I met up with anyone or anything threatening my girls out in that carpeted hallway, that person or thing wouldn't stand a chance.

The first night I sat there, I trembled like I was spastic, even though I had wrapped myself up in the patchwork quilt Ardis had made for us before her arthritis got bad. My mind was like a revolving door leading into a cave; in came one dark scary thought after another. I wasn't having a panic attack, though, it was more like a fear I knew wouldn't go away. How do we protect our girls? Why are there men (almost always men) who want to harm us? Who want to beat us up and rape us and even kill us? How could I love men so much and need to please them, and at the same time fear and despise them? I was sitting there shaking, wishing I could bore through these thoughts with illuminating and sharp thinking, all the while wondering if I dared sneak down to the kitchen for some mocha fudge ice cream. Did Plato and Aristotle and Seneca and all those guys enter some special neurological state where their minds could explore deep thoughts with no distractions? I like to think I have a good mind, but truthfully, it's hard to find any deep thoughts amongst all the clutter. It's like looking for my wedding ring on top of the dresser. I finally decided that I had no answers other than yes, to the question, "wouldn't some ice cream taste good about now?" I decided I could safely leave my girls for a few minutes and I left my post, tripping a little on the quilt as I stood up.

I was climbing back up the stairs with a big bowl of mocha fudge when a figure came out of Lin's room. Right away I knew it was Lin, but my heart had only needed a quarter second to nearly jump-start it into overdrive and I stood leaning on the banister, trying to get my breath back.

"Mom!" whispered Lin in a loud rasp. "You scared me!"

"Likewise," I said, breathing heavily.

"What are you doing?"

I held up my bowl. "What are you doing?"

"I woke up scared. I was going to climb in your bed." Her voice sounded years younger.

"Why don't we sit out here in the hallway for a while," I said. "You can help me eat this ice cream."

"Okay!" said Lin as if I had just asked her to the greatest party ever thrown.

We both sat against the wall with the quilt around our shoulders, holding the bowl on top of our bent knees. We took our time eating the ice cream in that gray fuzzy near-dawn light, passing the spoon back and forth, and we were nearly done when Lin said, "Why would somebody do that to Franny, Mom?"

In the long pause that followed, I heard the tickings of the house, the grandfather clock downstairs, the hum of the refrigerator. "I don't know," I said finally. "Sometimes it seems as terrible and cliché a thing as she was in the wrong place at the wrong time."

"That sucks," said Lin.

"I know."

"What if something like that happens to me? Or something worse? What if I got raped? Or what if I got raped and killed?"

I was instantly submerged in an ice bath of fear. "You won't," I said, scrambling for words. "You . . . you can't. You've just got to be careful . . . not take any chances . . . know how to defend yourself." I wanted to scream in frustration; I wanted to give her an answer that would calm her fears, and I couldn't. There was none.

A little cry came out of her throat, the kind that babies make that almost sounds like a cat's meow, and I held my daughter for a long time and then, softly, I began singing "Qué Será." It was a song I sang to both Lin and Darcy, but in my version, the girl doesn't ask her mother if she'll be pretty or sweet, but "Will I be the president? Or fly to the moon?"

"You're not the only one who can change lyrics," I told Dick after he heard me sing it to the girls.

"I never said I was. Besides, I like it."

"Really?"

"Sure. A feminist lullaby. It works."

So now I sat rocking Lin, not singing "Qué será, será" but what I believed were better answers.

> *"You will be my love, whatever you want to be,*
> *Just work hard and then you'll see,*
> *You can do what you want. You can go anywhere,*
> *You can do anything. And I love you so."*

I couldn't believe it, this fourteen-year-old fell asleep in my arms, and then I fell asleep, and Dick found us there in the morning, all humped over and sharing a blanket like two hoboes in a train car.

THREE DAYS LATER, to my surprise, I kept my scheduled rendezvous with Herr Professor Gerhart Ludwig. That's what I'd call him during our trysts—Herr Professor—and he seemed to like it. He liked ritual. He would tear off his clothes and then stand there naked, polishing his wire-rims with his undershirt. He had a scrawny, slope-shouldered body and yet the way he strutted around he seemed to think he was Michelangelo's *David* brought to life.

I found his striptease and glasses polishing exciting at first, but it seemed he couldn't start "class" without going through this little performance, and after the third time I began entertaining thoughts of skipping school.

In fact, the whole affair never had a lot of luster, but I wasn't willing to let it go yet, certain that it was still an adventure, and even if it was more like the Tilt-A-Whirl than the roller coaster, I felt any motion was better than none.

Herr Professor had just yelled "ey-yi-yi" like a guitarist in a mariachi band, so I knew we were done with our lovemaking.

He lit up one of his French cigarettes and watched his smoky exhale float to the ceiling.

"That was sweet, wasn't it?"

"Sweet," I murmured, even though I was miles away from Destination Orgasm. That surprised me—it usually doesn't take much.

"Divine am I inside and out," Gerhart said, his voice booming. "And I make holy whatever I touch or am touch'd from." He turned his head and looked at me with a little smirk. "Walt Whitman."

"Wait a second," I said, pulling my purse off the night-stand. "Let me get my pad."

I got out my checkbook and pretended to write something on a deposit slip.

"You said 'Walt Whitman'?" I asked, scrawling furiously. "So would what you said be then considered a Whitman Sampler?"

Gerhart stroked his beard (the only thing he stroked post-coitus) and said, "*Très amusant,* Devera. *Très, très* amusing."

I got up and started getting on my clothes. I don't care how beautiful a voice is, when it's used to say something condescending, it loses its power.

"Devera," he said, his voice as patronizing as a jewelry-store clerk who's certain you don't have the money to buy whatever you're asking to see, "we're not pouting, are we?"

"I'm not," I said, doing a little hop as my foot got caught in the leg of my underpants. "I don't know about you."

"Devera, *bitte. Kommen-sie.*" He often used foreign phrases but most often German ones. You'd think with a name like

Gerhart Ludwig he was as Deutsche as sauerkraut, but one vulnerable moment he confessed to me that he had changed his name from Gale because he thought it lacked masculinity. As far as I knew, he didn't have an ounce of German in him.

He reached for me then and I let him pull me back to the bed; I didn't know what I was going to do once I got my clothes on anyway.

I took a drag off his cigarette (he seemed to bring out all kinds of aberrant behavior in me) and blinked at the immediate headache it caused.

"What troubles mine paramour's mind?"

"What?"

"Me thinks melancholia has visited thy homestead."

I looked at him. "Why are you talking like a bad Amish poet?"

Hurt and irritation pushed down the professor's eyebrows. This was a man more used to reverence than teasing. Now it was his turn to get into his underpants, which were black bikinis, with a threadbare seat.

"Listen, Devera, I can understand you being upset about your friend's daughter, but please, don't take your feminine rage out on me."

"I'm not taking any *feminine rage* out on you."

"Yes, you are. You've been distant and uncommunicative—verbally *and* sexually, I might add—but I'm not a brute. I'm sensitive enough to realize that your unpleasant behavior is probably triggered by the assault of Francine LaWhatever."

"Francesca," I said. "Francesca LaFave." I leaned back against the thin lumpy pillow. "Her name is Francesca."

We kept the window shades down and our room now seemed wrapped in gloom. Our motel wasn't part of a chain but a mom-and-pop organization, and it was obvious mom and pop had interests other than interior decoration.

The room had water stains seeping from the seams of the faded lily-of-the-valley wallpaper; harvest-gold shag carpeting whose pile was matted and tangled like an old retriever's, and a dark walnut-veneer dresser, nicked and cut. The bed's mattress was concaved, so it was hard to get away from whomever you were in bed with. Maybe that was the point, though.

The room was not improving my mood any. "It just makes me so mad," I said, hiccuping. "So mad that men feel a compulsion to grind down women."

Herr Professor stared meditatively at his foot—the one that gave up a toe in a boyhood lawnmower accident. "Devera, most men do not feel a compulsion to grind down women." He flicked his fingers as if making quotation marks around the last three words, a gesture I hate. "Unfortunately, some men will always gain satisfaction from suppressing women," he said, his voice settling into his classroom lecture drone, "but I think you'll have to face it. The sexes will never be equal until women's physical strength matches those of men."

"Is that right?" I said, and in his boorish expression, I saw a challenge. "Okay, come on," I said, going to the walnut-veneer writing table. "Come on." I lifted my forearm and wiggled my fingers.

"You want me to arm-wrestle you? Are you serious?"

"Afraid I'll beat you?"

Herr Professor's smile was not a beacon of brightness. His elbow clunked against the table as he took my hand. "No, Devera, I would have to say that's not a concern of mine."

"Good. Let's go, then. On your mark, get set, go."

Gerhart's fake smile didn't last long, especially when our arms began quivering. His face went from red to scarlet and the loose skin on his chest trembled.

He shouted when I got him an inch away from the table, but that was no distraction, and I brought his arm down with one final surge of strength.

Leaning back in my chair, I clasped my hands and raised them over my head in the classic champion pose.

"One victory for the equality of womenkind," I said.

Gerhart looked at me with such loathing that I put my arms down. At home, in our little duels and contests, we get a lot of mileage over victories (and Dick actually seems to relish the few times I've been able to beat him arm wrestling) but Gerhart obviously wasn't enjoying my self-congratulation.

"That was quite a contest," I said. "Usually I get most people down in thirty seconds."

The professor was putting on his pants like a groom late for his wedding.

"I had no idea you were such an amazon." He zipped up his fly so quickly it sounded like something ripped. "I only lost because it was hard to concentrate with your breasts staring at me in the face."

I looked down. Goose bumps rose on my body; I had nothing on but my underpants. I was a millisecond away from making an apology, saying something to blunt his defeat, but then I thought, no way—why should I have to apologize for winning? Wasn't that just so typical?

Shivering, I gathered my clothes, thinking what a picture the two of us have made, arm wrestling with just our underpants on.

It's something Dick and I would have had a good laugh over, but obviously it wasn't a joke I could take home and share.

Gerhart and I were silent during the drive back to town until a semi started tailgating us.

"You'd better speed up," I said, "or else get out of the fast lane."

He didn't answer and so the words hung in the air and I began to think I had meant them for me anyway.

BiDi

WHEN THE BRUISES on Franny's face healed and I didn't have to be reminded of the incident every time I looked at her, it was easier for me to start picking up the pieces and reassembling them back into "normal life."

It was hard those first couple weeks. Dave Garner of the *Gazette* had written a story entitled, "Our Hockey Heroine Shows Her Real Strength" and I couldn't go anywhere without people asking me how Francesca was doing. I went from being the mother of a hockey star to being the mother of an assault victim, and I thought how weird it was, my having celebrity for reasons I would have preferred not having it at all. It brought back all those icky memories of when my dad left. I was only nine years old and one day he was playing Jarts with me in the backyard and the next day he was gone. He went the classic way, too—he said he was going out for some cigarettes. (One of the things I've always hated him for is his lack of imagination.) There was no one to help me or to tell me what was going on. My mother was thrown for a serious loop, barely able for a while to get dressed in the morning, and although my older sister, married at eighteen to an army guy and living in Frankfurt, wrote me letters, they were more "cheerer-uppers" than guides to coping. I was bereft—why would a man who tucked me in every night and gave me Eskimo Kisses leave me?

Kids at nine aren't exactly paragons of compassion

either, so I had to deal with Pam DeNeres asking me what I did that was so bad it'd make my daddy leave; or Billy Bracken informing me his mother said "Lon Wallstrom had always been sort of unstable and this sort of behavior didn't surprise her in the least." I am not ashamed to say that when Billy had his tonsils out that fall, I was the only fourth grader who refused to sign his get-well card.

I missed my dad terribly—he wrote us a few letters from California but my mother wouldn't let me answer them back—but almost as big as my grief was my anger at him for leaving us and making me *different* from the other kids. I guess in some ways, I've never forgiven him for that.

Don't get me wrong—I don't blame Franny for getting beat up—I just didn't like being thought of as a mother of a victim. I didn't like that my daughter was one.

When she went back to school they held a big Welcome Back assembly as if she were a hotshot alumnus who had gone on to become president of the United States, or at least a major corporation. There were only four days remaining in the school year, but nobody made her take any final exams. Francesca's always been an A student and one of her teachers told me that she could be absent two and a half months instead of two and a half weeks and she'd still know the material better than anyone else.

One small consolation: Franny wasn't eating as if there was no tomorrow; my daughter was actually losing weight and without me nagging her every step of the way. I even had to get out the old Singer and take in her waistbands.

No, I wasn't obsessively worried about Francesca. She's the type of person who will rise again no matter how many times she's knocked over. It was two men I was most worried about: Sergio and Big Mike. As I said, Sergio was acting like a tough little gangster; I wouldn't have been surprised if he started wearing black shirts with white ties and carrying a violin case to work. You know how it is with little guys; when threatened, they tend to overreact, like Chihuahuas or toy poodles. Just look through history—all the gangsters, including the political ones—seem to be short. At least I'm not remembering any big tall ones.

Sergio was hell-bent on revenge. He had stopped cooking, and every night, after the suppers I made (hot-dish concoctions courtesy of Grandma Smoland's flowered metal recipe box), he'd race off in his car, going as far north as Bemidji searching for a silver van and its driver. He called Sheriff Buck constantly, asking him if there were any new leads, and finally the sheriff dropped by to assure us that the moment he learned anything new he would let us know.

"But to tell you the truth, the trail looks pretty cold," he said, wrapping his long fingers around the glass of iced tea I served him.

"Well, you must heat it up!" Sergio exclaimed, his eyes opened so wide his eyebrows nearly met his hairline. "You must make a bigger effort!"

"We've done all we can," said the sheriff, who had taken to rubbing his sideburns in that nervous way he has, "but frankly, Sergio, I don't have the manpower to keep a simple case of assault on the front burner."

"Simple assault!" said Sergio, and then he got up and started pacing, blithering in Spanish just like Ricky Ricardo.

I smiled at Sheriff Buck—I felt sorry for him—and he smiled back, but in a red-faced, guilty way.

"I'll be getting back to my office, then," he said, unfolding his long, gangly legs.

As I said, Sergio had always been mild-mannered, so when he began to talk about arming ourselves, I got really worried.

"Sergio, I am not going to get a gun," I said, paralyzed at the very thought. "We live in White Falls, for crying out loud, not New York City!"

The stare Sergio gave me was positively sinister. Sergio has beautiful brown eyes, the kind that look liquid, but I felt a chill, like when I threw out the garbage one night and came across a raccoon sitting on the trash can.

"What exactly do you mean?"

"Well, come on, Sergio, White Falls is what I mean! I mean what place is safer than here? And who're you going to shoot at anyway? Alf Johannson? Or his wife, Violet, maybe? Or how about Bart the barber when he gives you a bad cut?"

Sergio slammed his hand down on the coffee table—I told you he had this scary smacking habit going, didn't I?

"Our daughter was beat up in White Falls, BiDi! So what do you mean, safe?"

He shot out the door like he was jet-propelled; off, I imagained, on another of his search parties. I prayed he never caught the guy because a husband in the slammer for murder was not something I needed at the moment.

So while Francesca and I held it together, the other man in our lives (however peripherally) joined Sergio in flipping out, and for reasons that made me absolutely positively sure that if things weren't rotten in the state of Denmark, they sure as hell were here.

Big Mike LaFave found God; I mean, he was born again in a big way. It happened, he explained over the phone in a voice like the one he used when we saw the Grand Canyon for the first time, when he was in the hospital with his burst appendix.

While Big Mike stayed home on Sunday mornings, reading the paper and watching golf tournaments on cable, his girlfriend Stacy had been going to a Pentecostal church. Big Mike had razzed her about going Christian on him and did that mean they couldn't have sex anymore? (He told me all of this, as if I were an old army buddy and I'd find it interesting.)

She hadn't minded his jokes. "It'll take more than bad jokes to break my faith," she said, and didn't mind either when he declined her every invitation to visit the church.

"But," he said, and I had to switch the phone over to my other ear, he'd been talking so much, "when I was laying in that hospital bed, BiDi, Stacy brought her prayer group in to see me. Now my first impulse was to ring for the nurse and have them kicked out, but before I knew it, they circled my bed and started praying."

"So what happened then?" I asked in the long pause that followed.

YOUR OASIS ON FLAME LAKE

"BiDi," he said, and I could hear he was choked up, "BiDi, I was visited by the Holy Spirit. I felt a warmth fill my body. I felt my heart open up to a love I had never felt." He blew his nose, a big honk, right through the receiver and into my ear. "I was saved."

When I hung up the phone, I noticed my hand shaking and I sat down feeling jittery, like I had the DTs or something.

We didn't get a hold of Big Mike until four days after Franny got beat up—he and Stacy were in Tennessee or Kentucky or someplace for a big revival. He drove up right away when we told him and got to our house·right in time for supper.

"You said she was severely battered," he said to me after Franny had gone to bed.

"Well, she was," I said. "Didn't you see her face?"

"I thought her condition was more . . . serious," said Big Mike. "I came out of some hockey games looking worse than that."

I couldn't believe it. I felt as if I were being scolded for our daughter's good prognosis. "Well, gee," I said. "I'm sorry to disappoint you. Maybe she'll lapse into a coma or something."

He had startled Franny when he came bursting through our back door. Sergio was out on one of his look-for-the-silver-van runs and Francesca was helping me set the table. Big Mike rushed over to Franny and put his hands on her face, asking the Lord to help her. Then he asked Franny to pray out loud with him—he's been in the house less than two minutes!—and Franny says, "I have to go to the bathroom," and runs out like she's being chased.

Now, before you go around thinking I've raised my daughter heathen, be advised that she has gone all the way through Sunday school at Hope Lutheran and she has been confirmed. Big Mike took not one ounce of interest in Franny's religious upbringing when he lived with us— "I'd rather go fishing" was his stock answer whenever I asked him to go to church with us—and now he expected her to get down on her knees with him and speak in tongues or something?

He was no comfort during his short visit, I can tell you that, and besides bugging everyone to let themselves be saved, he nearly ate us out of house and home.

SERGIO

IN THESE BAD weeks I have thought of many things. Many pictures and glimpses of the future jump into my mind and in one of these glimpses BiDi and I are in a courthouse, getting divorced. And besides being a little sad, I am more relieved.

Do not misunderstand me. I do not want a divorce, of this I am about ninety-five percent sure, but it is that leftover five percent that is bothering me.

And also, I am so wound up from what happened to Francesca, it would not surprise me if one day I just snapped in two like a dried-out wishbone. So what I am thinking is not always clear.

I stayed away from Cakes by Sergio for almost one week. It was not possible for me to get into that kitchen which I love, baking and talking to customers, also things which I love, while Francesca groaned in pain or fear during night sleep and naps. There was no way I could do anything but stay near her, be ready to run to her and hold her until her heart, which was like a wild bird in her chest, calmed down, until the back of her hair, tangled with sweat, began to dry.

It makes me almost ill again to think of those first few days—I felt I was standing on the edge of a deep black lake, holding on to Francesca, who had fallen in, holding on with one finger.

Everything was crazy—our water heater which has always rumbled like an old man's stomach—made its usual noises, but this time I would go down into the basement holding a hammer, ready to pound in the head of the intruder hiding by the canned goods.

I did not like all this fear and rage bubbling inside me like a red-hot poison brew, but how could I empty it?

I spent a couple afternoons sitting in a convertible in Dick's car lot, talking with him about what happened and how I was without power.

"Sergio, you've got to let it go a little," he counseled me. "Franny's *okay*. She wasn't raped, thank God, she wasn't maimed or—"

"But she was beat up, Dick!" I said, so mad I could have kicked in the windshield. "She was beat up by some stranger and left to die on the side of the road. Her ribs were cracked and her nose was broken! You saw her! My God, Dick, you are like everyone else saying, 'Come on, Sergio, she only got beat up!' "

Dick flicked his cigarette over the windshield, where it hit the bumper of the Seville in front of us and bounced off.

"My father was *only* beat up," I reminded him. "Only beat up and yet it ruined his entire life. It took away his voice, his singing, and all because he was *only* beat up."

"Oh, Christ, Sergio, I forgot about the history you've got with this sort of thing." Dick drummed his fingers on the steering wheel. "But I don't know . . . it seems we should be grateful for Franny not being more hurt . . . for her being okay."

"I am grateful," I said, almost shouting, "but I am so angry that I even have to be thinking about how it 'could have been worse.' It might be much worse than I even think. Francesca is healed on the outside, but how do I know how she is on the inside? The only thing I know for sure is that I am a wreck."

Dick jabbed at the radio buttons for a while even though the car wasn't running and no sound came out. "You're right, Sergio," he said finally. "Sorry. Maybe it makes me feel better to think it could have been worse instead of really seeing how bad it was. My God, if I stop and think of someone kicking and smacking Franny on the side of the County Road—"

"I can't stop thinking of it!" I shouted, and I must have shouted loud because Dick made this little face.

"My God," he said, "if I thought of one of my girls getting beaten to a pulp . . ."

"Exactly! Francesca is my girl and all I can think of is why and who did it? How can I find him so I can do the same things he did to her? So I can finish the job?"

It had been cloudy in the morning, but now the clouds had pulled away from the sun like a drawn curtain and I was aware of the drops of sweat on my upper lip.

Dick pulled out another cigarette. I had never seen him smoke a cigarette so quickly after just putting one out.

"What's the matter with us?" he said, punching in the dashboard lighter. "Why do men—or boys—beat up young girls—or women—or kidnap them, or rape them . . . ?" His voice trailed off as he lit his cigarette.

"*We* do not do those things, Dick," I said.

"Yeah, but we're *men*," he said, as if the word sickened him. "We're a part of the group that does."

"But that is absurd," I said. "Those men are animals . . . and we are . . . we are just men."

"Yeah, but you want to kill that guy that beat up Franny," Dick said.

The sun was still bright in the sky, but for a moment it seemed as if a dark cloud had scuttled across it, and in that moment I hated Dick. Then the moment passed and my anger was a big general one, aimed at everything.

"That is not the same thing, Dick," I said. "Not the same thing at all."

LOOKING FOR THE man I hated in the silver van, I got to know, as they are called, the highways and byways all around this area. I drove down freeways, through truck stops, past cows huddling in the rain, and up dirt roads that led to nothing but rusted-out car bodies and empty farmhouses.

Even though I drove as a vigilante, my fingers wrapped tight around the steering wheel like I was trying to choke it, driving was easier for me—at leat I felt I had a purpose—than being alone with BiDi.

My feelings were so scary to me, it was as if I had been one way in a room but then I walked through a door and was another way all together.

BiDi had cooked a dinner; well, she had boiled noodles and opened cans and crushed potato chips. (That's right! She crushes potato chips and puts them on top of these casseroles which, believe me, do not need any more additional salt!) I knew all about her cooking and it never bothered me before—I am enough cook for all of us—so why do I now bring it up in a mean spirit? I do now know, it is as if nothing about BiDi is safe from my anger now.

Well, this particular evening she cooked when Big Mike had come up and the strange, fractured family was all at the table. BiDi was flitting and fluttering around the kitchen like a busy little butterfly, definitely giving the idea that she liked cooking for both her husbands—past and present.

Big Mike asked us to hold hands and said a big long prayer—every time there was a little lull I would think he was done, but then he would say "Praise God!" He said at least eight "Praise Gods!"—I counted—before he got to the amen. I was ready to go to sleep before that amen came, and when it did, I made a big show of crossing myself (I didn't like the way Big Mike was pushing this religion of his around) and then, surprise, Francesca crossed herself, too.

"Franny," said Big Mike, "what's that all about?"

"What?" asked Francesca, pouring herself a glass of milk.

"You know what," said BiDi. "That crossing business. You're not Catholic."

Francesca pressed her still-swollen lips together. "I might be someday. And even if I'm not, what's the big deal? I like the gesture."

"Service to God is more than gestures," said Big Mike.

It was only good manners that keep me from giving him a karate chop right to the mouth—who did he think he was talking to us like a priest? Talking to *me* like that whose faith is solid as a rock?

"I believe, Mike," I said in my most even voice, "that the sign of the cross is a show of reverence and devotion. It is no simple gesture."

I couldn't believe it—Big Mike smiled and shook his head as if what I had said was something silly. "Sergio, when you are saved, you see all the nonessentials, all the doodads of worship aren't needed. All that's needed is an open heart and hands that clasp in prayer."

BiDi was looking at him, her blue eyes round as marbles. With her finger, she made a little circle right by her temple— *muy loco!*—which made Francesca and me smile. Big Mike, I guess, was too high on salvation to notice.

"He's like a different person," BiDi said later as she took all the little pillows off our bed. There are heart-shaped pillows, satin pillows with lace edgings, needlepoint pillows—like the pillows on the couches, these are like rabbits, always multiplying. Every night BiDi has to pile them up on a chair so that we can get to the real pillows, the ones we are allowed to rest our heads on!

"I swear, the only conversation we had about God or religion when we were married had to do with me nagging Big Mike to go to church. He always answered me with that 'opiate of the masses' quote. Now it's like someone's snuck into his body and taken over."

BiDi giggled as she pulled back the bedspread that also is too fancy to actually use, and when she climbed into bed she patted my side of the mattress the way a dog owner invites his spaniel over.

She was wearing this satin nightgown I had given her, so I should have guessed. She was in that rare mood for sex. Maybe not even mood; I have come to see that with BiDi, sex is a reward or a peace offering; always some strategy. Never would my wife open up her arms to me and say, "Come on over here, baby," just for the fun of it, just because she wanted me. And that hurts a person and soon that hurt turns to other things, which I was finding out.

The reason, I think, she wanted sex with me that night was because Big Mike was in the house and that excited her. I think she felt like the belle of the ball again.

She was so lovely, her blond hair curling so sweetly around her face, her beautiful body all smooth and curvy under that satin nightgown, as satiny as that nightgown, and I was torn for a moment. It is hard to say no when you are not so often given the opportunity to say yes.

But that desire could not rise (I mean that literally!) against hurt and anger and other feelings that I was full of.

So I got into bed and into a pose that was typical BiDi: the back turned toward the spouse.

"Sergio," said BiDi like a girl who wants to share a secret. "Sergio, I've got something for you."

Her fingertips ran along my arm up to my shoulder and down again.

"I am tired, BiDi."

"I'll wake you up." BiDi kissed my ear and her coconutty smell floated over me. But! For once I was not interested, was not going to let her use me for whatever her strange reasons were which had nothing to do with desire.

"BiDi." My words were strong with anger, making them sharp. "Good night."

She made a short gasp, I could tell she was surprised and mad when she began to fluff her pillows, with her fist, it sounded like.

"Fine!" Fluff-*pow*! "That's just fine." Fluff-*pow*! "But don't think I won't remember this!" Fluff-*pow-pow*! "And don't think I'll be so ready and willing the next time you come sniffing around!" Fluff-*pow-pow-pow-pow*!

Sniffing around. There it was—two simple words—what my wife really thinks of my sexual advances. I was a dog.

The next morning she acted toward me as if nothing bad had happened between us, in fact she was extra full of kisses in the kitchen and, I am sorry to say, probably because of Big Mike sitting there.

This time when Big Mike asked for us to hold hands for the morning prayer, I got up, taking my coffee cup with me, and leaned against the counter.

"You go ahead." I waved my hand at them. "I will say my own prayer my own way."

You might have thought I would have stopped there but I didn't. BiDi gave me a very dirty look and Francesca sort of winked at me without winking and Big Mike basically ignored me, and then they all held hands and Big Mike cleared his throat and said, "Dear Heavenly Father," and at that moment I started singing, "Ave Maria."

Everyone looked up at me with their mouths wide open, but I didn't stop, and after a few moments Big Mike started praying out loud again. I put my coffee cup down and sang louder, gesturing like the son of an opera singer I was.

"We thank you for the bounty . . ." said Big Mike.

"Ave Maria! Gratia Plena," I sang over him.

" . . . of both your love and . . ."

"Maria, gratia plena. Maria, gratia plena."

" . . . grace, and to these gifts . . ."

"Ave, ave, Dominus. Dominus te cum."

This went on until we had reached a powerful crescendo; Big Mike was shouting his praises and I was projecting as if I were trying to reach the back rows at La Scala.

I held the last beautiful note as long as I could, and there was a deep silence and it seemed as though Big Mike and I had planned our finales, my last *Ave Maria!* came right when he said "amen." I had to smile, it was so ridiculous, but then Big Mike said, "Oh yes, thank you for the mild weather, amen." He just had to get that last word in, and I left that kitchen, not wanting to be around the big cheater.

"HE MADE ME feel so weird, Sergie," Francesca told me that night, "like if I had Jesus in my heart none of this would have happened. And I mean, it's not like I don't have Jesus in my heart—well, I don't the way he does, but I still believe in Him, you know?"

"He is so wrong about things," I said, surprised that I was not shouting, I was so mad. "He is very wrong about saying that to you. It wouldn't have mattered if you were a Buddhist or a Mormon or a nun wearing a big black habit."

"Well," said Francesca, "if I was a nun wearing a big black habit, I probably wouldn't have been riding a bike, so it *wouldn't* have happened. I mean I'd have to worry about the skirt getting caught in the spokes."

"Well, then, maybe you would have been on a train to the convent and the train derailed, killing everyone."

There was a little dance in Francesca's dark eyes—there has never been a moment when she does not understand me.

"Of course," she said slowly, hugging to her chest the Snoopy pillow she has had all her life. "Of course if I were a Buddhist, I probably would have been off on some mountaintop chanting or something."

I nodded my head. "Yes, but the air might have been so thin that on that mountaintop maybe you would have passed out and been eaten by a Bengalese tiger."

Francesca laughed, and I was so happy, so happy that I could be a balm for her. Her good-night hug was strong and tight.

"Have you ever noticed," she said, whispering, "my dad has BO?"

"Tell me about it." I waved my hand in front of my nose. "Let us pray," I said, trying to make my voice deep like Big Mike's. "Let us pray that he finds a stronger deodorant."

DICK

THAT SUMMER WAS beautiful—almost hot, but not quite, lots of sun and skies a color that cannot be reproduced anywhere.

That perfect weather made it easy to think that life had gotten back to normal and I could relax a little; Darcy could walk down to the store by herself again and Lin could go out with her friends without having to call in every hour.

Business was good at the lot. I passed one afternoon talking about panda bears with a zookeeper from St. Louis, for cripes sake.

"They don't talk, you know," said Tad. "They have been known to make noises, but in all my years around them, I've never heard a peep out of a panda. Not one single peep."

"Is that right," I said. "I would have thought they growled."

"Nothing. Not a single peep."

We were sitting in a gleaming white Allante convertible, running down the battery, listening to music. We were like two guys on a road trip, drinking Mountain Dew from the office pop machine. The top was down and both of us—I let him sit in the driver's seat—had our arms propped up and sticking out of the open windows like chicken wings.

"You know what?" said Tad (don't ask me why a grown man would still answer to the name Tad), "I think I'm going to buy this car."

"Really?" I said. I had snuck hardly any sales pitches into the breeze we'd been shooting, so I was genuinely surprised.

"Yeah, Wendy can drive our trailor back"—he and his wife were vacationing at Dexter's Resort on Uncle's Lake—"and I'll drive this baby home."

"You sure?" I asked, and a sudden pounding in my head made me realize I had been sitting too long in the sun. "Well, if you're sure, let's go into the office."

This Tad the Zookeeper paid me cash on the spot for the convertible, laying out one-thousand-dollar bills on the desk like playing cards.

"I didn't know zookeeping was so lucrative," I said, watching the fan of money spread out and trying to keep from drooling.

"Well, it is and it isn't," said Tad, laughing. "At least not financially. But it feeds my soul." He folded up a still-substantial wad of cash that was left over and put it in his hip pocket. "You can thank 'Step Gliders' for my, shall we say, solvency?"

" 'Step Gliders'?"

"You haven't seen our ads on TV—'No butts about it'? Step Gliders are part of the family firm. Fitness equipment. Selling like crazy. If we ever go public, buy stock. You'll make a fortune."

A cash sale and a stock tip all in one beautiful summer's day.

Another thing was making me feel like I ruled the world— Your Oasis on Flame Lake (I was not going to shorten the name, despite Dev's protests) was scheduled to open the Fourth of July weekend. I was pretty confident that even competing against the fireworks and the annual boat and water show, the grand opening of Your Oasis on Flame Lake was going to be *the* hit attraction.

I had Devera make up the invitations—she knows how to do that fancy calligraphy—and I mailed them out to our friends and associates, as well as to my in-laws, who get an automatic invite to everything.

At the dinner table, I told Lin she could ask a couple of friends, but she looked as if I'd asked her to clean out the sump pump.

"Please, Dad," she whined, "you don't really expect me to spend the Fourth of July listening to you sing 'You Are So Pitiful to Me?' do you?" (Actually, this is one of my few parodies that Devera likes; I do a good Joe Cocker imitation and she cracks up.)

"No, no," I said, like of course, I didn't expect that; what was I, some sort of moron to forget that my daughter had a life of her own and it didn't include spending time with her father in his brand-new club on a national holiday?

"I'll be there with bells on, Dad," said Darcy. "You are going to let me emcee a little, aren't you?"

"Well, sure, Darce," I said. "Now how's about the two of us blowing this joint and getting a cone at the Dairy Maid?"

"Dick," said Devera in that warning voice that clearly says "don't play favorites," but I didn't care—loyalty has to be occasionally rewarded.

"Bring me back a Nutty Bar, will you?" she yelled behind us.

"Oh, sure, sure," I said magnanimously as I hustled Darcy out of the room. Lin made a request for a hot fudge shake, but we were already out the door and into the garage, far away enough for me to pretend I didn't hear.

A WEEK BEFORE the Fourth, Devera threw me a loop big enough to rope and tie a steer with. We were reading in bed; Dev some homework and me a wholesalers' appliance catalog.

"Dick," she said, sort of funny.

I was hoping to get some action going, but I couldn't tell by her voice whether she was going to kiss me or yell at me. To stall a little I picked up the book on her lap.

"Oh, Marcus Aurelius," I said, "didn't he play basketball for the Knicks?"

Saying "ha-ha-ha," Devera took the book and put it on her nightstand.

I leaned in to kiss her but she sat up, so that my lips only met her collarbone.

"Dick, I need to talk to you."

I didn't like this at all.

"Dick, I'm thinking of going down to the Cities next weekend."

I sat there for a minute and then I wiggled my finger in my ear. "Excuse me, but I thought you just said you wanted to go down to the Cities next weekend."

"I did."

"Dev, next weekend is the Fourth."

"I'm aware of that, Dick," she said, making little pleats in the sheet with her fingers. "It's just that there's this exhibit at the Walker that I'd like to see—and well, well, there's a play at the Guthrie that I wouldn't mind seeing either—*Private Lives?*—remember I stage-managed that play in high school and BiDi played Amanda?"

I was barely hearing any of this. How could Devera even think about going away?

"Devera," I said in my deepest voice, not wanting to be accused of whining. "Devera, you know Your Oasis is opening this weekend."

"I know, Dick." Her fingers were flying, she was a regular Betsy Ross making those pleats on the sheets. "I just thought—"

"Devera." I wasn't about to let her finish. "I need you with me. You weren't at the store for the Syttende Mai sale and I know that's no big deal, but this is and I need you." I felt stupid and needful and wanted to smack her for making me feel that way, but instead I sat there in a long painful silence.

"I know you do, Dick," said Devera finally. "I'm sorry. I'll be there for your opening. Of course I'll be there." She leaned over to kiss me, a long slow kiss I definitely thought was going to lead to more, but then she pushed away from me and rolled over.

"I'm still going to go away for a day or two," she said, pulling the sheet over her shoulders. "I'll just make sure I'm back by the Fourth."

She made good on her word. My wife, for the first time in our marriage, went away on a separate vacation. She was only gone two days, but time went haywire because it seemed those forty-eight hours took a year to pass.

"So, I take it you do not like being the Bachelor Father?" asked Sergio, after taking a long pull on the ice-cold beer I'd given him.

"Not one bit," I said. It was a relief telling the truth; that day in the lot and at the Top Hat for lunch, I'd pretended I was fancy-free, thoroughly enjoying my wife's absence. "I feel sort of strange. Like I'm missing something—a part of my body or something."

Sergio laughed, but it was the sort of laugh that doesn't encourage a person to join in. "You have got it bad, man."

"Got what?"

"Love fever."

I did laugh then; Sergio had cranked up his accent so he sounded like Don Juan: *loav feefor*.

"Same disease you suffer from, good buddy," I said.

"Sure," said Sergio, but he didn't get the bottle to his lips fast enough and I saw his smile disappear. "You know, this Oasis place is looking really good," he said, swiveling in a half circle on the bar stool. "Looks like a real club."

I nodded, smiling. It was true. The place looked great. Darcy and I had ordered all these movie posters (everything from *The Absent-Minded Professor* to *Repulsion*) and had hung them in frames around the room. There was a microphone in the middle of the stage and the piano both girls had taken lessons (and given up) on, stood to the left. Black curtains I'd ordered from a theatrical company in St. Paul hung at the back. I turned a switch on the light board, lighting up the main spot. Then I turned that off and lit up the red gel light.

"Just like Vegas," said Sergio.

"Thanks," I said, and for a moment I was happy as a kid, showing my best friend my new clubhouse. But then Sergio sighed and I knew it was my cue to ask him how things were going. So I did.

"Let me get another beer," said Sergio. He took two bottles out of the refrigerator behind the bar and handed me one. I was about to hold up my first one, showing him I still had half a bottle to go, but lifting it up I realized it was empty.

"Sergio, you are a true bartender." I said. "You anticipate a person's needs before he realizes he's got any."

"Would that be true for BiDi?" he said, sitting down.

I felt a flash of déjà vu and remembered hunting with Big Mike in that duck blind, remembered the shock of his confession that living with BiDi was not the perpetual turn-on I assumed it had to be.

"Sergio," I said, suddenly feeling I had to defend BiDi against whatever was going to be said, "you two have been through a hell of a lot with with happened to Franny. Things are bound to be weird for a while."

"Do you think?" he said, and his face brightened. I sat up a little straighter, feeling like an astute marriage counselor.

We drank in silence for a while; my daydream featuring a wooden sign with the words DICK LINDSTROM, FAMILY THERA-PIST carved into it. I liked the picture. If I hadn't inherited my business obligations I could easily see myself going into psychology. Hell, I majored in it. 'Course I did copy Vonda Ackerblade's papers all the time. (Why not make use of all those A students who had crushes on me?)

"Well," began Sergio, lacing his fingers around his bottle of beer and leaning close to me in that way that he has, "the problems are . . . well, I am seeing things about BiDi now that I do not like so much."

I peeled the label of my bottle with my thumbnail. I really hated this. "Hmm," I said, for lack of any words at all. "Hmmmm."

Sergio nodded eagerly, as if I had hit the nail on the head. "Yes, yes, and it scares me very much."

I folded my hands like a church, the steeple my two fingers made pressing against my lip. I was trying to look thoughtful, I suppose.

"You see, Dick, I think that Francesca needs her mother most now and BiDi is not ready to answer that need. And it hurts me very much to see Francesca suffer while BiDi goes on like nothing happened."

"That's how she's acting?" I said. "As if nothing happened?"

Sergio nodded. "Yes, yes, she has even told me that the sooner we put all this behind us the happier and healthier we will be. And so meanwhile, an even bigger barrier has grown between mother and daughter. And a small barrier has started to grow between BiDi and me."

He bowed his head and I braced myself for the worst—a guy crying—but he jerked his head up and his eyes were dry.

"BiDi thinks, you see, that the world turns for her, and when it turns in a way she doesn't like, she will not face it. She will go on, in the hopes that the world will make the adjustments."

"Wow," I said, not only impressed at how he had summed up BiDi, but thinking that pretty well summed up Devera, too. Okay, not totally, but there sure was a smidgen of truth there.

"And she does not care who she hurts when she is trying to put her own world back to where she wants it. The important thing is she gets her world back." He took a sip of beer and then a bigger one, nearly emptying the bottle. "Also, there is the fact she has a drug problem."

I stared back at him like a big dumb dog who wasn't sure if it had been told to sit or go fetch.

"Repeat that last part, please," I said when I remembered how to talk.

Sergio nodded his maniacal nod. "She always has had this . . . this energy, but now I see it is helped by pills. I caught her in the bedroom. She was standing by the dresser drawer with a bottle of pills—see, she hides them in her underpants drawer—and when I asked what she was doing with them, she screamed at me, 'Nothing! I am doing nothing!' Then I forced the bottle out of her hands—her grip was like a vise—and read the label. Amphetamines. She was jumping on me like a dog gone crazy, trying to get the bottle away, screaming, 'They're doctor-prescribed! They're doctor-prescribed!'

"I go to the bathroom with BiDi still fighting me and got them all flushed down the toilet. She looked at me with this crazy look in her eyes and said, 'I'll just get more, you stupid

bastard. I'll just get more!' " A shudder shook through Sergio
and he closed his eyes. When he began talking again, I had
to lean toward him, so soft was his voice.

"I told her I wouldn't let her get any more but that I would
help her so she wouldn't need them. She just laughed, and
Dick, it was a terrible laugh, and said the day wouldn't come
when she wouldn't need them, unless the day came when
she didn't have to answer to a greasy spic husband and a
daughter who's dumb enough to ride her bike in the dark and
get beaten to a pulp."

"Jesus Christ, Sergio, BiDi said that?"

He made a gurgling sound and slammed his fist against
the bar. I put my arm around him, thinking he'd be better off
crying than making these weird choking noises that sounded
like he needed a respirator.

"I could understand her calling me names," said Sergio
after he blew his nose on a Your Oasis napkin. "I mean wives
have called husbands names and vice versa throughout
history—but how, how could she say that about Francesca?
That poor girl is going through hell and her mother won't
even offer a hand to help her out. 'I never wanted to be beat
up,' Francesca told me. 'Why does she act like I did something wrong?' How do I have an answer for that, Dick? What
do I say?"

All illusions of being a top-of-the-line psychologist flew
out the window and I sat there, sitting on the tips of my fingers, swerving on a bar stool like an idiot. For the life of me,
I couldn't think of one word to say.

I wanted to call Devera down—Devera would know what
to say—but then I remembered with a sharp ache that
Devera was two hundred miles away, doing her thing in Minneapolis, whatever that was.

DEVERA

IN A STRANGE way, I welcomed Dick's retelling of that icky story; I thrilled hearing that BiDi was a speed freak (she wasn't really; she tells me *everything* and I'd known for years she took a pill every now and then to keep her energy up and her weight down; but from what I knew, she only took them now when she was really stressed). Still, I reveled in the nasty words she told Sergio. I know that makes me sound like someone twisted, but the truth is, hearing someone else's bad news made me forget—for a while—my own. And my trip with Herr Professor Ludwig was bad news.

Dick saw me off at the train station (when I hesitated before stepping onto the train, he kissed me hard and told me to live it up, which didn't help my guilt any). I got off in Little Falls, Gerhart waiting for me in the old rusty Bonneville convertible he calls Gladys. We giggled for miles, feeling like Bonnie and Clyde, on the run and looking for adventure. In fact, if Gerhart had pulled up to a bank and told me to keep the engine running, I would have, tearing up through the streets once he jumped back in with his bag of money, laying rubber as the police bullets whizzed by. That vision made me realize the strength and beauty of impulse and how I'll bet a lot of banks are robbed just because a person's hair was blowing in the wind and the radio was turned way up and a man and a woman knew that at least for an afternoon, they were invincible.

I could just hear my dad lecturing me through the wire-crossed glass window of the prison visiting room.

"See, Devera, that's what happens when you have an affair. First you cheat on your husband, then other crime starts to look inviting, and the next thing you know, you're involved in a shoot-out!"

We checked into a hotel along one of the freeways in Minneapolis—it was a Marriott and so of course I was pleased. This was definitely a step up from our usual dump.

We had lunch in the coffee shop and Gerhart asked me in his beautiful rich voice, did I wear contacts? And when I said no he said it was amazing; my eyes looked like emeralds in the shade.

Of course it's only now in retrospect I realize how stupid that sounds—I mean, how many times did he see emeralds in the shade as opposed to emeralds in the sun? As opposed to emeralds anywhere?

We went to the Walker art museum but it was free admission day and full of arty kids who all wore rummage-sale rejects and stood in front of paintings with their heads cocked at odd angles.

"Students," Gerhart whispered, rolling his eyes. "I am so tired of the insufferable youthful pretensions of students."

"Mais oui," I said, trying to look insufferably youthful and pretentious, but his eyebrows jerked in puzzlement, and once again he didn't get my joke.

We went outside then to the sculpture garden. It was so humid out it was sexy; I could shut my eyes and imagine myself marooned in Tahiti, wearing flip-flops and a scrap of cloth. We held hands as we wandered past cast-iron men with coats and giant spoons holding cherries and bronzed curves and hoops with names like *Challenge* and *Forgiveness*.

Gerhart was fairly quiet as we moved past the grassy plots, only occasionally murmuring things like "powerful," or "ironic." A part of me—the part that nodded—felt admiration for this man who saw meanings and intentions in art; the other part wanted to laugh, feeling a bit like a cliché.

We had lunch at a Japanese restaurant in downtown Minneapolis, Gerhart ordering sushi for the both of us while I sat with my hands in my lap, alternately feeling like an idiot

and feeling taken care of. It's a fine line and I can understand that men are confused about crossing it: Do I open the
car door? Do I light the cigarette? My theory: When in
doubt, answer this simple question: Am I doing something to
be nice or to be the boss?

I was letting the Herr Professor get away with things
I'd never let Dick do; this was my first affair, though, and
the rules were different. Besides, I still felt in control of the
big issue: the affair and its very existence was subject to my
say-so.

"Try some of this," said Gerhart, pushing a little dish of
green paste toward me.

"What is it?"

"Extra flavor," he said, nodding. "Just take this California
roll and scoop some up."

Like the good student I was, I followed instructions, but
my big approval-seeking smile changed with I got a mouthful
of the wasabi.

My eyes, I'm certain, were bulging as I pounded the table
with my fist. I'm sure I looked like a cartoon, but really, any
minute I wouldn't have been surprised to see flames of fire
shooting out of my mouth.

I scrambled for my napkin and spit out the ball of green
fire into it. Then I drank greedily from my water glass, and
when it was emptied, I helped myself to Gerhart's.

All the time my so-called lover was laughing uproariously,
as if tricking someone to take a bite of something flammable
was high humor. Herr Professor's laugh is not infectious
either, he sounds like a pig rooting for truffles.

I wiped my tongue with my napkin and waited for the
truffle-rooter to stop.

"Oh, my God," he said finally, wiping his eyes with a
curled finger. "I enjoyed that."

"Obviously."

"Oh, come on, Devera, you're not going to be like that, are
you? It was a joke. Admittedly on the broad side, but
nonetheless funny."

"Like I said, obviously."

Gerhart giggled. "*As* I said."

Was he suffering from a flash case of mercury poisoning because of impure sushi? First he pulls a silly prank on me and then he corrects my English?

"Let's get out of here," I said, thinking that if we got out of the restaurant things would improve.

"Calm down, Devera. I'm not going to waste two pieces of yellowtail and half a California roll just because you're in a bad humor."

By the time we got back to the hotel he had convinced me that my humor was suffering in relation to my nervousness about our tryst. Dick has occasionally called me a spoiled brat and I concede that I may relate a little strongly to the lyrics of "My Way." I'm not stupid, however, and I was not about to let some hurt pride and singed taste buds ruin what was supposed to be my enchanted getaway of Art! Music! Culture! And of course, Sex!

We took a nap after our naked-Herr-Professor-strutting-and-polishing-his-glasses ritual and then we decided to take a swim before we got ready for an evening at Orchestra Hall.

The pool was enclosed in a steamed-up glass dome. I took off my robe and put it on top of a patio chair.

"Last one in is a lemming," I said, and did a cannonball into the water. Gerhart jumped in after me, holding his nose, and when both our heads popped up through the water he said, "Race you to the shallow end!"

It couldn't have been a distance of more than thirty feet, but I accepted the challenge, good swimmer that I am. I swam quickly to the edge and waited, my elbows propped up behind me on the pool edge, as my lover did a crooked crawl over to me.

"I had a cramp," he said, turning. He had already started off in the other direction when he said, "Race you to the deep end!"

We had three races, with yours truly winning each one.

"Yes!" I said, after winning the third, holding up my arm in victory.

"Good Lord, Devera," he said, hefting himself out of the pool. "Don't make such a spectacle of yourself." He sat down on a chaise longue, pulling a pack of French cigarettes out of his robe pocket.

"Victory demands spectacle," I said, and smiled. I climbed out of the pool and squeezed the water out of my hair.

Gerhart stuck a cigarette in his mouth and with clenched teeth said, "One does not make a spectacle of oneself poolside when one looks like a spectacle oneself."

I smiled, certain he was trying to be funny. He had to be, using all those *oneselves*, didn't he?

"Are you serious?" I said, and it was only when he failed to smile back that I realized he was.

He shook his head slowly. "Devera, trust me. I've never seen you in this kind of light, and believe me, this kind of light does not flatter you. Dimples belong on the face, my pet, not the thighs."

His face was smug in the way that truly *not* funny people's are when they try to be witty.

"Is that right?" I asked, fury propelling me toward him. "Is that right?" I stuck my finger in a soft fold of his belly. "But they do belong on guts, huh?"

Beneath the scraggly hairs on his face, he blushed purple.

"How dare you," he said slowly and evenly.

I laughed. "What do you mean, 'how dare you'?" I remembered something my mother used to tell me as a kid, "Don't dish it out if you can't take it in."

"*I'm* not the flabby one," he said. "My God, Devera, the skin on your legs virtually hangs." He clenched the unlit French cigarette in his teeth (virtually all indoor places in Minnesota are "smoke-free") and looked me up and down. Everything that I disliked about him crystallized into a hard ball that hit me in the stomach, and I wondered how in the world I happened to hook up with a pompous ass like Herr Professor.

"Virtually hangs?" I said. How could I have *ever* been attracted to a man like this? "Hey, just because you're a lousy swimmer, don't take it out on me." I held up my middle finger, a favorite gesture of Dick's. "Why don't you virtually hang on this, twerp."

I dove into the pool, a pretty swan dive, not that he'd

notice. I swam lap after lap, pretending I didn't notice when Gerhart put his robe on over his big stomach and skinny little bird legs and walked out of the pool area like he was King Tut.

He left a snide little note in the hotel room, saying that apparently our *"affaire du coeur"* had hit an impasse and he'd find lodging with some university friends.

"Good riddance," I said, shredding the note. I had dinner at the hotel restaurant and then I swam until the pool closed, until I smelled as if I had been marinated in chlorine.

To say that I was surprised when Gerhart showed up the next morning would be an understatement. To say that I was flabbergasted when he wanted to climb into bed with me would be an even bigger one.

"You have got to be kidding," I said after he suggested we bury the hatchet under the covers.

"Devera, let's not make a mountain out of a molehill. We had some words and I left—by the way, the concert was lacking a certain strength I expect out of Beethoven's works—now, don't you think the adult thing would be to shake hands and make a little love?"

"Herr Professor, that's no longer part of the curriculum," I said as he wrapped his arms around me. "And let go of me."

"Devera, Devera," he said, tightening his grasp and kissing my ear, "you've got to learn when I'm kidding and when I'm serious."

"Likewise," I said, feeling like I needed a good deep breath. "Now get your arms off of me!"

He kissed me hard on the mouth and then his arms tightened around me. Panic welled up in me like water about to boil over a pot and I thought I was going to pass out.

"Let go of me!" I would have screamed but fear took away the power of my voice, so my words were rasps.

He responded, I could feel his arms loosen around me, but my reflex mechanism had been triggered and there was no way to stop my leg from jerking up and kneeing him in the crotch.

Once again his face purpled as he hopped backward, cupping his hand over his injured parts.

"You bitch!" he screamed. "What did you do that for?" He collapsed backward on the bed and curled himself up in a fetal position.

"I did it because I felt threatened!" I said. I took a step forward and then one back, torn between a desire to comfort him and the satisfaction of seeing him writhe.

"You have no reason to!"

"I thought I did!"

He groaned and rolled on the bed, holding himself, his face contorted in a grimace, like a Rebel soldier suffering from shrapnel wounds without quinine.

"I'm sorry," I said, "I just don't like to be manhandled." (Now there's a telling word for rough treatment.)

"I shouldn't have come back," he said, "but I'm the sort of chap who believes in giving people second chances."

That did it. That shattered any confusion, any thoughts I had that maybe I had overreacted and maybe I should go to him on the bed and start rubbing his back and suggesting an interesting way I could apologize, but this second-chances-chap crap was too much.

What was I doing in a too-cold air-conditioned hotel room with this pompous, pretentious, sexist creep whose Ancient Rome class was about as exciting as overcooked noodles and who confused assault tactics with foreplay?

I started throwing my things into my suitcase.

"Devera, heed this warning: If you walk out now it will end, and I mean *absolutely* end our relationship."

"We don't have a relationship," I said on my way to the bathroom to collect my toothbrush.

"We could have!" said Gerhart. "We could have had something that might have transformed you!"

I looked in the bathroom mirror and saw fear in reflection. The panic was taking my breath away, so to stop it, to try to fool it, I laughed.

"That's inappropriate!" called the Herr Professor, and for the first time I thought maybe he was seriously deluded, maybe he always thought he was in a classroom. "That's inappropriate behavior that doesn't help anything."

I gripped the bathroom counter and laughed harder;

laughed until I was doubled over the sink, watching my distorted reflection in the shiny faucet, until I heard the door slam.

"WELL, THIS IS a surprise," said Dick, as flushed and smiling as a boy on his first date. "I didn't think you were coming home until tonight!"

"I know," I said, setting my suitcase by his desk. "I got homesick, I guess."

"I think I see a customer," said Larry O'Herne, and he winked at Dick as he pushed himself away from his desk.

When the trailor door shut behind Larry, Dick gathered me up in his arms and kissed me, a vintage Dick Lindstrom kiss. I didn't want to let him go. I guess I had a lot of hopes pinned on that kiss.

When I finally did let go, Dick took a deep breath and said, "Wow."

We got hamburgers at the Top Hat and ate them in the little triangular park across from the fire station, and after Dick finished telling me how much he missed me, he told me what had gone on between Sergio and BiDi.

"She's coming undone," I said. "I'll have to talk to her."

Dick nodded solemnly. "She listens to you. She listens to you more than anyone."

That was true; even though she thinks I've let myself go, BiDi does seem to think I know the answers to the big questions. I find that flattering, and yet I can't help but think it's like asking a pilot who's flying upside down how to land.

I swatted at a mosquito feasting on my arm and it burst like a bloody blister.

"Here," said Dick, giving me one of those moist-towelette things. Dick's pockets are a paean to his Scouting days; he is always prepared.

Dick smiled back at me; it was one of those married moments when your spouse knows exactly what you're thinking. He took out a spool of dental floss from his other pocket. "You'll probably need this, too. The Top Hat burgers are getting awful gristly lately."

We lay down by the creek that wanders through the park and eventually spills over a cliff of white rocks before it joins the river. We started necking then; we were neckers from way back, and the noise of the creek water tumbling over rocks and the smell of flowering rosebushes planted by the Ladies' Auxiliary pushed me into a zone of happiness that made me forget, for a small moment, the anger and guilt that rose up underneath like noxious fumes.

BiDi

I GOT DRUNK at the opening of Your Oasis on Flame Lake. Not cute drunk, where I conduct seminars in the art of doing Rebelette back flips; not the kind of drunk where I burp and cover my mouth in surprise as if I'm astounded such a noise could come out of little old me.

No, I got the kind of drunk that makes people smile with clenched teeth and excuse themselves as you stagger toward them; sloppy drunk, puke-on-Jack-Cole's-shoes drunk, pass-out-on-your-way-home drunk. And as bad as it felt, it felt good.

I almost hadn't gone at all; Sergio had made such a ridiculous stink earlier in the day. He had come into the bathroom as I was taking some aspirin.

"You are not going to the party all doped up!" he said, grabbing my hand. I knew he would have pried my fingers open, so I saved him the trouble and opened my palm to show him the three big bad aspirin.

"Sí, señor," I said, imitating his accent the way Lucy Ricardo imitated Ricky's. "I mean, no, señor, I weel not go to de party all doped up like a beeg bad dopehead."

"You can make jokes, BiDi, but it is not going to change the fact that you are needing help. You should be in a rehabilitation center right now."

"Oh, right, Sergio. *I* should be in a rehab center. What exactly do you think I am? A heroin addict?" I washed the aspirin down with a swig of water. "I eat cauliflower more than I take speed, okay? And you know how much I eat cauliflower."

Sergio's face grew dark in that Latin way of his. "Any bit at all is too much. I don't want you to take them ever again."

I rolled my eyes. "We've been all over this before, Sergio. And over and over and over, yada yada yada. Really, it's getting a little boring."

Sergio scowled at me—was it my imagination or had he recently replaced looks of adoration with scowling? I didn't like it one bit, I felt like a Broadway star whose number-one fan had suddenly taken an interest in the understudy.

He left the bathroom muttering, and I locked the door behind him. Let him think I was in here with all my harmful pharmaceuticals. Ha! The truth was what I told him, basically. I hardly took speed anymore, it was only in times of duress. Like Franny's assault and Big Mike's visit. Okay, sometimes in the winter, when daylight lasts about four hours and snow piles up like old gray laundry; well, maybe then I open the bottle a little more frequently, but there was no way I was some out-of-control junkie scratching myself and wondering how I could score more. I controlled my Black Beauties and White Crosses the way I controlled everything: with precision and with flair. But I hated getting caught at something nobody knew I did, and when Sergio caught me that first time, I overreacted. Whew. I get a little sick to my stomach thinking of the names I called him and Franny; but hey, everyone deserves to flip out now and then and say horrible things that normally wouldn't cross their lips.

Speaking of lips, Sergio's were tight on our way to Dick and Devera's, but that was all right, Francesca was taking up the slack. She was fairly expansive, talking about the upcoming party.

"Darcy's doing this comedy routine," she said, her dark eyes flashing and I drew in my breath in surprise; she actually looked pretty. She had lost weight (it sounds cruel, but never underestimate the power of trauma to melt away those pounds) and her cheeks were a deep pink. She did have good skin; I've noticed Lin's nose and forehead practically drip oil—Devera says she goes through Clearasil by the gallon.

"She does all these impressions—she's pretty good, too, even though I don't know who half the people are."

Sergio laughed, his first of the day, I'm sure. "Dick says she does impressions of people he doesn't even know. TV and radio stars from the forties and fifties."

"I don't know how she can get up there and try to make people laugh," said Franny. "She sure is brave."

Sergio took one hand off the wheel and put his arm around Franny. "You're the one who faces hip checks and slashing hockey sticks," he said. "*That* is bravery."

Half the town showed up for the opening and it started out to be a blast. Devera always lays out a big spread, but without taxing herself—she always hires out. Yeah, White Falls has a caterer—Sheriff Buck's wife set up shop on Main Street—two stores down from Sergio's. Mary Lou's a great cook, but I'm getting a little tired of her rumaki and deviled eggs.

Everyone looked great, too—well, at least, dressed up. I mean, there is no way Connie Cole wearing one of her Laura Ashley puff-sleeved jobbies or Clayton Hagstrom with his shiny flammable leisure suits could be considered great looking. But everyone at least had made the effort and the air was spiced with aftershave and perfume and the excitement of a night out.

Devera looked gorgeous. She is, you know. Her face is beautiful in that fine-featured svenska/norske way and her dress didn't call any undue attention to her love handles or her flabby bottom. She was acting the perfect hostess; First Lady of the Lake, and when I caught up to her by the punch bowl, she smiled at me as if I was just the visiting dignitary she had been waiting for.

"Beed! You look great!" She was right of course, I had on this leopard-print dress I had whipped up the night before, low in the front and high-hemmed—just my style.

She poured me a cup of punch but I held up my glass to show I was otherwise occupied (Dick had mixed me up a nice vodka Collins as soon as we walked in the door).

"Some shindig," I said, looking around.

"Wait'll the entertainment starts!" Devera said. "You should hear what Dick's cooked up."

I gave her the fish eye; I knew Devera and I know how she wishes Dick would take his keyboard down to Leo's Pawnshop and leave it there.

"Hmm, can't wait," I said sweetly, and then raising the sweetness a decibel higher, I asked, "Gerhart here?"

A dark red cloud passed over Devera's face and she gave me The Look, the one my fish eye pales next to.

"No, he is not," she said, her tight mouth outlined in white, "and I'd appreciate it if we didn't talk about it here."

I pretended to zip my mouth shut and I held up my hand like a pledging FBI agent.

"Good," said Devera with an edge in her voice. "Now excuse me, I've got to mingle."

Not that I felt rebuffed or anything, but please! What was I—chopped liver? Who else was more fun at a party than me?

I finished my drink and had a second and then a third and flitted around the room like a bumblebee, knowing every man was hoping I'd light on him. Ted Erck in particular was on me like a shadow until I told him I was going to get in trouble with all the ladies in the room—and his wife in particular—for keeping him all to myself.

"You're right, I don't want to upset the boss," he said. He held his drink up high so he wouldn't spill it as he tried to press his old horny body against mine. "Especially such a jealous one."

I gave him a sorry-to-see-you-go face and a little wave, even as I thanked God for relieving me of the old bore. I was ready to sashay over to Larry O'Herne and upset his slutty girlfriend by flirting with him when Dick bounded up the stage.

"Ladies and gentlemen," he said, taking the mike as the lights dimmed. "Ladies and gentlemen, it is a distinct honor to welcome you to Your Oasis on Flame Lake—where your troubles take a breather and your problems melt like ice in a rum and Coke!"

There was applause and I felt one of those small thrills you get sometimes when you see someone's dream come true—and this club was Dick's. I was standing there, my heart pounding, thinking, Way to go, Dick!

He talked awhile longer, making a special toast to "his lovely wife, his rock, his one-and-only Devera" and "the two greatest daughters a guy could ask for," and then, before things got too sloppy, he strutted over to his keyboard and began playing "I Only Have Buys for You."

The crowd loved it, clapping and stomping as if a song about discounts at Viking Appliance was in a league with "Love Me Tender." Funny I thought that, because the next song he launched into was an Elvis parody.

> *"Ever since my laundress left me—*
> *I found a new place to smell.*
> *It's there at the bottom of my legs—*
> *It's Athletic Socks Hell.*
> *Oh, they are so stinky, baby,*
> *They are so stinky, I could die."*

Again, the crowd went nuts. Devera swooned by the stage and I thought, Hmmmm, is that how she swoons for her professor?

"How's Franny?" Devera's mom, Helen, asked me as Dick introduced the first act to the stage.

"Fine," I said, feeling my heart race. Even as an adult, I was still intimidated by Helen. Around her I never seemed to have an identity other than "Devera's friend." "Fine, Helen." (I purposely made myself call her by her first name even as I blushed.) "She's doing really well."

"I don't know, dear," she said. "These things have long-ranging consequences. I'm still suffering from the time Evan was robbed and pistol-whipped."

I can't count the number of times Helen has mentioned the robbery and the suffering it's caused her and yet she never talks about suffering over the death of her son. In fact, Devera tells me she never talks about her son at all; it's like the subject's off-limits. Oh well, different strokes for different folks, I guess. It's just not the way *I'd* want to cope with anything.

Helen was looking at me like a clerk watching a potential shoplifter. "You just watch Franny, BiDi," she said, nodding her head, her hair a swirled, unmoving helmet. "Don't let her fool you. Make sure she knows you're there for her."

I thanked her for her concern even as I wanted to tell her to butt out, capital B, capital U, capital double T, underline out.

Suddenly the party didn't look half so sparkling, suddenly the crowd of people who moments ago looked so happy seemed to be wearing looks of concern and pity, looks directed at me. I was so tired of this wealth of concern; it seemed nobody was willing to forget how the poor LaFave girl was so brutally beat up, and how's her poor mother BiDi doing?

Those vodka Collins started tasting extra good.

I remember getting hushed mimicking Jeannie Forstad, the librarian, as she scratched away at her violin; I remember heckling Glen Pauley as he did some ridiculously amateur magic tricks. ("Houdini's turning in his grave," I yelled to him, "unless he's already found a way out of it.") I remember whistling with my fingers as Darcy did a pretty good impersonation of James Cagney doing the twist.

My last memory is of Connie Cole, who somehow caught me as I was bouncing around the room like a pinball in a fast machine. She put her arm around me in her fakey chummy way and whispered there already was a stage show, so why didn't I just cool it on the entertainment?

I remember asking her, "Hey, what's the matter, where are those pictures of your beautiful Korean baby that you insist on shoving in everyone's faces every other minute?"

I remember looking up, laughing at my funny joke and seeing Sergio. The look on his face filled me with shame and yet I laughed louder and then I threw up all over Jack Cole's Hush Puppies.

DARCY

FRANNY SLEPT OVER the night her mom got bombed at the party and hurled all over the place.

"Does she ever embarrass you?" I asked her as we lay on those chaise-longue things out on the deck.

"All the time," said Franny. "Only I try not to let it bother me anymore."

We both had our heads tipped back, staring up at a sky that seemed to have a couple million more stars than usual.

"How do you do that?" I asked.

"I don't, I guess. She still bothers me."

"She was kind of funny at first," I said. "When she was meowing at the librarian, that was pretty funny."

"Yeah, but she always goes too far."

She did. I mean Miss Forstad *cannot* play the violin, but when BiDi meowed like a cat in heat, it was only for a minute that you wanted to laugh. Then you wanted to tell her to shut up.

"Whenever she's bugging me about my weight or why don't I get a perm or do something with my hair—well, if I get mad at her, she'll say, 'What's the matter, can't you take a joke?' like it's my fault that I'm not laughing."

"I hate when people say that."

"Me, too."

It was fun laying out on the patio on those comfortable padded chairs, our hands dipping back and forth into the leftover party food that sat on the little table between us. The bug zapper was busy frying mosquitoes, and for a while, each time a bug got zapped, we would say, "God bless you," the way you do after someone sneezed, but that got old fast.

When my mother decided (my mother always seems to make those kind of decisions) that Franny would sleep over, there was never any question who she'd sleep with; I mean she and Lin are the same age but they've got about as much in common as Katharine Hepburn and Carmen Miranda. Franny's and my friendship had really grown—especially now that we shared that BIG SECRET. "How come you and Lin don't get along?" I asked after I'd sucked all the yellow stuff out of a deviled egg.

"I like Lin," said Franny.

"Well, why?" I asked. "She's such a pill." It was a mystery how she had changed from a fun sister to such a snotty crabby one. My mom says it has to do with hormones. I have a theory about puberty: to punish teenagers for having all the fun, God gave them zits and periods and personalities that make Jekyll and Hyde look sort of stable. (I myself haven't shown any symptons of puberty yet and would like to skip them all together, although I wouldn't mind *something* in the chest department.)

"She's nice to me in school," said Franny. "She always says hi."

For a second I thought she was kidding—who wouldn't?— but she was looking the way my mother does when she watches those "Save the Children" commercials.

"She always says hi? Is that supposed to be a big deal or something?"

"Well, a lot of kids don't," Franny said. "Say hi, I mean. I'm too geeky for a simple hello is what it is." Her voice was gravelly but she didn't sound ready to cry—she sounded mad. "Sure, around hockey season, some people are nice to me, but just as many think I'm some kind of weirdo for being such a good player—not to brag or anything—and a lot of the girls—a lot who hang around with Lin—call me Bobby *Hulk*, or Bobby *Whore*—"

"Well, they're just trying to be funny, just using those old hockey players' names and changing them a little—"

"I know what they're doing!"

Franny hardly ever yelled, so when she did she really got your attention.

"Other times they call me the Big Dyke or Fat Franny or Puckhead—I'm surprised I didn't get beat up long ago, to tell you the truth, and by kids from my own school!"

Her arms jerked out—it was like her anger was too big for her words and jumped out of her body. She knocked over her glass of Coke and of course it crashed when it hit the deck.

That brought my mother out—she's got an ear for accidents—but when she opened the sliding-glass door she didn't say, "How did that happen?" but "Is anyone hurt?" which I appreciated.

"I broke a glass," I said before Franny got a chance to. "Which I wouldn't have done if you'd let us use plastic." My mom's got a thing for real glass.

"There are penalties to pay for luxuries," she said, "but most of the time they're small."

Franny and I both shrugged as Mom slipped back into the house; I mean sometimes there's no better response to an adult than that.

"Thanks for covering for me," said Franny.

"Anytime, pal."

My mom came back with a whisk broom and a dustpan and swept up the pieces of glass. She was out of her party dress and wearing this big old T-shirt that was torn and spotty with coffee and food stains. Dad says Mom can look like a punk rocker without even trying. She unwound a couple feet of hose that hung in a circle against the wall and sprayed the pop off the deck.

"Why am I letting you girls just sit there while I do all the work?" she asked. My mother's big on chore delegation.

"Because kids today are lazy good-for-nothings?"

Mom laughed. "I guess I just feel like cleaning up," she said, and turned off the water. "Sometimes after a party it just feels good to clean up."

"Sorry about my mom," said Franny. "You shouldn't have had to clean *that* up."

"Oh, Franny," said my mom. "Don't worry about it. I've cleaned up after your mom and she's cleaned up after me."

"Were you drunk, too, Mom?" I asked.

Mom laughed. "You think I'd tell you if I was?" She hung up the hose and sat on a deck chair next to mine. "No, what I was thinking about in particular was when I was pregnant with Lin. I threw up practically every day and twice, Franny, in your mother's car. She *hated* that."

"I'll bet," said Franny. "She freaks out at dust balls under the bed."

"Well, she got me back good tonight. I was cleaning up gallons."

"Yuk," I said, but I laughed. It struck me funny to be sitting out on the deck talking about heaving with my mother and Franny. They thought the same way, because we all laughed then and it was pretty cool, sitting under all those stars, inhaling that big piney night smell, just enjoying your friend and your own mom.

"Hey," said my mom, slapping at a mosquito that the bug zapper missed. "Let's take a boat ride."

Franny and I were off our deck chairs before you could say "last one in's a rotten egg."

We ran down the grass to the water's edge and pushed the rowboat in. We climbed in and laughed as the boat wobbled and the oars clunked against the sides The water was as black as the sky and I felt all excited, like I was doing something illegal, even though I was with my mom, who made us put on the life jackets that were lying on the bottom of the boat.

Franny and my mom took the oars and I sat in the middle, watching my mom row. Her hair stuck out, frizzy and curly, and she was wearing her dirty old VIKING AUTOMOTIVE—THE CADILLAC KING T-shirt, but I did not think in this entire world there could be a prettier, more fun mother. She started singing "Moon River," but it wasn't hokey at all, it was just right and I didn't have to turn around to know Franny felt the same way, because pretty soon I heard her voice. Well, I wasn't about to just sit there like a bump on a log and so I joined in, and both Franny and I sang in that way you do when you don't know the words, just bawling out a note or two that you think might fit in here or there.

I hate to quote a commercial but I was really thinking, "It doesn't get any better than this," but it did because when we'd finished our little concerto my mom told me to drop the anchor and then, totally suprising me, jumped into the water.

With her orange life jacket, she bobbed up like a cork.

"Come on in, girls," she said, "the water's fine."

Franny and I just looked at each other with stupid looks on our faces and then it was like some track official shouted, "Go!" and we rocked the boat, trying to jump off.

We formed a little bobbing circle and then the funniest thing happened; both Franny and my mom leaned back, sticking up one of their legs like members of a sychronized swimming team. I did the same thing then and we floated on our backs, lifting our legs or our arms like the Rockettes in water. I started singing "There's no Business Like Show Business" (a song I know all the words to) and we kicked and dog-paddled ourselves in circles and waved our arms. We were getting pretty good, too, till we started laughing and then we had to just float for a while because synchronized swimming and laughing at the same time is pretty tiring.

"A midnight swim," my mom said as we all lay there, staring up at the moon. "I've always found it's good for what ails you."

"What ails you, Mom?" The question popped out of my mouth like it had been Heimliched. I hadn't seen her freaking out since that day in the kitchen, and she seemed okay . . . but you never knew.

"Oh, lots of things, Darce," she said, sounding careful, like she knew I didn't want to hear too much.

"Like what?" asked Franny.

We must have been in the moon's path because my mom's face and Franny's seemed really white, almost waxy. It kind of gave me the creeps and I wanted to be back home and dry, under a blanket with the TV on.

"Oh, Franny," said my mom, "I guess it's just that life can be a pretty scary thing."

"That's for sure," said Franny. "And sometimes it seems

like the scary parts sort of push aside all the other parts. The better parts."

I was treading water like a toy that had been wound up too tight.

"Are you all right, Franny?" asked my mom. "Is everything all right with you?"

"Yeah," said Franny, and she laughed a funny little laugh. "I mean sometimes I still dream about getting beat up and I can't ride my bike past dark anymore, but yeah . . . I'm okay."

Little ripples of water fanned out from her dog-paddling arms.

"I hope so, Franny. But if you're not, I hope you know I'll try to help you any way I can. Don't ever feel afraid to ask for help if you need it."

My mom looked at me then and said, "Oh, my goodness. We'd better get back in the boat. Your teeth are chattering like castanets, Darcy."

I knew that I was the party pooper, that both my mom and Franny would have liked to stay in that soft black water, floating around or swimming like Esther Williams, but I was so scared. Franny knows who beat her up! My mom goes crazy sometimes! These were the two secrets that I thought they might tell at any minute, and I felt like the security guard or something and it was my job to make sure no beans were spilled. I don't know why I felt that way; I just did. And it was an icky feeling.

SERGIO

AFTER DICK'S PARTY, I drove BiDi home and put her to bed (even after throwing up, she was still drunker than I had ever seen her and walked like she had been shot).

Devera had insisted that Francesca stay overnight. ("She doesn't need to see BiDi like this," she said in the bathroom when we were sponging vomit off BiDi's leopard spots.)

When my wife began to snore—as loud as an old man!—I left the house to drive off my agitated feelings.

This time, though, I did not zip onto the freeways, looking for the thug in the silver van; instead my car drove into town like it had a mind of its own; past the dark and quiet Main Street, left onto Rosewood Avenue, the street where Noreen Norquist lives. I just wanted to drive by, to know this woman of kindness and welcoming arms was close by, but then I saw her light on in the window and so I turned off my car and sat in it, watching her window like an FBI surveillance guy.

I might have stayed there, too, in my dark cozy car, but then I saw Noreen pass by the window twice and that was too much for me, it was as if I had chomped onto the hook and was being reeled in.

My fingers drummed at her door—I had all my excuses ready if her husband or Emil Anderson were up with her— "Oh, hello, my car broke down," or "Say, Noreen, I know it is late, but did you find my shop keys?" etc., etc.

She peeped out the little door window and her mouth made a round O of surprise but just as quickly a big smile stretched it out. Noreen opened the door and took my arm, pulling me in.

"Sergio, what are you doing here?"

I looked around her messy but comfortable living room, shrugging my shoulders.

"It's all right," said Noreen, "Fred's asleep. So is Emil. I should be asleep, too, but I had to finish this book." She held up a book about a road less taken or something. "The only time I get to read is late at night."

I drew Noreen to me without a word, drew this big woman who has to look down to say hello to me, drew this mountain of love and goodness to me and kissed her.

She pinned me against the door and kissed me back and every single tension that had made my body seem like nothing but an engine revving at full throttle loosened up, and for giving me that great release I would have paid her one million dollars on the spot.

"Sergio!" whispered Noreen, her face flushed in that beautiful kissing and sexy way.

"Forgive me," I said, not wanting to use my lips to talk—my mouth only wanted to be back on hers that tasted of nacho chips. "I didn't mean to come here but I couldn't stay away."

"What's the matter?" asked Noreen, taking me by the hand and setting me on the bottom step of the staircase. You see, that's Noreen for you. It was a dangerous thing for me to be there—her husband or her boarder could wake up, or what about the neighbors—and yet on her face I saw only concern for the pain that I knew was on my face as clearly as whiskers.

I told her about the party, about BiDi getting drunk and sick; but that was only shallow water leading to the deeper parts; I told her how mad and afraid I was, how I wanted to kill the man who had beat up Francesca, how that desire seemed like a sore inside me, growing and getting worse. Noreen held my hands as I talked, her kind gentle eyes never leaving my face. I told her how sometimes I got so mad at BiDi I daydreamed about her getting killed in gruesome accidents—of being stampeded by a herd of buffalo or being swooped away by a tornado. We laughed a little then; it did sound ridiculous, but then I told her what scared me most was the possibility of not loving her anymore.

After all this talking, talking, talking of mine, Noreen kissed me and that led to more kissing and finally with us taking each other right there on the carpeted bottom step of the stairs that led up to both her husband's and Emil Anderson's bedrooms.

I had to stuff my fist into my mouth when I came to orgasm, without that barrier my howl would have brought wolves down from the Canadian border.

There weren't many clothes to put on—we mainly had moved things aside for access, and when things had been tucked in and zipped up, Noreen said, "Sergio, don't ever come here again. I'm too weak in your arms to ever deny you." (Why couldn't BiDi ever say these things?)

"But . . . but things are still the same at the shop?" I couldn't bear to think of stopping our closing-up ritual.

Noreen kissed her finger and put that finger on my lips.

"Things will always be the same at the shop," she said, smiling, "until one of us dies or leaves the baking business." Her smile left her face then. "But, Sergio, you need to talk to a counselor. You can't carry all this rage and pain around."

I nodded. I had been thinking that that was what I had to do; I needed a referee to keep me in bounds, to keep me from going crazy.

"I'll get you a list," said Noreen, the biggest helper of people in the word. "Fred's seen a lot of counselors; I'll find you a good one."

I nodded, too overwhelmed to say anything, and left Noreen's house, and as I walked to my car the crickets were quiet.

I didn't wait for Noreen's list. Three days later I had made an appointment to see a counselor down in St. Paul—I didn't want to see anyone in the nearby area, anyone who could walk into my shop, into my normal everyday life.

The psychologist's name was Cleo, she told me, short for Cleopatra. She had a twin brother named Marc Antony, and while they thought it was a curse when they were growing up, they wouldn't trade their names for anything now!

She told me all of this while we shook hands hello, and with the worst breath I ever smelled. Really, it reminded me of the time I opened a Tupperware container and found the pound of rare roast beef I had forgotten was there.

She motioned to a Naugahyde couch, which I sat on while she sat behind her own desk and held her pen like it was a cigarette. Her curved and frosted fingernails looked like little tiny garden trowels.

"Well, Sergio." She had to look down at her pad to remember my name. "Suppose you tell me what's on your mind?"

"Revenge," I said automatically.

"Revenge in what respect?"

"In the respect that I want to kill the guy who beat up my daughter Francesca, breaking her nose and ribs."

"And Francesca is—" said the counselor, holding her pen up in the air like a fork.

"My daughter!" I said. "Well, actually, my stepdaughter, although I could not imagine loving her more than I already do."

"That's very well and good." The doctor smiled. Her teeth were as long as a pony's. "But what I meant is, how old is she?"

"Oh. Fourteen."

"Was anyone ever charged in this assault?"

I tried to make myself more comfortable on that Naugahyde couch, but I just kept slipping and sliding around it.

"No. He has never been found. It was someone in a silver van, out on an old county road."

"Tell me, Sergio," said the doctor, "how is Francesca's mother reacting to this?"

I rubbed my earlobe and looked over her head at a painting on the wall. It was like one of those Rorschach test-pattern things, except that it was in color and written in flowing words were, SEE WHAT YOU SEE. IT'S OKAY.

"My wife is like most everybody else. Glad that it's over and that it wasn't worse."

"And you don't feel that way?"

"No! It was bad enough! Worse than bad! It has made me feel that I cannot protect my family, that there are people waiting in cars and vans or behind trees ready to get them!"

"So you're having a hard time letting go of your pain."

"Huh?"

"You're paralyzed by your impotence—"

"I never said I had that problem."

"I was referring to emotional impotence," Dr. Cleo said, laughing. "Now, Sergio, let's not be a pain hog. Let's let some of it go. Let's confront your daughter's attacker."

"Excuse me?" I asked, looking to my left and right.

Cleo the doctor smiled in her big-toothed way. "That pillow next to you. It's your daughter's attacker. You are allowed to do or say anything at all to it."

Well, that was all the permission I needed. I slid off the couch, threw the pillow to the ground, and stomped on it with all my might. When I felt I might have broken all its bones, I lifted it up and kicked it as hard as I could.

My aim was either very bad or very good; it flew right across Dr. Cleo's desk, knocking over a big vase full of tall and strange flowers. Water oozed out of the vase like blood from a cut, making a widening dark spot on her desk blotter, and Dr. Cleo pulled with franticness at the Kleenex box on her desk.

"I am terribly sorry," I said, going to help her. She waved me away with her long-nailed hands.

"You told me I could do whatever I liked," I said. "I am sorry for the accident."

"I believe there are no accidents," she said. "And in believing so, maybe I'm not the right therapist for you."

"You are dismissing me for knocking over your vase?"

"I am not dismissing you," said the doctor. "I am merely trying to save us both time and money. I don't have great success in treating your type of male anger and I don't have patience with patients who direct their hostility at me."

The words *patience with patients* made me smile, but I cannot say it had the same effect on the mad face of the doctor.

"I am confused," I said. "Don't you think you—that we—are giving up a little early?"

She piled more tissue on the spill, answering me by not answering me.

"So what should I do now?" I asked, because I truly didn't know.

She looked at me with grimness. "I treat mostly women and I do that because women are more open to treatment than men. It's been only for professional challenge that I've brought a few male clients into my practice, but I'll tell you right now, it's less a challenge than a chore. I suggest to you that you find a therapist willing to deal with your particular brand of antics, because frankly, I'm not."

Even as I felt like I had been told by the school principal to get out of the school, I knew getting out of the school would be the best thing for me. I walked to the door and then turned around.

"I am not willing to deal with *your* particular antics," I said, but I did not slam the door only because I knew she expected me to.

DICK

IT WAS EARLY evening and Dev and I were in the family room, playing around with the computer. We were making up the menus we'd have for Your Oasis if Your Oasis was a real nightclub with food.

"Chinese chicken salad," Devera said, typing it in.

"What?" I said. "I thought this was strictly a steak-and-chops joint."

"Think again," she said. "We'll have an international menu."

"No tofu," I said, and she looked at me and smiled, not touchy at all over jokes about the lifestyle choice she was unable to keep. "Eight-fifty?" I was reading the numbers on the screen. "Isn't that a little high for a salad?"

"Dick, are we going to be highbrow or lowbrow? Don't answer that, I've already picked highbrow."

I smiled and took a swig of beer. I was feeling real good, sitting thigh to thigh next to my pretty wife, watching her type into the keyboard. I nursed a little fantasy about her being my secretary who was more than ready and willing to tell the switchboard to take all calls and come into my office for a little private dictation.

Something had happened between us, nothing drastic, but Devera was pushing my hair out of my eyes, straightening my tie, doing those things that make a man think yup, she loves me. The extra attention was like a big dollop of cream in an already good cup of coffee and I was enjoying the hell out of it—especially after that cold spell we'd just been through. I wasn't asking why—dumb slob that I am—why ask why the sun shines, why the flowers grow?

There was some spaghetti sauce on her shirt from our supper and to me it was the cutest thing. So there we were, and I was getting a boner as she typed up *tender pieces of marinated chicken with the delicate flavors of sesame and ginger served on a bed of lettuce* when the phone rang.

Darcy was at a friend's house in town and Lin was at the mall doing whatever it is teenagers do there, so there were no kids/slaves to answer the phone. Devera rolled over on the wheeled office chair and picked up the receiver from the wall phone.

Her eyes went round as shooter marbles and a big dumb smile sort of froze on her face.

"What?" I asked, thinking maybe we had won the free ham at the weekly drawing they hold down at Sitz's Grocery.

Devera looked up at me and mouthed the word, "BiDi."

"Is she high or something?" I mouthed back.

Laughing, Devera covered the phone receiver as if protecting BiDi from my silent question.

"Listen, Beed, now calm down. Dick and I'll come right over."

"What?" I said when she hung up and was wearing this sly little elf smile.

Dev pulled her hair out of its ponytail and ruffled it with her fingers. "We're going to go to BiDi's house," she said. "She needs cheering up."

"Why?"

"Because," said Devera, and the elf smile on her face got wider. "Because she's pregnant."

NO SOONER HAD Sergio opened the door than he tackled us both in a hug.

"I am going to be a father!" he said. "I am going to be a dad!"

"Congratulations!" said Devera. "But let go of me, I can hardly breathe."

Sergio laughed and then, like a kid, took us both by the

hand and pulled us into the kitchen. I swear it was like he was skipping.

I felt like I was part of some happy but squirrelly trio—like Curly of Larry, Moe, and—but man, someone switched channels as soon as we got into the kitchen.

BiDi was slouched over the kitchen table, her face mooshed in her palm. She didn't look up to greet us but sat there inspecting the splayed fingers of her other hand. She reminded me of the snotty girls who used to sit in detention all the time.

"BiDi!" said Dev, racing toward her.

BiDi looked up the way those snotty girls looked at the poor-sap teacher who had the bad luck of being detention monitor.

"I told you you didn't have to come over," she said.

"As if I'm going to be talked out of a celebration," said Dev, opening up BiDi's refrigerator. "Hey, don't you have some champagne in here? Sparkling ale? Carbonated water?"

"I'll get something from the basement," said Sergio, and when he raced down the basement, I followed him.

Big Mike had refinished the basement in knotty pine; there were parts where the work was sloppy and the planks didn't rest flush against the ceiling molding. Lit-up beer signs were stuck up along the wall, along with a fifteen-pound northern, mounted on a plaque. I remember Big Mike and BiDi had a big fight over its custody—BiDi said she had caught it on their honeymoon, Big Mike providing just a little elbow grease in the last stretch. Big Mike had said funny what time does to a memory, he caught it on his own after BiDi had gone back to the cabin complaining of sunburn. Anyway, the northern was still on the wall, BiDi having won that battle.

Sergio poured a couple glasses of beer and motioned me to the Foosball table.

"You are in no hurry to get back up there, are you?"

"Well," I said, "BiDi doesn't exactly seem in the mood for company." I let the ball into play and we started shoving handles, which activated the little men.

"I do not know what she's in the mood for," said Sergio.

"But I guess pregnant women are like that. Up and down. Down and up. Moody." He was smiling as he said all this.

"But she's . . . happy about it, isn't she?"

Sergio's smile switched off and I almost scored, but then he got his concentration back enough to move his goalie. "Well, yes . . . I mean she is complaining about timing, and not feeling good and being too old. . . . Oh my—you don't think that she might be so unhappy to think about . . ."

Our play stopped for a moment as I looked at him standing there, his mouth hung open, unable to form the word.

"Oh God, Sergio, I wasn't suggesting anything like that. A lot of women aren't thrilled right away, I mean, it's a big thing, after all."

Sergio's cheeks dented in as he slugged down about half the beer. "You are telling me it's a big thing," he said, setting the bottle down. "I am going to be a father! The Herrera line will be passed down—I am sure it will be a son." His smile flared up and just as quickly disappeared. "She wouldn't do anything . . ."

"Nah," I said, like that was the dumbest thing I'd ever heard. "No way, Sergio. You're getting all shook up for nothing."

Sergio nodded and then blasted a shot at me that not only missed the goal but soared off the game board like a kick by Pelé.

DEVERA

DICK TOLD ME later about how Sergio had the ridiculous notion that BiDi wanted an abortion and I said to myself, Whoa, it's not so ridiculous, she brought it up to me herself. I would have told Dick but BiDi made me swear I wouldn't tell anyone, and even though I don't consider Dick "anyone," I decided to honor this particular request.

As soon as the guys had gone downstairs, BiDi slammed the edge of the table with one hand.

"Shit!" she said. "Shit, shit, shitty shit!"

"I take it you're not thrilled with your impending mother-hood."

"Don't you dare get smart alecky with me, Devera!"

"*Smart alecky!*" I filled the teakettle with water and put it on a burner. "Give me a break, Beed, you sound like old Miss Magneson, from Sunday school."

"I don't care how I sound—you should hear how you sound," said BiDi, and then she burst into tears.

This surprised me because BiDi is not a big crier, at least publicly. We took the girls to see that *Little Women* remake, and when Beth dies, we were all sobbing except for BiDi, who muttered things like, "As if you didn't see that coming a mile away," or "Oh, come on, she wasn't all that interesting a character anyway."

I've seen tears here and there, but the only times I've seen her really cry, really prostrate herself with grief, was when her dad left and when Elvis died.

We were only nine when her dad left, but my memories are very clear because it was so near the time my brother Don died. BiDi and I got into a big fight—she was pushing me on the tire swing in our backyard and we were arguing about her dad leaving and Don's death.

"It's a lot worse for me," BiDi said, pushing me so high I could touch the tree branches with my toes. "He was my *dad*."

"So what?" I said as I swung back toward her. "Don was my brother and he didn't just leave us, he *died*."

BiDi yanked at the rope, so that the tire lobbed wildly.

"My dad didn't leave me," she said, fury in her voice. "He left my mother. He would never leave me, he loved me!" She then pushed me out of the tire and we wound up fistfighting on the worn patch of dirt underneath the swing.

My mother came out, seperating us as she called us "little heathens." I staggered to my feet, my fists still curled. I noticed then that BiDi was crying and began to feel the stirrings of victory, but it then became apparent that she wasn't crying over what I did to her, but what her father did.

"I want my daddy!" she screamed, over and over again, flailing at the dirt with her arms and legs. Finally my mother, who seemed incapable of comforting her, called over Mrs. Wallstrom; who picked her up and carried her like a baby to their house, two blocks away.

She never spoke again of her father until she was an adult, and then in dismissive little jokes. The next man to mean so much to her was Elvis.

You have to understand, to be an Elvis fan when we were growing up was to be the opposite of cool, which in our jargon was *sad*. The Beatles were cool, the Rolling Stones were cool, but Elvis Presley was definitely not. So while I thought I wanted to marry John Fogerty of Creedance Clearwater one week and Roger Daltry of The Who the next, BiDi stood by her Elvis, shrugging off our teenaged ridicule by shaking her head and saying, "I feel nothing but pity for you, not being able to see all that there is in the man Elvis Presley."

She saw him in concert twice in the seventies, once traveling all the way to Vegas with Big Mike. She would have preferred that he hadn't gotten all fat and puffy, corseting himself in those fringed and spangled jumpsuits, but as she told me, "He's only human, Devera. You can't expect anyone to stay perfect all the time—not even Elvis."

I've come to admire BiDi's devotion; it's something bigger than I ever had for my teen idols, most of whom now play state fairs and let their cool old songs be used as commercial jingles. Maybe she knew all along something the rest of us were too immature to see.

But now she was crying as hard as she did when Elvis left the building for the last time, and I frankly didn't know what to do. My instinct was to hug her, but I've gotten burned so many times by following up that particular instinct with BiDi, so I just sat there next to her.

"Oh Devera," she said, the last deep sobs cutting her speech into little gaspy syllables, "I'll be forty next year! How can I have a baby when I'm going to be forty!"

"Beed," I said, taking her hand. For a change, she didn't pull it away. "Beed, a lot of women have babies when they're forty—even older."

"But not me! It's hard enough to stay a hundred and ten pounds as it is!" she wailed. "I don't want to get stretch marks or have my breasts get all sloppy with milk—I don't want to change diapers or teach another kid how to ride a two-wheeler or be a 'room mother' again and bake two dozen pink cupcakes for stupid Valentine's Day parties!"

Her complaints were certainly broad-based; the funny thing, every single one of them (except the stretch marks) appealed to me and I found myself thinking, Your luck, you get to go through that all over again. I started in fact, to tell her this, but she shushed me and whispered, "I can't say I haven't thought about an abortion."

The teakettle's whistle punctured the uneasy silence that hung in the air. I got up and made cranberry tea, slopping the water over the cups.

"So how far has that thought gone?" I asked, sitting down. BiDi wouldn't meet my eyes.

"It's gone really far," she said. She was wearing a pink chenille robe with lace edging and her blond hair was on top of her head, with some little wavy tendrils spilling down. She was in the midst of a major crisis and looked like Malibu Barbie at the breakfast table. Of course BiDi was in trouble, unlike Barbie, whose only problem for the last forty years has been her inability to get off her tiptoes.

I saw a figure flit by the hallway and a mini-flush of fear before I realized it was Franny.

"Hi, Franny!" I called.

"Hi, Mrs. Lindstrom!" came her voice, and I could tell she was already halfway up the stairs.

"Why does she always call me Mrs. Lindstrom? My kids never call you Mrs. Herrera."

BiDi smiled sweetly and batted her eyes. "I guess it's because my daughter's got better manners than yours."

"She probably does," I agreed.

I wrapped my tea bag around a spoon and squeezed it, watching the magenta streams drip into my cup.

"So," I said. "You said it's gone really far. What does 'really far' mean? You might go ahead and do it?"

BiDi stared into her teacup. "I would do it in a minute if . . . if it weren't for Sergio. If this wasn't Sergio's dream-come-true, yes, I would do it. In a minute." She shrugged and tears filled her eyes again. "But I can't, so I guess I'll just have to grin and bear it."

We sat for just a second, staring at one another, before we got the joke.

"*Literally,*" we said at exactly the same time.

BIDI

MY LIFE WAS starting to resemble one of my horror movies. Not one of the bloody, gory ones either, but the psychological thrillers that make you shake your head and think, Now, that's *sick*.

Sergio and I were sitting in the living room, knees to knees. We were a yarn-balling machine; he held the unwrapped skeins in his outstretched hands while I pulled the yarn strand from it and rolled it into a ball. I was planning on making an afghan—I had made one for Franny, Lin, and Darcy and now it was time for another.

No, I couldn't say the thought of this baby was the greatest thing since sugar substitute, but I was playing my old Scarlett O'Hara game (I only learn from the masters) of getting through the day by not thinking about it much.

Well, things were pretty cozy in that living room. School had just started and it was my favorite time of year; my New Year is actually how I think about it. I feel like I'm beginning something new, with all the hubbub of buying backpacks and pencils and back-to-school clothes (happy days—Franny was down to a women's size twelve from a sixteen) and that autumn tang just ready to pounce.

So, I was sitting there balling up yarn, and for someone going through a lot of turmoil, I was feeling pretty peaceful.

Then *ding dong*, that old harbinger of all sorts of things, and I thought later if only it had been Claire Stenvig the neighborhood leech looking to borrow some eggs, but no, there darkening my threshold was Big Mike and his girlfriend Stacy. I kid you not, darken is the right word; Stacy's black hair was a huge round puff—it looked like a big eclipse of the sun just sitting there on top of her head.

"Well, this is a surprise," I said, and anyone could tell by the tone of my voice what kind of surprise I thought it was.

"Well, we weren't just going to sit idly by—" began Big Mike, but before he could finish, Stacy Big-Hair shouts, "Don't do it!"

I turned to Sergio for some answers as to what Stacy didn't want done—had he just pulled out a pistol or a machete?

"What is this all about?" Sergio asked, armed with nothing more threatening than a skein of blue yarn.

Big Mike and Stacy had by now pushed themselves into the center of the living room like the uninvited guests they were.

"We won't let you do this!" said Big Mike, standing by the couch with his big arms folded across his big chest.

"We can't let you," said Stacy, trembling beside him.

"Look, you guys," I said. "I know being born again is probably a pretty stressful thing, but those of us who haven't gone off the deep end have no idea what you're talking about."

"What we're talking about," said Big Mike, looking at me with hate-filled eyes, "is you taking the innocent life of your child."

"We'll fight you every step of the way," said Stacy.

"BiDi," said Sergio, and there was a little jump of fear in his voice, "what is going on?"

"What's going on, Sergio," said Big Mike, "is we're here to stop Beverly Diane's abortion."

"Abortion?" said Sergio wildly. "What abortion? What are you talking about?"

"Get out of my house," I said, and I bent over to grab a ball of yarn. "Get out of my house right now!" I lobbed it with a good aim, hitting Stacy in the head.

"Yow!" said Stacy, jumping behind Big Mike, even though you'd need a cannonball to make a dent in that huge stiff hair.

"Franny wants this child!" said Big Mike. "She wants a brother or a sister and I won't allow you to take its life!"

"No one's taking anyone's life!" said Sergio, and he was a sudden blur, flying through the air, and to my great surprise, this blur knocked down the tower himself, Big Mike.

"They're fighting!" screamed Stacy at me. To them, she screamed, "Stop fighting!"

They were deaf to her pleas and I was of the mind to just let them go at it; after all, it did take the attention off me, but then they rolled over and slammed into the coffee table. I did not spend three hours on an arrangement of dried flowers only to have them knocked over, giving me a mess to clean up on top of everything else, and so I put my fingers into my mouth and blew one of my shrill, world-famous whistles.

I was a little surprised when, like obedient dogs, they stopped tussling and looked at me. Big Mike's face was a sweaty pink; Sergio's was just pink.

"Get up, boys," I said. "I don't have time for this kind of garbage." I went to the staircase.

"Franny!" I yelled. "Franny, get down here this instant!" I turned to the so-called adults in the living room. "Before Franny gets down here, I'd just like to say a few things to you, Mike, and to you, Tracy." I called her by the wrong name on purpose, and didn't even bother to acknowledge Big Mike's correction. "First of all, I am having this baby, and second of all, even if I wasn't, it wouldn't be any of your business."

"Babies are everyone's business," said Stacy.

"Hmm, isn't that funny," I said. "Franny wasn't much of Mike's business, was she, Mike?"

A blush seeped into Big Mike's beard and sideburns.

"He barely lifts a finger to be in her life and now he thinks he has a say in *my* family's life?"

"He wants to do the right thing for everyone," said Stacy.

"Oh, stuff it!" I was ready to say something with a little more zing, but I saw Francesca creeping down the stairs out of the corner of my eye and the censor jumped into action.

"Dad," she said, holding on to the newel post. "Um, Stacy. What are you guys doing here?"

"You called your father the other day?" Stacy said like a schoolteacher trying to coax out an answer. "You told him you thought your mother was going to have an abortion?"

I had already figured as much, having remembered Franny eavesdropping on my conversation with Devera. But my God, to call and tattle on me without even getting the facts straight? Betraying me, her own mother, to a man who only technically was her father?

"I, um, I," chanted Franny.

"Francesca," said Sergio, going to her. "This is *our* baby. BiDi's not going to do anything to our baby."

"Well, I heard her and Mrs. Lindstrom talking!" she wailed, falling into Sergio's arms. He brought her over to the couch, threw off a bunch of pillows, and set her down.

"What were they talking about, honey?" asked Sergio.

"Nothing," I said. "We were talking about nothing. I had just found out I was pregnant and I was a little upset and I was saying things just to get them off my chest." My cheeks felt hot, I felt like I was on the witness stand, facing four people who claimed they'd seen me at the scene of the crime. "I'm not having an abortion—I was just talking." I kicked at the basket of yarn balls. "Would I be making a baby afghan if I was going to have an abortion?"

"You must have misunderstood things," said Sergio to Franny, smoothing her flat black hair with his hand.

"She has some other misunderstandings, too," said Big Mike. "That's another reason we made the drive up here."

"Oh, I'm so glad you didn't waste the trip aborting a nonexistent abortion," I said.

"You don't have to be so snotty," squeaked Stacy.

"Tuh," I said. "Don't even get me started."

Big Mike had moved over to the recliner and sat down. He was never one to stand when he could sit. "Franny asked me," he said, and then cleared his throat with a cough, "if it was all right if Sergio legally adopted her."

"What?" said Sergio and I together.

"It just about broke Michael's heart, hearing you ask that, Franny," chirped Stacy.

"Would you just butt out?" I said. I sat on the other side of my daughter, who was spinning her birthstone right around and around her finger. "Franny, you want Sergio to adopt you? Why didn't you tell us about this?"

Franny sniffed. "First of all, I wanted to see if Dad would agree to it. I really think he wouldn't mind, I mean it would get him off paying child support."

"Of which he pays a minuscule amount," I added.

"BiDi," said Sergio.

"I mean, what do you care, Dad?" said Franny, finally looking up from her hands. "I don't mean that much to you—I hardly ever see you, so what do you care?"

"Franny," said Stacy. "Your father cares very much."

I was *this* close to slugging that woman.

"That's not true," said Big Mike. "You're my daughter, Franny, and I won't let another man adopt you. You're a LaFave, and that's all there is to it."

"That's not all there is to it!" said Franny. She jumped up and ran to the staircase. "There's a lot more to it and you'll never figure it out and I don't even consider you my father, so what does it matter anyway?"

She raced up the stairs and we all sat there in a creepy silence until Big Mike said, "Stacy, let's go."

"Great idea," I said. "And next time, call. Or better yet, don't make it a next time."

"Francesca's a wonderful girl," said Sergio, following Big Mike and the woman I was dying to get into a cage match with. "I would be honored to be her father."

Big Mike stopped at the front door, and when he turned around, I got scared, knowing that look and that temper.

"Well, you're not ever going to know that pleasure," he said, holding a big fat finger in front of Sergio's nose. "And don't you ever forget it."

"Yeah," said Stacy, and I did one of those false little steps like I was coming to get her and she yelped and pushed Big Mike's back, and they blew out my front door like the plagues they were.

DARCY

I WAS AFRAID Franny was losing it, so I called her up to ask her.

"Franny, you're not losing it, are you?"

Her voice was low over the phone. "Losing what?"

"Your grip. Your marbles. Your hold on reality."

"What are you talking about, Darcy?"

"About you calling your dad to stop your mom's abortion that wasn't going to happen in the first place."

She kind of drew in her breath and I thought for a minute she was going to start crying or yell at me, but instead she laughed. Well, maybe not laughed. Chuckled.

"Oh, you heard about that one. It figures—you usually hear about everything, don't you?"

"I have my sources," I said in my best spy voice.

"Sure. I'll bet you stood outside your parents' bedroom door and eavesdropped."

"Franny!" I said, wounded. "It wasn't outside the bedroom door, it was outside the kitchen door."

She chuckled again and I did, too, mostly from relief that if she was losing it, she sure didn't sound like it.

Her telepathy kicked in then and her voice got soft and serious.

"Darcy, I know it sounds like I overreacted, but I did hear my mom talking about an abortion and I just wanted to make sure I did everything I could to change her mind—if it had already been made up."

"Still . . . to call your dad—"

"Darcy," interrupted Franny. "I want a brother or sister, okay? I didn't care what I had to do to make sure I got one, okay?"

And then she hung up on me, which is a pretty radical thing for Franny to do.

I would have called her back but I had to pack my junk to go over to my grandma Ardis's. Lin and I had passed the age where we needed to stay over because my parents were having a late night out, but I still liked what she called "our little slumber parties."

We always made popcorn in this big heavy pan that never burns a single kernel and we made rootbeer floats with one scoop of vanilla ice cream and one scoop of chocolate. But the thing I liked best was just spending time alone with her. I mean, she loved me in that you're-so-special grandmotherly way (which is like having your biggest fan be related to you) and I don't know, she just knew how to have fun like a kid. My grandma Helen is nice but kind of distant. I mean, it doesn't take much for you to start bothering her. I could never picture her playing dress-up, which was sort of what Grandma Ardis and I were doing; mainly because she doesn't allow messes of any kind, even if you tell her you'll clean up as soon as you're done with whatever mess it is you've made.

"Oh, Grandma, this is really cool!" I said, trying on a plaid swing coat with brown velvet collar and cuffs.

Grandma smiled. "I wore that to a Duke Ellington concert. It was your grandfather's and my fourth date. The one that turned the tide."

"What do you mean?"

"Here, this goes with that," she said as she dug a brown velvet beanie out a trunk and handed it to me. "What I mean," she continued, watching me model in front of the big oval mirror that stood on a stand, "is that your grandfather had a rival. Or so I let him think."

"And?" I asked, watching her put on a blazer with big padded shoulders.

"I was also dating Ralph Ronning," she said, trying to

button the buttons but unable to with her gnarled-up fingers.
I did it for her. "Ralph Ronning farmed over past Uncle's
Lake. I found him boring as all get-out, but your grandpa was
afraid he was going to lose me to him . . . and of course, I did
nothing to persuade him differently."

"Why, you old conniver."

"When your grandpa took me to Duke Ellington—well,
the concert was in Minneapolis, and Duke Ellington—this
was no polka band! So I knew it was a *serious* date. Sure
enough—Vernon proposed!"

"What happened to Ralph Ronning?"

"Oh, I dropped him like a hot potato," she said. "After all,
I got the one I wanted."

She stood by me and we both looked in the mirror. I like
to try to see the kid in old people's faces and I could kind of
see it in Grandma's—I mean her cheeks were pink and her
eyes looked sort of excited. In her red blazer, I could see the
young woman Ralph Ronning and my grandpa fought over; it
was easy to forget the old lady who made little squeaks of
pain as she climbed the attic steps (even though she had told
me she felt the best she had in weeks), easy to look past her
hands that were twisted like they'd been broken.

"Darcy," she said, "you look wonderful in that outfit."

"I was just about to say the same to you, Grandma."

"I loved that little beanie. It made me feel like a career
gal—like an executive secretary . . . or a copy writer." She
smiled, but this smile came with teary eyes. "Your grandpa
liked it, too. In fact, he liked hats just like you do. Said they
were the dessert to the whole meal."

"He said that?" I asked. About the only memory I had of
my grandpa Vern (he died when I was six) was of miniature-
golfing. We were tied, and then in the last hole he got the
ball in with three strokes; it took me five. But he looked at
the scorecard and said, "Oops—I never was much good at
math. I added all wrong. You beat me by two points!" Then
he flashed the scorecard in front of my face, too quick for me
to see anything.

I wish I had more memories, but that's a pretty good one. I

mean it sure beats Amber Wilkerson's, who told me her grandpa once showed her his thing at Paul Bunyan World.

"Your grandpa," said Grandma, "said a lot of wonderful things. Now, what do you say we pack this stuff up—unless you want any of it?"

"Want any of it," I said. "Are you serious?"

"It's yours for the taking."

And so I took: cashmere sweaters with jeweled embroidery by the neckline, circle skirts and big wide-cuffed pants, jackets with padded shoulders and peplums, and most of all: hats. I scored eight hats, including the brown velvet beanie.

"Grandma, why didn't you tell me you had all this great vintage stuff?"

She sort of petted the sleeve of the plaid swing coat she was folding up. "I didn't know it was 'vintage' stuff. I just thought they were my old clothes."

I, OF COURSE, got harassed by the morons at school. I don't know, sixth grade was bad but seventh grade's like Conform-to-the-Norm City. Maybe it was because the middle school and the high school are in the same building, so we get all the bad influences of those kids. *Whatever the reason*— our school was not exactly a place that breeds creative expression.

I was wearing this blue suit—the jacket had big padded shoulders and a little peplum and the skirt went almost to my ankles. (Grandma Ardis isn't much taller than me, but I knew it would look better after I grew a couple inches.) I wore a matching blue toque with a gold buckle, which I had to take off in homeroom because there's some dumb law about not wearing hats because you can conceal weapons in them. Yeah right, as if I was totin' a forty-five on top of my head.

"Halloween's not till next month," said Shara Nelson, who gets my vote as "Most Likely to Stay a Snot."

"Then that'll give you plenty of time to change out of your costume," I said. Shara just kind of tsked at me; I mean, she really isn't worth sparring with because her insults are so lame.

I had to stay late after school for the first debate-team meeting of the year. (I drew the topic "Defending an American's Right to Burn the Flag" for the next week's practice session—gee, I can't wait to get started on that one—yawn.) Anyway, I was running down the big wide staircase by the gym, minding my own beeswax, when who do I run into but a bunch of hockey players. They were all standing by the trophy case, making lewd comments about a trophy the football team had won.

"Pussy sport," said someone, I don't know who.

"Loser sport," said another, "stupid, *pussy* loser sport."

"How hard is it to catch a ball and run? Even a girl can do that."

There was a sudden hush as the group of apes smelled an intruder and I was hoping they were just going to let me pass in that smirky silence, but then one of them said, "Well, look who's here, Bette Hepburn."

"That's Bette Davis," I said. "And Katharine Hepburn."

"Same diff," said the imbecile.

I kept walking, and really, my heart was banging away like I was trapped in the jungle without my Land Rover.

"Either way, you look like a dork," someone said, and that really burned me, enough so that I stopped and turned around.

"Well, maybe I think people who are walking billboards for Nike are dorks," I said. The dumb guys looked at each other in their sweatshirts and jerseys that said Nike! Nike! Nike! (or occasionally Adidas). It wasn't hard to figure out why these unimaginative morons had nothing better to do than dress the same and bother some poor seventh grader who chose not to. Figuring I had made my point, I was about to turn around when who do I see among the stupid faces but the stupidest face of all: Pete Arsgaard's. I looked at him right in the eye and his face turned red.

Believe me, I was dying to say all sorts of things to him, but couldn't. I had promised Franny. So instead I just stared at him for about five seconds, shaking my head like I couldn't believe what I was seeing and then I left, not caring at all what those jerks said . . . well, not caring *much*, 'cause really, knowing you're right is a kind of protection, like a shield or something.

DEVERA

IT JUST GOES to show you I don't know anything about anything: Your Oasis had become my oasis.

"Isn't it just the greatest place?" I had asked BiDi and Sergio one night as I sat them at one of the tables by the big picture window.

"It's like one of those nightclubs you see in old movies," said Sergio.

"And you were the one who said the name was too long and the whole idea was stupid," BiDi reminded me.

Whatever there was to be rubbed in, BiDi always found it, and the nearest open wound to rub it into.

"Guess I was wrong!" I said, bright as a hundred-watt bulb. The only way of dealing with BiDi is to rise above.

The "club" was only open Friday and Saturday nights and I found myself looking forward to every weekend. It was like being on a date, only we didn't have to drive anywhere. Dick and I both dressed up—I actually wore heels and jewelry and perfume and Dick usually wore his nice blue suit that brings out the color of his eyes. We spent the half hour before Your Oasis opened putting the linen on the tables, lighting the candles, and setting up the bar. (Remember, our customers had to bring their own liquor, but Dick and I supplied the mixers, ice, and clean glasses.)

The club was always full—full of our friends who, invariably, dressed up, too.

"See," said Darcy. "Glamour is *not* dead. Pretty soon women will be wearing hats and gloves again and guys will be sticking boutonnieres in their lapels."

"Oooh, can't wait," offered Lin.

It was Dick's policy that anyone be allowed to perform, but most people only needed to get on stage once or twice and then got it out of their system, leaving the lion's share of stage time to a small group of regulars; Dick, Darcy, Kirby Horvig—the school superintendent who fancied himself the Mort Sahl of the Upper Midwest—and the "song stylings" of Mac Connors and Bunny Vold.

They had been coming, separately, to the club every Friday night, each with a song to sing. Hearing the other, a fan club of sorts had developed, and around September they started singing duets. Bunny's got a fill-up-the-church kind of voice, while Mac plays around with the lyrics in a sly sort of way; he reminds me of a French cabaret singer, except for the fact he sings in English.

They sang "Fever," and "Autumn Leaves," and "Someone to Watch Over Me"—all those great old standards that made the club seem, at least while they were on stage, like the only place to be on earth. We had candles lit on every table and Dick always made a point of recruiting someone else to run the light board when Mac and Bunny sang so that we could sit together by one of the big windows. It was like a sweetened, condensed honeymoon, sitting in that candlelit room listening to two voices singing those classic songs, with a view of the night sky and the moon reflected on the lake.

It wasn't as if I had ever stopped loving Dick; I just think my fiasco of an affair with Herr Professor made me realize why and how *much* I loved him.

All of the things that had really begun to bother me about him, all of the things I thought were so immature—his goofiness, his cheerfulness, and his insistence on having fun— were so refreshing after being trapped in Herr Professor's vacuum of pretension.

BiDi was right in her assessment of him, but I wasn't about to give her the satisfaction of telling her so. That's one of the things about her that I both admire and am annoyed by: her first impressions are usually right on the money. Once, after I had told her she was too judgmental after she had described the new church secretary as "shifty," she told me, "If you don't like the preview, you usually won't like the movie." And it turns out she was right about the secretary, who ran off with all the profits from the Christmas bazaar.

When she grilled me for details with Gerhart, I just told her it was over and there wasn't anything to talk about. Who wants their face rubbed in something that already makes them sick?

And I do physically cringe every time I think about being with Gerhart, wondering if I had been teetering on mental illness when I started our affair. I'm not kidding when I suggest mental illness played a part in my "indiscretion." I had been so on edge with those panic attacks—who knows?—maybe some reasoning part of my brain was affected. I know a jury might have a hard time with that defense, but I would still use it to plead my case: I wasn't in my right mind.

Another reason I love Your Oasis so much is that since it opened, I haven't had one panic attack. One thing may not have anything to do with another, but to me it feels like a safe place. In my research I learned that attacks often leave as quickly as they come on; but I still can't believe my good luck, that maybe they're gone for good. I'm knocking on a lot of wood lately, thankful . . . but still wary.

"YOU WATCH," I said to Dick one night as our resident Steve and Edie crooned "It's Only Make-Believe" to one another. "If they're not an item already, they will be soon."

"Mac and Bunny?" said Dick. "Get outta here."

Dick had been working with Bunny on her campaign song, a parody of "Fools Rush In," so maybe it was too much to ask him to see this political workhorse as a romantic figure.

"Bunny's never been out with a man as long as I've known her," Dick said, and then lowering his voice to a whisper, added, "In fact, it wouldn't surprise me if she's a citizen of the Isle of Lesbos."

"Isle of Lesbos," I muttered, shaking my head. "Why don't you grow up, Dick?" I looked onstage at Bunny and Mac, who were almost nose to nose, singing to each other. "And after you're done growing up, take a look at them and tell me they're not in love."

They were; I caught them smooching, as my father would say, on the outside steps leading to the deck.

"Hey, you two," I said, "you need a blanket or something? It's cold out here."

They untangled themselves as quickly as caught teenagers.

"Devera," said Bunny.

"None other," I said, unable to wipe a big smile off my face.

"We were just—" began Mac.

"I saw *just* what you were doing," I said, shifting the bag of garbage whose disposal had brought me outside in the first place, "and I knew it was coming."

"You knew *what* was coming?" asked Bunny.

"Love," I said, lifting up the trashcan lid. "It's written all over your face whenever you sing."

"It is?" asked the lovebirds in tandem.

I laughed. "In bold captions."

The next day Bunny called me, her voice as furtive and whispery as Mata Hari's.

"Devera, listen, Mac and I are both sort of new at this . . . thing, and we'd appreciate it if you kept it to yourself."

"Too late, Bunny, I already called the *Gazette*."

For once Bunny didn't have a snappy comeback.

"I'm kidding," I said. "I'm kidding. I won't say a word to anyone. Although I already told Dick."

"Well, Dick's all right," said Bunny. "I guess you know who I want to keep this a secret from."

"I really don't, Bunny."

"My dad."

"Mister Vold?" Bunny lived with her father, an old man who always wore a felt fedora and whose good posture I always pointed out to the girls whenever we saw him at the Snack & Gas. "Why would he care if you have a boyfriend?"

She giggled, something not in character. "Well, he just doesn't want me to desert him. It's been just the two of us on that old farm since my mother died. He's afraid if I find someone, I'll leave him all alone."

"And how old are you, Bunny?"

Her laugh was sheepish. "Fifty-two."

"Don't you think it's about time you found someone? It's not fair of your father to ask you to give up your whole life."

"I know." Bunny sighed. "But there was nothing much to give up before. And the older dad gets, the more unreasonable he is."

"Well, you've got to decide what's more important to you, Bunny. Loving Mac or pleasing your father."

"Can you believe we're even having this conversation, Devera?" Bunny's voice cracked. "I feel like such a fraud—a big part of my platform is moving ahead for women's rights, and now you find out how I'm afraid to stand up to my own father. But he's getting so old, Devera, and he's got no one in the world but me."

"Oh, Bunny." I swallowed down a lump that had formed in my throat, thinking of my own father and the ties that bind us. I couldn't even go away to college after that creep robbed and pistol-whipped him. "Oh, Bunny," I said again, gathering my thoughts. "I think what your dad would like best is to see you really happy. And if Mac makes you really happy . . . well, you should go for it."

"You're right, Devera." She sniffed, and I could tell she was starting to cry. "Who'da thunk it, is all I have to say."

"THINK MY GIRLS will ever be that loyal to their old man?" Dick asked after I told him about our conversation.

"God, I hope not," I said.

Dick got this wounded look on his face for a second but then he nodded and said, "I agree. I'd feel bad if I somehow stopped them from doing something they really wanted to do. Or loving some guy . . . unless of course he was a total jerk."

We were sitting on the couch, sharing a bowl of popcorn and watching a diving competition on TV.

"Yeah, my dad warned me about those total jerks." I said, wiping my buttery fingers on a napkin. "But I married you anyway."

Dick got my head in the crook of his arm and rapped on my head—what we call "giving noogies"—and I tickled him, trying to get out of his hold, and that's the way Lin and Kyle found us when they walked in.

"Just ignore them," Lin advised. She got the clicker and turned the TV channel to MTV. A band jumping around shirtless was trying to outscream their guitars. "Just ignore them and maybe they'll go away."

Dick grabbed the clicker and turned it back. "Hey, we were watching this," he said. "And if you made us miss the Chinese guy, you're in big trouble."

"Divers," said Kyle, "cool."

I passed him the popcorn and Lin put her feet up on the coffee table, and that's how we managed to spend a little quality time on a Saturday afternoon with a daughter who didn't believe such a thing existed with her dorky parents anymore.

SERGIO

WE HELD OUR own little ceremony the night after Francesca's father and his girlfriend left.

"Just because it isn't legal doesn't mean it's not important," said Francesca.

"Amen to that," said BiDi, blowing out a match. "The legal part doesn't mean diddly."

"But candles, Mom?" said Francesca, laughing. "Don't you think you've overdone it with the candles?"

BiDi held her arms out. "What can I say? I've always loved a ceremony."

There must have been over fifty candles lit—okay, at least thirty! I was touched deep; thinking all those little flames of light were tiny compared to the big flame I had in my heart for BiDi and Francesca. And the bambino to come—my son! (I know it will be a son, making my life complete!)

BiDi set up a video camera on a tripod by the side of the fireplace and we were ready to begin.

"Wait, wait," she said as we stood there, shy and nervous, pulling at our fingers and our collars. "Hold everything."

She ran upstairs and came back wearing an old choir robe from the year she had been talked into being in the bell choir.

"Okay," she said, "both of you stand here, by me."

This was BiDi at her finest, the rose among her thorns, the sun before the storm cloud. It was the BiDi who could make me able to imagine old age with her.

It had been her idea for Francesca and I to write adoption vows, and now she stood in front of us like a priest and asked Francesca to read hers.

Francesca unfolded a square of notebook paper.

"I wanted to type this up on nice stationery," she said, "but I guess I didn't." She shrugged her shoulders, blushing.

I put my hands behind my back, not wanting them to see how much I was shaking.

"I, Francesca LaFave," she began, her voice a little bit wavery, "do take you, Sergio Herrera, as my adopted father because you feel like a dad to me, because you care about me and love me, and because I care about you and love you back."

My body had a live wire in it, surely they could see how I shook? And my heart! It was like a Kentucky Derby winner galloping toward the finish line.

"I promise to love, cherish, and obey—well, only obey as much as a kid should obey her dad when she's a teenager going through her rebellious stage."

Here Francesca smiled and we laughed, longer than necessary, but it was good to break the tension.

"These things I solemnly swear to. Sincerely, Francesca LaFave, but in her heart, Herrera." She pushed aside her black bangs with her fingers and I could see the little shake in them, too. "Was that okay?" she asked BiDi and me.

The tip of BiDi's nose was pink and there were actually tears in her eyes. This pregnancy is seeming to bring out her good emotions.

"I have never heard anything more beautiful in all my life," I said. "Well, maybe my wedding vows come close." Even though my wedding vows were straight out of the book, I did not want BiDi to feel left out.

I had not written any lines; I had a pretty good idea about what I wanted to say, but now I stood there like a dummy, my mouth not hinged properly. My head felt like a buzzing TV set that had no show on it. I cleared my throat, rubbed my forehead, and retucked in the back of my shirt, hoping that some antenna would go up and I would get some reception!

"And now," said BiDi as if I wasn't aware I was supposed to speak next, "we will hear from Sergio."

"What is a father?" I almost looked around to see who was speaking, my own words surprised me so. When I saw that there was of course no other man speaking in a rather high-pitched voice, I went on, also thanking God for giving me a question I could answer.

"A father is a man whose job it is to be a father."

I know BiDi couldn't help that little yip of laughter and I was glad she did because she made me focus my eyes on Francesca and then all the words I needed came.

"A father is a lucky man," I said, taking my daughter's real hands, and in my heart the hands of my unborn son, "lucky if he has a child, the best flower in the world's garden, a child like you to love, to watch over, to protect, to learn from, to guide, and to help.

"Francesca, my love for you is a happy lodger in my heart—one that will never move because it could find no better place!" I almost shouted this, so I took a deep breath to calm myself down. "I pledge to be there for you in your trials and tribulations, which I hope there will not be many more of. I pledge to be there with all my love, my warm coat of love, which I will hold open for you always."

Well, you can see I am the son of an opera singer.

"Wow," said BiDi when it was clear to her I was done and had no P.S. to add on. "You're a poet, Sergio." She straightened the white collar of her robe and put her hands over Francesca's and mine. "And now, by the powers vested in me by the State of Love, I now pronounce you father and daughter. Francesca, you may kiss your dad, and Sergio, vice versa."

It was really a celebration! We opened a bottle of bubbly water (because of BiDi being pregnant and Francesca being underage we did not get champagne) and clinked our glasses together and made a pizza and then watched the video we made of the ceremony.

We laughed at how high my voice sounded—I would not have stood out in a group of Castrati Brothers—but really, as they say, when the tape ended, there was not a dry eye in the house.

It was a perfect evening. There was nothing, not a word, not a breath I would change, so I was surprised when I couldn't go to sleep. I had not done it for at least a month, but I felt a compulsion to do so now. The grass was wet and the night sky was black as ink when I got into my car. Not wanting to wake anyone, I didn't start the engine until I had rolled in reverse out the driveway and then I drove for an hour or so, looking for that silver van—or any trouble at all that might be waiting for me and my family.

BiDi

ON COLUMBUS DAY (a day that gets absolutely no respect here in the Land of the Vikings), Lily Erck came back from her Ladies' Auxiliary meeting to find her husband in his easy chair, watching an R-rated movie on cable.

"Ted," she scolded him, "you're a little old for those monkeyshines, aren't you?"

When he didn't answer, she repeated the question, and when he still didn't answer, she said, "Oh no, your hearing's not on the fritz, too, is it?"

"I'll never get over that," she told Devera's mother later. "I was teasing him about his impotence and there he was—dead!"

It was a massive coronary and his funeral was the biggest I'd ever seen; after all, Dr. Ted Erck was a pillar of the community. A *leaning* pillar, but still, next to Devera's dad Evan, he was probably White Falls' most revered citizen.

Helen and Evan sat with Lily in the church, Evan's arm stretched across the pew, a shelter to both women. The Bergdahls and the Ercks had gone through a lot together, what with the death of their sons in that paper-shack fire.

After the burial, everyone had lunch in the church basement; the smell of tuna and hamburger casseroles made me want to upchuck, but Sergio said it had nothing to do with my pregnancy—the smell made him sort of sick, too.

I was showing a little and suddenly I was Miss Popular—everyone had something nice to say, except for Connie Cole, who said I looked cute "plump."

"Wish I could say the same for you," I said, breezing by her, wondering why she's always go to get her digs in. There's no way I could be called plump—I could still wear my jeans, I just had to leave the zipper halfway down.

Sergio was getting me a piece of cake (he donated three to the luncheon) when Lily Erck sat down next to me and squeezed my hand so hard I whimpered.

"Beverly Diane, if I weren't so aggrieved, I would slap your face."

Bunny Vold, who had been reminding everyone Election Day was coming up, leaned in close, her eyes wide.

I had no idea what Lily was talking about, but she was newly widowed after all, so I had to humor her.

I smiled at Bunny. "I'll vote for you if you make like a tree and leave."

"Say no more," she said. She stood up, her plate on top of her coffee mug, and went to another table of constituents.

One look at Stan Nilsson and his wife was all it took for them to clear the table.

"Lily," I said quietly, not wanting to draw any more attention than we'd already drawn. "I have no idea what you're talking about, so why don't you help me out and give me a clue?"

Her veiny hand trembled as she lifted the square gold clip of her big square leather purse and pulled out a brown padded envelope, the kind my VCR tapes are mailed in. She pushed it toward me.

"This is from Ted. It's addressed to you and I found it in our safety deposit box. I probably would have read it, but it says right here on the envelope, see?" She pointed to a scribble. "It says, 'Lily don't open this, it's none of your business.' "

We stared at each other and I felt like I was in that old show *Bewitched* where Endora freezes all the people so she and Samantha can have a private chat.

"Well, I'm glad you honored his wishes," I said, sliding the mailer toward my own purse, which thankfully was big enough to hold it. "Excuse me for a moment, won't you, Lily?"

I walked as calmly as I could to the women's room, hearing the buzz in the room grow.

"BiDi, what is it?" asked Sergio, jogging over.

"I don't know." I pushed open the door. "I'll be right out."

I locked the door (fortunately this was just a single-toilet bathroom, so the herds couldn't follow me in with the excuse that they had to go, too), shivering like the temperature had just dropped forty degrees. I tugged at the stapled flap, pricking my finger with the sharp end of a staple.

"What the hell?" I whispered as I opened the envelope. It was half-filled with that Styrofoam popcorn packing stuff, which I scooped out to find the real treasure, or what the good doctor had supposed I'd think was a treasure: a posthumous stash of Dexedrines and Bennies. I sat back on the toilet, completely flummoxed. What could possibly have been on that old drunk's mind?

He didn't leave me completely in the dark—there were two notes tucked to the side and the first one, dated just over a year ago, said:

> My Dearest Beverly Diane:
>
> It probably was no secret how I felt about you all these years—you who put the flame in Flame Lake, and I, so smitten with that fire. I found myself hoping you'd develop any virus that was going around—how I loved flu season!—just so I could treat you! How I loved listening to your heartbeat through my stethoscope! How I loved tapping my little hammer on your lovely knees! How I loved sharing our amphetamines adventure! You just watch, once the AMA gets off its puritanical keister, all of America will be on, in safe doses, to the wonderful, energizing beauty of speed!
>
> A lot of things make a man's life worthwhile, B.D., and you were one of those things to me. When you throw yourself these pill parties, think of me as your host. With great affection, Dr. Ted.

If I didn't have such a strong constitution I probably would have fainted right there. Really, I had no idea White Falls' beloved family physician was such a druggie—let alone a pervert. Sure, he always seemed happy to see me, but what man didn't? *Tapping my little hammer on your lovely knees!*

Ugh!

I unfolded the second note just as someone knocked on the door.

"BiDi, are you all right?" asked Sergio.

"Fine, hon!" I said as brightly as if I'd been opening birthday cards. "Be out in a second."

The second note was dated over twenty years ago and written on a prescription form.

Dear Beverly Diane,

Today I gave you your senior-high-school physical, and my mother, Mrs. Virginia Erck, was sitting in the waiting room, as she likes to do, keeping up with my patients and just passing the time. After you left, she told me what a nice young lady you were and how you had spoken to her so respectfully—uncommon for teenagers in this day and age—and that she'd like to give you something. She gave me the enclosed pearl necklace, which has been in her family for years.

"Tell her it's just for being nice to an old gal," she said. My mother is impulsive like that—especially as she's gotten older and finds giving away her things gives her more pleasure than keeping them. And so, here it is, with both my mother's and my best wishes.

Dr. Ted Erck

I fished my hand in like Little Jack Horner, and sure enough, pulled out quite a plum—a string of pearls. The clasp was a pretty little filigreed thing, slightly tarnished.

Again the banging on the door. "BiDi!"

"Coming, Sergio!" I said. I stood, ripped up the weird doctor's first note, and let it flutter into the toilet bowl. Then I held up the padded envelope, and like a cook adding ingredients to an already strange brew, I poured out a stream of pills, saving only a few for whatever rainy days might lie ahead. I flushed the toilet and watched it all swirl its way into our sewer system.

I grabbed up the Styrofoam popcorn and put it back in the envelope, along with the necklace and the second note; the one that got me off the pretty big hook the first one almost speared me on.

I looked in the mirror, put on a dash more lipstick, and stood there admiring myself for a moment before I went out to face the lions.

"I NEVER KNEW Ted's mother to own any pearls," said Lily Erck, examing the necklace. She and the rest of White Falls were crowded around me in that church basement like I was a visiting bishop, or whatever they call a Lutheran bigwig.

I shrugged my shoulders; after all, how was I to know more than what the note told me?

"Good pearls, too," said Marshall Naslund, who owned Naslund Jewelers on First Street. "Come in for an appraisal, Beverly Diane."

"Oh," I said, "I don't need them appraised. Their sentimental value is worth more than money to me."

The crowd nodded appreciatively.

"Did he leave anything else?" asked Devera, of all people.

"Nothing but the note and the pearls," I said, shaking my head at the mystery.

Now, to tell you the truth, there's nothing more I wanted than to take that necklace to Duluth or down to the Cities and cash them in, but I had an audience and I knew I'd better play to them. Lily had just given them back to me, and I stared at them for a moment, letting myself get misty-eyed, before I stood up, looked over the crowd until I found my target, and said, "Francesca? Franny, honey, come over here. I want to give you something."

The crowd again made noises of great approval as my daughter, red as red on a face gets, poked her way over.

"Francesca," I said, standing up, "I'm sure if Mrs. Virginia Erck had ever met you, she'd want you to have this." I fastened it around my daughter's neck and the room exploded in applause.

"Miss Virginia never really liked me," I heard Lily complain to Devera's mother as they walked to the dessert table.

"NICE SPEECH," SAID Bunny Vold as we gathered our coats from the big rack. "If there were an election today, you'd win, hands down."

"Well, thank you, Bunny," I said. "But I'm not really the political type."

"Like hell you aren't," said Bunny, and I was just about to ask her what she meant by that, but then her father, old Mr. Vold, started hollering at her.

"You'd better find me a way home," he said, angling his fedora on his head, "because I'm not riding home with that mailman!"

"Oh, Dad," said Bunny. "You rode here with him, remember?" She looked at me and rolled her eyes. "Men. What are you going to do?"

I rolled mine back. "Anything you have to, I guess."

DICK

THE HALLOWEEN PARTY (costumes required) we threw at Your Oasis started out great. Devera and the girls and I went through spools of orange and black crepe paper; it criss-crossed the ceiling like the web of a giant tiger spider (if there is such a thing). Ghosts and black cats and witches swung on little bobbing strings and the candleholder for each table was a jack-o'-lantern. Clayton Hagstrom gave us a bunch of pumpkins—he's got a bumper crop this year. Guy always manages at least one annual bumper crop of something.

Devera was dressed as a gypsy. She wore a long skirt and a scarf tied around her head and gold hoop earrings big enough for a hamster to jump through. She went around talking in this gypsy accent—she's pretty good at accents (you should hear her Australian; in my mind one of the hardest)—reading people's palms and predicting futures.

"What about me?" I said, pressing her up against the kitchen wall as she opened a bag of candy.

"Dick, you're going to make me spill this," she said, and just as she kissed me a stream of candy corn pelted the floor.

"Geez, you're good," I said, kissing her back. "Tell me more."

Darcy was dressed in a tuxedo my mother, arthritic fingers and all, had fashioned out of an old black suit of mine. Her hair was stuffed up into a top hat and she had penciled a mustache and sideburns on her face. Our emcee.

Lin wore a gopher suit—from her role as the Minnesota state mascot in a 4-H presentation a couple years ago. She had cut the feet off the costume to give her more leg room and wore his rubber half mask—big cheeks and buckteeth. She was cute, in sort of a grotesque way. Her boyfriend Kyle was unable to break away from their teenaged fashion and wore a black suit and shirt, but at least he lightened things up with a white tie.

"Here, waiter," I said, handing him a tray of rumaki. "Pass these around."

"I'm not a waiter," protested Kyle, "I'm the Shadow."

"Pass 'em out anyway, would you please?"

Bunny Vold cut in on Devera and me while we were dancing to some Johnny Mathis.

"Aren't you bewitching?" I said, taking her green hand.

"Shut up, Dick, I hate these things. I've got no imagination when it comes to costumes."

"Costumes," I said, looking at her peaked black hat and long black dress. "You're in a costume?"

Bunny Vold laughed her ho-ho-ho Santa Claus laugh.

"Yeah, and I'm sure this is how I look to a lot of people. Come to think of it, though, it's more often 'bitch' than it is 'witch.' "

I nodded. "True. So next year come as a cocker spaniel."

"Pit bull's more my speed." She growled, and Mac Connors, unable to be away from his new love for longer than half a song, cut in.

"Sorry, Dick," he said, "but I'm under her spell."

BiDi was dressed as a princess and her high-waisted costume perfectly accommodated her pregnant belly. God, she was lovely—I mean she always has been but I'm a sucker for pregnant women, with their flushed full faces and bright eyes and, of course, their nice ripe breasts.

Sergio was a prince, with a robe trimmed with ermine (cotton batting with black construction paper) and carrying a scepter no less. He held it in front of me like a barrier.

"Peasant—I command you to fetch a drink for my fair princess!"

"I'm a pirate, not a peasant," I said, unsheathing my own plastic sword. "Now, en garde."

We thrust and parried for a while, what the hell. Party entertainment, you know how it goes.

"All right, break it up, boys," said Devera, pulling me aside. "Dick, we're out of Scotch."

"You're kidding me," I said. "Who's the lush?"

"No one. I just forgot to get some. We're also running low on beer."

"I'm gone, I'm gone."

I hate a party that skimps on the libations (that was the last time I'd let Dev be in charge of the liquor order) and it would only take me fifteen minutes to get to Norse Man Liquors and back.

It was a crisp cool night and the air smelled of rotting leaves and lit jack-o'-lanterns that lined the steps and driveways on Lake Road. It was perfect Halloween weather and I wished I'd brought a carton of eggs to lob at cars and houses, or a bar of soap to make my mark on store windows.

Whatever happened to those good old pranks? Smearing lard on doorknobs, TP-ing a house? Kids today seem as if they can't be bothered—or if they are bothered, their fun goes beyond prankishness and into violence. Too much crap on TV is my guess—you watch, I'll bet in thirty years there'll be so many restrictions on television programming you won't believe it. Or maybe they'll ban TV all together.

I pushed down the accelerator—put me in a car at night with just the dashboard lights for company and I'm Mr. Philosophy.

Noreen Norquist was in the liquor store buying a case of expensive Dutch beer.

"You sure are partying hard tonight, aren't you?" I said, sidling up to her at the cash register.

"Well, Mr. Earp, it is a holiday," she said, counting out her money.

"Does Wyatt Earp wear a ruffled shirt?" I asked. "I'm a pirate."

"Oh," said Noreen. "Sorry."

I invited her on to Your Oasis, but she said she and Fred and Emil were involved in a high-stakes poker tourney, and besides, she liked being home for the trick-or-treaters.

I watched her go, thinking what a nice woman she was, but man, what a big ass. Really, it was like she had a couch cushion rammed in her pants.

I shot the breeze for a little while with the kid from State working the register. Dad Evan always hires from the college and gets burned by at least one of them a year, but come on, the temptation to lift a keg or two for a frat party must be pretty great. Another college kid carried the booze out to the car—Dad Evan believes in service, that's for sure.

I was lighting a cigarette out in the parking lot, enjoying the sense of déjà vu—how many times have I lit up in a parking lot!—when a guy wearing a cape and tights and a weird hat slammed the passenger door of a crappy little Toyota and staggered to the store. A woman wearing Indian war paint stuck her head out of the driver's side and shouted, "Don't forget the cigs!"

The guy stumbled past, but then he stopped and back-pedaled a couple steps until he stood directly in front of me.

"Let me guess," he said, his words overly precise. "Errol Flynn in *The Swashbuckler*."

"Nope," I said. "Just a generic pirate." I dropped my cigarette butt and crushed it with my foot. "And you? Spider-Man?"

The guy pulled himself up as if I had offended him. "My good man, I am Lord Byron." He struck a pose, holding his hand up and focusing his bloodshot eyes on a point past my shoulder. " 'Who loves, raves, 'tis youth's frenzy, but the cure is bitterer still, as charm by charm—' "

"Well, have a good one." I turned to walk away from this bore and was almost to my car when he grabbed my arm. I thought, oh geez, he's going to finish the damn poem whether I want to hear it or not.

"You're not *The Swashbuckler*."

"I never said I was."

"No, no, I know who you're dressed as." He started snickering; a drunk, ugly laugh. "You're the—you're the Cuck-olded Husband!"

"What's that supposed to mean?" I said to this jerk with the stupid costume and the scraggly beard.

"Yoo-hoo," yelled the woman in the car. "What about my cigarettes?"

"Yoo-hoo yourself," snarled the guy. He swayed a little and pushed my chest with his fingers. "Ask your wife, my good man. Devera will explain it all to you."

My blood turned cold at the mention of my wife's name—how did this creep know my wife's name—*who* was this creep who knew my wife's name?

The guy staggered off and I thought about going after him and then beating the shit out of him, but I just stood there, watching him until he had gone into the store. I gunned the Fleetwood out of the parking lot, my heart racing, trying to keep up with my brain. I was almost home when I slapped the steering wheel, realizing who it was I had been talking to.

Gerhart Something or other. Devera's Ancient Rome pro-fessor from last term. But what the hell did he mean I was a cuckolded husband? My mouth felt like it had been wiped free of all spit and all the liquid transferred to the palms of my hands—did he mean him and . . . Dev?

I shook my head at the suggestion—it was ridiculous. Dev and that asshole with the gray teeth? No way. Impossible.

The party was in full swing when I got back—Evan and Helen were there (dressed as Raggedy Ann and Andy—pretty pathetic costumes for a couple in their sixties, if you ask me); the Coles were there, the Arsgaards, the Pauleys, and the Opdahls. Larry O'Herne was sawing off a piece of the huge submarine sandwich we'd laid out and was feeding pieces of it to his nurse girlfriend, who—lots of imagination there—was dressed like a nurse.

I smelled Devera beside me before I saw her—even under perfume or hairspray, that woman cannot hide her essential scent from me.

"So where's the Scotch, hon? And weren't you going to get some beer, too?"

"It's in the car. I guess I forgot it in the car."

"Well, you don't have to yell at me."

I concentrated on watching Darcy and Lin leading a conga line out on the dance floor.

"Dick," said Devera. Standing behind me, she clasped her arms around me like a belt. "What's the matter?"

My hand pushed through hers, breaking her grip.

"Dick—"

"My sword was digging into me."

Devera moved and stood in front of me.

"Dick, look at me. What's the matter with you?"

I could almost hear the creak in my neck as I forced myself to look at her. My beautiful, traitorous gypsy.

"Dick . . . what?" She pulled me out of the room, nodding at the party guests we passed. She steered me toward the utility room but there was a dinosaur kissing Frankenstein by the washer, so taking a quick turn, Devera pulled me into the sauna and onto the cedar bench.

I wiped my eyes with the ruffled cuff of my stupid pirate shirt.

"Dick," she said, her voice soft as a new mother's. "*What* is the matter?"

"I saw your old professor at the liquor store," I said, my voice slow and dull.

"You saw—" The catch in her voice told me everything I needed to know.

"Yeah. The Lusty-Minded Professor. Only he was dressed as Lord Byron, the asshole. But he seemed to see more in my costume than I intended. He thought I was dressed as—and this is a direct quote, Dev—as 'The Cuckolded Husband.' "

Devera spoke in slow motion. "Oh, my God."

Pain poured through the top of my head, through my neck, and into my chest. "How could you, Dev? How could you . . . cuckold me?"

A quick laugh, like a bark, shot out of Devera's mouth and then she covered her face with her hands.

"Oh, God, Dick," she said, crying, "I am so sorry. It didn't mean anything—nothing at all—I can't stand Gerhart Ludwig and I have no idea why I went to bed with him—we only did a few times. I never did with anyone else, Dick, I guess I was just looking for a change—this past summer I just thought everyone was either ganging up on me or taking me for granted and then you know I was having those panic attacks, and I don't know, my life seemed so scary . . . so in need of change. Oh, Dick, I am so sorry, I wish it never happened, please forgive me."

She had no air left and took a deep ragged breath and then sobbed all the harder.

Her crying seemed to cancel out my need to and I sat there, my back against the wood planks, staring past her shaking shoulders, at the girls' swimsuits dangling by their straps on the door hook.

What do you do when your world turns out to be something totally different than you thought it was? Dev's and my marriage was like a top-of-the-line Brougham, pure smooth running quality, and then BOOM—all of a sudden it was all smashed up, spewing hot water from its punctured radiator, its fenders crumpled and hanging on to the frame by sheer aluminum threads. And all the time I was just cruising, staying in my lane, obeying all the traffic lights.

I'm sure I would have sat in that sauna all night, oblivious to everything, but Darcy ferreted me out.

"Dad! We've been looking all over the place for you—the show's about to start and—hey, what's going on in here?" She must have noticed we weren't exactly throwing our own private party.

"We were having a little quiet time, that's all," said Dev. Her voice was light and easy, as if that was exactly what we had been doing.

Normally Darcy wouldn't have taken such a crock-of-shit answer, but she didn't have time to grill us—"the show must go on," is a credo she's taken to heart.

I blinked when we got back to the party room—it was like stepping back onto the midway after being stuck in the Haunted House.

"Happy Halloween, all you ghouls and ghosties," said Darcy, scampering up the stage, "and thanks for spending

Halloween at Your Oasis—too cheap to stay at home and pass out candy, huh?"

My daughter, the lounge comedian.

"We've got a really big shoe for you tonight," she said, dipping into her Ed Sullivan. "So without further ado, let's bring up the Big Cheese, the Music Man who *rewrites* the songs, my father, Dick Lindstrom!"

Apparently Darcy hadn't taken notice of the violence of my head shaking and there was nothing I could do but let the wave of applause push me up on stage. I stepped behind the keyboard and launched into "My Girl," the old Temptations classic, only my lyrics were adjusted to match the title "My Boil."

I hammed up the choreography and the audience couldn't get enough of my dips and attempts at moonwalking, and when they begged for an encore, staying in the Temptations mode, I sang a soulful "Just My Indigestion."

> *"Dear Lord, hear my plea,*
> *Don't let another belch escape*
> *From out of me,*
> *Or I would surely die. . . ."*

To my loyal fans at Your Oasis, I was Mr. Showbiz and I wanted to shout into the microphone, "See? See, Devera?" but when I dared look at where she had been standing, she was gone.

Darcy

THE THING IS, it started out to be such a great party. Adults in costumes are always so much more fun than adults in normal clothes; it's like they figure they can cut loose because no one will recognize them. My grandparents came as Raggedy Ann and Raggedy Andy, and my grandpa walked around with stiff arms and legs, like a doll come to life. In a suit and tie you couldn't get him to skip two paces.

After I loaded him up a plate from the buffet table, he told me to be a good girl and get him a gin and tonic. I said, "Don't get so bossy, Andy, or I'll knock the stuffing out of you." He laughed, and boy, I could never say anything like that to him in real life. He's a fun grandpa, but still, we always know we're supposed to be respectful to him.

My grandma Ardis didn't come and that kind of bummed me out because I hate to think of her always alone in that adjustable bed of hers, taking her Advil and playing solitaire. She helped me with my costume—a really cool tux—and I'm sure she could have whipped up something great for herself, but she told me no, her party days were over, and besides, she never much cared for all the drinking.

It's not that my parents host a shindig for Lushes, Inc., but there is plenty of whatever joy juice gets you in that gala mood, if you need joy juice to get you there in the first place (which personally I can't ever see myself needing). I just think that Grandma has spent too much time inside her own house so that she's sort of afraid to leave it. Which makes me feel bad, but if a leopard can't change its spots, how are you supposed to?

I was really excited about emceeing the show—I'm definitely either going to be a comedian/actor or an anthropologist. Franny can't believe that I like to get on stage—especially with no set lines—and try to make people laugh. Like it—I love it! I feel like I can do anything up there, sort of all-powerful. When Dad's little spotlight hits me, I feel, uh-huh, this is where I'm supposed to be. Franny says she'd be so scared she'd faint and I asked her what the difference was shooting a puck in front of an audience or telling a joke?

"The difference is that it's not just me out there," she said. "Someone passes me the puck or I'll pass it to someone—I'm part of a team."

And that *is* the difference, I guess, because I like that it's just me up there. I don't have to share my lines with anyone and I get all the credit. I get all the silence, too, if a joke bombs, but that hasn't happened yet, and if it does, I'll just figure it's the audience's fault and not mine. Hey, I realize we're talking *ego* here, but it's like cake frosting—I'd rather have a little too much than not enough 'cause you can always scrape some off.

I wish it was something you could loan out—I'd love to give Franny some of my extra ego. Boy, I never knew how much she really needed it.

That piece of crust Arsgaard has not once talked to Franny about the night she got beat up and yet she's still hopeful, she still thinks maybe things'll be like they used to and he'll stop by her locker and ask her if she thinks Lemieux will ever outscore Gretsky, or do you think Dallas will ever be as good as when they were the North Stars? It's pathetic if you ask me; if I were her I'd hope he'd stop by my locker just so I could shove him in and lock it with a lock no one knew the combination to. Just last weekend we were walking down Main Street after loading up on chocolate at Cakes By Sergio and who should be coming the other way but Ben Opdahl and the Butthead himself.

I really thought I was going to have to try to remember all

that emergency CPR stuff we took in 4-H—little speckles of sweat popped out above Franny's lip and she was all red in the face and breathing like she had about one eighth of a lung.

"Be cool, Franny," I said, thinking, Is it four compressions and fifteen breaths or the other way around? "Just relax."

Franny had this wild look in her eye, but she nodded and her throat moved as if she had swallowed a tennis ball.

"Hey, Franny," said Ben as they got near us, "first practice's less than two weeks away."

Franny nodded her head so hard I thought I heard her teeth rattle.

"Hope I can play more offense this year," he said.

Franny kept the head bob going.

Ben looked at me for the first time. "Nice hat, Lindstrom."

I was wearing an old hat—the kind fur trappers used to wear—that I'd found in the secondhand store by Uncle's Lake.

"Thanks," I said, assuming he was complimenting me rather than insulting me.

"All right," said Ben, after we all stood around not saying anything. "See you guys later."

Little Chicken Turdface hadn't said one single thing. Just stared at the ground the whole time, his ugly little coward's face getting almost as red as Franny's.

We walked a ways and then I said, "Franny LaFave, if I ever see you act like that again I'm going to kick your gluteus maximus."

Franny burst out crying.

"Okay, okay," I said, "So I won't kick it."

"He hates me!" Franny wailed. "He hates me and I don't blame him!"

I steered Franny across the street to the little park by the falls. My mother could have thought of something good to say—something that consoled Franny as well as sort of slapped some sense into her—but I was not my mother, and for once, I was speechless. Really, the way her face looked and the sound of her voice, well, she would have knocked the words out of Barbara Walters herself. So I just sat her down on the park bench and really, I think I was shaking as bad as she was.

"I'm not going to play hockey this year," Franny finally said after she'd lost about a quart and a half of fluids through her tear ducts and nostrils.

"What are you talking about? Of course you are." I kicked the cement leg of the park bench with my heel. "If you let one slime-blooded creep keep you from doing the thing you love, well then, Franny, you're a real sad sack, sadder than I could ever believe."

Franny shrugged, like so what?

I decided to try something different. "If you don't play— and screw up White Falls' chances at any kind of season— then I'll just consider it my civic duty to tell everyone the real reason you don't want to play. I'll tell them the truth about what happened that night."

Franny didn't have to tell me I would cease to exist for her if I did, 'cause her face said it for her.

BUT THAT NIGHT, at the party, Franny was having as much fun as anyone else was. Her costume was letting her throw away some of her shyness—she was dressed as a loon, from this dumb *Hail to Thee, Minnesota* pageant she and Lin had been in—and she was walking around really funny, sticking out her butt and her beak and making these weird loon calls. Plus Lin was being nice to her—I mean she actually asked her to help start up this dance line. For Lin to even bother to ask you what time it is is a big deal. I had been noticing a little of Lin's old niceness coming back—not often, but flashes here and there that reminded you she did have a personality once upon a time and maybe it wasn't squashed permanently under all her teenage yuckiness.

It was like there was a mini Mardi Gras going on in our basement—people in costumes dancing, drinking, singing, and eating—and when we were all doing the hokey-pokey I got the hiccups from laughing so hard.

But then the fun took a little detour when I found my

mom and dad sitting in the sauna of all places. When I opened the door they both tried to rearrange their faces into normal-looking ones but there was that second or two when I saw how they had been looking, and it scared me. I knew they had been talking about something really heavy but I tried to convince myself it was nothing more than planning a surprise Christmas vacation to Borneo or Baja or something. Yeah, right.

Well, as they say, the show must go on, and even though I was feeling pretty weird about my parents—I mean except for when I thought my mom might be going crazy, normally they're not the kind you worry about—I knew there were people who wanted to be entertained, so I jumped on that stage like the trouper I am and got things cooking.

Dad sang some funny songs and Clayton Hagstrom, Jr., did some pretty cool birdcalls and Bunny and Mac kept to the Halloween theme and sang songs like "It's Witchcraft" and "Bewitched, Bothered, and Bewildered."

I did a couple of impressions (my Eartha Kitt getting huge applause from those who knew who Eartha Kitt was) and then exited, stage left, just as Lin and Kyle were running up the stairs.

"Where are you guys going?" I asked.

"To the fire station," said Lin. "We're gonna catch the rest of the Halloween party there."

Every year the fire department throws a party at the old firehouse for kids who are too old to go trick-or-treating or get bored at their parents' parties. People come from the whole county, so it really rocks.

"Oooh, can Franny and I come?"

"My sister's picking us up," said Kyle. "She's got a full car."

Lin looked up at me, and believe it or not, something close to concern came into her eyes. "She really does, Darcy. She's picking up Heather and Megan and everyone who lives around the lake. Why don't you ask Dad? Maybe he'll take you guys over there."

It took me a while to find Dad. He was standing out on the

deck, staring out at the black lake. I was kind of afraid to intrude upon him—you know, when someone's having some deep thoughts you don't want to interrupt him by asking if he wants to come to a weenie roast or something. But anyway, when I asked him, he seemed to think that was the best idea he'd heard in a long time.

"Sure, why not? I could go for a little drive."

I tracked Franny down—she was picking the onions out of Bunny Vold's hoagie (Bunny couldn't do it herself with her green rubber witch gloves)—and then Sergio, who had just lost a game of darts to Violet Johannson, said could he go along, and everything just sort of snowballed. And I mean snowballed, because it was the start of the avalanche, the rumbling had already begun, and the chunks of snow were about to break off the cliff ledges, but how were we supposed to know?

SERGIO

IT WAS NOT all my fault but about seventy-five percent, which is pretty bad. Dick has tried to take the blame, saying, "You're not the one who put the pedal to the metal, Sergio," and while that is true, I *was* the voice screaming in his ear to go faster, Dick, go faster.

The girls had run ahead of us to the car and I took a deep breath, thinking how if there were an aftershave that could get the smell of a autumn night by a lake just right, then it would be a big hit! I was not given much time to enjoy nature when my friend Dick grabbed my arm and I felt the way field mice must when they are grabbed up in the talons of big hungry hawks.

"Ow," I said, trying to pull away. "Do you mind, Dick?"

"Sergio," he said, pulling me closer, and again with such a grip I grimaced out loud again. "Sergio, Devera's having an affair."

"Devera's having an affair?" It was a reflex of surprise that made me repeat the words. "What do you mean?"

"I met her lover in the parking lot." Dick's voice cracked like a choirboy's who shouldn't try to sing tenor anymore. "In the fucking Norse Man Liquors lot! He's one of her professors!"

I was shocked, to tell you the truth. There are some marriages that seem immunized against the big diseases of unfaithfulness or betrayal and Dick and Devera's was, of course, one of them. What could Devera be thinking about?

This was a time when my friend needed my counsel—or at least an arm around his shoulder—but by now the girls were in the car, blaring the horn at us to hurry up! Hurry up!

Dick kicked at a soccer ball that was sitting on the front lawn and it flew down the small hill that leads to the lake.

"Nice shot," I said, even though I knew this was not the time for jokes but feeling a need to say something. I don't think he heard me anyway. He was racing to the car, his bright red pirate pants making a sound like someone rubbing their hands together.

The girls were humming with excitement in the backseat.

"Of course we won't dance with just anyone," Darcy was saying. "Only the ones who ask us!"

Francesca thought this was the funniest thing ever said and she tipped back her head to laugh, her loon beak pointing at the ceiling.

But Dick was not having as good a time. His vise grip was now on the steering wheel and he stared straight ahead like a student driver testing for his driver's license.

"Dad, you could just drop us off and we could find a ride home with somebody. I mean there's bound to be lots of kids there."

Dick did not respond to Darcy and for a moment I thought he hadn't heard her, but then he said, "Fat chance, Darcy. Fat chance," so loud that Darcy asked him if he thought she had a hearing problem or something.

"No, I do not," said Dick, and his voice was not his usual friendly one. "But you're not going home with anyone but me and Sergio. We'll wait in the car for you."

"We will?" This was a surprise to me. "What about our party?"

"It's nine-fifty," said Dick, pointing at the dashboard clock. "Darcy and Franny can stay until ten-thirty."

"Dad, that'll only give us a half hour!"

"You're lucky we're taking you at all!"

In the silence of the girls' pout, Dick turned on the radio. The song "Monster Mash" was playing and we drove along Lake Road, passing lit jack-o'-lanterns who smiled their leering smiles at us. White sheets hung from the Johannsons' big oak tree and the slight wind that was blowing pushed them sideways, so they looked more like ghosts than I cared for. The moon, too, was playing its part on this Halloween night—it wasn't full but almost—and strings of wispy clouds moved across it like smoke.

Did I have a premonition about what was to happen? No, I am attuned to many things, but like my mother, I am not attuned to things of a psychic nature. My uneasiness came from my worry about my friend. I knew Dick was all of a sudden in a strange place he had never thought he would visit, and frankly, I did not know what sort of directions to give him.

"Dad," said Darcy, "it's the first time Franny and I have ever gone to the firehouse party. Can't we stay until at least eleven?"

Dick braked so hard that we slid a little on the road that was covered with wet leaves.

"Dad!" protested Darcy.

I knew Franny had to be wondering what was going on with this man normally so mild-mannered. I stuck my hand between the seat and the passenger door. Finding it, Franny squeezed it.

"I would like one thing," said Dick, straightening the car out. "I would like a little peace and quiet while I'm driving, okay?"

"Well, geez, Dad," said Darcy.

Dick didn't exactly want peace and quiet because he turned the radio up. It was Elvis singing "Heartbreak Hotel" and I could just hear BiDi laughing and saying, "Thank you!" Anytime she comes across an Elvis song on the radio, she thinks it's her own special present.

Maybe Elvis was a tonic for Dick, too; by the time we got to town his jaw wasn't quite so clamped and his knuckles weren't white from the strain of his grip.

"Wow," said Darcy, who must have figured it was safe to break the code of silence, "look at all the kids!"

There were lots of kids, too, spilling out of the firehouse

and sitting on the hoods of cars parked along the street. There was a Darth Vader and a Little Bo-Peep (or maybe Goldilocks) but most of the kids didn't have costumes on, being at that funny age when they don't know what to do with Halloween anymore.

We drove down First Street, looking for a parking spot, and were just about to take a left on Main when an old Impala screeched to a stop, missing us by just inches.

"What an idiot," mumbled Dick, and as he shifted the car into reverse to give the other car room to pass, the passenger in the Impala opened his door and yelled, "Get the fuck out of our way!"

"I *am* out of your way, you little punk!" Dick shouted back, jerking his door open, but he was stopped from getting out of the car by Darcy's words.

"Oh, my God," she said, and I looked back at her to see the fright in her voice was on her face, too. "Oh, my God, Dad, those are the guys who beat Franny up!"

So much happened in that next moment. Francesca yelled "Darcy!" and Dick said, "What?" and a black cloud of anger started filling up my chest, taking my breath away.

"It's them!" said Darcy. "Guy Hammond and Ricky Walsh!"

"But that's not a silver van," I said, so stupid, even as the rage got bigger and bigger.

Everything felt slow motion. I felt myself opening my car door, but then I felt the tug of Dick's hand, pulling me back. Dick told me later that all the time I was doing this I was "bellowing"—he said I sounded like a wounded animal.

The Impala, its passengers probably realizing who was in our car, jerked back and then going from zero to forty mph, squealed around the corner.

"Go after them, Dick!" I yelled. "Go after them!"

I thought later how lucky we were that they took Third Street out of town; there was no traffic at all, so other drivers were spared our reckless speeding.

They turned left on the new two-lane highway, going sixty according to what Dick's speedometer read.

"Why aren't they going faster?" I asked, thinking if I were being chased, I would step on it.

"That old Imp probably can't get any faster," said Dick, his voice as calm as a pilot's. "Look at all that exhaust."

I must admit, the chase at this time was exciting. A chase always is, even if it's not the Indy 500. It helped me to be involved in the chase, too, to tell Dick what he obviously could see himself—"There they are!"—because my mind was not yet ready to think about the big things I had just learned: that Francesca had lied about a stranger beating her up, and why?

We followed them a few miles and then they made a wobbly turn toward Veil Lake.

"Man, if they're stopped, it's going to be DWI time," said Dick. "I'll bet they're bombed out of their minds."

At least once a year there is something in the paper about plans to pave the road around Veil Lake, but it is never done, the tourists like the "rusticness" of gravel and tourists are the bosses of Veil Lake, where only twenty-five percent of the homes are occupied year-round. It is much bigger than Flame Lake but not half so pretty.

The road started climbing. Only for about one third of the way is it level with the lake and then the road starts climbing up an incline. It is above the lake by about two hundred feet and people must build long stairways to get up and down to their cabins.

We never once caught up to them enough to bump their fender or whatever it is we would have done. ("What would we have done?" Dick asked me later. "I don't know," I answered, and I didn't. All I knew was that we had to catch them.)

We were quiet now that we were off the freeway. It was so dark and it seemed we needed all our concentration just to keep the Impala in sight. Their backlights were getting father away and I thought we were losing them when something happened that made me doubt my vision. White lights instead of red were suddenly facing us, and getting bigger.

"Dad, they're coming after us!" screamed Darcy.

"Are they crazy?" hollered Dick.

The charge of excitement that smelled of metal was wiped away by a different smell, sort of like that of a small dead animal. The smell of fear, I guess.

I can't remember if the big Cadillac was still moving at that time or had braked, I was hypnotized by those lights coming at us, getting bigger and bigger, and just as I thought they would swallow us up, Dick swerved the car all the way to the right and everyone's voices were choked off by one big gasp and then BOOM, the Impala smashed into the side of the car and Darcy was thrown over to Francesca. I heard glass break and Dick shouting and then a gunning of an engine and a squeal of metal ripping away from other metal and then the flooring of an engine and then the strangest noise of all, a big whoosh like an airplane flying low, only it wasn't an airplane, it was that Impala, and I knew they were going over that cliff. Seconds later we heard that terrible sound of a great weight smacking against the ground. After that I heard nothing else but the noises in our own car. Dick had somehow gotten in the backseat and was holding Darcy. He was whining like a hurt dog.

Francesca's loon beak was crumpled and hung around her neck from its string. She had moved to the corner where Darcy had been sitting and her face was as milky white as the moon.

"Francesca, are you all right?"

She looked at me and nodded, but her eyes were like those children in war zones you see in *Life* magazine.

"Dick, I'm going to get help!" I said, sliding over to the driver's seat. I started up the engine I didn't even know Dick had the sense to turn off, but when I put it in drive and pressed on the accelerator, it only groaned in a funny way. It felt like it was trying to move but couldn't, the way a toddler must feel when he wants to run away but his mother is holding him by the back of his shirt.

"Dick, I'm going to get help at someone's house!" I punched the button of the glove compartment in, and sure enough, there was the flashlight I had hoped to find there.

Dick is always prepared. When I opened the front door, Francesca said, "I'm coming, too!" and after trying to open the back passenger door, she scrambled over the front seat.

Neither Francesca or I had a jacket over our costumes but I felt that I was burning up, and when I asked Francesca if she was cold she shook her head and said, "Hot." Later I learned it had dropped below freezing that night.

We held hands, the stream of light from the flashlight cutting through the dark like a sword. We started running at the same time. I think we would have run straight down the hill that leads to the lake but it was too steep and the night was too dark to risk it. We ran along the road until the flashlight found us a rickety wooden staircase leading down to the lake.

I said a silent prayer of relief, but it must have been out loud because Francesca said a very serious, "Amen." We practically tripped down the stairs leading to the house that was lit up and where voices were coming from.

"Oh, my gosh, is that you, Sergio?" said someone standing on the deck and holding a flashlight which was shining right into my face.

"Yes!" I said, turning off my flashlight and wondering who I was speaking to. "There's been an accident! Dick Lindstrom and his daughter are up on the road, in the car!"

"Come in," said the person, taking my arm, and as soon as we stepped into the light I could see it was Madge Peasley, who came into the shop every month to pick up a caramel fudge cake for her book club.

"Wes and Bill are out there now," said Madge, nodding vaguely. "We heard the crash and didn't know what was going on. It was the scariest thing I've ever heard."

"I've got to call for help," I said, going toward the telephone.

"I already did," said Madge. "Someone should be here in a couple minutes." She looked at Francesca and me with her head cocked. "I'm going to get a towel for that cut, Sergio. You two sit right down."

I looked down and saw that the trim of my king's robe was bloody and suddenly I realized there was a spot on my head that was throbbing and felt open, like it was getting air. I touched it, and when I looked at my fingers they were covered in blood.

I pressed the towel Madge gave me to my forehead.

"You say Dick Lindstrom and his daughter are up on the road?" asked Madge, and when I nodded she asked, "Do you know who's down at the bottom?"

"Kids," I said. "Two kids from . . ." I couldn't think.

"From Elgin High," whispered Francesca. Madge's son Bill came running in, calling for blankets, and then I heard the sound of sirens and I thought that was just about the right time to sit back and close my eyes.

DEVERA

BIDI AND I were sitting at the kitchen table, tossing Halloween popcorn (dyed black and orange in the kernel) into the air and trying to catch it in our mouths. We were placing wagers on each try and little towers of nickels rose in front of BiDi. She hadn't missed a single toss, even when she did fancy things like throw the kernel from behind her back. It was maddening.

"Do you practice or something?" I asked as she gulped another kernel out of the air.

BiDi smirked at me and with one finger dragged a nickel away from the diminishing center pile over to hers.

"The Popcorn Queen wins again," she said.

I had told BiDi about Dick meeting Herr Professor and we were both acting giddy and silly—like shoplifting kids who are putting on a brave front in the store's holding room before their parents show up to pick them up.

"You're like a trick dog," I said, laughing.

I knew it was in the calm before a very big storm, so I was playing it up for all it was worth.

Connie Cole emerged from the basement steps. "Devera, we've got to go," she said, her voice overly apologetic. "It's time for Sarah's feeding."

"What's a matter?" asked BiDi. "Doesn't your baby-sitter know how to heat a bottle?"

Connie smiled what my mother called a sour-pickle smile. "It's a bonding thing, BiDi," she said. "Sarah likes her mommy to hold her when she eats."

"And how do you rate?" BiDi asked Jack Cole, who stood in a clown suit, picking at some bean dip on the counter.

"I feed her—" said Jack, but he was interrupted by BiDi, who got up from the table and ran toward him, cupping her hands.

"Oh, God, I feel sick!" she said, and then pretended to throw up all over his big clown shoes.

"Good humor," said Connie, tossing back her platinum wig. (She had obviously come as Marilyn Monroe, but BiDi had made a point of calling her Myra Breckenridge all evening.)

"You still owe me for my other shoes," Jack said, laughing, but Connie, who I think holds the twisted perception that BiDi has a crush on her husband, pulled him out the back door, muttering her thanks for a good party.

About two thirds of the guests had left shortly after Dick and Sergio took the girls to the firehouse. It's not that they felt the party was over if Dick wasn't there; the majority of our guests are not what you'd call party animals, always choosing to leave a little after ten. I can't imagine that any of them usher in midnight even on New Year's Eve. The stalwarts who remained downstairs were being treated to a request concert by Mac and Bunny, a concert I denied myself the pleasure of listening to because I felt I didn't deserve to. I knew I'd be paying a self-enforced penance for a long time because of my affair (or because of Dick's discovery of my affair) and I thought I might as well start right away.

So there I was losing money to a woman who had a caninelike ability to catch a thrown object in her mouth, when the phone rang and once again I shared with BiDi the terrible experience of getting the news that one of our daughters was in the hospital. But this time was far worse; this time it was my daughter.

If the grim reaper has a voice, it would sound like Dick's did on the phone.

"Devera," he said, "there's been an accident. You've got to come to the hospital now."

It was as if a match had been tossed inside me, igniting a furnace blast of fear. "Who's hurt?"

"Darcy."

"Oh, God," feeling the words catch in my throat, feeling I couldn't catch my breath. I hung up the phone and BiDi was already at the back closet, pulling coats down off their hangers.

BiDi drove to the hospital and she said I kept muttering, "Lightning does strike twice, lightning does strike twice," but I think she made that up because the only memory I have of that drive is thinking I'd never been more cold in my life.

THERE WAS THAT awful emergency-room bustle going on when we got there and I wanted nothing more than the nurses to go behind their desk and file their fingernails while making personal phone calls, wanted the doctors to be reading the paper in the vending-machine area that served as a cafeteria, wanted it to be a typically slow night in the White Falls Hospital.

"Oh, God, BiDi, I'm going to pass out."

"No, you're not, Devera," said BiDi, holding me by the arm. "But if you do, I'll catch you."

I looked around wildly, but I could make no familiar face out in the motion of people running around.

"There's Dick," said BiDi finally, steering me toward the admitting desk, which, oddly, was vacant.

My knees did turn to water then and I began to sink, but BiDi, true to her word, clutched my arm tighter, and pulled me up.

Dick, looking like a pirate who had just lost a high-seas battle, came to me wordlessly, enveloping me in his big arms.

His hug seemed to be consoling me for too big a thing and I felt hot and breathless with panic. "Where's Darcy?" I said. "Where's my baby? I need to see my baby!"

"They're working on her," said Dick, his mouth pressed against my ear. "She'll be all right, Devera. I know she'll be all right." He gave a little gasp then, like someone had

jumped out at him from behind a corner, and I felt his body
shake. BiDi had disappeared somewhere, so there wasn't any
ballast and we both slid against the wall, crumpling to the
floor in our despair.

Dick tried to tell me what happened, but each time he
started, a new gale of emotion would sweep over him and we
were still against the wall, crying into my gypsy scarf, when I
felt a body sit next to me.

"Devera," said Sergio, "Dick." He paused until we both
looked up. He must have seen a question in my eyes because
he touched a bandage on his forehead and shrugged, sig-
naling me that his was no big wound. "I was able to grab Dr.
Holland as he was rushing between rooms. Darcy will be
fine."

"What hap—" I began.

"All I know is that she will be fine," said Sergio.

Relief gushed through me and I couldn't understand why
Sergio's face and voice were so sad. A sudden sick feeling,
one of the many sick feelings that had struck me within the
last half hour, centered in my stomach.

"Sergio," I said, feeling shame that I had only now thought
to ask this question. "Where's Francesca? Is Franny all
right?"

Sergio made a face like it was the silliest question and yet
the most welcomed one he had ever heard.

"Francesca is fine," he said. "Not a scratch on her. She's
with BiDi and the sheriff in the chapel."

An awful sense of déjà vu washed over me: A daughter
hurt . . . the sheriff . . . the chapel.

"Sergio," I said. "Tell me everything that happened."

IT WAS ALMOST as if people related to central characters illus-
trated the story as Sergio told it. When he was telling about
first coming across Guy Hammond and Ricky Walsh, a
couple I later learned were Ricky Walsh's grandparents came
in, looking so lost and bewildered I wondered how they had
found their way to the hospital at all.

Then Penny Hammond, escorted by a deputy, came rushing in. Her rabbit-fur jacket was half off her shoulders and her hand, cocked at her side, held a cigarette. I recognized her only because we had gone to the St. Francis Autumn Fest in Elgin one year and she had been wearing a name tag as she worked at the pulltabs table.

A minute later I heard the kind of wail I hope to never hear again and I knew immediately her son, Guy, was dead.

"Oh, Dick," I breathed, and we clutched each other's hands as if they were towropes tossed to us in a wild ocean.

The thoughts reeling in my head almost made me dizzy. A boy named Guy Hammond was dead? A boy who with his friend beat up Franny? Why did Franny lie about them? Why would she want to protect them? Why did Dick chase them in the car? Could he be held liable for Guy Hammond's death? The question that kept pushing aside all the other ones finally propelled me upward to find someone who could answer it: how is Darcy?

My timing was good; just as I was about to barrel into the off-limits area, a nurse appeared and told me to follow her to see my daughter.

Sergio disappeared, into the chapel, I think, and Dick and I went into the room where Darcy was. The nurse led us past a curtained area and I saw two pair of feet that I recognized as belonging to the elderly couple.

When the nurse pulled back Darcy's curtain, both Dick and I raced to her bedside, both of us sobbing.

A huge purple egg grew out of the middle of her forehead, above her shut eyes. Her mouth looked distorted, the mouth of a clown who didn't know how to put on her makeup.

"Oh, Darcy," I whispered to my daughter. Why had they told me she was all right? She was not all right; she was hurt and mangled and, as far as I could tell, unconscious.

"Dick, is she sleeping?" I asked.

Dick shrugged his shoulders helplessly, but my question was answered by Dr. Holland, who seemed to have taken form by the end of the bed.

He was Ted Erck's replacement, hired out of Bismarck,

North Dakota. He had a boyish face on a prematurely balding head.

"She must be sleeping," he said. "She had regained consciousness on the way to the hospital and was able to answer the questions we asked her. She had taken her seat belt off during the chase, she said, so she could look through the back window better. She wanted to make sure you knew that she was wearing it most of the night, Mrs. Lindstrom. Unfortunately, not at the time of the crash."

A sob ripped out of me—how many times had I been the seatbelt monitor, how many times had I said, "It only takes a second to have an accident?"

The doctor patted my hand. "She was lucky, though, in that she was wearing her hat down low on her head; we had to cut it to get it over that goose egg. She could have been injured worse if it hadn't been for that hat. You can't really see the way her mouth is swollen up, but she will need extensive orthodontia." The doctor looked down, and I could see the overhead light reflected on the top of his head. "It's the strangest thing," he said, adjusting his stethoscope before looking up again, "six of her upper teeth broke off and we couldn't find any of them. A deputy examined the car from top to bottom and couldn't find a single tooth . . . or piece of tooth. We could have called in someone to reaffix them if we had, but they've disappeared. She may have swallowed some; they may have just fallen out of the car in all the commotion. But there's no skull fracture, no broken bones or internal injuries. She's a lucky little girl."

"Thank you," said Dick and I simultaneously, and the doctor nodded deeply, almost bowing, before slipping through the curtain.

"She had such pretty teeth," whispered Dick, brushing a lock of hair away from her face.

"No, she didn't," I said. "Or at least she didn't think so. Remember how she always said her teeth were too small for her mouth? How she said she was the only person she knew who had baby teeth for permanent ones?"

Dick smiled. "Let's give her the biggest teeth possible. Let's let her pick out huge big choppers. Big Bugs Bunny teeth."

Always mindful of good timing, it was at that moment our darling daughter chose to awaken from her faked sleep, to mutter through swollen lips, "What's up, Doc?"

BɪDɪ

NEEDLESS TO SAY, all hell broke loose. The *Gazette* headlines read ONE ELGIN BOY DEAD, ANOTHER PARALYZED. Dave Garner wrote a big spread on Guy Hammond's hockey career (twice voted MVP by his teammates) in the sports page. *Francesca LaFave did not care to respond when this reporter asked why she hadn't implicated them as her assailants,* he wrote. He didn't add that she didn't care to respond to anyone.

When we took her home from the hospital, Sergio and I sat up with her and she sobbed and sobbed, rubbing her eyes with the heels of her hands until I thought there was a serious chance of her detatching her retinas. When she was drained of tears, she laid her head on what passed for my lap (I can't tell you the last time she did that) and I petted her hair until it crackled with electricity. For one brief moment her mood lifted and that's when the baby kicked and Francesca said, "Ouch."

"Sometimes it's like a soccer match," I said, and we laughed a little but it was only a few syllables of *huh-huh-huh.*

"Franny, honey," I said when she finally stopped crying and a rhythmic hiccup blipped out of her every twenty seconds, "why did you make up that story about the stranger in the silver van?"

Her wail was immediate.

"Okay, okay," I said, patting her back, "it's okay."

That's the closest we got to any kind of answer. When my

legs started to cramp up from the weight of Franny on them, I passed her off to Sergio, who held her nearly an hour. When she finally fell asleep, Sergio eased himself out from underneath her and she whimpered a little when I covered her up with an afghan I had crocheted from a kit.

When Sergio and I went up to bed, he did the oddest thing: he put *Viva Las Vegas* in the VCR.

"I don't want to think of anything right now," he said, watching that glorious Technicolor splash over the screen. "I don't want to see the pictures in my mind or hear the sounds in my head!"

We sat shoulder to shoulder against the headboard, watching Elvis cavort with Ann-Margret, and I thought it was doing the trick (Sergio even laughed during that waiter scene) but then he buried his face in his hands.

"It's all my fault!" he cried. "I kept telling Dick to go! Go faster! Go faster! When I found out these were the boys who beat up Francesca, I wanted to kill them—but I didn't want them to die!"

Sergio turned around then and beat his pillows until I thought the stuffing would fly.

"But why did they go after us, BiDi? Why did they turn their car around and run straight into us?"

"They were drunk, Sergio. Sheriff Buck said there were empty beer cans all over the car—"

"Still," said Sergio, who now clutched the beaten pillow to his chest, "why would they do that? It was more than drunk—it was crazy. And if I hadn't said anything, they'd be alive right now!"

"Who knows, Sergio? If they drank that much, maybe they would have crashed into a median or another car—and besides, how could you not have gone after them after you found out who they were and what they'd done?"

Sergio hung his head. His face was so sad it reminded me of that blue guy Picasso painted; the one my twelfth-grade art teacher lectured on for a whole period.

"You're right—I don't think we could have *not* gone after them—who wouldn't have?—but still, if only we hadn't . . ."

We talked and talked, and when I looked up at the screen and saw that it had turned to fuzz, I was startled. Really, I can't ever remember giving Elvis less than my full attention.

OF COURSE, OUR camp wasn't the only one under siege. Ricky Walsh may or may not walk again, but it looks like there's more weight to the may-not side. And look at Penny Hammond—her only son gone. I heard she went on quite a bender after Guy's funeral, but who could blame her? I did hear that she had a booze problem to begin with—one her son inherited, apparently—but obviously, I don't hold it against anyone if they need something to help them get by. I wrote her a sympathy card but then I tore it up because I couldn't think of any words to sign my name to. She did have my sympathy, but she also had my rage—what was she doing bringing up a thug like Guy Hammond who beat up girls to nearly an inch of their lives? Maybe if she hadn't been logging so many hours at the bar, she could have raised him better. I know that's mean, but I can't help it. If grief is like a slough, then anger is a pair of boots that help you walk through it. At least that's how it worked for me. Francesca was incommunicado, Sergio was full of guilt, and I was casting huge aspersions on a poor alky who had just lost her son.

Things were bad over at the Lindstroms', too. Dick was going through the same guilt Sergio was going through, but I think his was even greater because he was the driver and his daughter had been hurt. Plus he had Devera's infidelity to brood over, and from Devera's phone call, that's exactly what he was doing.

"I didn't wake you, did I?," she asked, calling me at seven-thirty the morning after the accident.

"You know I'm always up." It's true—I'd wake up at six even if I went to bed at five.

"Isn't it terrible?" she said. "I can hardly believe it happened."

"Are you home?"

"No," said Devera. "We stayed overnight at the hospital.

Lin did, too—when she got home from the firehouse party, my dad told her what happened and she had him drive her right over. It's so weird to think that there were parties last night and now . . . this."

"How's Dick holding up?"

"BiDi, he's a wreck. They moved Darcy to a room—she gets out later today, by the way—and we both slept in there—if we slept at all. Sometimes he would start talking to me and then he would get this funny look on his face and say, 'How could you?' and I'd get frantic, thinking Lin or Darcy were awake and would hear that. So he's not just dealing with feeling responsible for this accident, or whatever it was, he's dealing with me cheating on him." Devera's voice gurgled a little bit. "Listen, BiDi, I'm using the phone in the waiting room and I really can't say much more. I'll call you when we get home. You guys can come over then."

We stopped at the Dairy Maid to get a milkshake for Darcy, and when we got to Dev's, Helen answered the door and took the milkshake like we were delivering it at the servants' door.

"Everyone's in the den," she said, making a swooping, lady-of-the-manor gesture with her hand, and I thought, Well, la-di-da.

Darcy acted as if the milkshake was on a par with getting a diamond. I gotta hand it to that kid—she could barely move her mouth but she had me cracking up doing an impression of Boris Karloff without his dentures.

"I look like a hockey player, don't I, Franny?" she asked, opening her mouth enough so that we could see all the spaces in her smile.

We had dragged Franny along because I didn't dare leave her alone in the house the way she was feeling. Lin decided it wouldn't damage her reputation to be nice for a change and took both Franny and Darcy up to her room.

"You want to shoot some pool, Dad Evan?" asked Dick. "Sergio?" They retreated to the basement.

Devera and I wandered into the kitchen. We didn't even have the distraction of cleaning up the party mess because

Helen and a few of the guests had straightened up after we had gone to the hospital.

"Hey," I said, looking at the wiped-down kitchen table. "I wonder what your mother did with all those nickels I won?"

"Probably pocketed them," said Devera. "She assumes any money lying around is hers."

"I heard that," said Helen, coming through the door, and both Dev and I put our hands to our mouths, like little kids going "Uh-oh."

"I put all the change in that dish on the shelf," said Helen. "You can count it if you like."

Devera laughed nervously. "Oh, Mom. We were just joking."

"I don't think a joke at someone's expense is necessarily funny."

Honest, I felt like we had slid back in time about thirty years and we were kids getting yelled at.

Devera threw me a little shrugged-shoulders look and then asked the favorite Minnesota ice breaker, "Coffee, anyone?"

She had barely sat down after pouring everyone a cup when Helen started in on her.

"Look at you, Devera," she said. "You're biting your fingernails again."

I watched as Dev placed the coffeepot down and turned to her mother, a frozen smile on her face.

"I guess I've been under a little stress lately, Mother," and I couldn't help thinking, Ooh, Helen, if only you knew.

"Then you have to find a less damaging way to manage your stress," she said. "After all, a woman's hands tell a lot about her character."

That frozen smile remained on Dev's face even as she sipped her coffee and I thought she was just going to give Helen the silent treatment, when she set her coffee cup, very carefully, on the table. I steeled myself against the onslaught.

"Mother, do me a favor and shut your mouth."

This doesn't sound like much, but believe me, the delivery was deadly.

Helen did shut her mouth and then opened it as if ready to speak, but Devera wouldn't let her.

"All you can tell by a woman's hands is whether or not she

bites her nails or uses harsh dishwashing liquid or likes jewelry. My character comes out in many different ways, but trust me, chewing my nails isn't one of them."

Helen opened and shut her mouth again, but this time words came out, in a furious little whisper.

"How dare you talk to me like that?"

Devera made a noise between a tsk and a laugh. "What does it matter how I talk to you—you never listen anyways. You haven't listened to me since Don died."

Again Helen and I did our parts in the gasping choir.

"Well, I don't care anymore," Devera continued. "It's not my problem. You can tune me out like you always do, but I'm going to talk to you *how* I want to talk, not how you want to hear."

As much as I was horrified by this, I was loving it. It was like seeing Miss America and her first runner-up duke it out at the coronation.

I was prepared for Helen to say something really venomous, or slap Devera or something dramatic, but instead she rubbed her forehead as if she had a headache and said, "I was worried about Darcy, Devera. She could have been killed. Why wasn't she wearing a seat belt, Devera? You know how we've always stressed the importance of wearing seat belts with you, what with Dad being in the car sales business. . . ."

Dev looked at her mother as if she were crazy. "If you must know, Mother," she said, very slowly, as if speaking to someone who just doesn't quite understand, "she was wearing it most of the time, up until they were at Veil Lake. Then she unbuckled it so she could see what was happening out the back window." She looked at me and, shaking her head, rolled her eyes as if she couldn't believe she had to spell all this out to her mother.

With a trembling hand, Helen raised her coffee cup to her lips and I thought she was just fortifying herself with a little caffeine before she really lashed into Dev, but she just sat there, nothing moving but her shaking hand as tears began to roll down her face.

"Mom!" said Devera.

Helen put down the coffee cup, which seemed ready to fly out of her hand. "Oh, Devera, I miss Donald so much! I couldn't bear to think of you having to miss Darcy as much as I miss Don!"

Devera didn't waste a second getting to her mother and they sat there holding one another, each sobbing louder than the other, and it was then I decided I'd better go downstairs and see who was winning the pool game.

DICK

SERGIO AND I offered to pay for Guy Hammond's funeral and his mother accepted the offer. She had called me up the night after the accident, so drunk I could barely understand her, screaming that she was going to sue me for wrongful death. Sheriff Buck had warned me that she might try to get a lawsuit going but he said she had no case; I hadn't done anything illegal.

"Is this blood money?" Sergio asked me as he wrote his check for half the expenses.

"I don't know," I said, not liking the question at all. "We're just trying to help out, that's all."

I had asked Penny Hammond if she wanted us at the funeral. She laughed a crazy laugh and said it would be better all the way around if we stayed the hell out of Dodge. I could have kissed her for that—going to that boy's funeral was the last thing I wanted to do—but I was trying to do the right thing, even though I didn't have a clue as to what the right thing was.

Darcy had told Devera and me the whole story behind Franny's assault—how that chickenshit Arsgaard had run away and how Franny lied to protect him. Pete Arsgaard! A kid I had mentioned to Lin several times, in the context of why can't you go out with a boy like Pete Arsgaard? Hockey player, first baseman, freshman class president—it seemed to me he was an all-around A-class type of guy. I vowed to be nicer to Lin's friend Kyle; maybe I was wrong about him, too, and he wasn't some worthless slacker.

"Why won't Franny tell anybody about Pete?" Devera asked. BiDi and Sergio hadn't been able to get anything out of her.

"I don't know," said Darcy. Her blond bangs covered her shrinking goose egg, so that injury wasn't as obvious as her missing teeth, which made her look like an an old woman with an eerily preserved face. It was unnerving and I looked forward to taking her down to St. Cloud to start her orthodontia work. "It's like she has this code of silence and she thinks it's more important to keep it up than tell the truth. She didn't want to get him in trouble."

"Unbelievable," I said, shaking my head. "All of this could have been avoided if she'd just spoken up at the beginning."

"Dad! Don't blame Franny!"

"Yeah, Dick, I really don't think that helps anything."

"And I really don't need advice from you right now," I said, pointing my finger at Devera. I must have sounded as menacing as I felt because Darcy burst into tears.

"I'm sorry," I said, reaching out to comfort her, but it was Devera's arms she sought shelter in. "I'm just so tense about everything. I know Franny's not responsible for the accident and she wasn't responsible for getting beat up—I'm just trying to make sense of the whole thing, that's all."

"I don't think there's sense to be made," Devera said quietly.

Darcy couldn't see me, so I gave Dev the finger. I knew it was immature, but what the hell. There she was, making sane comments as she rocked our daughter whose messed-up face and teeth I had a big part in creating.

"Darcy," I said, trying to keep my voice soothing even though I wanted to punch out the whole world, "I've got to tell Sergio and BiDi about Pete Arsgaard."

Darcy lifted her head from her mother's shoulders. "I know. I mean, I don't think it's really squealing anyway. It's just telling the truth." She sniffed and wiped her nose. "I just hope Franny won't be mad at me for the rest of her life."

I happened to look at Dev then and I could tell by the way she was looking at me that she was thinking the same thing

Darcy was thinking, only the person she hoped wouldn't carry a lifelong grudge against her was me.

I sort of tossed my head, a gesture that said, "You wish."

THE FIRST SNOW of the season—and it was a big one—fell on the day of the funeral. I was glad that my part had been spelled out; I paid for the funeral but I wasn't supposed to attend it. Other people were confused as to proper etiquette; Tom Emery, the White Falls hockey coach, called me asking me what I thought he should do.

"See, there's a couple guys who want to go and, you know, honor a fellow hockey player, and then there's a couple of guys who think we shouldn't go out of respect for Franny and what those guys did to her."

"What camp are you in, Tom?"

"I really don't know. I guess I'll just tell them that it's not going to be a team choice, but a personal one."

"But how about you?"

A long pause was followed by a big sigh. "I look at it this way, Dick. He was a hell of a hockey player, but chippy as hell. Now, a lot of good hockey players can be chippy, but in my eyes, if you beat up a girl on the side of a road, I've lost my respect for you. So . . . I'm not going."

" 'Preciate it, Tom," I said.

DAVE GARNER FROM the *Gazette* told me later that about a half dozen of our hockey players went and the car they were in slid through an icy intersection and got into a fender bender with a car full of Elgin High cheerleaders. No one was hurt, but it freaked out both carloads. Dave said the church was packed and that Guy Hammond's hockey coach eulogized him, calling him a boy who was "one hundred and ten percent there for his teammates on and off the ice, a high-spirited young man who enjoyed practical jokes and good times."

I wonder if I had been there, would I have stood up to offer a protest? Something like, "Yeah, that sure was funny when he tried to run us off the road. Almost as funny as when he broke a couple of Franny's ribs." Oh, those darn high spirits.

Dave said it was pretty hard to look at six pallbearers all wearing their letter jackets, trying not to slip down the church stairs as they carried the coffin to the hearse.

I told him how hard it was to look at Darcy's face. He apologized in a hurry.

Forgiveness was like an anchor I couldn't pull up. Of course, it wasn't just Guy Hammond I was having a hard time forgiving. I moved into the guest room the night after the accident; when Lin and Darcy asked me what was going on, I told them I thought I got a little whiplash from the accident and didn't sleep well at night, and rather than disturb their mother, I chose the guest room.

I don't know if they believed me or not, but since I couldn't tell them the truth—your mother is an adulterer—I couldn't worry about it.

CLAYTON HAGSTROM SEEMED to be coming to the lot more than ever and I spent hours sitting in new models with him, listening to him rail against the Republicans, who didn't have the "brains of an elk herd" and had sent us into everlasting debt with all that "Star Wars horseshit." Larry O'Herne and I played endless games of cribbage and I'd wander from the lot to the appliance store, down to Sergio's for a slab of cake and some BS, and then on over to the Top Hat for some coffee and more BS. I began to realize how ax murderers could be described by their neighbors as "just a nice, normal guy," because I thought I was smiling and keeping up the usual wisecracks while inside I was Mount St. Helens, ready to erupt.

"Dick," Devera said when she was able to corner me one day (I had the fine art of avoiding her down to a science), "we can't go on like this."

"So what are you suggesting?" I said, trying to hide my fear in a shout. "A divorce?"

Tears welled up in Devera's eyes. "No, that's not what I'm suggesting, Dick. I love you. I want to keep this marriage forever. But maybe we should get counseling."

I shook my head. "I don't need counseling. I'm mad for a legitimate reason. Maybe you should get some counseling to help you figure out why you needed to 'cuckold' me."

THE ONLY BRIGHT spot in that dim season was Thanksgiving. It's always been my favorite holiday—nothing to buy but a lot of food, nothing to do but unpack all the pinecone turkeys and papier-maché cornucopias the kids have made through the years, nothing to do but sit back with the family and enjoy the best meal Devera makes all year and then unbelt my pants and watch football all afternoon. Okay, that's the glib synopsis, and while it is true, the big charge I get from Thanksgiving is this feeling of reverence that's with me the whole day. Really, it's almost like a religious experience—I feel like I'm the luckiest guy in the world, full of thanks for everything from the taste of the gravy to how the weak winter sun still feels warm on my face when I'm sitting in the recliner watching the game. This year there were Darcy's new teeth to be thankful for. They were a little bigger, a little whiter than her old ones, and she couldn't stop smiling. She said she had whittled her career choices down to two but now she had to entertain the idea of being a model, too.

"I know it's a shallow profession," she said, "but I can't deprive the world of this." Her smile took up one half of her face.

We were having dessert and coffee a couple of hours after the big meal—my mother had brought one of her famous sour-cream raisin pies and Dev's mom, Helen, had contributed her lefsa—and I sat at the table looking over my family and feeling like I could bawl into my napkin.

It's at dessert time, too, that our usual tradition unfolds—the girls present whatever craft they've made at school or on their own. As I said, we've saved them all and they're displayed all over the place—on the dining-room table, on the sideboard, on the wall. They've gotten a little more sophisticated as they get older; there're less Indian headdresses and pilgrim stuff and more personal expressions of thanks.

Darcy read the poem she had written.

"Uh-um." She cleared her throat and smiled her toothy smile. " 'Thanks Again,' " she read. "By Darcy Lindstrom."

"Helen," said Dad Evan, "where's that coffee?"

"Grandpa!" whined Darcy.

"Sorry," said Dad Evan, accepting the thermos pot from Helen.

Darcy cleared her throat again.

"Thanks again for laughter—I know it keeps us sane.
Thanks again for seasons—winter snow and spring rain.
Thanks again for ice cream—and while I'm at it, cake.
Thanks again for my family—and living on Flame Lake.
Thanks for all these things—and for those I didn't list.
Well, thanks again for not getting really, really pissed."

"Darcy!" said her grandmothers together.

"Well, I couldn't think of anything else to rhyme with 'list,' " said Darcy, dropping the defensiveness in her voice to laugh along with the rest of us.

"What about 'gist'?" said Helen. "You could have worked 'gist' in there somehow."

"It was wonderful, Darcy," said Devera, and I smiled at my wife because I was in agreement, but the relief in her face reminded me I wasn't letting her off the hook yet and so I looked away.

"Okay," said Lin, placing a small ribboned box on the table. "Dig in."

There was some hesitation over who should open it, so Darcy grabbed the box, but then, showing a suprising amount of restraint, she passed it to me.

I don't know what kindness possessed me, but I passed it to Devera. She actually blushed as she accepted it.

"Well, then, here goes," she said, and after she unwrapped the box and lifted its lid, she let out that universal pleased-parent coo.

"I made them myself," said Lin, "in art class. I got to use the acetylene torch and everything. Mr. Parish usually only lets the seniors use the torch. There's one for each of you."

The box was passed around and we each took out the ring that was labeled with our name. Each was the same style, but unique in its rendering: three narrow brass bands braided together.

"I wanted to get different metals—maybe some silver—but Mr. Parish said silver wasn't in the school budget."

"Thanks, Lin," said Darcy, holding out her hand to admire the ring. "I love it."

There were more thanks as all of us tried on our new jewelry.

"It's symbolic, too," said Lin, playing with the matching ring she wore on her finger. "See, one band is for the Bergdahl side of the family, the other is for the Lindstrom, and the third is for our family: what the Bergdahls and Lindstroms made together."

Well, if that wasn't going to set the emotion meter off, I don't know what would.

"It's beautiful," said Devera, wiping her eyes with her napkin. I couldn't help but notice the blur of whipped cream on her cuff.

"Really special," said Helen.

"Fits me like it was custom-made," said Dad Evan.

My own mother had lifted her watch-on-a-pendant necklace off over her head and asked Darcy to open it.

"My knuckles are too swollen to wear it," she explained, "so I'll just wear it around my neck."

I was too damn touched to say anything. My daughter, whose favorite activity was banning family events, had made these?

Later, in the kitchen, I asked her about them. We were doing the dishes (that was traditional, too; Dev took care of the menu and the girls and I had KP) and we had a nice peaceful cycle going. I washed a plate, Lin dried it and passed it to Darcy, who put it away.

"So what made you make such a wonderful gift?"

"Well, Dad, I'm not a complete slob, you know," she said.

"You're not?" asked Darcy.

"No, I'm not. I mean, I can appreciate a good thing when I see it."

"She must want money, Dad," chirped Darcy.

"Are you saying we're a good thing?" I asked, heartened beyond words.

Lin shrugged. "You'll do."

"Why, Lin," I said, "that's the nicest thing you've ever said to me." I put an exaggerated tremor in my voice for both comic effect and to cover up the real tremor I thought might be there. Really, I felt like Sally Field at that Oscar ceremony where she told the audience they really, really liked her.

"When I showed Kyle, he wanted me to make him one, too."

"And did you?" I asked.

Lin shook her head. "I told him he's not in our family."

Taking a side with the family against her boyfriend! I thought I might have to sit down.

"What did he say to that?" I asked.

She tsked that way teenagers do. "He can be such a baby sometimes."

I didn't pursue the subject and Darcy had the grace to follow my lead. That reverential Thanksgiving feeling was on me big time, I was just so grateful to be washing dishes with my girls, with Lin confiding in me like the old days, and Darcy telling her usual jokes. Man, I would have got down on my knees, but I didn't want to scare them.

SERGIO

FRANCESCA THREATENED TO never speak to me again but I had to think that was idle threatening. There was no way I was not going to speak to this Pete Arsgaard. BiDi thought we should take an ad out in the paper—*Need a Coward? Call Arsgaard*—and even though I could see the satisfaction in something like that, I knew it just was not going to be done. After consultation with Dick and Noreen and my own consciousness, I decided I would speak to Pete alone.

"You're not even going to let his parents know what a loser they have for a son?" she asked.

"BiDi, you know Ned and Teresa," I said. "You know they're good parents, they love their son. How can it help anything if I tell them?"

"I think they should know! If they knew, then they could punish him! If Franny did something like that to someone else, I'd want to know!"

"Would you?"

"Damn straight," she said, crossing her arms over her big belly.

It was not that I wanted to protect Mr. Pete Arsgaard from anything, but really, I thought if I confronted him with his parents, they would be too much of a distraction to me. I wanted Arsgaard *mano a mano*.

I knew he worked at Scheckler's Hardware on Saturdays, so the weekend after the funeral I went to pay him a visit.

I stood by him while he was putting screws into little drawers.

The color went out of his face like a light inside him had been switched off. His eyes darted back and forth, exactly like a cornered animal's, and I knew he was figuring out which aisle to run down.

"Meet me at my shop on your lunch break," I said, keeping my voice low and pleasant so Old Man Scheckler wouldn't think anything was going on. "If you don't meet me, you will be sorry."

"Cake?" I asked him when he came by, flushed and breathing a little hard. "Coffee? Or do you athletes try to stay away from these sort of things?"

He shook his head and shrugged at the same time, and I smiled to myself. What was a little teasing when I just as easily could have tortured him?

"Let's go in the back room, then," I said, and I gestured toward the swinging door. Noreen had just taken a cake out of the oven, and seeing us, she nodded, set the cake on a cooling rack, and went into the store. I led Arsgaard back toward the time clock, where there is a little cardtable.

"Sit," I said, like a good host, but when he sat down, my pleasantness said adios.

"You know why you are here, don't you, you little lowly worm?" (Later when I repeated the conversation to Dick, he laughed, saying I had just called Arsgaard the name of a beloved children's book character.)

Arsgaard must not have read the book; he looked at me in fear, his Adam's apple going up and down in continuous swallows. He nodded.

"Why did you do it?" I asked. "Why did you leave Francesca on the side of the road to get beaten up by those barbarians?"

Arsgaard's nostrils flared back and forth.

"She could have been killed! She could have been killed and yet you did not do a thing!"

"I . . . I . . ." His nostrils flared more and his eyebrows were moving like caterpillars and then his chin quivered—I was watching his whole face fall apart—and then suddenly, he let out a wail and rested his head in his arms and bawled.

I sat there, my hands in my lap, watching him. He cried for a long, long time and I thought seriously of getting a glass of cold water to throw on him when he finally lifted his head.

"Oh, God, Mr. Herrera, I am so sorry," he said, not even able to open his eyes to look at me. "I don't know why I did what I did—I was just so scared."

"Don't you think Francesca was scared, too?"

"Yes." Tears oozed out of his eyes, but he wiped them away with his sleeve. "Yes. I know she was scared. I just—I don't know—I was just so afraid to get involved. It just seemed so much easier to . . . to walk away."

"Don't you mean *ride* away?" I asked. "Don't you mean ride away as fast as you could, you cowardly piece of shit!"

His mouth moved up and down, up and down, like a fish taken out of the water. "You don't know what it's like, Mr. Herrera," he finally said. "You don't know how hard it is to like Franny, how much crap everybody gives you—"

"It would be anyone's honor to like Francesca!" Pure fury ejected me out of my chair. "What she ever saw in a weakling like you, I can't figure out!" My arm was raised as if I was going to slap him. "If I am ever aware that she likes a weakling like you again, I will stop the relationship like that!" I snapped my fingers and the noise was as loud as two dry twigs breaking. "Now let me tell you something else," I said, sitting back down. "I would not mind at all to have everyone knowing what a coward you are, but I have figured the important people already know. Francesca knows. Her family knows. Dick Lindstrom and his family knows. And you. You know. So you don't have to be sick with worry that one day your sad little story will leak out. It won't. And it won't only because Francesca doesn't want it to. And we all love Francesca. She is finer than anything you will ever know." I couldn't believe it, but suddenly I was doing the same thing Arsgaard had done five minutes ago, sobbing like a lost little boy.

I cried thinking of how much I had wanted to kill the person who beat up Francesca and how my wish, in its strange way, had come true. How I knew the agony of that saying, "be careful what you wish," but there was no going back, and a part of me would always be stained with this wish that somehow reached out to a drunken seventeen-year-old boy and killed him. The rational part of my being fights these thoughts, but it is just as easy not to be so rational when something like this happens.

I don't know how long I cried—it felt like I could not stop—and then Arsgaard touched my arm and said he was really sorry and could he go now?

I waved him off, not lifting my head. With my face buried in that little pillow my arms made, I could smell my deodorant and my cologne and it somehow gave me comfort, to just sit there and smell my smells.

Noreen came in after a while and put her hand on my hand and we sat there until we heard the front doorbell tinkle.

"I'll get that," said Noreen. "Why don't you take a little break?"

It was a good idea she had and I decided to walk over to Dick's lot.

We got in a blue Coupe de Ville and I told him all about my meeting with Arsgaard and he said I should have roughed the little prick up a little and then I asked him how was it going with Devera, and he said it was hard and I started a little speech about a little affair not meaning much in the big picture of his marriage. He got all red in the face and yelled what did I know about anything—BiDi wasn't off boffing the mailman, was she?

"Mac Connors?" I said. "You think BiDi could compete with Bunny Vold?"

Dick did not appreciate the lightness I was going for, but I was not the sort to make my own confession to make someone else feel better. Not at the expense of Noreen.

"So what are you going to do?" I asked finally.

"What can I do?" said Dick, and his voice cracked. "I love Devera. I have always loved Devera. But how do I go on if she doesn't love me?"

"Dick, I know for a fact Devera loves you. Anyone who knows the two of you knows that."

"Well, maybe no one knows jackshit."

I talked to him about temptation and how affairs in a marriage can mean all sorts of things, and in Devera's case it seemed to me an experiment in doing something wild, something not like the usual Devera. People do all sorts of things when they are under a strain.

"So what strain was Devera under? Was it so terrible being married to me? Being mother to our girls?"

"Dick, haven't you ever felt bad inside when everything on the outside seemed to be going great?"

Dick looked at me like I was crazy.

"No," he said, and then we both laughed because we knew it was probably true.

I have always admired Dick's big enjoyment for life, for loving the cars he sells, the music he makes, the woman and girls he lives with, and I was hoping this thing was not going to make him sour—believe me, that is a side of Scandinavians, too. They are most often friendly and helpful, yes, but they can lock themselves up and away from you, too.

"Oh, crap, there's Clayton Hagstrom," said Dick, watching the old man walk through a row of cars. "Ready to pretend he wants to buys a car. Thanks for letting me bend your ear, Sergio."

"Anytime, amigo," I said. I got out of the car, too, and watched as Dick came to life, hitching up his pants and putting a little salesman swagger into his walk and clapping Clayton Hagstrom on the back as if he'd been waiting all day to see him.

IN CHICAGO, I flashed my MasterCard like it was an FBI badge and I was busy breaking up speakeasies. (I love that gangster lore of Chicago; I cannot walk the streets without thinking of Al Capone and Eliot Ness!)

Did I spend money! Why not! I needed a big release after all that trouble and I was making money! Well, not so much yet, but when the Chicago store opens, look out!

It was the second week of December and I guess what put me in the spending mood were the lights strung up along the

Magnificent Mile and the carols being piped in and the snow that was floating down just like God was up there with a big sifter.

Noreen looked so pretty, too—her eyes were shiny and her cheeks were rosy from the cold and then from the heat of the stores.

She helped me pick out lots of things for Francesca; sweaters with colors she said would flatter her, earrings (Francesca and Darcy, with Lin's help, pierced each other's ears in our downstairs bathroom!), and a pair of boots with little heels on them. And books—a complete works of Dickens and Twain, which Noreen says are long-term invest-ment presents to be appreciated long after the clothes are out of style and the earrings are lost.

We split up when we did the shopping for BiDi and Noreen's husband, Fred—that would have been stepping into a no-trespassing zone, I think. Afterward we met in a little bar that you had to climb down steps to get to.

"To spending money," I said, holding up my whiskey and water. (See, I even drink like a gangster in Chicago!)

"To having fun," said Noreen, clicking her glass to mine.

But we didn't have to make a toast to having fun—we were already having it. So much fun, I wanted the day to never end; well, I did want it to end, because that would mean it would be night and we would be in our hotel doing what we do best with each other.

Everyone in town knew about the trip, so it was not as if we had snuck off with one another. What everyone thought, though, was that it was a business trip, pure and simple. After all, Les and Myra Lund were with us, too, and the four of us had busied ourselves for three days interviewing people and demonstrating recipes but also taking time for shopping and touristy things, too.

We were all going back to White Falls the next day, and to tell you the truth, it was not an idea that had me jumping for joy. It had been such a relief to be away from all that trouble, to think of nothing but business and pleasure.

After our lovemaking the night before, Noreen had asked

me if maybe we should break up our affair. I gasped like I had stepped into a cold shower.

"Why?" I asked.

Her red hair was gray at the part and spilled over her naked shoulders. "Well, you and BiDi are bringing a new baby into the world and maybe . . . maybe you need to be more . . . unified."

I rolled over to face her and pushed some of her hair behind her ear. "This is the funny thing," I said. "I had been thinking the same thing." This time I heard her gasp and I laughed. "No, no, I only thought it for about five minutes. I thought maybe it was time I was loyal to my wife and our son we have made, but then I realized I must be loyal to myself, too. Unified, as you say, because without you, Noreen, there is too big a piece missing in my life."

"I'm glad I'm that piece for you, Sergio, because you're that piece for me," said Noreen, and then her voice got a little bit playful. "Now, tell me one thing. What are you going to do if your baby is a girl?"

"It won't be!" I said, and then we both laughed at my adamance. "Don't get me wrong," I said, stroking her hair. "I love girls. I love Francesca as my own. And so I know what it is to have a daughter. Now I want to know what it is to have a son. He will be a boy."

"Will you love it less if it's a girl?"

"It will be a boy," I said, "and I will love him with all my heart, but there will still be space for me to go on loving you."

Noreen's sigh had a funny musical note to it and we had no more words then, just long kisses that tasted of the cashews we'd bought in the lobby candy shop.

People might understand Noreen's need more than mine. She has a husband who can't do much of anything anymore but sit and complain about his army disability checks being late. "He can be a wonderful man," Noreen says, "he was always wonderful before the war." I believe her, but believe me, I have never seen this so-called wonderfulness. I believe in many ways BiDi is a wonderful woman, but she is not so wonderful in the way she doesn't like to love me with her body and I am a believer in finding what it is that you are needing.

I know my church would shake many fingers at me saying, "You are wrong about this one," but I truly think God saw the goodness between Noreen and me and of course we see its goodness and those are the only votes that count. It might just be a big excuse for something very wrong, but it feels very right.

So on our last vacation night together, Noreen snuck into my room at nine-oh-five. We giggled like teenagers on a school trip—Myra Lund says by nine o'clock she and Les are always out like lights, so we always waited a few minutes after to visit each other, not wanting to run into the chaperons in the hotel hallway.

I had just opened a bottle of champagne and we had toasted to our successful business trip ("May we always be in business," Noreen said) when the phone rang. It was Devera, telling me BiDi had gone into labor.

"But that's not supposed to happen until February," I said.

"Well, Sergio, it's happening now."

Noreen said later I moved so fast getting all of my things packed that it made her a little dizzy to watch.

BiDi

ELVIS WAS SINGING "It Won't Seem Like Christmas Without You" and Francesca and I were in the nursery, stenciling bunnies along the wall, when my water broke. A warm gush sprayed down my legs and I stood there dumbly, wondering for a half second how Franny had knocked over the paint can and why was it warm? Deep down I knew right away what it was, but my mind still scrambled for excuses.

"Oh, shoot," I said, looking down at the dark water that was surely going to stain our newly installed carpet, but then my housekeeping concerns were overtaken by fear and I whispered, "Franny!"

She must have thought I was going to yell at her again for painting outside the stencil because she didn't respond.

"Franny! Call the doctor! My water broke!"

She was out of the room in a flash and back in a flash later.

"Mom, I don't know the doctor's number! Where is it?"

"Calm down," I said, not wanting her panic to feed my own. "Call Devera instead."

"Okay," she said, her head bobbing. She disappeared again and I stood there, leaning against the wall (careful not to smudge any bunnies). I had this funny idea that everything would be okay if I just stood there.

By the time Dick and Devera put me into their car, I was having my first contraction.

"Dev, this isn't supposed to be happening."

"I know," said Devera, squeezing my hand. "Just hold on."

"Mrs. Herrera, you're in labor," diagnosed the perceptive Dr. Holland after examining me.

"I know that, Doctor," I said, bracing myself for the contraction that had started to build, "but you've got to stop it. I'm not due until the second of February."

"It's too late to stop it," said the doctor. "But what I'm going to do is put you into an ambulance and get you down to St. Cloud. We don't have the facilities for a premature baby."

I had one instruction to Devera, who with Dick and Francesca was going to follow me in their car: call Sergio.

THE CONTRACTIONS DECIDED not to pussyfoot around but I found myself distracted, even excited, by the ambulance ride. Those things are fast, boy, and when you're laying on your back and can't see where you're going; well, it's a wild sensation. To me it felt like a fast, downward slide, like one of those log-in-a-chute rides, except of course, I didn't get wet. Some paramedic was chattering to me until I asked him if he'd mind putting a lid on it; I just wanted to enjoy the ride.

"Well, excuse me, ma'am," he said. "Just trying to do my job."

Sergio hopped on the first plane to the Twin Cities and drove, he said, beyond the speed limit by about thirty miles per hour, but he was not quick enough to witness the one event that would have been his own personal Fourth of July: the birth of his son.

It was a pretty easy labor as far as labors go; fast and hard. Since they're all going to be hard anyway, I'd rather have mine fast. The strange thing was, even though I didn't have any drugs, I was . . . well, detached from the whole thing. It wasn't like a near-death experience; I mean I didn't feel myself hovering above everything like some human cloud, but in a way I felt I wasn't there at all. I knew those contractions were humdingers but the nerve centers that process pain seemed to be off duty. I was aware of how much it hurt, but only aware, not bothered. To tell you the truth, I think I was so anes-thetized by fear that I could have had a root canal without novocaine. (Not that root canal is more painful than child-birth, but I want to give an example men can understand.) When the doctor told me to start pushing and after marshaling all my concentration into four teeth-gritting, bone-crunching pushes, my baby saw the fluorescent light of day.

"It's a boy!" the doctor said, and they bundled him up and swooped him away. In that swoop, though, a nurse I'll always be indebted to held him close enough to me to let me touch his face. He was as blue as a plum.

"Oh, my baby," I said, touching his tiny little cheek with my finger, "my beautiful baby boy."

The baby had been out of my room for less than an hour when Sergio came flying through the door. Really, it didn't seem like he ran toward me as much as zipped, feet off the ground.

"BiDi! BiDi, we have a son!" he said, practically throwing himself on the bed to hold me in a hug. "We have a son!"

I didn't know if my cheek was wet from Sergio crying, or from me. I was about to ask him to pass me the Kleenex, but then my whole body shuddered and my voice rose up in a moan.

"Oh, BiDi," said Sergio, holding me tighter. "It will be all right! Our son will be fine!"

But he wasn't. And it wasn't his lungs—what the doctors were most worried about—that sent him by helicopter to the University of Minnesota—it was his heart.

"He needs immediate surgery," one of the doctors who was making decisions about my child's life, but whose name I didn't even know, told us. "We're happy about his lungs—they're in better shape than we thought they might be and he's a good weight—almost four pounds—but there is a hole in his left chamber that we need to repair."

I felt that the gift Sergio wanted most in the world—the gift only I could have given him (well, legitimately) was a child, and now not only had that child come into the world before he was done, but with a bad heart. And all because of those few doses of speed I took when I *thought* I might be pregnant. Okay, when I *knew* I was pregnant but hadn't had my suspicions validated by a test. And then there was that time at the opening of Your Oasis when I got so bombed. Oh my God, I couldn't even think about possible fetal alcohol syndrome.

I did not enjoy the sensation of guilt at all, no sirree. Not only was it a feeling I was unfamiliar with, but it was spreading into a general all-around dislike of myself. That's pretty hard to take for someone who's lived their life not only tooting their own horn, but leading a full-piece orchestra. The thing is, the more bad things I thought about myself, the worse I felt. How could I be thinking about myself so much when my baby's life was in jeopardy? Why wasn't I spending every thinking moment praying for my son? What was the matter with me?

Of course, I had an answer for that, too. I knew Sergio was praying full speed ahead and why weaken God's reception by my little discombobulated thoughts and prayers? I know that sounds sacrilegious; I mean if God can make us and everything else, surely He can sort out who's praying for who and how sincere their prayers are. But I felt sort of out of my league; prayers for a very sick baby seemed so huge and daunting compared to my usual dumb requests for an Elvis sighting to be proved real or a weight loss for Francesca.

IN THE UNIVERSITY of Minnesota waiting room, where I got lost twice just trying to find my way back from the ladies' room, Sergio was exactly the opposite of how I thought he'd be acting. He sat calmly, holding my hand, making sure I was warm enough ("Devera, can you get BiDi a blanket?"), fed enough ("BiDi, how about some soup?"), comfortable enough ("Do you need another Tylenol?"). Dick, on the other hand, was pacing like a new tiger in the zoo.

"Dick, honey, why don't you sit down?" asked Devera. "I'll get you some hot tea."

"That sounds good," said Dick, but no sooner had he sat

down and taken a sip than he was up again, hands folded not in front of him, but behind his back, walking back and forth behind the couch.

I thought Devera raised her eyes at me, giving me some sort of signal, but it was hard to see through the mist from my constant tears. I don't know, they just kept coming. This was a marathon of tears, a siege, a deluge. It was as if all the sadness of the world had pointed its finger at me and decided it was my turn. I wasn't cutting myself any slack either, my mind churned out pictures and memories and words said years ago.

I cried thinking of those letters my dad sent me all those years ago that always started with *How ya doin' Tootsie Pop?* I know my mother was dealing with some pretty heavy stuff, but couldn't she have just let me write back once? I cried thinking of the many times he must have gone to his mailbox, filled with hope that maybe I'd finally written back. I finally got his address by using my head and fishing out of the trash the crumpled envelope of a letter he'd written, but it took me months to write the perfect letter, the letter that would bring him back to me, and when I did, it came back to me with a *Return to Sender/Address Unknown* stamp. It's the only song of Elvis's I can't listen to. I cried remembering the telephone call we got from his sister Ruby, telling us "Lon had passed on in Bakersfield." I hadn't cried when we got the news—it was the night of our winter prom and I was Sno Daze Princess and I didn't want to spoil my big night out. I cried over all those times I wanted to tell him I loved him, all the times I wanted to hear that he loved me.

When I got done crying over my dad, I cried over my child-hood dog, Heidi, getting hit by the Bookmobile and the way she tried to drag herself across the street with one bent leg; I cried remembering when Big Mike told me he wanted a divorce and the way he kept shaking his head back and forth, as if he couldn't believe he had married me in the first place.

My afterbirth contractions were strong enough so that they gave me something I could concentrate on, but then zip, I'd get another picture sent my way care of Sadness Unlimited. Pictures of mothers: my own, when she flew up from Florida to my wedding to Sergio and told me how lucky I was to get a second chance at love because she sure never did; Ardis and the way her fingers looked all big and mishapen holding her glass of punch at Lin's confirmation party; Helen and how the tears rolled down her face, thinking of her son, Don.

I thought of Mr. Vold and how, after his wife died, he used to row to the middle of Flame Lake every night and sit there until way past sundown; the way his daughter Bunny sounded singing "Autumn Leaves" one night at Your Oasis.

"The world's too sad a place," I said to Sergio at one point, and he nodded, letting go of my hand to put his arm around me. He smiled at me and squeezed my shoulder and I looked at him, trying to gain strength from this kind man who loved me no matter how mean I'd been. But it was not enough to stop the album from flipping its sad and lonely pictures in my head, and the ones it kept coming back to were two faces: my son's blue one and Francesca's, the way it looked after I had asked her once at dinner if she was going to play another boys' sport because wasn't the wrestling team short a heavyweight?

DEVERA

I HAD MADE a vow that I was not going to sully myself by ever again acknowledging Gerhart Ludwig's existence—but the day after Guy Hammond's funeral, I snuck behind the statue of Longfellow by the English department (his minor in history makes him qualified—he says—to teach night classes like Ancient Rome and the France of Louis XIV). I fell in step with him as he skipped down the sanded stairs. His step was jaunty, I imagined, because of an upcoming tutorial with some coed.

"A warning, asshole," I said through the side of my mouth, and he looked at me so startled I almost laughed. When he saw it was me his face relaxed into its usual expression of condescension, but I had seen that initial fear and my confidence swelled like a rogue wave.

"Devera," he said in that pompous paternal voice, "what inspires such sharp words?"

Two students passed us on the icy sidewalk, walking in choppy little step so they wouldn't slip. Snow had begun to fall again and I watched the flakes alight, like little tiny stars, on Ludwig's coat lapels.

"Do me a favor and shut up," I said, and immediately Herr Professor's arm was on mine, steering me to the side of the statue that faced the science building.

"Devera," he said, changing his tone and his tack, "something must be really bothering you."

"I'll say." I looked at him, baring my teeth like a dog's. "I just want to know what you possibly gained by telling my husband of our cheap lousy little affair?"

The professor's rheumy eyes bulged. "What are you talking about?"

I looked up, rolling my eyes at Longfellow, wanting a witness to the feigned innocence of the unbelievable twerp that was Gerhart Ludwig.

"Halloween night?" I said. "Lord Byron spilling his guts to Dick in the Norse Man Liquors parking lot?"

Gerhart sagged a little, holding on to the toe of Longfellow's concrete foot for support.

"Devera, I was drunk as holy hell on Halloween night. You're saying I met up with your husband and told him—"

"Told him he was cuckolded."

The professor folded and refolded his gloveless hands.

"No . . . Devera, believe me, I have no remembrance of anything I said or did to anyone that night and I can assure you—"

"No. No. Let me assure you." I looked him square in his soulless little eyes. "One more word to Dick—to anyone—and I'm going to your department head, to the dean of the school. They have 'guidelines' against teacher/student relationships, don't they? I'm not so concerned about myself, but I worry about all those young girls in your English-comp. class. When I get done with you, you won't be able to teach letterwriting by correspondence course, got it?"

Gerhart nodded, his head a jiggle of motion.

"One more word, Ludwig, drunk or sober, and you're finished."

His head kept up its bobbing and I turned around, my dramatic exit flawed only slightly by a slip on the ice.

Would I have told Dick about my affair if Herr Professor hadn't beaten me to the unfunny punch line? I have thought about that question a lot and I believe that I would have. Of course, once you've been caught it's easy to think you were right on the verge of confession anyway.

Dick set up camp in the guest room, which really scared

me because it was a public admission to our girls that something wasn't right. He made up some excuse about his back but the girls didn't believe him for a minute.

"Mom, what's going on with you and Dad?" Lin asked. I was watching her cut out a hat she had designed for Darcy's Christmas present. (She makes all her presents and, unlike me, usually has all her Christmas stuff done by Thanksgiving.) Lin's not only a talented artist, but she's a great sewer (BiDi taught her how a few years ago) who blindstitches her hems and meticulously finishes all her seam allowances. When I sewed, or tried to, most of my projects met their end as a wad of fabric crammed in the back shelves of the linen closet.

"He hurt his back." I flushed at the speed at which I corroborated Dick's lie.

"Mom." She set down her pinking shears and sat next to me while I brushed a scrap of velvet with my fingertips, unable to look my daughter in the face.

"Lin," I said finally, "your dad and I are having a fight and neither one of us knows how to make up to the other yet." I do try to tell my girls the truth, but this truth was too big to tell.

"At least I'm glad that you and Grandma aren't fighting so much anymore."

I smiled, genuinely pleased. "You noticed?"

"Mom, I know Darcy's your 'unusually perceptive kid,' but I see things, too, you know."

"Lin, who's ever said Darcy—"

"It's okay, Mom. It's just nice not having you and Grandma at each other's throats all the time."

Right after Darcy was in the accident, we'd had this blowout that led to her finally talking to me about Don. We had made a few baby steps toward each other and I hoped we'd be taking more.

"Well anyway, I'm glad you confided in me about Dad," said Lin, taking my hand. It took me a minute to realize she was serious. "I mean I am old enough for you to tell me things, you know."

"Does that work both ways?"

Now it was Lin's turn to blush. "Sure. Except I don't have anything to tell."

"Good," I şaid, and we both laughed, understanding the subtext perfectly.

"How come you wear a men's watch, Mom?" she asked, twisting my watchband the way she used to in church when she was a toddler. She never made a peep if she could just play with my watch; she'd pull at the band until she eased it off my hand and then twist it and study it, holding the glass face inches away from her eyes.

The question stumped me for a moment; I had been ready to counsel Lin on how she should always turn to me whenever she has *anything* to tell, particularly about boys.

"I . . . I guess it's because your uncle Don had a watch like this."

"Dead Uncle Don," Lin said quietly, and then there was a quick blurt of laughter from both of us. When the kids were small, they always remembered my brother in their bedtime prayers: ". . . and bless dead Uncle Don."

"He wasn't wearing his watch when he had his accident, although I've never figured out why, because he used to wear it all the time," I said. "Mom and Dad looked all over for it— they wanted him to be buried with it on but they couldn't find it anywhere."

After I didn't speak for a while, Lin asked, "Where was it?"

"I had smashed it up," I said. "I had taken it into the woods and stomped on it until it was unrecognizable. Until the springs were flattened and the glass was ground."

"Why?" Lin's question sounded like a hiccup.

I drew a line in the velvet with my thumbnail, buying time while I tried to articulate my thoughts. "Well . . . I guess because he loved it so much. There was this contest at Naslund Jewelers when it first opened and he won it—he guessed the exact number of jelly beans in a jar, the *exact* number. I remember he said it was a precision watch for a precision mind."

"And you smashed it all up?"

I nodded, and when I couldn't find a Kleenex in my pocket, I blew my nose on a velvet scrap.

"I was just so mad at him, Lin. I wasn't grieving like my mom and dad because I never felt he really had time for me. I was sad, but mad, too, because I felt he had wrecked everything. My mom's life. My dad's life. And I didn't want him to be buried with that watch. I wanted to have something he loved; some of his love, I guess."

"So then why did you smash it?"

I shrugged. "I don't know, Lin, I was just a kid." I balled up the fabric scrap and tossed it at the wastebasket. "But I guess that's why I wear a man's watch. For Don."

"Weird," said Lin, but her voice was as tender as a cherub's.

In the midst of all the snow, the weather went crazy the other way and we had a two-day heat wave. The temperature actually got up to fifty one day and I approached Dick tentatively, in the hallway as he was coming out of the bathroom.

"Things are warming up out there," I said. "How about in here?" I reached out to touch his chest, but he intercepted my hand and tossed it aside like scrap paper. I watched him walk down the hallway, shamed as the adulteress I was.

I tried to think, how would I handle Dick's affair? I actually laughed then, because the idea was so preposterous, and then in that laugh, I understood the size and breadth of Dick's anger. He had no doubt felt the same preposterousness, the same absolute sense that no, my spouse would never, *ever* sleep with someone else; it was too ridiculous to even fathom. But then I did the preposterous, the unfathomable, and what was Dick left with? How could he believe anything? But even as I understood his rage, I could not soften it. I had apologized over and over; using the words *I'm sorry* as a greeting, and *please forgive me* as a salutation. I pleaded with Dick to talk to me alone, with a professional counselor, with an audience of scorned husbands and a talk-show host as a moderator—I didn't care—I just wanted to talk.

I have no idea how long Dick would have frozen me out; I do know Carlos's early arrival helped speed the reconciliation. And later, when BiDi told me she and Sergio wanted Dick and me to be his godparents, I told her I'd be honored, but in a funny way I thought the roles were reversed, that Carlos was my godfather, looking after me.

DARCY

WELL, MY NEW teeth are in and not to brag or anything, but I'm better looking than I ever was. They're whiter than my old teeth were, and shapely, if you can think of teeth as shapely. They just have softer edges than my real ones did. So I thrill the world at large by smiling a lot, and sometimes I even mean it.

Boy oh boy oh boy, sometimes I wish I could have just fast-forwarded through these last few months, or even better, pressed the erase button. But as Ms. Metcalf, my English teacher, says, "All of our life experiences make us who we are, and who we are should come out in our writing." Well, duh. Who else is supposed to come out in our writing, the ghost of Chico Marx? Get a grip, Metcalf. We're "journaling" in her classroom, which I think is a bogus idea. I mean, who wants a teacher grading your inner-most thoughts? So I write about things she expects—typical where-do-I-fit-in adolescent crap—and she gives me A's, even though I'm as sincere as a cashier telling you to "Have a nice day." But I'm not about to unload to Metcalf (even though she's not all bad, I mean she did put *A Good Man Is Hard to Find* on our reading list) "who I am." She'd probably send me down to the school nurse on the double. I'm not saying I need psychiatric intervention, but some of my thoughts are not exactly sunny-side up at all times. How could they be?

I could have handed in a real confessional, but Franny

would never let me. It was a letter she got from Ricky Walsh, a couple weeks after the accident.

"Wait'll you see what I've got," said Franny. We were sitting at the bar of Your Oasis having a snack before we started cleaning up. My dad paid us five bucks apiece to clean up the joint, even though it was never very messy. I mean there were empty glasses and scrunched-up napkins and stepped-on peanuts, but it's not like the place was trashed.

She dug out a letter from her jeans pocket and handed it to me.

"Good handwriting," I said, squinting at the envelope. "How'd it even get delivered to your house?"

"Just read it," said Franny.

It was pretty shocking and I'm not talking about the terrible spelling or the bad grammar, which is typical for a boy, if you ask me. Nope, this got to you because, as Metcalf would say, "the writer spoke from the heart." Which was a big surprise, because I wouldn't have thought Ricky Walsh even had one.

Dear Fransheska Lefave, (it read, and the spelling and grammar haven't been corrected because I don't think you should tamper with the way someone says something important):

My name is Ricky Walsh and Im one of the guys who beat you up and than ran into your car. Im sorry for both of them. Im writing because Im getting treatment now for alcahol abuse and were supposed to epolojize to people who we hurt by drinking. But I think I would have epolojized to you even if no one made me. I know you must think its hard to beleive but its true. I feel real bad for what happened. I feel real bad for Guy not even being around here any more and bad about my legs all though my vertabray issent crushed after all and I will prolly walk out of this place. Maybe with a cane but Hey sure beats the chair! Me and Guy liked to drink alot, I gues the only time we dint drink much was playing hockey which we loved I know you did to. Why did we beat you up. I have asked myself that question over and over. Guy and I dint talk about it ever I gues we did feel shame but man we were so drunk that night and then coming across you on that rode it just seemed like fate. We had been driving and driving over all thes little back rodes that night thought we were going out with our girlfrends but our so called girlfrends cansulled and than there you are! and you had made us so mad during that one game scoring the winning goal and making us look bad. At least thats what we thought than. You being a girl and all wernt supposed to play like you did that was our game. So we beat you up and I now this is no excuus but Guy could always make me do anything its like I always wanted to impress him by how tuff I was cause he was like a star. I have always been kinda a dumb shit like that about needing to impress people and always in the rong way I gues. I threw up on the way home. We joked that it was the beer but I realy was sick from what we did. Then seeing you Halloween night in that car, we were scared but drunk to so just took off and than when you guys chased us it got to be like a movie almost and we were scared but wild to. Laffing and stuff. It was fun to be in a chase seen. Why Guy turned around and headed strait for your car Ill never now I was scree-ming at him What are you doing? but he kept laffing and floored it man I count beleive it. I tryed to grab the wheel but you now Guy was big and strong and he just pushed me away. The only thing I thouht to do right was buckle my seat belt I was so scared but I thouht do it right now man! And I did and it prolly saved my life. I miss the fucker man Im sorry he had to go but what he did was pretty stupit for every one invollved. Im really sorry I say that again. I now I cant take away what happend but I sure hope you get over all this and move on with your life the same way I am doing with mine. Ive never seen a girl play hockey like you did and its a gift and I hope you use it cause youl bring White Falls the state champinship yet! Go for it! I herd your girl frends face was messed up in the crash I hope shes all right Im sorry for her to. Sincerely, Ricky Walsh.

"Stylewise," I said, "he reminds me of Fitzgerald."

"Or Hemingway," said Franny.

Our way of making a joke—it was like laying a few bricks of a dike to protect us from getting whomped by this huge wave of sadness that was ready to crash down on us. We both laid our heads down in our arms, the way you do in school when you're taking a secret vote or something, but a second later, Franny nudged me and said, "Oh, let's not cry. It seems all I do is cry."

"All right by me," I said, wiping the one tear away that had already snuck out. I picked a bunch of M&M's out of the trail mix, before shoving the dish toward Franny.

"Is my face really messed up?" I asked Franny as I examined it in the big bar mirror.

"You look better now than you ever did," said Franny. "Your lip's a little bigger on that one side but it looks cool."

I nodded, admiring my movie-star smile and then I ate my M&M's, watching as Franny picked out the sunflower seeds.

"Do you really like those?"

She shrugged. "You took all the M&M's."

I set a little pile in front of her and we grazed away for a while like a bunch of cows, and then I asked her, "Do you accept his apology, though? Do you forgive him?"

I watched Franny in the mirror. She'll never be pretty in that easy way Lin is, but there's something about her I think is beautiful. She's so dark and her face has so many angles—the bump on her nose from where she broke it does add character, I don't care what Franny says—she looks like she came from a country I've never heard of.

"I do accept his apology," she said slowly. "I mean, I think he's really sorry for what happened. But I don't know if that's the same as forgiveness . . . forgiveness seems like a pretty big thing and I don't know if I'm ready to give it away yet. That might take me awhile."

I put my arm around my friend's shoulder. "I know what you mean, Franny. I don't know if I could ever forgive them—especially Guy Hammond, I mean he definitely seems like the bad guy here. 'Course, he's dead and it's a little easier to forgive a dead person."

"A lot easier," nodded Franny.

* * *

FRANNY DECIDED NOT to join the hockey team. The coach
came to her house a couple times to hold powwows with her
and her parents and then some rah-rah even wrote an edito-
rial that was printed in the school paper, begging Franny to
find her school spirit and pay her debt to her school. That
ticked Lin off so much she wrote a reply that said the
trouble with jocks is that they assumed their world of sports
was the only world and to wake up and realize that there
were a lot more important things than catching a ball or
shooting a puck and that Franny didn't owe anything to anybody or anything and why didn't they just trade in their
pom-poms and their school banners for something that
meant something.

I was proud of Lin, but when I asked Franny didn't she
think that was great, she just shrugged and said she was tired
of everyone making such a big deal of her.

"I played hockey because I loved it, not for the attention I
got. Now I'm getting attention for not playing, which is not
the reason I decided not to play in the first place."

"Why did you decide not to play?"

Franny looked like I had punched her in the stomach.

"Oh, Darcy, do I have to explain it to you, too?"

I thought for a moment and then shook my head. "Not
really."

It *was* kind of hard to understand; I *love* getting attention for something I'm good at. I mean that's why I'm in
every school talent show and why I hog the stage at Your
Oasis. But I don't get the grief for being funny and entertaining that Franny got for being good at hockey. Still,
there are all those stories about people who had to put up
with constant rejection, who were told "you're no good,
you'll never work in this town, blah blah blah," and they go
on to become Bette Davises or Phyllis Dillers or Barbra
Streisands. But then, they didn't have to worry about teammates either; they were solo acts. Still, a part of me wanted
Franny to tell everyone to shove it, saying "I don't care
what happened or what you think, I'm playing hockey." But

she wouldn't. And so White Falls got back to being a mediocre all-boys team whose record by the New Year was 4–7–2. And Pete Arsgaard, the biggest coward on the face of the earth, was having his best season ever, with four goals and two assists. And life's a bowl of cherries if you can ignore all the pits.

At least we were a little distracted that crappy winter by the drama of Franny's little brother. Franny stayed at our house the weekend our parents were at the hospital in Minneapolis. Grandma and Grandpa stayed with us and they are about as lenient as baby-sitters can get without someone calling social services. I mean we could watch videos all night long and have caramel corn and fudge for supper, which we did the night they went over to the Johannsons to play rook.

"You kids'll be all right now, won't you?" asked Grandma, spritzing behind her ears one final blast of the Emeraud she always carried in her purse.

"Sure," I said coughing, and waved away the stink bomb, "we'll be fine."

"There's some pizza in the freezer, and some potpies."

"Okay, Grandma."

Grandpa honked the horn—the Johannsons only lived a few houses down, but it was too slippery a walk in the winter.

We went into the family room off the kitchen and put an Elvis movie Franny had brought over into the VCR.

"Whoever wrote this screenplay should have his Writers Guild card taken away," I said, watching Mary Tyler Moore run around in a nun's outfit.

"His what?"

"His Writers Guild card. All those people who write movies belong to a union. I mean if they're writing for a union production."

"A union production?"

"Sure. They've got unions for actors, for writers and directors—even producers. You know, to get them health care and good working conditions and millions of dollars for three weeks' work."

"How do you know so much about that stuff?"

"Why, Franny, I'm the queen of Hollywood," I said in my best Mae West voice. "I might not have been crowned yet, but that's only a formality."

"Whatever." Franny laughed. We got back to watching Elvis, who was cute all right, but it sure wasn't like watching Gary Cooper or Clark Gable at work.

When Lin stomped into the kitchen, scattering snow all over the place, Franny and I had just turned off Elvis and were on our way downstairs for a game of pool.

"Brrrrrr," she said, which is sort of the thing everyone in Minnesota is programmed to say when they come in the door in the winter.

She dropped her jacket and mittens on the floor and kicked her boots so they flew across the kitchen floor.

"I thought you had a date," I said. Lin had turned fifteen and could now officially go out with Kyle by herself, even though his sister or his parents still had to drive them places.

"I'll tell you all about it," said Lin, following us, "but first I need a Coke." Her voice was all mysterious, and when I stopped in the middle of the steps to ask her what was up, Franny bumped into me and Lin told us to keep moving.

Lin got us Cokes (this was something, my sister acting as waitress!) from behind the bar and we all sat down at a table by the stage.

"So what happened?" I asked.

"Well," said Lin, as if we were dying to hear what she had to say, which of course we were. "Kyle and I broke up."

"You what?"

"I'll put it to you in language you can understand," said Lin. "It's Splitsville. We're finished. The party's over. My dance card is free again."

"What happened, Lin?" asked Franny, her dark eyes round.

Lin took a sip of Coke and then turned the bottle in little circles. "I don't really know. We were on our way to Amelia Thompson's party and he was going on and on about this old

Mustang he's going to buy when he turns sixteen and all of a sudden the idea of listening to music and slow dancing with him made me want to beef. Major beef. So I told him I felt sick—which I guess wasn't a lie, actually. I don't know, it was just getting to be the same old thing all the time. It wasn't that fun anymore." She leaned back and looked up at the ceiling fan and I did the same, wanting to copy her, she looked so glamorously wounded. "There's a lot of fish in the sea, as Dad says, and I decided it was time to throw the net out."

"Just watch out for those sharks," said Franny. She was staring up at the fan, too, when I looked at her, surprised—I mean, I think she meant it to be funny, but it sounded so weird, so adult.

A good entertainer can always sense when the mood needs to be lifted, so I jumped up on the stage, taking the mike off the stand. "Hey," I said, in my best lounge-lizard voice. "Looks like we've got a younger crowd here tonight at Your Oasis. Where you from, pretty ladies?"

Lin and Franny just looked at each other, so I got down off the stage. "Don't be shy, pretty ladies. We're all dying to know where you're from."

Lin leaned toward the mike I held out and said in a funny (for her) old-lady voice, "Uh, Cleveland. My friend and I are visiting here from Cleveland."

This was encouraging, I couldn't remember the last time Lin didn't think she was too cool to goof around.

"Cleveland!" I said. "So what brings you senior citizens to Lake Country?" I held the mike in front of Franny.

"We're on vacation," she said in a nasally voice.

"On vacation," I said. "Vacation from what?"

"From our men," said Lin. Both she and Franny laughed.

"That's right," said Franny. "We're on vacation from our men . . . and the law."

"The law! What, did you ladies park in a no-parking zone?"

"Oh, no," said Franny, "it's a little more serious than that."

"Now, Francine, don't spill the beans," said Lin.

"Well, Lin . . . erva, you know how I like to talk."

"Francine" and "Linerva" laughed like they thought they were Martin and Lewis.

"Ladies, I know I speak for the entire audience when I say we're dying to know your secret."

Lin nudge Franny. "Tell her, Francine."

"Well . . ."

"Go ahead."

Franny smiled a shy smile. "Well . . . we plugged 'em."

"*Plugged* 'em?" I said, out of character.

"Yeah," said Lin. "They were bad boys and so we did them in."

"It felt so good," said Franny, "even though we knew it was a sin."

They clinked their Coke bottles together in appreciation of their wit, I guess, and then Lin upped the surprise ante by jumping on the stage and turning on Dad's Casio.

"They were bad boys and so we did them in," she sang, playing one of the few chords she remembered from piano lessons. "It felt so good, even though we knew it was a sin."

"Ladies and gentlemen," I said into the mike, "the lady from Cleveland can sing!"

Lin waved Franny up on the stage.

"So why'd you do them in?" I asked in a funky Aretha voice.

"They were bad!" said Lin.

Two long chords were played and then Franny sang, "They were bad and they made us sad!"

"A familiar story," I half said, half sang, walking the edge of the stage. "And these soulful sisters are here to sing about it."

Lin played a blues riff; well, it was close enough.

"Oh, his name was Kyle," sang Lin. "And I thought he was my man."

"He was her man," echoed Franny.

"But he started boring me, till I wanted to . . ."

"Kick him in the can," offered Franny.

They smiled at each other and sang together, "Kick him in the can."

I guess it was one of those you-had-to-be-there kind of things. Really, it was magical in a way. Not that the lyrics would have Cole Porter worried—or even my dad—but for my sister and Franny, it was pretty spectacular. I turned the houselights off and shone the spot on them as they sang about "men can be so cruel—they spit you out like gruel" and "we won't take their abuse—we'll make them sign a truce." Once again, this was all improvised right on the spot, so cut them some slack. I think it helped Lin to sing about how "Kyle brings up the bile" and even though Franny let Lin lead the direction of the lyrics, at one point she let it rip and sang, "I didn't ask for anything, I didn't ask you to stay, so why did you have to run away?"

When the song finally petered out, Lin and Franny took a bow and I clapped like I'd just seen the greatest show on earth. We all stood there for a while, wondering what we should do for a finale until Lin came up with the fabulicious idea of taking a sauna.

"Whoo—am I sweating," I said after we'd been in there awhile.

"That's good," said Lin. "That gets all your impurities out."

"Gross," I said, but I liked that Lin knew about these sort of things.

We sat around in the heat, not saying much, baking like a bunch of potatoes.

"I've got to get out of here," I said finally, "or I'm gonna fall asleep."

"Me, too," mumbled Franny, and then Lin had another bright idea.

"Hey, you guys," she said, "let's do what the Scandinavians do."

"What's that?" asked Franny.

"That," said Lin, "is running naked through the snow."

"I guess that's one way to wake up," said Franny.

We stood by the door leading to the driveway. Lin had her hand on the doorknob, but she couldn't quite seem to turn it and we were laughing like crazy. Then Franny's towel slipped and she said "oops," and the way she grabbed for it made us laugh even harder and Lin sort of leaned/fell against the door and all of a sudden it opened and she stumbled out, her towel falling to the driveway.

She stood up, this look of shock on her face, and then she hollered, "All right, let's party!"

Franny and I threw off our towels, and screaming, we followed Lin as she ran across the driveway and into the yard.

There's a lot about winter that can be a real drag, but sometimes there's nothing like it. A full moon was glowing like Kryptonite and lit up the whole sky like a night-light. Plus it was snowing, and the snow was that Christmas-card stuff; flakes that are big and fat and lacy.

In between our screaming, we were laughing as we ran around the house. It was a weird sensation; my feet didn't feel like they were freezing as much as they were burning, and even though we were running, I felt I was moving in slow motion. I could hardly breathe and yet I didn't want to stop running—under that Kryptonite moon and that falling snow I felt so free, as if I were on the top of the world—the North Pole or something—and the rest of the world was below me. I was cold but it didn't matter because of all the other things I was feeling.

I thought Lin was headed for the front door and I was kind of disappointed that we were going inside, but then she veered off into the yard and plopped down on her back, fanning her arms and legs in the snow.

"Angels!" cried Franny, and suddenly she and I were on our backs in the snow, too, making skirts and wings for our angels.

We all scrambled up then as if we all of a sudden realized, "Hey, this is *cold*," but not before standing still for a moment, admiring our beautiful angels. I mean they turn out a lot better when you're not wearing bulky parkas or ski pants.

Then we ran back to the house, howling like a pack of coyotes.

* * *

WE WERE PORKING out on popcorn and fudge and rootbeer floats when Grandma and Grandpa came back from the Johannsons. Grandma was carrying our towels.

"Say, what were these doing out on the driveway?" she asked.

"Oh," said Lin, "we took a sauna and ran naked through the night."

"Very funny," said Grandma.

"Turn out the lights when you go to bed," said Grandpa.

We put sleeping bags in the family room and watched the rest of that bad Elvis movie. Every now and then I'd hear a kind of smooching noise and knew someone had just got another little popcorn remnant out of their teeth. We had the fake fireplace going (the only one that doesn't have gas jets is in the living room) and after we laughed about who was farting (it wasn't me; well, not all the time) we talked low about everything from what it'll be like in the year 2000 to shoe styles to Franny's new little brother.

"I think he'll be okay, Franny," said Lin. "I just have this feeling."

"No offense," said Franny, "but I don't think 'feelings' have anything to do with what'll happen to Carlos."

She said it in her usual nice Franny way, but still, I was shocked. I mean it's not very polite when people are trying to reassure you and you shoot them down.

"So do you think he's going to . . . die?" asked Lin.

"I don't know," said Franny after a long pause. "I just know that how I feel really has nothing to do with whether he does or not. I mean, I can wish and wish that he'll be okay, but I don't think those wishes find a way from my head into his heart, you know?"

"So do you think praying does any good?" whispered Lin.

I clamped my teeth shut so they'd stop chattering.

"I don't know if it does," said Franny. "I've prayed for so many things all my life—to not be such a big dork, for my dad to acknowledge my existence, for my mom to quit bugging me so much . . . and I don't know, none of those prayers ever seem to be answered."

"You're not a big dork!" I said.

Franny's laugh was like a sneeze. "Thanks."

"That's right," said Lin. "You're not a big dork at all."

"That night I got beat up and Pete ran away, I was mad and scared, but most of all, I thought, 'What'd you expect, Franny? Why shouldn't those guys beat you up? Why shouldn't Pete run away?' "

"Oh, Franny," said Lin.

"And then when Guy Hammond was killed, I thought: 'Of course.' Why shouldn't worse things happen? Why shouldn't the trouble go on and on? Why shouldn't my brother die?"

She made a little choking sound and I heard little swishing sounds as Lin moved around in her sleeping bag, moving closer to Franny. In the semidarkness, I saw her put her arm around her.

Both of them were sniffling away; not big-time crying, but still, I didn't want to, I couldn't listen to it. I got up and turned on the radio to this station out of Minneapolis that plays big-band music. "String of Pearls" came on and then some Tommy Dorsey and Frank Sinatra and then Peggy Lee sang "Fever."

Franny had stopped crying and she asked me, "Who sings that?"

"Peggy Lee."

"Oh, I thought it was a man."

"Yeah," I said, "she sounds like a man in a lot of her later songs. She sounded more like a woman when she was younger."

EVERYONE ELSE FELL asleep before me, as usual, and I lay there, my fingers laced behind my head, watching snarls of snow untangle themselves outside the big picture window. I laughed a little, thinking how that snow felt on my naked skin, but then a shiver kind of zapped through my body and I thought: What were we, crazy? What if someone had come across us, some maniac rapist murderer, seeing three girls, nude, running through the snow? I could see him, some big creep standing before a judge saying, "I didn't mean to do it, but it's not like they weren't asking for it. I mean, they were all buck naked."

Joy is a pretty big word, I mean it's not your everyday feeling, but I really think that's what I was feeling out there with Lin and Franny, making angels in the snow. Now I couldn't bring that feeling back or even the memory of it. I was shivering too hard. I was wearing pajamas inside a sleeping bag with the fake fire crackling away in the fireplace, but still, I was shivering like I was going to freeze.

DICK

THE FIRST WEEKEND BiDi and Sergio's baby was in the University Hospital in Minneapolis, Dev and I rented a room at a downtown hotel where a guy dressed like a jester opens the door for you. We spent three nights there and closed the lounge bar every night. It was just so god-awful depressing.

The baby had the Last Rites read to him before he was even a whole day old, but he rallied. In fact, his pediatrician says he has the same life expectancy as any other healthy baby boy. Imagine that—a premature infant has open-heart surgery in his first forty-eight hours of life and not only survives it, but *has the same life expectancy as any other healthy baby boy*. Modern medicine; sometimes it seems like a religion all its own.

Carlos Lon Herrera is what they call him, named after both grandfathers. He's a cute kid, too—he's got Sergio's dark eyes and BiDi's dimples.

Sergio was a wreck those first few weeks; he was afraid to sleep, thinking that the baby would die if he did. He lost fifteen pounds which he couldn't afford to lose and he said his hair was falling out by the handful.

But when they brought the baby home and started believing the doctors; yes, the baby *was* thriving, Sergio said that was it, no more, he had used up all his worry and he wasn't going to waste another minute thinking about what *might* happen.

"Carlos needs me in the here and now!" he told me as

he stood rocking his sleeping son, who was dressed in a miniature New York Rangers jersey. "This is all there is—the right now!"

BiDi seemed to be doing great (she got her figure back, it seemed, before she got out of her hospital gown) but Devera told me she was going through hell, thinking that her doses of speed and the few drinks she had when she knew she was pregnant were responsible for Carlos's early arrival and that little part in his heart that didn't fuse.

"Beed, you'll never know the answer," Devera told her. "There are women who have healthy pregnancies and unhealthy babies and the other way around. You just don't know. You can't torture yourself about something you can't ever know."

"I'm sure Sergio thinks I'm responsible," said BiDi in a small doll's voice, but Dev said if he did, he never said anything to her. Same here, I told her, I never heard Sergio blame anyone.

"If Carlos had . . . died," Sergio said, "I would have blamed everyone but most of all God. But Carlos is okay! The only things I have to worry about right now are do his diapers need changing? Is it time for his feeding? I'll bet he could use a burping!"

Carlos's sickness was like a jail, and when the door was unlocked—when he got better—we shot out of there like freed lifers. Everything seemed possible, all throttles were wide open.

This sounds kind of stupid but it's a fact: on the coldest day of the year—we're talking thirty-three below zero with the windchill factor—things between Devera and me finally started to thaw.

We had just spent the day with Sergio and BiDi in the hospital waiting room while a team of doctors sawed through Carlos's breastbone (did they even need a saw with a newborn like that? With cartilage so new and soft—couldn't they just use a file?) and stitched up that hole. Needless to say, it was not *fun*. Every time we heard footsteps you could see BiDi flinch and Sergio white-knuckle the armchairs. Remember,

Bidi had just given birth—she should have been in a hospital bed herself—and she would start leaking milk and Devera would take her away to the bathroom so they could "express" it into bottles she'd brought along. So when BiDi wasn't flinching, she was expressing, or crying, or asking God to "help my little baby."

I had to keep moving; anytime I thought I might sit down I could feel the bile push up in my throat, and so instead of vomiting all over everything, I paced. When the doctor finally came in and said she couldn't have hoped for a smoother operation, well, we all whooped and grabbed each other and bounced around the room.

So when Dev and I went back to the hotel (the shifts had changed and a new jester was holding the doors open) we were so high we fell on our bed and did something we hadn't done since I'd heard of her and Ludwig. We made love, and true to form, *great* love. My God, it was like her body was the Eighth Wonder of the World and I had just discovered it. (She had made many advances during the standoff but I had said no to every one of them.)

Afterward, we both bawled like babies, apologizing and accepting apologies, making promises, and a truce was forged from those apologies and promises, more of which were made in long talks in the lounge bar (if I never have another honey-roasted peanut in my life, it won't be soon enough). The next thing I know, we're making plans to renew our vows this May for our eighteenth wedding anniversary. We'll even be doing it at the church—in wedding attire, no less.

Either I'm the biggest chump in the world or there should be a St. Dick, patron saint of forgiveness, I don't know. I love Devera, what can I say? And the more we talked about this vow-renewal thing, the more it sounded like a good thing.

Reconfirm our love, tell the world if we had it to do all over again, we would. I did tell Dev, though, that this time there's no rule bending—she cheats on me again and I'll be seeing her in Divorce Court.

She cried when I said that, even though I had meant it as

a joke (the kind of joke that's totally serious). She said she
had learned her lesson—was I ever going to truly forgive her
and go on or was there always going to be this thing hanging
over her head like a guillotine?

I said a guillotine over the head still wasn't as bad as a
knife in the heart and then we got into it and were ready to
call the whole thing off. Dev got up off the bed, grabbed her
pillow (she's got a loyalty to this one pillow you wouldn't
believe—imagine a grown woman taking "her" pillow with
her to a fancy Minneapolis hotel!) and was ready to flounce
off and sleep who knows where, but then she somehow got
her foot tangled up in the bedspread and she hopped twice
before falling to the floor. She was furious for a minute, muttering as she tried to free her foot.

"Stupid bedspread. This is supposed to be some kind of
classy hotel and they still use polyester fiberfill bedspreads?
Who wants to pay to sleep under polyester fiberfill? I'm going
to ask the manager if he's ever heard of this thing called
cotton."

I picked up the telephone. "Get me housekeeping now!" I
shouted. "I've got one question for you, buddy—who wants
to pay to sleep under polyester fiberfill?"

Dev stood there for a minute before she realized I was
talking to a dial tone, and when I hung up the phone and
opened my arms, she tumbled right into them.

BUNNY VOLD SAID renewing our marriage vows inspired her to
go ahead and marry Mac Connors. It was a complete surprise; we got a postcard from Cheyenne—a picture of a
cowboy trying to rope a calf—with the message *Guess you've
gotta lasso love when it comes wandering in your backyard . . .
if you let it run off you've got no one to blame but yourself. So
we went ahead and made it legal out here in the Wild West
where anything's possible. Now I've got a built-in campaign
manager for the next mayoral race! Love, and there's lots of it,
Bunny and Mac.*

Yeah, Bunny did lose the election to Jerry Bydell, despite
my hard labor. I must have passed out at least two hundred

of her "Hop to It" buttons. Bunny says next time she'll use a clearer slogan.

I've been working on a song to sing to Devera in our (re) marriage ceremony. It's not even a parody, it's got an original tune and everything. I can just hear the whole congregation gearing up to laugh and then being disappointed that the lyrics aren't funny plus they can't even recognize the tune.

The ceremony's still two and a half months away but Lin and Darcy are running around as if it's next weekend. They're both going to be Devera's bridesmaids along with BiDi, so they're looking through catalogs and pattern books for dresses, arguing about sleeves and hem lengths and whether or not they should wear hats (Darcy of course says yes, "but not those dorky bridesmaid's hats") and a bunch of other things that seem to matter to them. Still, I'm happy to see them getting such a kick out of this thing. It was pretty rough for the girls for a while—they didn't know about Ludwig, but they knew something was up—poor Darcy writing me little notes that I'd find in my pants pockets or tucked beside my keyboard downstairs; notes telling me she loved me, everyone loved me, and I wasn't going to move away and divorce anyone, was I?

Lin tried to be the perfect daughter, lasting for about a month in a role I know must have been a real stretch for her. There was no lip (which I sort of missed), no begging for longer curfews, no more beating up on her sister. She even brought back the concept of color to her wardrobe, and even though it's still mostly Addams Family black, those occasional reds and purples and blues are like the first spring tulips.

When she called me a doofus I was thrilled, knowing she was feeling secure again and that things were getting back to normal.

I had thought that I might move out for a while, but in truth it would have taken me finding Dev in bed with the entire faculty of White Falls State, the debate team, *and* Larry O'Herne to do something that drastic. So I'm a pushover, I could be worse.

The only thing that still *really* bugs me is knowing that Devera could run into this Gerhart creep anytime. She's taking some more classes—in women's studies, no less—and could easily see him. Dev says she doesn't think he teaches night school anymore and not to worry, if she sees him, she'll go the opposite direction. Why couldn't she have picked some stranger, some cherry picker from Willmar—some roofer from Cloquet? Some guy that wasn't in the same town as us?

I even thought about taking a little visit down to this guy's office and throwing around a couple threats and a punch or two, but I could never coordinate the action with the thought.

Sergio probably would have punched him right there in the parking lot the minute he heard the word *cuckolded*, but I'm not Sergio; my temper is like a gas flame set at medium low, if that high.

But enough about my marital soap opera. I trust Dev that it's over and she's sorry. Brooding about what happened will only give me an ulcer or worse. However bad things were, they are on an upswing now.

Extra proof: Today I pulled off the coup of my entire sales career. I sold Clayton Hagstrom his first Cadillac. Not a nice respectable Sedan de Ville or a stately Brougham but the flashiest car on the lot, the beautiful cherry-red Eldorado convertible. I sell him the quintessential summer car in the middle of winter!

"You finally did it, Lindstrom," he said, clapping his hands in their cotton-farmer gloves. I didn't know if he was applauding me or trying to get the circulation in his fingers going.

We were standing by the Eldy, tears filling the corners of our eyes from a wind that was so cold it seemed every gust was a bite.

"There's not too many men can convince me of anything—but you convinced me I should own this car."

For a moment I was speechless (a rare enough event), and then I finally managed to ask, "How?"

Clayton Hagstrom narrowed his wily blue eyes at me and with his fingers, tapped his chest.

"Passion. I loved coming by here just to hear your passion. It was more than the usual car-salesman baloney— you made me believe I was missing out by not driving one of these."

"I must be good," I said, half under my breath.

"Hey, now," said Hagstrom, pulling down the earflaps of his hat, "don't go thinking you performed a miracle or something. I needed a car—the trucks are for the farmwork and I don't do much of that anymore, and besides, the Dart's almost ten years old."

"So why not a new Dodge? Say a Viper? Or a Coronet?" I couldn't help myself, I wanted to bait him even as I wanted his praise.

The white stubble on the old farmer's chin moved as he rolled his tongue under his lower lip. "I'm getting old, Lindstrom. Eighty-two next birthday. I thought it was time for a little style."

"And that you'll have driving this baby down Main," I said. "I can just see you breezing around with the top down, the wind blowing through your hair, the gal of your choice sitting next to you."

"I haven't signed any check yet. Keep talking foolishness and I won't."

I could have kicked myself. Clayton Hagstrom was a man totally devoted to his wife Nellie, even though she'd been dead for fourteen years. There was no way he'd appreciate allusions to an active social life and I felt like an amateur for thinking he would.

I cleared my throat, trying to sound businesslike. "Let's go in and have a cup of coffee. Get you all set up."

We finished the transaction without further incident, and a half hour later Clayton Hagstrom drove the Eldorado out of the lot, smiling bigger than I thought his mouth was capable of. I felt like a justice of the peace who'd just married a couple who was perfect for one another.

So I was feeling pretty damn good when I got home.

Devera helped me celebrate by opening up a bottle of champagne left over from our New Year's Eve party (it was a formal affair—the guys wore tuxes and the women wore gowns, Mac and Bunny sang Gershwin and Cole Porter and the *Gazette* wrote us up like Your Oasis was the ballroom at the Plaza and anybody who wasn't there was definitely square).

My wife toasted my "superior powers of persuasion."

"Oh-ho-ho," I said like that French skunk in the cartoons, "so I guess I could talk you into joining me in the sack right now?"

Devera laughed. "We're already drinking champagne at three-thirty in the afternoon—we're supposed to be completely decadent and go to bed, too?"

We probably would have, but the old sex inhibitors—kids—came tumbling into the kitchen, laughing and littering the floor with scarves and jackets and mittens.

There were a bunch of them—two of Darcy's friends and at least four of Lin's (no Kyle; he is, as Lin says, "not a force in my life anymore").

"Dad, the ice is awesome," said Darcy, "and you should see—I did a double axel!"

"You did not," said Lin. "You don't even know what a double axel is."

"Well, I spun around twice in the air!"

"She did," nodded one of Darcy's friends. "I saw her."

Lin's contingent started making sandwiches, Darcy's hot chocolate, so figuring our chairs were more wanted than we were, Devera and I left the kitchen and I was thinking hmmm, maybe we really could get in a little Afternoon Delight, but then the phone rang and the way Dev said *Trish!* (a fellow classmate from Women Poets or Women Composers or Women Lathe Operators—one of those women classes Dev takes) I could tell that she was going to be on the phone for a long time.

I wandered downstairs and got a beer to wash the taste of champagne out of my mouth.

Settling on a bar stool, I almost laughed out loud at how unbelievably sweet life can be at times.

That struck me as song material, so with an energy that surprised me (it takes a lot to get me off a bar stool with a freshly opened beer) I jumped up, my mind running through rhymes of life—strife, rife, knife; but on the way to the stage, I passed the window and a movement caught my eye. I stood there in the dim, winter afternoon light of Your Oasis, squinting out at Flame Lake and the motion I saw on it.

The sky was gray with an undercoat of pink and the pines that flank our property stood tall and black against it. The snow was dappled with blue shadows and drifts of it pushed up against the shoreline from where we'd shoveled to make an ice rink. In this pastoral picture skated Franny—I could tell immediately it was Franny.

We were all bummed out when she decided not to play hockey this year—in fact there had been a silent agreement in both families to boycott the high-school hockey games—but with getting my marriage back on track and Carlos's troubles to worry about, Franny just wasn't preeminent in my thoughts. A few nights back, though, Darcy and I had watched an old movie with Yvonne DeCarlo in it and something about her reminded me of her.

"How is Franny doing, Darce?" I asked.

Darcy shrugged. "All right, I guess, okay. I think she's getting better."

I was relieved at her answer and didn't pursue it any further because I didn't want the answer to change, but now as I watched Franny out on the ice, I knew that the damage done to her—to Darcy with her big false teeth, to all of us— was more than a tear that could be stitched up and considered mended. I knew that it was a deep jagged wound that might get infected over and over, in countless small ways, before the scar tissue could finally grab hold and start to heal.

I swayed a little under the weight of knowing this as I watched Franny stick-handle the puck, her red hat and gloves bright as berries against the darkening sky. She looked around, dodging imaginary opponents, and then, with that tremendous burst of speed that had earned her ribbons and mentions in Dave Garner's column, she zipped across the ice and lifted her stick to shoot.

The puck sailed up—a small dash of black against the gray winter sky—and landed in snow far past the boundaries of the shoveled rink. It must have landed where Franny had aimed, for she lifted one leg and arm, pumping them both in victory, as if she had just scored.

Your Oasis on Flame Lake

LORNA LANDVIK

A Reader's Guide

A Conversation
with Lorna Landvik

Q: Where did the idea for this story come from?

A: I really don't know. The characters just came into my head and said, "Here we are. We want a story told about each of us!"

Q: Your first novel, *Patty Jane's House of Curl,* was rejected many times by publishers. Did you ever doubt yourself as those rejections piled up?

A: I didn't mind the rejection because I knew I was involved in a process, that the book was being seen, and that rejection slips were going to be inevitable. There were times I felt discouraged, but I also figured the manuscript just hadn't landed on the right desk at the right time. The process by which a publisher chooses a manuscript can be so serendipitous. An editor who turns you down on Monday might see merit in your manuscript on Friday. Occasionally, for solace, I would page through *Rotten Rejections,* a book that contains copies of rejection letters sent to the authors of some of the greatest literary masterpieces ever written.

Q: You alternate among five narrators to tell your story: BiDi and Devera (friends since childhood), their husbands, Sergio and Dick, and Devera's daughter, Darcy. Darcy is not the only child in these two families, so why did you choose her to be the voice of the younger generation?

A: I don't know. I've always let the characters lead me, and Darcy was the one who asserted herself. I tried to make Franny one of the narrators, because her story is one of the central events of the novel. She just didn't want to talk. Some readers have said they think it would have added to the story to have Franny as the narrator. Others say it lends her a certain power to not have her voice heard but to have her story told through everyone else's eyes. I feel secondary to the wants of my characters. I can't push them around. They're the ones that push me around.

Q: How do you find and latch on to those different voices?

A: They just come to me. I never base my characters on specific indi-
viduals but rather on the stew from which all writers write—our
imagination, our experiences, and the people we've met. As each
chapter ended, the characters asserted themselves as to who would
go next. It was a relay in which the baton passed from character to
character.

Q: **What are the advantages of writing with more than one narrator?**

A: You get more access to each character. Using multiple voices allows
you to explore not only what the characters say but also what they
think.

Q: **Did you find it difficult to write in a man's voice?**

A: All I did was sit around in my underwear and boss my spouse
around. Inspiration then came quickly. Actually, I enjoyed writing
in the male voice. It was fun allowing these characters to be so
honest and to say things people might otherwise be too polite to
express. That's also why I like to write in multiple voices. It gives
me the freedom to let my characters show all their rough edges.

Q: **What do you like about Franny?**

A: I like her because she's so strong. I like her ability to keep a firm
sense of herself while people are telling her she should change and
be more like everyone else. I've always been drawn to people who
follow their own path and refuse to listen to all the "traffic cops"
in their lives. Franny is like that when it comes to ice hockey.

Q: **Your debut novel was well received by critics and reviewers.
What sort of pressure does this place on you to produce an
equally successful follow-up?**

A: My first novel, which received a tremendous response from readers
all over the country, was a very emotional story. I was a little worried that people would be looking for the same kind of emotional
roller-coaster ride, because I knew *Your Oasis on Flame Lake* was
going to be different. It's a more thoughtful story. While I don't
want to write the same book again and again, I do want to write
stories in which the characters seem real, characters in whose lives

the reader can become engaged. I want my stories to have a good touch of humor, and if readers reach for a Kleenex every once in a while to wipe away tears, then I think I've done my job.

Q: Do you find your experience as a stand-up comedian coming into play in your writing?

A: I do. I've done stand-up and improv and know how important timing is in live performance. In writing, I'm very aware of the rhythm of a sentence. A wrong word can lay a rotten egg on the page as surely as a bad joke can lay an egg on the stage. The right word, on the other hand, makes the joke.

Q: You wrote the screenplay for your first novel, which was optioned for a movie. Do you prefer writing novels or screenplays?

A: Writing a novel is much more fun than writing a screenplay. A novel allows you to take a long trip with your characters—going down as many side streets as you want. Screenplay writing follows a more precise format. You always have to think, "How will this look on the screen?" The enforced focus on visuals takes you away from your character's thoughts.

Q: Why does Franny decide to stop playing hockey? Will she eventually play again?

A: Franny was never a hotdog kind of player. She loved to play just for the sheer joy of the sport. But being the only girl on the team made her a target. After she was attacked, she wanted to remove herself from the situation that had given her so much pain. I really don't know what she'll end up doing, but my personal opinion is that in a year or two, Franny will get back on the ice. I think she'll eventually realize she can't let the attack lock her away from something she really loves to do, but for now she needs to take a break.

Q: What advice do you offer for beginning writers?

A: Write every day. Once you've written something and decide you want to get it published, never give up! Don't ever let someone else's "no" stop you from doing what you want to do. Beginning writers also need to know what moves them as a reader. If they can get a handle on that, it will help their own writing. And they need to closely consider their characters. A writer always has to ask, "Are my characters strong enough? Do they seem real to me?" If they seem real to the writer, chances are they'll be real to the reader. One final word of advice: eavesdrop as much as possible. Listen to the way people talk. Don't try to make great art out of dialogue. Just make it sound real.

Q: Has the success of your books changed your life at all?

A: It hasn't changed it in any grand way. I'm still writing at my kitchen counter. Of course, it's enormously rewarding and validating to have your work published and to have people like it. I love being able to say, "I'm a writer," without having people roll their eyes and ask me how I *really* make my living. Although if I hadn't been published, I'd still be writing . . . and working temp jobs.

Q: Describe the evolution of this story.

A: When I lived in Los Angeles I wrote a lot of performance comedy, stage shows, and sitcom scripts that were never produced. To keep my hand in the world of fiction writing, I wrote short stories. Unfortunately, my short stories were never really that good. *Your Oasis on Flame Lake* was one such effort. I sent it to an editor, who wrote a letter back saying he found the writing spectacular but couldn't make heads or tails of the story. I put it back in the drawer, but the characters kept yammering at me to get them out. They wanted a fuller accounting of their lives. When I realized what they wanted, and where they wanted me to go, I was able to transform the short story into its current incarnation.

Q: Are you planning a sequel to either of your first two books?

A: I don't know. I've fielded a lot of questions about sequels to both novels, and there are some ideas percolating inside me about revisiting the House of Curl. I'm very curious to find out what's happened to Patty Jane and the crew. So far, however, I'm directed by the characters in the book I'm currently working on.

Q: Is writing easy or hard for you?

A: I classify writing as "fun"—rather than "easy" or "hard"—and enjoy it tremendously. I'm not the greatest disciplinarian, however; I like to take long lunch breaks, longs coffee breaks—long breaks in general!

Q: Are there any parallels between your own household and the households of BiDi and Devera?

A: Well, I do have a big-hearted husband. I also have hockey-playing daughters, but they hadn't started playing when I wrote the book.

Q: Why doesn't Franny name her attackers?

A: Because she didn't want to get that weasel, Pete Arsgaard, in trouble. In many ways, Franny is incredibly strong but was weak in that she wanted to preserve her relationship with this guy, no matter how small it was. I was actually very troubled that Franny tried to protect him. If it had been Darcy who was attacked, she would have come forward right away.

Q: What do you mean when you say you were troubled by Franny's failure to come forward? Aren't you the one controlling her actions?

A: The old writer's cliché—that the characters take on a life of their own—applies in this case. Writers, to me, are like airplane pilots. Although they guide the plane to its final destination, they don't necessarily control what each of the passengers is doing. It's a joy when your characters become so real that you can't control them. They're like real people, with all the complexities, doubts, quirks, and desires. It's great fun to try to figure them out and see why they're doing what they're doing.

Reading Group Questions and Topics for Discussion

1. Why do you think Landvik has written this book from several perspectives? Do you find it easy to follow the action, or does the multi-narrator format take getting used to?

2. With which characters do you most closely identify? How would you describe each of the main characters in this story?

3. Why do you think the author chose Darcy as the narrator representing the younger generation? Do you think it would have been more effective to have Franny tell her own story rather than having other narrators tell it for her? What do you think the biggest difference is between the two generations presented in this story?

4. There are two people having affairs in this novel: Sergio (with Noreen) and Devera (with Professor Gerhart). How do their affairs differ, and how are they same? Why do you think Landvik has chosen to make one of the affairs benign and the other more harmful? Do you think Sergio or Devera has good reason for having an affair?

5. Other cultures think Americans overreact when it comes to human sexuality and extramarital affairs. Are Americans too straight-laced? When we find out about public figures committing adultery, how much should we care? Do we pay too much attention to the private lives of our public figures?

6. What would you do if you found out a married friend of yours was planning to have an affair? Would you try to talk the friend out of it? Would you tell the spouse?

7. How would you describe the relationships that exist between the children and their parents?

8. Why does Franny choose to tell her stepfather that she's started menstruating rather than her mother? What does this say about Franny's relationship with her mom? Why do you think BiDi is so jealous of Franny's hockey success?

9. BiDi wears form-fitting clothes to flaunt her body and considers flirting a recreational sport. What do you think of her behavior? Is

it acceptable to play the "game" the way she does? BiDi also says the people who call her a tease are the ones who are angry because she refuses to play the flirtation game by *their* rules. Do you think BiDi's right?

10. Do you see BiDi as a shallow character? How does having the baby change her character? Is she heading for a redemption of some kind?

11. What do you think went through Darcy's mind when she saw her mother, crouched under the table, in the midst of a severe panic attack? Devera talks openly and honestly with Darcy about the attack. Should she be so forthcoming about something that so obviously terrifies her daughter?

12. Sergio is determined to find, and even kill, the guy who beat up his stepdaughter. How would you react if someone you loved had been attacked? Is Sergio's eye-for-an-eye philosophy the answer?

13. BiDi is clearly unhappy about having another child. Why doesn't she tell Sergio about her feelings? She goes along with being a mother even though she really doesn't take too well to the role. Are parents like this hurtful to their children in the long run? Do you think parents are able to keep their unhappiness about being parents from their children?

14. Was Franny right to tell her father that she overheard Bidi talking about considering an abortion? Should she have talked to her mother first?

15. Why do you think Franny decides to give up ice hockey? Does this mean that the people who attacked her have won? Do you think she'll take up hockey again?

16. Franny eventually gets a letter of apology from one of the guys who beat her up. She says she accepts the apology but doesn't feel ready to forgive him. How would you react under similar circumstances?

17. Who do you think is responsible for the auto accident? Should Sergio have let the boys go? Was he irresponsible, considering that he had two other kids in the car with him? What would you have done?

18. Was Sergio right to confront Pete Arsgaard? Should he have spoken to Arsgaard's parents first? How would you have handled the situation?

19. Dick eventually decides to forgive Devera after finding out about her affair. However, he says, "Either I'm the biggest chump in the world or there should be a St. Dick, patron saint of forgiveness." Do you think Dick is a chump, or suitably forgiving?

ABOUT THE AUTHOR

Writing and theater were Lorna Landvik's twin passions
when she was growing up in her home town of
Minneapolis, Minnesota. After graduating from high
school, she and her best friend traveled in Europe and settled briefly in Bavaria, supporting themselves as hotel
chamber maids and English tutors. When she returned to
the States, Landvik briefly attended the University of
Minnesota before moving to San Francisco, where she
performed stand-up and improvisational comedy.
Another move took her to Los Angeles, where she
worked as a stand-up comic at the Comedy Store and the
Improv, then temped at the Playboy Mansion—"I felt like
Margaret Mead studying a secret society"—and scouted
bands for Atlantic Records.

After six years in California, Landvik married Chuck
Gabrielson, whom she met at a high school dance back in
Minneapolis; their first daughter was born a year later. In
1986, the trio walked across the country with the Great
Peace March for Global Disarmament. "A thousand people started the march on the West Coast, but we were
stranded in the desert and a core group of about four hundred decided to go on," Landvik recalls. "It ended nine
months later with a candlelight vigil at the reflecting pool
in Washington, DC." After the march, Landvik and her
husband decided to go home to Minnesota.

Landvik, who writes her novels in longhand, has continued to nurture her interest in theater since her return to Minneapolis, appearing in several plays, including *Bad Seed*, *Lunatic Cellmates*, and *Valley of the Dolls*. She also wrote and starred in *Glamour Queen*, a one-woman show, and *On the Lam with Doe and Rae*, a two-woman show. Landvik made her debut as a novelist with the critically acclaimed *Patty Jane's House of Curl* (1996).

More excerpts from reviews of Lorna Landvik's *Your Oasis on Flame Lake*

"A hard-to-put-down novel that finds complexity and intrigue in the simplest of everyday lives and the simple friendships that offer comfort and support . . . Very clearly character driven, the storyline evolves from the nature and motivations of the people Landvik renders."

—*Middlesex News*

"The novel builds to a well-crafted and suspenseful climax . . . [It is] a fine, original novel, leavened with humor; very readable."

—*Louisville Voice Tribune*

"The story is freckled with laughter, sadness and life in general. It will often remind you that those small things you take for granted are the ones you will remember fondly in years to come."

—*Rocky Mountain News*

"In *Your Oasis on Flame Lake*, each of the characters tells his/her own story. Lorna Landvik skillfully weaves each of these stories into one interesting and attention-holding book."

—*Marietta Journal*

"Some writers do comedy really well. Others pen drama best. Luckily for us, some manage to combine true wit and intense conflict in one narrative. Lorna Landvik . . . manages this feat with aplomb in her latest novel."

—*Boston Tab*

Don't miss this wonderful novel by Lorna Landvik

PATTY JANE'S HOUSE OF CURL

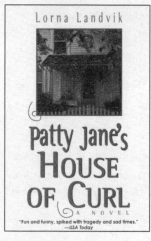

It's been said that a good haircut can cure any number of ills, and before long Patty Jane and Harriet—two sisters from Minnesota—have opened a neighborhood beauty parlor complete with live harp music and an endless supply of delicious Norwegian baked goods. It's a wonderful, warm-hearted place where you can count on good friends, lots of laughter, tears, and comfort when you need it—and the unmistakable scent of somebody getting a permanent wave. . . .

**"FUN AND FUNNY, SPIKED WITH TRAGEDY
AND SAD TIMES."
—*USA TODAY***

Published by Fawcett Books
Available in your local bookstore